Painting Venus

Richard John Mitchell

By the Same Author

Stealing Venus

Copyright © 2024 Richard John Mitchell
The right of Richard John Mitchell to be identified as the author of this work has been asserted by him in accordance with the Copyright, Designs and Patents Act 1988.

Any references to historical events, real people, or real places are used fictitiously. Other names, characters, places and events are products of the author's imagination, and any resemblances to actual events or places or persons, living or dead, is coincidental.

No part of this book may be reproduced, or stored in a retrieval system, or transmitted in any form or by any means, electronic, mechanical, photocopying, recording, or otherwise, without express written permission of the publisher.

ISBN: 9798879022599

For Harriet, Flora, Leo and Zak, with love.

PROLOGUE

It was a beautiful hotel room, painted in cream and burnt sienna and gold. Above the bed there was a framed print of the customs house by Turner. Will Bentley thought it an odd choice to put an English painter on a Venetian hotel wall, but this wasn't his room. He had no time for idle thoughts.

The wardrobe doors were still open from his search, but he was tidying up now. He straightened a pair of men's black shoes and closed the wardrobe hurriedly, wishing his thudding heart would quieten. A lady's coat had caught in the wardrobe door and he tucked it back inside. He went across and closed the balcony door. Sunlight touched the tops of the hyacinths in a balcony pot so they glowed like gas flames.

Time to escape. He peeped through the spy hole on the room door. All clear. He unclicked the dead bolt and opened the door a crack, his hands feeling a little damp inside the latex gloves he wore.

No-one in sight.

He was halfway into the corridor when he saw the woman coming round the corner. He stepped back into the bedroom and leaned on the door, forcing it to close against the resistance of its spring.

He knew her.

His heart threatened to burst out of his chest, for he was unused to such exploits. He had recognised the woman. It was the filmmaker he had met at the wake...what was her name?

Rachel!

His mouth twisted into an ironic smile despite the gravity of the moment.

She hadn't seen him. Her eyes had been lowered as she hunted for her key card in her purse, but any second now she would walk in and find him in her room.

That couldn't happen.

He knew there was nowhere to hide. The bed had no space underneath. The bathroom had a bath, a shower and a toilet, but nothing else. There was the wardrobe, but he imagined her opening it and finding him squashed inside.

The only place to go was the balcony, so he ran across the room, unlatched the door and stepped out, sliding it closed as he heard the room lock bleep. He looked around desperately for escape but he was two storeys up. The balcony was separated from the next by a spiked grid. He pressed himself to one side as if trying to melt his body into the bricks, and saw Rachel enter her room without looking his way. He held his breath, afraid that even the slightest movement would attract her eye.

She took her coat out of the wardrobe, vindicating his instinct not to hide there. She put the coat on the bed, then turned her back to him and went into the bathroom, pushing the door half closed. When she came out she couldn't fail to see him.

There was nothing else for it. A memory of his studio roof in Cambridge flickered into his head. He patted his pocket to make sure the package he had retrieved from the room was safe. Then he licked his lips, stood on the metal balustrade, took aim and leaped into space.

1

And as the cranes go chanting forth their lays,
Making in air a long line of themselves,
So saw I coming, uttering lamentations,
Shadows borne onward by the aforesaid stress.

DANTE, The Divine Comedy

1475, Florence

It was a crisp January morning in Florence and the sun haloed the three-storey cream buildings bordering the Piazza Santa Croce. As it reached the basilica the old brown stone seemed to glow in turn, and when its rays touched the stands of the wooden amphitheatre newly erected in front of the church, dew steamed off the wood. There was no wind and chimney smoke painted vertical lines on the sky. The square in front of the wooden amphitheatre where the joust was to take place was already thronged with spectators, but the amphitheatre itself was only now filling up with guests of the Medici.

Sandro Botticelli was on his feet and leaning on the seats in front of him. He was cold because he was hungry. He had intended to grab leftovers from the evening before, stuffed eggs with a hint of ginger, but they had vanished, presumably into the gullet of his greedy brother. Instead he had left the house for fear of being late, and the half-hour walk from via Nuova had plagued him with cooking smells as his fellow Florentines broke their fast.

Behind him sat Andrea del Verrocchio, a silversmith, sculptor and painter, ten years his senior. His friend.

"Is there anything to eat or drink in this desert?" he asked Botticelli plaintively. "If Il Magnifico has paid a fortune in honour of his little brother, you would think he would feed his guests."

He was a rotund man with a fleshy chin, unlike the lean figure of Botticelli, yet strangely nimble and precise despite his bulk.

"Well it's not just for Giuliano," Botticelli said. "When I was getting background for my commission I talked with Lorenzo and he said we are honouring the new alliance."

"With Venice and Milan? Yes, I heard that too. I hope it will last more than five minutes this time. And I hope we won't be subjected to long speeches about how wonderful it is and how we should all be so delighted."

Botticelli shook his head. "He won't do that. Lorenzo is a showman, so he'll perform for the people. This won't be pomp and circumstance, it will be a spectacle to remember, and Giuliano will charm everyone with his usual brotherly good humour. Simonetta will dazzle, as she always does. I'm looking forward to it."

At this point Botticelli saw the young poet, Angelo Poliziano, pushing his way through the assembly towards them, past the painted wooden sign saying 'Posti degli artisti'; the artist's seating area. In his hand he held a slab of bread piled high with roasted pork.

"Angelo, well met indeed," Botticelli said, clapping him on the back. "Where did you get that meat? Andrea and I missed breakfast."

The boy was ten years his junior, dark haired and heavy browed, with an aquiline nose and full lips. He had an imperious demeanour which commanded respect, and ambition to accompany it. He was very clever. He was attending at the request of Lorenzo to capture the scene in words, and such a request from the Lord of Florence was a command.

"Andrea doesn't look like he needs to eat anything for a week," Poliziano said through a mouthful of pork, not looking very imperious at that moment. "But you'll find a young maid down there." He gestured vaguely with his free hand. "She told me it wasn't yet ready, but I flourished a coin and she gave me this to get rid of me."

"Ha," said Botticelli, sweeping his cloak around him. "In that case she can get rid of me too. Where exactly is she?"

Poliziano pointed vaguely again and he set off purposefully, with a cry from Verrocchio echoing in his ears: "Bring a bone for me to gnaw on."

When the painter returned with two loaded hunks of bread he handed one to Verrocchio and found that during his absence a wench had brought hot spiced wine and his friends had secured a goblet for him. Some minutes passed while they ate and the amphitheatre filled up with the nobility. The young poet finished first and took out a red silk cloth to wipe the grease off his chin. He took off his matching red cap for a moment and ran his fingers through his hair before replacing it. Then they held up the Val d'Elsa glasses and toasted.

"Salute!"

"I may survive another day," Verrocchio admitted, rubbing his stomach.

Botticelli nodded and then looked more closely at his old friend.

"Now then, tell me about Giuliano's armour, Andrea. How was your commission? Are you pleased with it?"

He patted his arms to indicate imaginary metal cladding and looked around in hope of seeing Giuliano de' Medici himself, sheathed in gleaming metal, but none of the Medici had yet arrived. A band of lute players started up beside the amphitheatre and the music drifted over the square, almost drowned out by the cacophony of the growing throng. Street vendors had set up around the roped-off enclosure and were plying a lively trade of bread, cheese, meat and wine.

"Silver body armour, topped with a splendid helmet," Verrocchio said. "Sparkling with jewels, dear boy. No expense spared."

"If it is beautiful, then I shall write about it," Poliziano declared, looking into the middle distance as though his thoughts were elsewhere, his leg marking time with the lute music. He turned to Botticelli.

"What brings you into this august company, Sandro? Did you paint the seating signs, perhaps?"

Botticelli grinned.

"I *am* the august company, Angelo," he said. "I'll wager you that by the end of the day I shall have a new commission, if not more than one." He waved a hand expansively at the growing audience. "In fact, I must mingle. I refuse to be banished to the artists' row with you two, particularly when there are so many more beautiful people for my discerning artist's eye."

"Then we shall be able to have an intelligent conversation while you are gone," Verrocchio said gravely, and Botticelli looked back over his shoulder, spreading his hands and giving them a bow with his head only, a smile on his lips. Then he was gone, descending among the nobles and opening his arms in welcome so that they smiled and greeted him. He was well known in the court and La Signoria, Florence's ruling council. He cut a distinguished figure, still in the full bloom of manhood, just turned thirty and handsome. His hair was long and had a natural curl. He had a look to him which could be commanding, or completely disarming when he was jolly, which was most of the time. He liked to be the entertainer in any gathering, and he possessed a quick wit that held no arrogance. Men found him professional and women found him attractive. He was one of the more sought-after bachelors in Florence, though he claimed he had once dreamed he'd married, then woken up in grief and walked the streets all night lest the dream should revisit him. Some accused him of keeping a boy, but this was a commonplace slander aimed at politicians and those with money. Meanwhile his growing reputation as a master painter was well earned and his studio grew busier each year.

As he moved through the crowd, taking in the line of a nose here or the slant of a brow there, he smelled roasting songbirds and hogs, smoke from the cooking fires and chimneys, the acrid scent of unwashed bodies and the unmistakable odour of horses. He saw a seated dog watching the spitted hogs mournfully, and imprinted the image in his memory.

The front row of the amphitheatre had no name on the painted sign, simply the Medici coat of arms comprising a V of five red balls topped by a blue ball on which were painted three Florentine fleur-de-lis. As Botticelli managed to make his way to the front, Lorenzo de' Medici himself arrived. Il Magnifico was an ugly man in his mid-twenties with long straight black hair and the classic Medici hooked nose, but he had undeniable gravitas which fascinated women and garnered respect from men. No-one was voted into the Signoria without his approval. Today he wore a crimson cloak – Medici colours for a Medici day. He nodded to the nobles as he passed them and when he reached Botticelli he smiled a welcome and touched him briefly on the arm.

On Lorenzo's arm was Simonetta Vespucci, twenty-two years of age and said to be the most-beautiful woman in Florence. Botticelli knew her well, as she had sat for his painting which would be displayed for the first time that very day. Lorenzo's ugliness seemed to emphasize her beauty. Her pale hair was wound in delicate braids about her head and held in place by jewels. Her long neck rose from the collar of her pale blue dress in such a way that the nape was exposed, making Botticelli want to caress it. His mouth went dry when she caught his eye and smiled.

"Maestro Sandro! I am so excited to see my portrait! I am hoping that you have done me justice! You have been most cruel in refusing to let me see it until today."

"My lady," Botticelli said, colouring and inclining his head respectfully. She was the only one in the world who called him Maestro Sandro, but how could one correct La Bella Simonetta? "I hope you enjoy the surprise."

She smiled, gave him a little nod and then followed Lorenzo. Her husband Marco Vespucci followed behind her. He was two years her senior, and cut a short and uninspiring figure. Lorenzo's brother Giuliano was rumoured to be having an affair with Simonetta, though it was presented as platonic love and not one of cocks and hens. Giuliano would be carrying her emblem in today's joust.

The lute players finished their piece, and after a short interlude a flourish of trumpets sounded from outside the ground, signalling that the joust was to begin. The crowd quieted.

Botticelli hurried back through the curved rows of seats. He nodded to the Albizzi family and they nodded back, then to the Pazzi family, who didn't. He regained his position in the artists' row, and realised that Verrocchio was already in drink when he made a *sotto voce* remark about a passing wench's behind.

It was quite a view across the piazza. To the left of the amphitheatre a line of stands went along the side of the square, decorated by the Guilds in bright Florentine colours, and to the right people stood three or four deep, jostling while they waited for the joust to begin. Two small boys battled earnestly with stick swords despite the flourish of trumpets only moments before. A grey cat sat on a stone pillar, washing itself and ignoring the hungry curs that prowled below in search of a bone.

The far side of the square had a deeper crowd, punctuated at intervals by minor nobles on horseback. One of these great men had earlier been pitched off his mount to the general merriment of all. A boy had slapped his horse hard on the rump and then disappeared nimbly before a servant could lay hands upon him.

Every window overlooking the piazza was filled with faces looking down, and every balcony was thronged with onlookers. Botticelli sighed with impatience, keen for the joust to begin. He knew he wouldn't get any painting done that day, so when the maid passed by with her jug he held out his glass and she filled it. She caught his eye and blushed prettily when he winked at her.

There was a second flourish of trumpets, this time with a sustained roll of tambourines in accompaniment. The procession commenced and everyone fell into an expectant hush. There was no central tilt barrier. Instead the jousters would ride about the ground and attempt to unseat each other in a melee that usually resulted in several injuries and much entertainment.

The thirteen jousters entered the ground in a solemn parade, flanked on either side by tambourinists and pipers, who serenaded them with gusto. There were nobles from Florence, Venice and Milan, then men-at-arms who went to the corners of the arena, followed by sundry relations, and finally some *buriassi*; the trainers who were there to observe the rules of the contest.

Il Magnifico's brother, Giuliano de' Medici, was fourth in the line. It was not the Medici way to appear to lead or rule, only doing so behind the scenes. His silver helmet and armour sparkled and Botticelli patted Verrocchio on the shoulder.

"A fine job, my friend."

Verrocchio looked pleased, leaning forward on his seat to see the dazzling spectacle. Everyone on the stands began to applaud and the crowds surrounding the arena cheered encouragement, shouting *'Palle! Palle! Palle!'*.

The horsemen made their way to the front of the amphitheatre and slowed almost to a standstill as they passed Lorenzo and La Bella Simonetta, seated in front of the stands. Botticelli caught sight of the Pazzi family and saw that they were applauding too, though somewhat half-heartedly, forced by public courtesy. He smiled. They were a miserable lot, always complaining that the Medici overstepped their authority and behaved like royalty, but he felt sure Lorenzo had their measure. When Giuliano reached the stands in front of his brother he stopped and bowed as low as he could while on a horse. In his hand he held a banner of Pallas in a white shift, painted by Botticelli. Pallas was a perfect likeness of Simonetta Vespucci. The sound of the applause grew and spontaneously the entire crowd of nobles stood up, many of them turning in their seats to where Verrocchio and Botticelli stood smiling and nodding, and Poliziano did the same even though his contribution had not yet begun.

"You should probably sit, Angelo, while we gather the praises," Verrocchio said with his usual deadpan humour. The young man laughed.

"People will be reading my verses long after your armour is made into horseshoes, Andrea, and Sandro's banner has been used to wrap fish."

"These would be the verses he hasn't yet written," Botticelli said to the silversmith with an innocent smile.

"Imaginary verses," nodded Verrocchio gravely.

Meanwhile Giuliano was exchanging words with Simonetta and when she had responded, a page collected the banner and stepped clear.

After more ceremony and compliments from Lorenzo about the city states of Venice and Milan, there was a pause for the musicians and relatives and *buriassi* to clear the arena. Then the first bout began and for a while there was nothing but wheeling horses, clouds of dust and cries of triumph or frustration. Occasionally one of the jousters would be unseated and pages would run forward to assist him and recover the horse, but there were no broken bones and after the first bout there was wine and beer in profusion. The scent of the sweating horses wafted over the stands. Botticelli was regaling his colleagues with stories of his studio and some joke he had played on an unfortunate student named Biagio, acting out the various moves to illustrate his tale.

It was a good day and despite being January it was warm. The second bout began and was again played out with good sport and no serious injury. Botticelli suspected that the Florentines had been urged not to challenge their Venetian or Milanese counterparts too strongly; the idea was to build bridges, not break bones. After round two it was time for lunch. This time Lorenzo had added food to the free-flowing wine and beer, and the crowd formed benevolent groups. At times an altercation would break out, fuelled by alcohol, but always the men-at-arms would step forward and stop the affray before it developed, marching away the guilty parties.

Botticelli went walking again among the nobles. The wine had made him loquacious, but he was in good company. Almost the entire crowd within the amphitheatre had drunk more wine than was sensible, with the exception of the children that weaved in and out of the adults, and some of them had sneaked a glass. During the midday break the barriers around the arena had been opened so that the space was available to the public, but men-at-arms were now stopping newcomers at the entrances to the Piazza to prevent too much of a crush.

Botticelli observed the people and their exchanges, the little dogs that danced at the edges of the crowd, and the solemn-faced guards who kept order. The colours were rich. Florentine cloth was the finest in the world and everyone had turned out in their best. Splashes of red marked the nobles, but every other colour was woven into the human tapestry.

"Maestro Botticelli!"

He turned at the sound of his name and bowed to the woman who had spoken, racking his brain to remember who she was. She was an attractive signora of middle years, surrounded by three children who obviously wanted to run off and play but were under stern orders to remain. She wasn't a familiar face in Florence and yet he remembered her from somewhere. Then he looked at her daughter's face and had it: the young girl was Semiramide d'Appiano, promised in marriage to Giuliano de' Medici even though she was only ten and he already twenty-two. Botticelli particularly remembered the young lady for her unusual name, after the legendary Babylonian queen Semiramis, mentioned in the Divine Comedy. Botticelli had come across Semiramis in his studies of Venus, with whom there were mythological associations. This little princess was far too young to demonstrate any of the 'sensual vices' referenced by Dante Alighieri, but somehow her name had stuck in his head.

He returned his gaze to her mother.

"Madonna Campofregoso!"

He spread his arms wide in welcome and stepped forward, bowing. She offered her hand and he took it in both of his, so that she felt the pleasant warmth of his enclosing fingers and coloured a little at the sudden intimacy. "How charming to see you once more!" he exclaimed, but then noted her flush and released her hand. He switched to a subdued and earnest tone: "My dear lady, I was so sorry to hear of your loss."

Her face adopted a look of remorse. She was a handsome woman – one could see where the little girl got her pretty looks. Botticelli had visited the family in Piombino on the promise of a large commission, but then her husband Jacopo III Appiani had died in March of the previous year, before confirming his contractual intentions, and it had all come to naught. Botticelli had liked the man and his regret was genuine. Jacopo, despite being the bastard son of Emanuele Appiani, had possessed none of the bitterness that so often accompanies the illegitimate, and spent money on the arts despite his reduced financial circumstances.

"That is the very thing I wanted to discuss," the Madonna said. "Before he was taken from us, Jacopo intended to commission portraits of each of the children." She indicated the three of them who stood sullenly beside her; Jacopo the fourth, who must be about fifteen, a younger boy of perhaps thirteen whom she introduced as Gherardo, and Semiramide.

"May God rest his soul," Botticelli said, "and of course I remembered his intentions, but I did not wish to presume…"

He waved away the end of the sentence with his hand.

"I quite understand, Maestro. But now that my affairs are in order I would *myself* like to commission you to complete those very same portraits."

"It will be my pleasure, madonna," echoing his earlier bow with an inclination of his head. "Do you reside in Florence for long? We should meet to discuss the matter, and I should make sketches of the young lord and his siblings."

"That would be satisfactory," Battistina Campofregoso said. She was clearly a woman accustomed to getting what she wanted. She glanced left and right, then leaned in a little closer and spoke in an undertone. "Forgive me, but my husband handled previous commissions. Perhaps you could tell me what I need to consider?"

Botticelli marshalled his thoughts, unused to plunging quite so quickly into business, but responded quickly.

"We should discuss it in privacy and comfort," he said, waving a hand at the noisy crowd below in the square. "But you should consider the size you would like, and your budget, and whether you would like separate portraits or a family group. Whether you would like panel or canvas." He hesitated. "In addition, you may wish to give thought to the use of ultramarine, which as you may know is of lapis lazuli and therefore can affect the necessary funds."

"I see you are as skilled with the sale as with the brush, Maestro Botticelli!" she said with a smile, not alarmed by talk of coin. "I would like separate paintings and I would like you to begin with Semiramide. We are here until the end of April so that she can familiarise herself with the Medici court, and the courtiers can call upon her. You will recall that she is to marry Giuliano when she becomes a woman." She indicated the little girl with her hand and Semiramide curtseyed to Botticelli.

"I remember the young princess," Botticelli said. "And I should tell you that my ultramarine is imported from the Levant and is the first yield from several soakings, so it is the richest of blues you can imagine, almost violet, positively glowing from the panel. Such quality may come at a price, madonna, but it will set your paintings afire and will demonstrate your discernment when viewed by court visitors."

"Then we must have it," she said, and again the smile came, making him think she was amused by him.

Botticelli winked at the young girl beside her mother and suddenly she returned his smile, losing her earnest expression.

"Are you not a little young to be pledged in marriage to the brave Giuliano?" he asked with a twinkle in his eye. Immediately she became the imperious young princess.

"Our marriage will unite the Appiani and the Medici names forever, Maestro," she said to him, clearly quoting her mother, and he inclined his head in deference, showing that he knew his place.

It was arranged that he would call upon Madonna Campofregoso the next day at the Medici palace, where she and her retinue had rooms, and after a pleasant exchange about the pageantry of the joust, they parted.

Botticelli continued to work the crowd, nodding to acquaintances and exchanging a word with everyone. At one point he encountered Verrocchio and leaned into him conspiratorially.

"*Three* commissions from the same woman," he whispered. "It is a productive gathering. And you?"

Verrocchio looked around to make sure they were not overheard, then replied in a similar low tone.

"The possibility of an ornate silver altar, to fit a side chapel as a gift from a lord." He smiled at his friend. "It would be expensive, so he must have sinned mightily."

The joust continued and Giuliano predictably won, bowing low to the crowd's loud cheers of appreciation, and then to his brother Lorenzo. To Simonetta he presented a posy of white cyclamens, their stems wrapped in silk to prevent sap from staining those slim fingers. It was a charming gesture – flowers in January – and Botticelli nodded in quiet appreciation. Yet when Simonetta's husband Marco turned his face for an instant, perhaps it was only the keen-eyed painter who perceived his furious expression.

There was to be a *festa* afterwards at the Medici palace in via Larga, and the nobles made their way there in carriages while the crowd settled in for a party of its own in the Piazza Santa Croce. Botticelli was invited to the *festa* as an honoured guest. He decided to clear his head by walking to the palace, as it was only on the other side of the cathedral. He passed neighbours gossiping in the lengthening afternoon shadows and drew his cloak around him as a light breeze cooled the January day. There was the constant clatter of carts and the barking of dogs that chased them, together with the stately rumble of coaches as the nobles passed by. The streets were full of artisans: leatherworkers, weavers, dyers, stonecutters and other craftsmen of all kinds. Someone was hammering metal – a ringing sound. Children played in the streets and boys hurried past him bearing packages or sealed letters. At one corner he heard a couple arguing in an upper-floor room; the man's voice angry and the woman's raised and shrill. He passed a musical instrument shop where a man sat on a stool playing a viola da gamba. A small boy beside him held out a bowl and Botticelli dropped a coin into it.

His senses were alive with images that his mind translated into paintings. He felt invigorated, as if he could feel the blood coursing through his veins. His nostrils were assailed by strong odours. On the pleasant side were baking bread, roasted almonds and sweetmeats from *pasticcerie*, while at times a lady's perfume might reach his nose. But these divine aromas competed with the stench of stale blood from a butcher's shop, horse dung in the street and the reek of urine from the woollen-cloth fulling mills that lined the Arno. He passed a large tenter shed, open to the air on each side so that the cloth inside could dry, and paused to watch the workers stretching new cloth on tenterhooks.

Once he reached the cathedral it wasn't far to the palace, where nobility and gentry were still emerging from coaches in the Via Larga. He was admitted immediately with them, recognised on sight by the door guards due to his frequent attendance at the Medici Court. He followed the footmen to the great hall where all were assembled, and a goblet of wine was handed to him as he came through the great doors

"Alessandro di Mariano di Vanni Filipepi, detto Botticelli," the herald announced him formally to the throng. The familiar hall was as magnificent as ever, in contrast to the deliberately modest exterior of the palace. It was full of people in every shade of Florentine silk, several of whom were clients who nodded to him and raised their glasses.

"Sandro Botticelli!" cried a voice at his elbow, and he turned to see a man of Poliziano's age, but with a firmer jaw, a thicker neck and brown curls to the shoulder. He had an aquiline nose like the Medici, and Botticelli raised his eyebrows, unable to place him.

"I believe we are neighbours," the man said, holding out his hand. "Amerigo Vespucci at your service."

Botticelli shook the proffered hand.

"The pleasure is mine, sir," he returned formally. "I have heard of you from Fra Giorgio, who commissioned a piece from me last year for the Monastery of San Marco."

"My uncle," the youth said with a grin. "Fra Giorgio has spent many years trying to educate me, but had more success with my brothers, as I am but a humble clerk in the Medici Bank."

"Hardly humble as a Vespucci," Botticelli said. "And I hear you have been befriended by Lorenzo himself."

"Ah yes," Amerigo said, neatly grabbing a goblet of wine from a passing footman. "Lorenzo and I have discussed geography together. He has a fascination with everything – or at least anything which has mercantile possibilities."

"Geography? You mean trade with other states?"

Amerigo smiled. "Other states of course, but other countries, too. "I have an obsession with maps, I must confess. Are you interested in cartography?"

Botticelli inclined his head ruefully. "Too much geography for me," he said. "I have only recently come to accept the rotundity of the earth."

"Indeed," said Amerigo with a gleam in his eye. "Well just last year I saw a map by Paolo Toscanelli, of the whole world in the form of a globe. May I call you Alessandro or do you prefer Botticelli?"

"Sandro is my preference with friends," Botticelli said, "and you are my newest friend." They clinked the Murano goblets together, which made a sound like a bell. A footman replenished their glasses. When he had gone, Botticelli turned to Vespucci again.

"I only live in the via Nuova so I invite you to visit my workshop," he said. "After my studio closes would be best, when the students have cleared up and it is less cluttered. An hour or so before vespers. Are you close by?"

"Borgo Ognissanti," Vespucci said. "You must visit me in turn and I'll show you my maps. I already have quite a collection."

"I'd be delighted," Botticelli said, privately thinking that he wouldn't be captivated by maps, but liking the young man nevertheless.

After more discussion they were interrupted by some minor lord and his wife, both of whom were quite as drunk as Botticelli himself now felt. They were interested in a portrait of their granddaughter, so Botticelli made his apologies to Vespucci and spoke with them, trying to pull his wits together. When the conversation was over he felt a sudden urgent need to use the jakes, but in his inebriated state he forgot the way and wondered down the wrong passage, admiring the paintings and peeking into empty rooms.

It wasn't until he was inside the third room that he saw the couple. They were quite oblivious to his presence, locked together. The woman's dress was hoiked up to her thighs with the man's hand between her legs. His remaining hand caressed her neck as he kissed her. It was Giuliano de' Medici and La Bella Simonetta. Botticelli may have been drunk but he had a strong instinct for self-preservation, so he backed quietly out of the room as swiftly as he had entered, mercifully remaining unnoticed. He closed the door behind him with exaggerated care.

He felt suddenly miserable at such vulgarity. He located the jakes and relieved himself, wondering how he could have missed it with the other men heading in that direction. There was a fountain and he washed his face, deciding that he should go home. But when he emerged into the corridor he saw Giuliano's departing back, returning to the party. Somehow the room where he had seen the lord with Simonetta drew Botticelli back. He heard coughing as he approached.

The door was open and he found Simonetta standing just inside. She was coughing into a silk handkerchief and it went on for fully half a minute before she managed to stop and wipe her mouth. She leaned on a small table, swaying, then sensed his presence and turned to look at him.

"Bella Signora, are you ill?" he asked with concern.

"Maestro Sandro," she said, shaking her head. "You should not wait too long to paint me again, I think."

He caught her arm to steady her.

"The coughing," she explained after a moment. It makes me dizzy, but I'm all right now."

She didn't look all right. He released her and stepped to one side so that she could pass. He watched as she went down the corridor and slowly ascended a staircase until she was out of sight. Then he looked down and realised she had left her silk handkerchief behind on the table. He picked it up and saw that it was stained with fresh, crimson blood.

2

A work of art is above all an adventure of the mind.

EUGENE IONESCO

February, Oxford

It was a cold day close to the end of February and Will Bentley was nervous. He wasn't used to addressing the capacity audience filling the St. Ebbe's lecture theatre, and the students weren't used to him. He had done this at Cambridge, but never at Oxford. Almost all of their lecturers were professors, as he had seen from the History of Art Department's syllabus. He had been incongruously squeezed into the Hilary Term because he could talk in detail about how to forge an Italian Quattrocento masterpiece, and what had started as an eccentric idea from a lone professor had been welcomed with enthusiasm and oversubscribed. This was partly because there is something rather intriguing about art forgery, but also because Will himself had been splashed across newspaper front pages following the events of the previous summer. At that time he had made the headlines in connection with the theft of a Botticelli masterpiece, and his own paintings had begun to sell as fast as he could paint them.

He looked for the remote which advanced the slides and then realised with embarrassment that he already had it in his hand. He turned to the screen, which was still displaying the title page: 'Forgery of Quattrocento Art', and pressed the button on the remote, breathing a sigh of relief when it worked and the screen filled with a painting of a Venetian galley in full sail.

"To paint a very fine line such as is required for rigging on maritime paintings, the idea of the rigger brush was invented," he said.

The screen filled with a close-up of the head of a size zero sable rigger, with long brush hairs and a thin pointed body.

"The rigger is the forger's friend because as you can see here, the long hair permits him or her to rest a guiding finger on the canvas and any hand tremor is absorbed by the length of the hairs, permitting an extremely fine line to be created.

"The difference between the copyist and the forger is also an extremely fine line," he said to the sea of intent faces. "The difference is that the forger, or perhaps a dishonest dealer involved in the subsequent sale, attempts to pass the copy off as the original."

A hand went up. He had told them he would like it to be interactive.

"What about the provenance of the painting?" a young man asked. "Doesn't that provide evidence of its authenticity?"

"It does," Will nodded, and lifted his gaze to take in the rest of the audience. "The provenance is the paper trail that records every previous sale of the painting. But there are problems with provenance. For example, the provenance may be forged as well. In fact it is a relatively easy task to forge an old document, especially if you are already skilled at reproducing an exact copy of a painting. But the other difficulty is that there may be little or no provenance. If the painting were found in an attic where it has resided for two hundred years, who's to say what happened before that?" He looked around the audience and one or two people nodded. "This brings me to my next point."

He clicked the remote and a picture of Botticelli's Primavera filled the screen.

"Who has seen the actual Primavera?" he asked, and several people in the auditorium raised their hands.

He nodded. "It's quite a sight, isn't it? It hangs in the Uffizi gallery in Florence, in the same room as the Birth of Venus. The first thing you notice when you see the real thing is its size. This is a big painting. It's over ten feet wide. It would be extremely difficult and very time consuming to attempt a copy of Primavera, and of course it would be entirely pointless. Raise your hand if you have never before seen this image."

Every hand in the room remained down, either because they had all enjoyed a good education, or were reluctant to confess their ignorance in front of everyone.

"Exactly," Will said. "This painting is one of the best-known images in the world, so even if we made a perfect copy of it, we wouldn't be able to sell it as Primavera itself, even to a private collector, because we would have to get the original out of the Uffizi, which I suspect would be a bit tricky."

There was a ripple of laughter.

"That of course is a shame, because Botticelli has done a great deal of work here beyond just painting the image itself, and that's what I want to come on to now. Notwithstanding his extraordinary skill as a master painter, Botticelli was highly versed in secular tales of history, and experts today, probably some of them in this very room, have analysed this painting *ad infinitum* in an attempt to identify the many allegories that it represents.

"For example, Primavera is thought to be a wedding celebration of some kind. We see the three graces holding hands on the left, with Cupid firing his dart of love into the heart of one of them. We see the husband, cast as Mercury to the left of the three graces, and look! His red cloak bears golden flames or rays, which are associated with Saint Lawrence, and that in Italian is Lorenzo, the same name as Lorenzo the Magnificent, or perhaps his nephew Lorenzo di Pierfrancesco de' Medici; both of them patrons of Botticelli. In the background we see bay laurels as further symbols of Lorenzo, and citrus fruits known as Medica mala. Medica, Medici. This painting is full of allegory and we have hardly begun. Many books have been written about this one painting. So this brings us to an important thought, ladies and gentlemen."

Will paused for dramatic effect. He was enjoying himself now, nervousness forgotten.

"Our forger won't attempt to reproduce this masterpiece even if she or he has the skill."

He paused.

"By the way, I say 'she or he' to be inclusive, but the fact remains that most known forgers are male." He smiled. "This could be because women aren't foolish enough to do it, or that they are so very good that none of them get caught."

There was another ripple of laughter.

"So our forger doesn't want a Primavera that they can't sell, but they might want to paint something *in the style of* Botticelli, and have others interpret it as his on their behalf. This is an interesting idea and is the most common approach of the forger. Our forger has a challenge, however. He – and forgive me if I say 'he' – now has to be not only a master painter, but also a master of allegory that would have been understood in the Renaissance, so that academic experts such as your professors are tricked. That is a tall order indeed."

Another hand went up; a young woman this time, with blonde hair and blue-rimmed glasses.

"But what about modern technology?" she protested. "Can't it easily identify a real painting from a fake?"

"Another excellent point," Will said. "If you put a modern reproduction to the test it will be found out. But it is expensive because the equipment is highly specialist, and the masterpiece has to be transported to wherever that lab might be, which is not always convenient. So many paintings are never tested. The trick of the forger is to avoid the well-known master and instead to go for a lesser-known artist who still has value. And the painting must be painted on an old panel or canvas, never modern. The sides of the painting may have been photographed for security purposes, as they are normally concealed inside the frame, and so the sides must be identical to the original if a true copy is being made. Now we see the value of painting a different picture in the same style. The forger could use an old support, which is the panel or canvas the image is painted on, but he will struggle to reproduce the back and sides exactly as they should be."

The girl in the blue glasses nodded and he continued with his pitch, now bringing the discussion to Botticelli's Mars and Venus by putting up an image of the painting on the screen. There was a momentary buzz of whispered conversation across the audience and heads turned to each other for a few moments.

"I see that some of you recognize the significance of this particular painting, which is the one I was involved with last year, together with an insurance investigator named Lucy Wrackham. Now we don't know the exact date of Botticelli's Mars and Venus, but best estimates place it at about 1483, towards the end of the Quattrocento. We can surmise it may have been painted around the same time or just after Primavera. Both of them are painted on panel, as opposed to the Birth of Venus which may have come a year or two later and is painted on canvas. Canvas was becoming increasingly popular in Florence at that time."

He pointed to the screen.

"Here we see Venus, dressed and demure, and Mars unconscious after his amorous advances; a regrettable occurrence which may be familiar to some of the gentlemen in the audience."

There was another titter, this time more from the women.

"The paint is egg tempera, so Botticelli was capable of achieving fine precision. Let's have another show of hands: who has seen *this* actual painting?"

This time quite a few hands went up.

"Good for you," Will nodded. "It's much easier for us to see Mars and Venus of course, because it's just down the road in the London National Gallery, and you can pop in any time rather than having to queue for tickets. So if you haven't seen it yet, go along and see what you think."

He moved the slide on to a close-up of Venus lying in repose.

"Again we see allegory," Will went on." Venus is fully clothed this time, her hair is made up, and she has a pearl brooch at her breast. Perhaps therefore she represents a married woman, who out of respect would not be shown naked as in the Birth of Venus. It's thought that Botticelli's muse was Simonetta Vespucci, a young beauty of Quattrocento Florence, and it could be her, for she was indeed married."

A hand went up, distracting him this time.

"Yes?"

"We don't actually know that his muse was Simonetta Vespucci, do we?" asked a young woman. She had long dark hair and a slight Italian accent. She seemed a little older than the other students.

This was an unexpected question. Will tried to marshal his thoughts.

"Well, we don't absolutely *know*," he agreed. "But Botticelli did ask to be buried at her feet on his death, which is important. And there is another clue over here to the right."

He used the laser pointer on the remote to point at an area to the right of a conch shell that one of the little satyrs was blowing into Mercury's ear.

"Here we see wasps, again perfectly reproduced in great detail, flying in and out of the bough by Mercury's head. The Latin and Italian for wasp is *vespa*, so again this could be an allusion to the Vespucci name."

"Or it could just be an extension of the joke that even wasps won't wake him cos he's shagged out!" the girl responded, and this time the whole audience erupted and Will laughed with them. Her Italian pronunciation of the English slang somehow made it charming.

"You are absolutely right," Will said gallantly when order had been restored.

"After all it was five hundred years ago, and we can't be sure of anything. We can only make educated guesses."

The screen filled with a close up of the folds of Venus's dress just above her right hand.

"Now let's take a closer look. You can see here how intricate the painter has made this simple cloth, so that the light and shadow fall perfectly as the eye expects they should." He clicked again, bringing up a picture of the wasps. "Here we see the wasps we were talking about a moment ago. Botticelli didn't just paint them in roughly; they are anatomically correct from life, right down to their black-striped bodies. Academics have even identified their likely *genus*.

He clicked again, this time showing a close-up of the conch shell.

"Perfectly painted," he observed. "But again, full of allegory, and this time it has helped us date the painting." He looked around the audience. "Bear with me on this. It's a bit of a convoluted tale but quite fascinating, so listen carefully."

Some of the students literally leaned in closer.

"Why a conch shell?" Will asked, raising his eyebrows. The close-up of the magnificently painted shell filled the screen. "The shell was used in antiquity as a trumpet, as it is being used here. According to myth, the god Pan used one to produce a fearful sound that put the Titans to flight in the middle of a battle with the Olympian gods. It induced the confused terror that we call 'Panic', after Pan."

He paused and there was a momentary buzz of conversation as much of the audience turned over a familiar word and examined it differently.

"Now we come to the date of the painting. This myth about Pan and the conch shell was described in an extremely rare ancient work purchased by the poet Politian from the inheritors of Toscanelli, who died in 1482."

People were frowning with concentration, looking for the link but not seeing it.

"I did warn you that the story goes on a bit," Will said. "So let's summarize where we are."

He held up a finger.

"One. Our story starts with one these satyrs – that's the little cherubs with goats' legs – trying his very best to wake up Mars by blowing in his ear with a conch shell."

He added a second finger. "Two. The myth tells us that a conch shell was used by the great god Pan to induce Panic in the Titans. So it would be a good way to wake up Mars, wouldn't it?" He opened his hands in question and several of the audience nodded in agreement.

He added a third finger and carried on. "Three. We know that Toscanelli, who was an Italian mathematician, died in May 1482. And when Toscanelli passed on, his inheritors didn't have much use for all his academic books and papers, so they sold them all off. One of those papers was a very rare manuscript recounting this legend about Pan and the conch shell. It's thought that only two copies of it were ever in existence.

"Now we are almost there," he said, forgetting to count on his fingers anymore. "Along comes Politian and buys the rare manuscript containing this story about the conch shell. That means he is one of the very few people acquainted with the story. And what we also know for sure is that Politian knew Botticelli. Lorenzo the Magnificent was patron to both of them so they would have seen each other at court. Except they wouldn't have called him Politian like we do. Does anyone know his name in Italian?"

"Poliziano!" cried the dark-haired girl with the Italian accent.

"Exactly!" he said. "So if Politian or Poliziano recounted the little-known story about the conch shell to Botticelli, then we can make a good guess that Botticelli would have remembered it. He might even have decided to put it into his Mars and Venus painting because it is a good tale."

He looked around the audience. "I expect it would have taken a little while for Toscanelli's inheritors to get his books onto the market, and we can imagine that Botticelli would have taken some time to create this magnificent artwork, so this probably gives us an earliest date of 1483 for the completion of Mars and Venus."

He paused and there was another buzz of conversation which slowly quieted.

"We begin to understand the secrets hidden in these great paintings, which enables us to look at them with new eyes, both in appreciation of the art, and in appreciation of the intellect that drove that art. The forger only obtains all that allegory if he copies an original. If he paints something in the same style, he must make up his own allegorical allusions, so the point I am making is that it isn't as easy as merely being a good copyist. You need more than a good rigger brush."

He clicked the remote and brought up the full painting again, glancing surreptitiously at his watch and finding that he had just a minute left. It was time to get to the finale.

"Now you may have heard about my experience last year and how my old friend Alfred Smith, a master forger, painted a copy of Mars and Venus?"

Several people nodded.

"Well, we recovered photographs of the forgery from the London house where he was staying. He paused for dramatic effect. "And now I should confess that I have been deceiving you a little, because all the slides of Mars and Venus that you have seen tonight are of the copy painted last year by Alfred Smith. The folds of the dress; the wasps; the conch shell – ladies and gentlemen, you have been admiring a forgery."

3

Her robe was white and delicate as lace;
And still her eyes, with silent speech and rare,
Talked to the heart, leaving the lips at peace:
Come to me, come, dear heart of mine, she said:
Here shall thy long desires at rest be laid.

LORENZO DE' MEDICI, Sonnet translation by John Addington Symonds (1888)

27th April 1476, Florence

It was a warm Saturday afternoon, almost into May. Sandro Botticelli watched the funeral procession pass his workshop; first the clergy bearing torches, then the bier bearing the body of Simonetta Cattaneo Vespucci, clad in a white dress with perfect braided hair, open to view by all. They had left off the canopy despite the rising heat so that all could take a last look at La Bella Simonetta. Only last week he had spoken with Maestro Stefano, the doctor sent by Il Magnifico to care for her, who had said that by the grace of God she would recover. Yet last night she had passed away in the early hours and was with God. Botticelli realised dumbly that his cheeks were wet with tears for this lovely young woman, snatched away by consumption, the thief of time. He still remembered her at the joust the previous year, and afterwards at the palace when he had heard her graveyard cough.

The via Nuova wasn't wide and her bier passed within ten feet of him. He could see that her face was pallid in death but the *beccamorti* – those who had prepared her – had used rouge to colour her cheeks. Her face in death was drawn, her cheekbones too angular, her body too thin. He had painted that face and knew every contour of it in life, and now he recognised the emptying of the sanguine humour from the vessel of her body. That was why many called consumption the white plague.

The pallbearers walked at a steady pace and bore her towards the mouth of the street where it opened into the Borgo Ognissanti in an explosion of sunlight. The family mourners followed, led by Simonetta's husband Marco and other close relatives, then Giuliano himself, clad in sombre garb. The Medici lord bore a tragic expression, and Botticelli's keen eye noted it. The artist recognised the familiar face of Sforza Bettini, suddenly almost next to him in the throng, and took his arm so that Sforza turned and saw him, putting his hand over Botticelli's for a moment in a consoling gesture.

"A sad day, my friend."

"Sad indeed," Botticelli replied. "Is Lorenzo still in Pisa? He will find this a cruel cut."

"He is," Sforza said. "I have this morning penned a letter and sent it by horse, so he should know by tonight. But forgive me, I must walk on."

He dipped his head in a slight bow, Botticelli released his arm and the cortege moved away. He followed behind the less-important mourners and they all emerged onto the Borgo, where the press of the crowd was more intense and a wailing ululation came from the women, clamouring for the Virgin's aid.

They moved up the street until they reached the rough square of untidy grass which sloped down to the bank of the Arno in front of the Convent of Ognissanti. The procession stopped and a short requiem mass was conducted out in the open before them all, for the church knew when to take advantage of an assembled multitude. Botticelli chose to hang back with the crowd rather than be recognised by the assembled lords. He did not want to talk. His tongue was stilled with grief. He wanted only to bear silent witness and honour the dead.

When the short mass was over and the bell tolled mournfully in the *campanile*, the bier was lifted and Simonetta Vespucci's body was carried by the pallbearers for the last time out of the sunlight and into the candle-lit gloom of the church. Botticelli could have followed but he had seen enough. As the crowd began to disperse he walked down to the bank of the Arno, where there were four cypress trees. He stood beneath their cool shade by the muddy bank, watching a cluster of exploding bulrushes float cream-coloured down on the breeze. The river slid by and he let his mind drift with it.

4

O for a Muse of fire, that would ascend
The brightest heaven of invention.

WILLIAM SHAKESPEARE, Henry V

February, Oxford

After Will completed his presentation, everyone decamped to another room where there was an opportunity to mingle. The History of Art Department had stumped up some wine for the occasion. The pretty girl who had quizzed Will from the audience was waiting at the door with two glasses of red wine. She pounced on him before anyone else had the chance.

"Mr Bentley, I hope you like wine," she said with a smile. "My name is Alessa Cooper, and I was hoping to grab you for a minute."

She held out a glass.

"That's very kind but I have to ride a motorbike tonight, so I'll say no. How can I help?"

She turned and offered the unwanted glass to a student just coming through the doors, who took it gratefully.

"There," she said with a smile, and then leaned in conspiratorially. "I want to talk to you about Botticelli, but not right here."

He raised his eyebrows.

"Why not here?"

"This place is full of academics desperately looking for something to write their next paper about," she said. "I can say that because I am one. If you have half an hour I promise you will find it interesting. We could meet in the Blenheim."

"The Blenheim?"

"It's a pub just up the road. I'm meeting my fiancé there but we could have a quick chat afterwards."

"That would be very nice," Will said, but I'm meeting someone in London and I can't hang around."

He wondered why he had said 'someone' instead of 'my girlfriend'.

She had an infectious smile and she used it again. "I need only fifteen minutes."

He shook his head. "I do need to get off, I'm afraid. But I promised your professor to stay here for half an hour, if that helps. Let me get something non-alcoholic to drink first."

He excused himself and made his way to the table which had been set up as a temporary bar. He got a sparkling water and turned to find Alessa Cooper still waiting for him, but now she had been joined by several other students. She wrinkled her chin and looked exasperated.

"If you change your mind," she said, "I'll be at the Royal Blenheim on the corner." She leaned in again. "It would be mutually beneficial if you come, I promise."

She held out a card. "Otherwise give me a call."

He took the card and put it in his pocket, and she was gone before he could say anything else.

The other students descended upon him.

"We were wondering if you could tell us what happened last year with the National Gallery painting," said a young man.

"It sounded very dramatic," said the girl next to him. So Will briefly recounted the story he had told many times before. When next he raised his eyes to look round, a woman in her thirties held out her hand and introduced herself.

"Rachel Blake, Mr Bentley," she said. "I'm a film maker and freelance journalist. I heard you'd be here and talking about forgery so I managed to sneak in."

"Oh yes?"

Will looked around evasively. In his experience, journalists generally wanted to ask him about his own history as a forger, even though it was long ago, and he didn't want someone dragging all that up again.

"Oh don't worry, I'm not going to give you the third degree," she said. "I'm not working for a tabloid or anything." She had mid-brown hair in a bob, very red lips and tattooed eyebrows. He looked around desperately for escape.

"Yes, forgery certainly is fascinating," he agreed, "but the topic of today's session was really about Botticelli, so we should stick to that."

"Botticelli and how your friend forged his painting," she said, pinning him so that his mouth twitched into a slight wince. "I thought the theft would make a fascinating story. Interviews and some on-location work to show people the places they may have read about. Luxley Park, that sort of thing. It would make you even more famous!"

She had done her research. She gave him an unmistakeably flirtatious look.

"I suppose so," he said politely, "but I'd rather be less famous, not more, and I don't have any time to contribute to a documentary film."

She tried a few more gambits but he managed to put her off and she wondered away to talk to someone else.

There was a general hubbub as the assembled art department, made garrulous by wine, swapped gossip and carried on a dozen different conversations, mostly on the subject of the Italian Renaissance in general or Botticelli in particular. Will was dragged into several of them and was already aware that he had been there for almost an hour. The wine ran out and after ten more minutes the students started to thin.

A grey-haired man wearing a blue shirt, a navy-blue jacket and a bow-tie came over to him and held out his hand.

"Milton Flynn, Mr Bentley," he said, his voice a condescending drawl. "Interesting talk."

"Glad you liked it, Mr Flynn," Will said.

"Professor. Yes, it's always interesting to see how non-academics approach an academic topic."

"Invigorating rather than dry and dusty, I hope," Will said, taking an immediate dislike to him.

"Rather melodramatic," Flynn said," but I suppose we need something to liven up Hilary."

"Who's Hilary?"

The man gave him a pitying look. "Not a *woman*, Mr Bentley. The Hilary Term."

"Ah yes, I saw that on the agenda. Why isn't it just called the spring term? Is it some kind of secret code."

"A cypher of sorts? Keep the riffraff out? Yes, I suppose you could say so. The second academic term is named after St. Hilary of Poitiers. Have you heard of him?"

"Can't say I have," Will said, feeling in no mood to be talked down to. "Must have been tough having a girl's name."

Professor Flynn smirked. "Hilary is from the Latin *hilarius*, as we are told he was a man of cheerful disposition. We don't know for certain as it was the fourth century, but we celebrate his feast day on the fourteenth of January."

And what earns St. Hilary this honour?" Will asked.

"It's from the legal system," Professor Flynn said. The law courts arrange their sessions into four terms: Michaelmas, Hilary, Easter and Trinity. The university doesn't have an Easter term, just the other three."

"I expect everyone's away at Easter eating chocolate," Will said gravely.

Flynn eyed him.

"I would have thought that with your history Mr Bentley, you would be very familiar with the court system," he said. He raised a glass of wine in a sardonic toast and turned away before Will could think of a cutting reply. Irritated with the man, he drained the last of his water and decided he'd had enough. He went to shake the hand of the professor who had invited him. Due to a mix-up he had arrived that morning for a ten o'clock slot, but then found he had been squeezed in at four in the afternoon since he was extra-curricular. Now it was almost six and he had left Cambridge at half past seven that morning, so it had been a long day. The professor thanked him warmly for an entertaining afternoon and so did the colleagues clustered with her, so he felt slightly mollified, despite Milton Flynn. It had been a pleasant day on the whole.

"Did you manage to park at the back as I suggested, Mr Bentley?" she asked.

He had done so, so she showed him to the rear exit, thanked him again and bid him farewell. He called his girlfriend Lucy before stepping outside into the cold, but she didn't pick up. He was about to dictate a text message to her but then the phone vibrated as she called him back.

"Lucy?"

"Will! How did the lecture go?"

"Pretty well, I think. I've just finished so I should be in Richmond in an hour or so."

"Ah. Will, I'm awfully sorry but I'm at the airport. I tried to call you earlier but your phone was going to voicemail."

"The airport?" he said, raising his voice in surprise. "My phone was switched off while I was doing the talk. What are you doing at the airport? I was really looking forward to seeing you."

He realised too late that he sounded plaintive.

"I know, but I need to be in the New York office for Hoffman's. It only came up today and I managed to get the last flight so I'm on the seven twenty-five. I'm about to pass through security. In fact they are threatening snow so I hope I get off the ground."

Lucy worked for a global art insurance company called Hoffman and Courtland. He looked out of the window and saw a few snowflakes drifting down. He felt exasperated but tried not to show it.

"Yes, the snow's just starting here. Well that's a shame. What's going on in New York?"

"They've got some insurance scam going on and they want me there," she said. "Will, I'm very sorry, but work comes first."

"Work comes first," he repeated.

"Well, you know what I mean. I can't just refuse."

"No, of course not," he said. "I was just looking forward to seeing you. We aren't getting together very much, Lucy. We could do with a catch up."

"I know we could," she said. "But it's difficult with me being in London and you stuck in Cambridge."

There was an awkward silence until he broke it.

"When are you back?"

"I'm away all week," she said. "Back on Saturday morning early, unless they change it. The red eye."

"OK then," he said, feeling grumpy now. "Well, I guess I'll just go back up to Cambridge tonight, then. Have a good trip."

"I'll call you, but I'm at security now so I need to get my laptop out and take my shoes off. Talk soon!"

She disconnected before Will could say goodbye and he looked at the phone for a moment before putting it back in his pocket.

"Hmm," he said, shaking his head and tucking away his phone. He stepped out through the rear doors of Littlegate House. It was several degrees colder than it had been that morning when he had come down. He pulled his jacket tight and buttoned it up. A few snowflakes settled on him. He pulled out his phone again and checked the weather, which was destined to worsen as the evening progressed. It was already dusk. His Triumph Bonneville motorcycle was in a covered rack next to a large number of pedal bicycles, and he knew the trip back was going to be unpleasant; gritter lorries spraying salt in his face and the snow worsening. Not much fun on two wheels. He had thought about buying a car lately, and considered it again now: bikes were fun in the summer but horrible in the winter.

He felt miserable. He wanted a drink and something to eat, and he had been expecting exactly that after an hour's ride to Lucy's house. He looked at his phone again and saw that tomorrow it was due to warm up and rain would wash away the snow. He decided on the spur of the moment that he would stay the night in Oxford and go back the next day. Sandy, his principal model, had already been cancelled but he could probably get her back again if she were not busy. She life-modelled for several art and sculpture classes these days, so he had to book her in. He went back into Littlegate House and called her. She picked up almost immediately, seeing his name on her phone.

"Hi Will, how did your talk go, all right? The weather's about to turn nasty up here, according to the telly. What's it doing down there?"

"The talk went well but Lucy can't make it so I'm coming back up."

"Oh *Will*. What's up with her then, has she got another fella?"

The question threw him a little as he realised he wasn't entirely sure.

"Well I hope not. She's just got to go to New York for her company."

"All right for some."

He smiled. He knew Sandy didn't much like Lucy. She thought his girlfriend was snooty.

"Yes. So there's no point in going down to London and I'm coming back. I think I might wait until tomorrow, though, because it's starting to snow here."

"Is it really?" she said, surprised. There was the sound of movement, and then the squeaky sound of steamy window glass being rubbed.

"Blimey! It's snowing here too!"

She sounded excited. She loved snow.

"There we are then. I don't really want to ride the bike in snow and it's supposed to melt tomorrow."

"OK, then. Well ping me when you get back if you want me to come in."

His next call was to his friends Anna and George Levy in Cambridge, and George picked up.

"Hello Will," he said. "Aren't you supposed to be heading down the London road in pursuit of passion?"

"Supposed to be," Will said shortly, "but Lucy can't make it so I'm coming back in the morning. I know I asked you to pop into the studio to feed Beauty and the Beast, but I'll probably be back to do it myself."

Beauty and Beast were his studio cats, and had originally come as strays from George's wife Anna, a vet who styled herself patron saint of all good causes to do with animals.

"I'm sure Anna will want to go anyway," George said. "We're just having a glass of wine and eating taramasalata, but we're going to pop over in a bit and make sure they have food in their bowls."

"You don't need to, but thank you."

"Okay," George said. "Sorry to hear about Lucy. Everything all right?"

"I think so, she just had to go on a trip for Hoffman's. Thanks for looking after the cats."

They ended the call and he put his face to the window. It was dark but he could see snowflakes falling, illuminated by the outside lights. He went along the corridor and checked with the man on the front reception desk of Littlegate House. He was assured that as a guest lecturer it would be fine for him to leave his bike there until the next morning. He went out of the front exit and stood in the doorway, stuffing his hands in his pockets as protection against the cold. His breath clouded in front of his face. It was already nearly seven and he needed a hotel, but he didn't know Oxford. He saw a piece of paper had slipped from his pocket and fluttered down to the paving stones. He picked it up. It was the card the Italian girl had given him, with the History of Art Department's name and address emblazoned on it. It wasn't personalized to her, but she had hand-written her name and a mobile phone number on the back.

"Alessa," he said to himself, trying the name on his tongue, and then shook his head. She was much too attractive a girl for him to be meeting in a pub when his relationship with Lucy was struggling. But on the other hand, she would know Oxford, and she wanted to talk with him about Botticelli, and he could do with a pint. The truth was, he felt cross with Lucy. He looked around and saw a pub on an intersection with another street, so he crossed over, leaving footprints in a thin smattering of snow. A bus passed slowly, snow suddenly very evident in the beams of its headlights. At first he thought from the pub sign that it was the White Horse, but as he approached he realized that underneath the White Horse name and logo it said, 'Royal Blenheim'. It was on the corner with Pembroke Street, built of red brick with black-and-white mock Tudor above. He went in and the warmth and buzz of conversation was especially welcoming after the freezing February evening outside. He made his way to the bar, looking around for the Italian girl. She wasn't in sight but he decided to have a pint anyway, even if she had already left. He inspected the pumps and ordered a pint of Village Idiot, simply because he liked the name. He took a pull and it was good ale.

It was a large pub, but after a minute he saw the Italian girl at a half-round table in the rear. She was sitting with her back to him, talking to a man in his late twenties who was presumably her fiancé. Will examined him surreptitiously. The man wore a white open-necked shirt and a black jacket to match his slick black hair. He was full-lipped, high cheek-boned and good looking. Will vaguely recalled seeing him at the reception after the lecture, chatting to that pushy filmmaker woman. It appeared from his expression at that moment that he and Alessa were having an argument about something, so Will decided to stay at the bar and leave them to it. He parked himself on a stool.

His thoughts returned to Lucy. Back in August it had all been so romantic. The weather had been gloriously hot and they had just had the drama of the art theft and then plunged into a relationship as a result of it. Lucy wasn't really an ideal match for him. She was tidy and precise and organised, and the clutter of his studio drove her crazy. But she was clever and beautiful and he had fallen head over heels in love with her. Now he felt injured, because he was slowly coming to the realisation that she might not have the same feelings for him. He drained half of his pint, feeling moody. Certainly she *liked* him, and she was happy to spend time with him. But she didn't seem to want to spend the rest of her life with him – she had another whole life without him which revolved around the art insurance company that she worked for. He drank the rest of his pint much faster than he normally would, and then the Italian girl's fiancé strode past him without looking left or right and went out into the night. There was a momentary draught of cold air. Will waited for a minute but the girl didn't follow. He couldn't see her from where he was sitting, so he slid off his bar stool, leaving his empty beer glass on the bar, and walked round to her table. She was typing something into her phone and didn't see him approach. There was a half-full bottle of wine and two glasses beside it; hers nearly empty and her fiancé's apparently untouched. When she saw his legs beside her at the table, she looked up sharply, then jumped a little as she realised it was him.

"Will Bentley, that's a surprise! I'm sorry to glare at you. I thought you were someone else for a moment."

"Not a problem. You wanted to have a chat, and I had a cancellation, so here I am."

She paused for a moment to gather herself and then nodded and stood up.

"Of course, sit down. But will you just excuse me for a minute? I need to freshen up, but don't you dare leave!"

She had that Italian way of ending each sentence with an almost-indiscernible 'a'. She grabbed her bag and disappeared into the Ladies, leaving a grey coat on the seat where she had been sitting. He sat down as invited. He wanted to get another pint but he couldn't leave the table, as in her absence he was in charge of her coat. He slid the full glass of red wine in front of him carefully to one side, then looked around. The wall was half-timbered and incongruously wallpapered above in a motif of large pineapples. The framed photograph above the table was an old rowing eight from the 1900s which was rather good. On the table there was a menu and a beer mat, enabling him to discover that the White Horse was the name of the brewery and not the pub.

Alessa Cooper returned after a few minutes, smelling of perfume. She sat down and dumped her bag beside her without looking where it landed.

"Sorry about that," she said. "I thought you weren't coming, and then I ended up having a stupid row with my fiancé." She flashed her infectious smile at him and whether it was the beer or her he didn't know, but suddenly he was just happy to be there. She held out her hand across the table. "Call me Alessa," she said. He shook her hand and told her to call him Will.

"Thank you for coming," she said. "But I thought you had to dash off to London?"

"I did, but my girlfriend couldn't make it, so I thought I might stay in Oxford given the weather situation."

She peered around but there was no window in sight.

"What's the weather situation?"

"Starting to snow, and it's due to get worse. So I thought I'd stay the night rather than go back to Cambridge on these roads. I'm on a motorbike and I don't want to end up in the ditch."

"Well you'll be all right finding a hotel in February," she said. "Oxford's choc-a-bloc in the summer but not right now. "You ought to book somewhere, though. Do you have anywhere in mind?"

"Not at all," he said. "I don't know Oxford."

She suggested the Museum Hotel, only a few minutes away at St. Aldate's, and he managed to book the last room over the phone. Then he excused himself to get another pint and asked her if she wanted anything.

"Do you want some wine instead?" she asked, putting a hand on his arm as he was about to get up. "My fiancé Lucas didn't touch his glass and I can't possibly drink a whole bottle."

"That would be very nice."

She slid her fiancé's wineglass over to him.

"I swear he didn't even take the tiniest sip."

He lifted it and they clinked glasses. He sipped and then nodded appreciatively.

"Very nice," he said again. "So what did you want to speak to me about, Alessa? You mentioned Botticelli, but you probably know much more about him than I do. I just know certain bits very well."

"I want you to meet my father, actually. Papà is a professor, but long retired. They're thick on the ground around here. He's an alumnus of the University, but he's quite ill now so he doesn't get into town very much. He's got diabetes and his sight's failing. He's in a wheelchair."

"I'm sorry to hear that. Is your mother still around? It must be tough on her."

"Mamma died of breast cancer when I was fourteen," Alessa said. "She was a lot younger than him but she went first. She was from Udine in Northern Italy, so that's where my strange accent comes from."

"It's not strange, it's a good accent," he said, meaning it. "But I'm sorry to hear about your father. It must be hard for him, spending his whole life as an academic but with his sight failing. Why do you want me to meet him?"

"Papà is a Botticelli expert," she said. "In fact you could probably call him a Botticelli nut. He's written a book about him and he's trying to write another, but these days he has to dictate and I type it out for him. He even named me after the man. Alessandro di Mariano di Vanni Filipepi, you see? My full name is Alessandra, but I stick with Alessa because it's easier for the English to say."

"Well if he's an expert then he's way out of my league. I'm simply a painter. I just ended up doing a few lectures because I was good friends with Alfred Smith, and you heard all about last year I suppose?"

"Yes. That's why he's interested and wants to meet you. He thinks you might be able to solve a mystery for him, and he can't do it himself because he's not very mobile these days."

"What mystery?"

"Well, I don't want to give away all the details, but suffice to say it's about Botticelli's muse."

"Simonetta Vespucci."

"There you go again! Just like I caught you jumping to conclusions in your talk today."

Will grinned. He picked up the bottle to pour wine for the two of them, but then paused.

"Do you have to drive anywhere?"

"No, I live here in Oxford."

He nodded, feeling very mellow as the wine followed the beer and soaked into his veins. He could tell she was getting over her earlier argument with the fiancé.

"I recall pointing out that you were talking nonsense," he said affably, toasting her with his glass.

"I certainly was not!" she said hotly, and then laughed and blushed as one or two of those standing in the now-crowded pub glanced over at their table.

"You didn't, and I wasn't," she said in a more moderate tone, leaning closer to him to be heard above the hubbub. "You said it must be Simonetta in Mars and Venus because of the wasps, and I said that is just one interpretation."

"And I pointed out that he was buried at her feet," Will added, looking at her over his wineglass. "Do you suppose he painted someone else as his muse for his entire life, and then just as he was about to curl up his toes he decided to get buried at the feet of La Bella Simonetta?"

"The burial part is a wrinkle, I agree," she said. "But think about it! Simonetta dies of tuberculosis in 1476. He paints Mars and Venus in 1483 or thereabouts. Do you think she's still his muse seven years after she's dead and gone?"

Will thought about this and realised she was right – the dates didn't make sense.

"I do see what you mean," he said. "Well, maybe he just kept her in his mind's eye. She was supposed to be the most beautiful woman in all Florence after all. Or maybe he didn't have a muse at all. I don't have a muse, I just paint my model, but she isn't a muse, just a nice young lady."

He looked thoughtful, nevertheless.

"The artist muses that not everyone has a muse," she said.

"I mean a muse in the classical sense as you very well know. And if it wasn't Simonetta, then who on earth else could it have been?"

"Aha!" she said. "There we get precisely to the point. Papà has a theory that it *was* someone else."

Well, who?"

"You'll just have to come and talk to him, won't you? Otherwise you'll always wonder who it was and every time you give this talk you did today, you'll feel cross that you never followed up your one golden chance of finding out."

He shook his head. "This is crazy! What do I care who Botticelli's muse was?"

"So you admit he had one?" She dipped her chin and widened her eyes at him.

"I do *not* admit that he had one. And if he did, I don't care who it was."

"Of course you do."

"I don't."

"You must! You cannot just *not know*."

He sighed and looked at her. She tossed her dark curls but her mouth was almost breaking into a smile. What he wanted to do was to lean across the table and kiss that mouth, but he couldn't. There was a long silence while he sipped wine and thought about her point, and she looked back at him challengingly.

"Oh all right then," he said, giving in, and then added suspiciously, "Where does your father live? He's not on the Isle of Wight or anything, is he?"

"The Isle of Wight? Whatever gave you that idea? He's in Islip, which is a village a bit to the north of Oxford. It's only about twenty minutes and on the right side for you to get back up to Cambridge. I'll give you the address and you can pop round in the morning. I've got to get over there early. We'll make you some lunch and perhaps the weather will have had a chance to clear up before you go back."

She wrote the address of her father's cottage on the back of a White Horse beer mat and he slipped it into his pocket. At the door of the pub they paused to do up their jackets, for it was now past eight and the snow was coming down more thickly.

"I hope this will have calmed down by morning," she said, waving a hand at the weather and shrugging in a very Italian way that must have come from her mother.

"Me too," he said.

They parted at the door of the pub as they were going in different directions, shaking hands a little awkwardly. Will thought that when you meet someone you like, their touch can seem electric. As he walked the short distance to his hotel, guided by his phone, he realised that he had a text waiting. Seven words from Lucy had arrived about three quarters of an hour ago: 'Made it. Pilot says last flight out!'

He realised guiltily that he hadn't thought about Lucy even for a moment since he had walked up to Alessa Cooper's table in the pub.

5

There is something in humility which, strangely enough, exalts the heart, and something in pride which debases it.

ST. AUGUSTINE, Christian Doctrine

1480, Florence

Botticelli walked the last few steps to the Convent of Ognissanti but paused in the morning sunshine with his back to the church, looking across the grass to the trees beyond which the Arno flowed. He remembered standing under them on the day of Simonetta Vespucci's funeral, just four years before. Now her bones resided in this same church.

He had not yet heard the Terce bell marking the third morning hour and the intended time of his meeting, so he went down to the water's edge and stood beneath the cypresses, just as he had done on that spring day. It was June now and much hotter than it had been that April. Flies maintained a constant buzzing, and bees passed along the wildflowers at the foot of the wall marking the bank of the Arno, nodding the blossoms with their weight. The distinctive resin smell of the cypresses was evocative and he looked back at the old church, seeing in his mind's eye the procession of Simonetta's bier, the cluster of mourners and the solemnity of the crowd. If he reached back still further in his memory, he recalled Simonetta's laughing eyes glancing at him in the amphitheatre at the joust – only five years ago but it seemed like a lifetime. Many people he knew had died since that event, and he had created many paintings. He realised that he no longer had a complete memory of La Bella Simonetta's face; just fragmentary impressions and the reminders of old paintings.

The Terce still had not sounded across the city and Botticelli's thoughts turned to Giuliano de' Medici, riding out in the joust with his infectious smile and boyish wit. He should have hated him for stealing Simonetta's virtue, but one could never have hated Giuliano – a perfect blend of fun and flamboyance – especially now that God had taken him too. He had been murdered in the cathedral just two years previously. Botticelli shook his head at the memory. He had been painting in his workshop at the time and had only heard the tale of the murder and the subsequent attempted coup recounted to him by Angelo Poliziano, who had been present at the time of the attack. Afterwards his friends had teased him that while all Florence was up in arms, Botticelli had been painting a picture and had only discovered anything was amiss when a boy came to shout the news through the streets that the Medici had triumphed over the Pazzi family.

Giuliano had been suffering from an injured leg and had almost not gone to the mass, but had been persuaded by two of the conspirators, Francesco de' Pazzi and Bernardo Baroncelli, to join his brother Lorenzo. While Lorenzo had chatted in the ambulatory of the cathedral with Poliziano and others, the sacristy bell had tolled and all at once there had been a great commotion. Two priests standing with Lorenzo had drawn daggers from their robes and one of them had succeeded in wounding Lorenzo in the neck before he had leapt back out of harm's way and drawn his sword, slashing at the incompetent priests and forcing them to fall back in alarm in the face of his speed and fury.

His brother Giuliano had experienced no such good fortune. While Lorenzo had made good his escape through the sacristy, passing perplexed priests donning their vestments, the two conspirators with Giuliano had commenced a vicious attack. Unarmed and weakened by his injured leg, Lorenzo's brother had been an easy target. Pazzi and Baroncelli struck him down savagely and then continued to thrust their knives into him as he sank to his knees, his life blood pooling onto the floor of the cathedral. They continued to mutilate his body long after he was dead.

After hearing of the murder, Botticelli had gone out late in the day with Poliziano to the Palazzo della Signoria. There he had witnessed the bodies of no fewer than five of the conspirators hanged on ropes from a window of the tower. There was the naked body of Francesco de' Pazzi, Archbishop Salviati beside him and three other conspirators whose faces were too choked and distended for Botticelli to recognise. Poliziano had filled in the bloodthirsty details and Botticelli, never much of a one for real-life blood and guts, had almost sicked up in the street. Angelo had told him that he had seen the Archbishop, still kicking, fix his teeth into Pazzi's naked corpse – a last act of hatred following the ill-fated coup that he had been persuaded to join. Botticelli had subsequently been asked to paint effigies of the hanged on the Bargello tower, lest anyone should forget, for which he had been paid two hundred florins. God moves in mysterious ways. Over the last two years the Pazzi family's estates had been seized and their dolphin insignia had been systematically obliterated from everywhere it could be found.

"Maestro Botticelli?"

It took Botticelli several seconds to bring his thoughts back to focus on the present moment and look at the diminutive friar before him.

"Yes?"

"Maestro, I am Fra Martino. I am the one that wrote to you, and we were to meet at this hour. I was waiting for you at the door but I saw you pacing beneath the trees."

"Of course, brother," Botticelli said. "I was awaiting the Terce but I was having troubling thoughts. Please forgive me."

"The Terce bell has already tolled," the friar said with raised eyebrows, and Botticelli looked at him in surprise.

"Forgive me," he said again, absently. "I was recalling the passing of Giuliano."

The friar nodded in understanding.

"We have seen troubled times," he said. "But we are here to continue God's great work, and that is what I wish to discuss with you. Will you accompany me, maestro?"

Botticelli followed the friar across the grass towards the church. Trade carts were still coming in from the Porta al Prato and they had to wait a moment, so out of habit he studied the friar, absorbing a memory of him that he might put into some future painting. The friar was one of the Umiliati, an order of Benedictine friars that ran the Convent of Ognissanti. He was disfigured by smallpox scars on his face and had crooked brown teeth. He was a short man, reaching only to Botticelli's shoulder, dressed in a greyish-white habit of undyed cloth. He was tanned brown as if he worked in the fields, but his fingers were stained dark with oil, and his letter had said he was some sort of locksmith. He was an odd person to be commissioning a painting. Botticelli noticed that a slight smell of oil lingered on him. As the painter mounted the steps and they entered the gloom of the convent, he saw a large bunch of keys that clinked on the friar's belt, confirming his role as locksmith to the convent. He followed the friar down the nave and into dark rooms at the rear, where they eventually stopped at a workshop filled with metal devices and tools of all kinds. It was lit by a single shaft of light from a high unglazed window, and motes of dust and small flies danced in the light beam. There was a stink of candle tallow but none of the brown candles were burning.

Botticelli frowned in perplexity. Normally a church had a reception room draped with tapestries into which he would be welcomed, and such things as artistic commissions would be discussed in comfort over a glass of wine. He supposed that this room reflected the simple life of the Umiliati.

"Please be seated," Fra Martino bid him, and Botticelli sat on a bare wooden chair. The friar settled before him on a wooden stool, and began without preamble.

"Maestro Botticelli, the Order wishes to commission a painting from you. We have two panels which have been prepared and already mounted. Maestro Ghirlandaio is to paint St. Jerome on one of them, and we wish you to paint St. Augustine on the other. My brothers and I have discussed it, and we are thinking that both saints should be placed in their studies."

Botticelli sat and considered the request. Fra Martino waited patiently, not prompting him to react, but watching and waiting. The painter stared unseeing into the middle distance, his eyes slightly raised, his mouth a little open, with the tiniest frown creasing his forehead.

"Writing some text or sermon of rhetoric, perhaps," Botticelli said at last. "I could surround him with theological works, and perhaps an astrological device such as a zodiac globe to add attraction to the eye."

"Yes," agreed the friar. "And a clock showing the hours from sunset."

"A clock?"

"To show the precise hour of the day."

The friar looked a little ill at ease but Botticelli couldn't immediately see why, though his keen eye noted it.

"I will explain, but first I need to show you where the painting is to be located," Fra Martino said cryptically. "If possible we would like the work begun very soon and finished in time for the 28th August."

"Saint Augustine's feast day. That should be possible if it is not too large. We should also discuss the matter of the fee for the commission, Fra Martino, but not until I have judged the size of the panel. Who is the patron?"

"You may know that the Vespucci family has a private chapel on the south side of the nave," the friar said, and Botticelli nodded. He had correctly guessed that the Umiliati Order itself was not the client.

"Where Simonetta Vespucci is interred. I have visited once or twice."

"Yes, the people say that she is your muse, maestro."

"She is and she isn't," Botticelli said with an enigmatic smile, realising with surprise that he had never before put this into words. "She was while she lived, but now she is several years with God and my memory of her grows faint. How can I explain, Fra Martino? I paint people from life. It is the only way to make them true."

"You need the living soul to bring life to your paintings," said the friar, inclining his head and drawing the sign of the cross. "Then may she rest in peace through the grace of God. But I mentioned the Vespucci for another reason. Amerigo di Nastagio di Vespucci speaks highly both of you and Maestro Ghirlandaio. He wishes to pay for both commissions, to which of course we have gratefully agreed." He smiled. "In fact, he suggested to me that a certain rivalry between the two of you might present our convent with two particularly fine works."

Botticelli chuckled. He and Amerigo had become friends and the man had his measure.

"I fear he has detected the sin of pride in me," he said. "But that will be satisfactory. Will you require ultramarine?"

"That won't be necessary," the friar said. "Saint Augustine renounced a misspent youth for less earthly pleasures of the mind and soul. We do not need to dress him in bright silken raiment, for his strength is of the mind. But perhaps you could add the Vespucci insignia to the picture? Signor Vespucci indicated that this would be a boon in honour of his deceased father, Ser Nastagio."

"A blue stripe bearing golden wasps on a red shield," Botticelli said. "That can easily be furnished, but I will at least use a base grade of lapis lazuli for the stripe, or it will fade with time and insult our patrons. Fear not, Fra Martino," he added, seeing the friar's alarmed look. "It will be a small area, not the Madonna's robe. Please take me to see the bare panel now, and you can explain your reference to a clock."

Fra Martino led him back through darkened corridors into the church and showed him the two empty panels.

"This is to be the site of Saint Augustine," he said pointing, for I have already allocated the other panel to Maestro Ghirlandaio. As you can see they are on corresponding sides of the choir wall, each as pendant to the other, so we would ask that you and Maestro Ghirlandaio produce complementary works."

Botticelli inspected the panel carefully, humming to himself as he thought about the possibilities. At last he nodded.

"It can be done," he said simply. "Now as regards the fee..."

"Before you name a fee, Maestro, there is a complication," Fra Martino said, peering around in the gloom to ensure that they were not overlooked.

"Yes?"

"May I have your word that this is in complete confidence?"

Botticelli looked blankly at him.

"You may have it."

"Then God shall be your witness, Maestro Botticelli. Do you understand and agree to tell no-one of this?"

The friar actually held out the cross that hung on a chain around his neck and Botticelli touched it.

"God is my witness," he said, his brow wrinkled, his look intense. "What is this secret?"

In answer, the friar moved a wooden platform close to the panel, created to facilitate the painter, and clambered up onto it, his breath coming stertorously, his knees cracking. He reached up and pressed several points on the stone one after another. There was a faint click and then the panel shifted, drifting slightly out on the right side as if hinged. Again the friar looked furtively up and down the nave, but no-one was in sight.

He clambered down again, grasped the edge of the stone panel and pulled. It was heavy and the backs of his fingers turned white. The panel swung slowly outwards to expose a cavity within, the height of a tall man. It was empty.

"Who do you want to hide in there?" Botticelli asked in a low voice.

"Not who, but what, maestro," the friar said. "Let us return to my cell and I will tell you, but remember that I have your word, for this is of utmost importance to the Order. We must reset the lock before we close it. Can you climb up in my stead? You are a younger man than me."

Botticelli hopped up onto the wooden platform with considerably more grace than the friar had exhibited, and inspected the locking mechanism.

"Pull up the knob on the inside," the friar instructed. Botticelli did so, feeling the increasing tension of a spring until the lock clicked.

"Very well, the lock is primed," the friar said. "Come down and close the panel."

Botticelli jumped down and landed lightly, then turned and inspected the panel. It swung freely on a metal hinge coated in oil. Light began to dawn on him.

"So this secret is why I am talking to *you*, Fra Martino. And is this why we met in your cell and not the usual greeting room?"

"A lock from a locksmith," Fra Martino nodded, still looking around. "But please close it now, for no-one must see."

Botticelli gripped the panel and applied his weight so that it swung slowly inwards. As it aligned once more with its frame, there was a dull metallic click from within and it remained in place.

"Very ingenious," he said. "And somehow this is connected with the clock that you mentioned?"

The friar nodded but put a finger to his lips. He checked that the panel was closed, then led the way back to his cell. This time he closed the door and locked it. None of the other cells in the corridor even had doors.

"Our Order has the sacred bones of San Giovanni da Meda," the friar said in a low voice. "But relics are too often pillaged, maestro, so we wish to hide them and keep them safe."

"San Giovanni da Meda?" Botticelli said, ashamed to admit that he didn't know of this particular saint's significance.

"One of great importance to the Umiliati," Fra Martino said, "though no longer in the mind of Rome."

"And the clock?" Botticelli prompted.

"The clock," Fra Martino repeated, standing and walking over to a workbench shrouded with cloth. He removed the cloth and Botticelli saw a complex metal mechanism with sliding parts."

This is a replica of the lock in the panel," the friar explained. I made two identical locks, but this one is for you."

"For me?" Botticelli said, confused.

"To measure, maestro. By the slightest pressure on these five levers in correct sequence, so…"

He demonstrated and the sprung-loaded locking bar clicked back. "…the lock opens. My idea is that these levers could be incorporated into the painting. You will observe that they are arranged in a circle."

"Like numbers on a clock," Botticelli said, understanding now. "So by pressing numbers on the clock face, the lock would be released. Ingenious indeed, Fra Martino." He knelt down in front of the mechanism, studying it with ferocious concentration, then nodding. "It could be done, I think. Do you have paper and ink? I need to make an impression of the levers."

After a short period he had a perfect tracing and he stood up.

"It can be done," he confirmed, as he had said in front of the panel. "But I will need to inspect the panel again. It need not be opened but I must measure exactly where the levers are positioned on it, so that I can make the composition work. We must then test it once the painting is drawn and again when it is completed. Tell me, does Ghirlandaio have a similar hidden mechanism and concealed cavity?"

"He does not, maestro," said Fra Martino, shaking his head in emphasis. "Only you, so it is important that you do not discuss it with him or allow him to see the cavity."

Botticelli felt ridiculously pleased that the secret was to be entrusted with him and not with Ghirlandaio.

"It will remain our confidence," he said gravely.

It was early August when Botticelli was putting the finishing touches to the St. Augustine painting, but Fra Martino had disappeared. Botticelli had not seen him for ten days, which was very unusual because the friar normally visited him every other day. He had asked for him but received only evasive answers. "Fra Martino isn't here." "Fra Martino has just slipped out, he will be back soon." "Fra Martino cannot come to you now as he is outside the walls."

He had been painting the lines in the book of mathematics above St. Augustine's head at the time, and had been seeking almost anything to write, knowing nothing of mathematics, so he painted in their feeble excuses: '*Dov'è Frate Martino? È scappato. E dov'è andato? È fuor dalla Porta al Prato*'.

Botticelli had used the clock in the painting to show the twenty-fourth hour, representing Compline, the time of sunset. At this moment, according to legend, St. Augustine had been in his study writing to St. Jerome, and had a vision coincident with Jerome's death in Jerusalem. Thus Botticelli had woven the clock into the painting to report the exact hour of the vision, not merely included it without explanation. Fra Martino had been duly impressed.

The friar had lent him a key so that he could come and go at any hour while working on the painting. He still had this key. One evening he let himself in after the Compline bell in the late evening when the friars had gone to bed and none still walked the halls. Botticelli checked his completed painting first by instinct, then inspected Ghirlandaio's completed St. Jerome and liked what he saw. After that he followed the corridors with a candle, having trouble finding his way in the dark but eventually recognising the door to Fra Martino's cell. A friar was snoring loudly in the next cell so he was very quiet. The door to the locksmith's workshop was ajar and he stepped inside. The cell was much as before, even to the detail of the second lock beneath the cloth which Botticelli had now studied many times. There was no sign of Fra Martino and the rough bunk in the corner contained no sleeping figure. Yet there was a smell that Botticelli recognised. He wrinkled his nose and sniffed. A sour smell of iron and salt. The smell of a butcher's shop. He lifted the bedding and at the head end, beneath a simple pillow of straw, there was a black pool of dried blood, and he knew why Fra Martino had not been to visit him. Someone had discovered the secret of the relics, or perhaps they had tried but failed to discover it. He would never know.

Botticelli shivered, realising that he may be the only soul who knew of the relics. On instinct he replaced the friar's bedding and looked round the cell, his eyes falling upon the spare locking mechanism. He removed the black cloth which was draped over the lock, then replaced the mechanism with a large pot of grease and covered it up with the cloth. Then he picked up the locking mechanism and tucked it awkwardly under his cloak. He returned through the corridors to the choir, all the while mercifully unobserved. Leaving the spare lock on the floor for a moment, he climbed up onto his painting platform, which was yet to be dismantled. He pressed the correct sequence of numbers on the clock face: II, XIIII, XXII, VIIII and I. The mechanism of the lock clicked open and the panel released. He jumped down and opened the panel. Behind it now was a brass-bound box bearing pictures of religious figures, its lid raised into a peak like the roof of a church. A ruby was set into the peak at each end. Botticelli opened the lid and saw inside the skull and bones he had expected to see.

He shut the box, closed the panel, picked up the spare lock and let himself quietly out of the side door of the church, locking it and pocketing the key. Then he made his way down to the Arno and hurled the intricate lock mechanism far out into the water, where it instantly sank. When he got back to via Nuova he let himself into his workshop, shut the door behind him and leaned his back against it, wiping his brow. After a minute he went to a cabinet in his room and poured himself a glass of wine with shaking fingers. Then he bowed his head in the direction of the convent and toasted the sacred bones of San Giovanni da Meda.

6

Wine is a turncoat; first a friend and then an enemy.

HENRY FIELDING

February, Oxford

Will didn't have a high tolerance for alcohol and felt hung over when he awoke the next morning in his Oxford hotel room. He took a long shower, scrubbed himself with the Happy Buddha soap provided and then used a disposable toothbrush he had obtained from housekeeping. There was a bathroom scales provided by the hotel, so he stood on it and found to his surprise that for the first time in his life he was three pounds heavier than normal. He decided it must be the scales and not him, but it instilled a doubt. He shook his head dismissively but then wished he hadn't. He dressed thoughtfully, wondering whether his waistline felt tighter or if he were imagining it.

He went down to breakfast but tried to eat sensibly, eschewing the sausages and bacon and sticking with eggs. After poached eggs on toast and two cups of coffee he began to feel human again. Having nothing to pack he was able to leave quickly.

Outside the snow had settled in the night but was now melting rapidly. Every surface was dripping. He picked up his motorbike from Littlegate House without any trouble, dried the seat with a cloth he kept in the back, put on his leathers and set off. It took him twenty minutes to get to the village of Islip, and then a further five to locate the cottage. It was built of grey stone with dormer windows and it was called Mill Cottage. Will parked the Bonneville in a corner next to a five-bar gate. He locked away his leathers, secured his helmet and then knocked on the door. After a few moments

Alessa opened it, her face breaking into a smile.

"You came!" she said. "I was afraid you wouldn't. Come in, you must be frozen."

He followed her through the hall, passing a sitting-room to the right and then a kitchen, but she turned left into a study and he went in after her.

An old man was seated in a wheelchair beside a crackling fire, protected by an antique brass peacock's tail fireguard. The room was filled with books, and any part of the dark-green wallpaper which was not covered by books was filled with paintings; mostly small watercolours. There was also a portrait in oils of Alessa when she had been a teenager. There was a roll-top writing desk with lots of little drawers and a computer on it. The window overlooked an untidy back garden with a patch of snow still melting on the lawn. On the window shelf there was a black-and-white photograph of a beautiful woman, and another beside it of the same woman, this time with grey hair, beside a much younger and sprightly version of the man in the wheelchair.

"Papà, this is Will Bentley," Alessa said to the man in the wheelchair, and turned to Will. "This is my father, Professor Humphrey Cooper."

"Mr Bentley, thank you for coming," the old man said, and held out his hand. "Call me Humph. Everybody does." His breath came in a wheezy rattle, almost like a whistle. He had grey hair, curly and thick, and dark-brown bushy eyebrows above timeworn features. He wore large, black-rimmed spectacles with pebble lenses.

Will shook his hand and then sat down on a sofa opposite the wheelchair, with a low table between them. "Call me Will," he said.

"I wasn't sure if you would visit me," Cooper said. "I thought it would sound like a fool's errand, but I mentioned it to Alessa and she said she would give it a try."

"Your daughter is extremely persuasive," Will said, and Cooper laughed, his laugh turning into a minor coughing fit.

"Don't I know it!" he said.

"Would you like some tea or coffee, Will?" Alessa said. "What about you, papà? The kettle's boiled."

"Tea would be good," Will said, and she disappeared to make tea for the three of them.

"How did your lecture go yesterday?" Cooper asked. "You were talking about Mars and Venus, I believe?"

"It seemed to go all right," Will said, "but I'm surprised you even heard about it."

"I'm an alumnus of the History of Art department so I'm on their mailing list. It was in their newsletter and it caught my eye, because I specialise in Botticelli." He gestured around the room and Will remembered what Alessa had said the previous evening. He now spotted various books with Botticelli in the title, some of which he recognised.

"I've written a book about him, but that was mainly about the paintings.

Now I'm trying to write about the man himself," Cooper went on. "It's difficult with these not working very well anymore, though." He used two fingers of one hand to indicate his eyes. "Losing my sight."

"I'm sorry to hear that."

"Damn nuisance, but we're not here to talk about me. I gather Alessa told you something of my quest?"

"She did, but she was quite cryptic. She argued with me a lot during the talk when I said that Simonetta Vespucci was Botticelli's muse. Then she said last night in the pub that you had an alternative theory, but when I asked what it was she said I'd have to talk to you. So here I am."

Alessa reappeared at that moment with three mugs of tea.

"I'm sorry," she said. "I know I ought to be doing the whole teacups and teapot thing but then the tea goes cold and anyway it's a hassle and I don't want to miss anything. *Have* I missed anything? Do you want any sugar?"

"Thank you," Will said, taking a red polka-dot mug and placing it on the table before him. "No sugar, and you didn't miss anything yet."

"Botticelli painted the Birth of Venus, and Mars and Venus, and Primavera, most likely in the early 1480s," the professor went on as if there had been no interruption at all. "Simonetta Vespucci died of tuberculosis in 1476, so she had been gone at least five years when he started to produce those extraordinary pagan paintings with the young woman who always has the same face."

"But he asked to be buried at Simonetta's feet," Will said, beginning to feel like a broken record.

"And so he was, when he died in 1510, thirty-four years after Simonetta. But we don't know more than that. For example, was he devoted to her for that entire period? For *thirty-four years*? Or did he ask on a whim to be buried at her feet when she died in 1476, and someone remembered all those years later? Perhaps he indicated his wish in a long-forgotten will. You see, it isn't definitive that she was his muse once we consider the facts."

Will pursed his lips and rocked his head from side to side a little.

"I suppose so," he admitted grudgingly.

"All right. So who might he have been painting in those three secular paintings? They would have been expensive, likely commissioned by Lorenzo himself or by the Vespucci family acting as his agent. For what occasion might you buy a very expensive painting in those days?"

"I don't know much about those days," Will admitted, shaking his head. "People imagine I'm a renaissance art expert, but I only really know about Botticelli's Mars and Venus painting. I can tell you about clients today, though. They usually buy for an investment, or a nice picture on the wall if they can afford it. Or it could be a family portrait, for a special occasion."

"A family portrait is getting close," Cooper said. "Lorenzo the Magnificent was patron or tutor, however you want to interpret it, to his younger cousins, Lorenzo di Pierfrancesco de' Medici and his brother

Giovanni. He paid for their education. Their father had passed away you see, so Il Magnifico had become their ward."

"They called themselves the Popular branch of the Medici family," Alessa added. "*I Popolani*." She passed her father's tea to him and he took it gratefully, continuing to speak in between sips.

"A bit of early self-marketing," Cooper said with a wry smile. "Now Lorenzo The Popular – let's call him Il Popolano or too many Lorenzo's get confusing – Il Popolano got married in July 1482. We also estimate that Pallas and the Centaur, and possibly Primavera itself, were painted in 1482. So what could be more likely than that Il Magnifico commissioned one or both of those paintings from Botticelli as a wedding present, perhaps in response to the dowry from Il Popolano's bride-to-be?"

"A wedding present?" Will repeated.

"Yes," Cooper nodded. "Think about it. Primavera is all about cupid's dart of love piercing the heart of one of the three graces, while Mercury looks on and Venus is in attendance. We also have Flora, representing fertility, and the whole painting is covered with allegories referring to the Medici."

"Yes. I talked about some of them in my lecture," Will said, frowning. "I don't really know the Pallas picture, though. I've seen it in the Uffizi in Florence, but I haven't looked into it."

"Pallas is a young woman with that same face we keep seeing, and the painting is all about her taming a wild and unruly centaur, which could be a metaphor for bringing Il Popolano into line by marrying him."

Will nodded slowly.

"Okay," he said. "Let's suppose you're right. But I must confess that I have only ever really studied the Mars and Venus picture in detail. I got interested after the whole forgery thing last year, and people kept expecting me to be an expert about it, so I picked a few things up. What can you tell me about *that* painting? It was likely painted a year after Il Popolano got married, in 1483."

"Yes, 1483," Cooper agreed. "Some suggest as early as 1478, but I disagree. Now Mars and Venus as you know is all about fertility. Clearly its two subjects have just had sexual intercourse, and the young woman again has the same face that keeps cropping up. She is dressed, just as she would be if she were married. It would not be proper for her to be undressed, you see. In fact, if you wanted to commission a painting to encourage the gods to grant Il Popolano and his new bride a clutch of children, Mars and Venus is exactly the sort of thing you might ask Botticelli to create."

"So I presume what you are saying is that the married woman in the painting was Botticelli's muse," Will said. "That the artist was placing Il Popolano and his *wife* into all these secular paintings."

"That is precisely what I am saying," Professor Cooper said, sipping tea so that it steamed up his glasses.

"And what was the name of this woman?"

"She was called Semiramide d'Appiano," Cooper said. "She was Simonetta's niece, as it happens, and it was a political marriage. She was originally promised to Il Magnifico's brother Giuliano, but he was murdered in 1478."

There was a silence while Will thought about it.

"The Pazzi conspiracy," he said. "The one who was killed in the cathedral, you mean?"

"The very same."

"Giuliano had popped his clogs so they married Semiramide off to Il Popolano instead," Alessa added. She pronounced it 'pawped his clawgs'. "Semiramide was bringing her own line of aristocratic blood to the table, as her family was married into the Aragonese dynasty of Napoli."

Will tried the new name on his tongue.

"Semi*ra*mide. Is that how I say it?"

"Yes, exactly. Emphasis on the 'ra', and 'day' on the end."

Will nodded. "All right then, so Semiramide is an interesting idea, but she seems to be conjecture. Have you got any actual evidence?"

"There you have hit the nail on the head, Mr Bentley," Cooper said, evidently not yet feeling sufficiently comfortable to call him Will. "There is no evidence at all, but if there were, that would be dramatic news indeed. To prove that Botticelli's muse was Semiramide Appiano rather than Simonetta Vespucci would be a wonderful chapter for my new book. And that's where you come in."

"Me?" Will said. "I only just heard about this woman a minute ago."

Cooper seemed unperturbed. He turned to his daughter. "Show Mr Bentley that print-out, Alessa."

She stood up and riffled through the writing desk for a few moments before emerging triumphantly with a printed-out email. It was a Google Alert.

"Alessa is very clever with computers," Cooper said, "Whereas I struggle to find the 'on' switch. However, we were discussing her academic studies and she told me all about Google Alerts and the way you can set up a search for anything at all. So I asked her to set me up an Alert for 'Semiramide Appiano'. We had to include 'Appiano' because otherwise you get a deluge of responses about Rossini's opera. Anyway, I got a lot of responses and I followed them all up, but there was nothing I didn't already know. Time went by, but the interesting thing about these Alert things is that they email you when something new comes along."

He handed the sheet of paper to Will. "This arrived a few days ago."

Will read it. It seemed to be some kind of digitised book entry. The title was 'Medici letter written by Semiramide Appiano' and the yellow highlights contained the phrase '…Lucian's tale of Alexander and Roxana…' It was from a book entitled 'The Classical Origin of Science Fiction' by Frederick Pocock, written in 1957, and the sub-text below said that it was about the writings of Lucian."

Will looked up blankly.

"I'm sorry, but I haven't a clue what this is about," he said. "Science fiction?"

"Perfectly understandable," the professor said. "So let me explain. The British Library seems to have scanned this old book into their computer and now they can search the words in it. So it turns out the book contains this reference somewhere and it's rather interesting. What it means is that this man Pocock was writing about science fiction and he was obviously using Lucian as an example."

"Obviously?" asked Will with irony, and the professor looked a little abashed.

"Yes, I suppose it isn't obvious, sorry. Lucian authored a satirical treatise which he called A True Story, in which he wrote about aliens and outer space, even war between planets."

"Well there was a lot of that sort of thing in the forties and fifties," Will said. "Dan Dare, for one."

"No, you misunderstand, Will," Cooper said, warming to his theme and becoming less formal as he did so. "Lucian of Samosata wrote his True Story in the second century after Christ. About 150 AD."

Will sat back, astonished.

"Oh!"

He read the piece of paper again that Alessa had handed to him.

"That *is* actually amazing. So this man Pocock wrote a book pointing out that Lucian had started science fiction way before any of us could possibly have imagined. But I don't understand the connection between Semiramide and Lucian. How does that work?"

"Well, I haven't seen the full reference," Cooper admitted. "But here is what I think happened. I think Pocock had read this reference somewhere and used it to demonstrate that not only did Lucian write about aliens and outer space rather sooner than Dan Dare, but also that a member of the Medici family in Quattrocento Italy – Semiramide d'Appiano – was familiar with Lucian's tale of Alexander and Roxana. Obviously I don't know what final point he was making, because we didn't get the full text of the book, just this snippet."

"That seems logical," Will said, frowning. "And I vaguely remember something referring to these Alexander and Roxana people, but I can't remember what. How do they come in?"

"You probably came across it last time you looked at Mars and Venus in the National Gallery. Alessa, have you got that bit you printed out from the National?"

She had a piece of paper already in her hand, knowing how the story would unfold. She handed it to Will. It was a description of the Mars and Venus picture, though he noticed that the National referred to it as 'Venus and Mars'.

PAINTING VENUS

A lost Classical painting of the marriage of Alexander and Roxana was described by the 2nd-century Greek writer, Lucian. It showed cupids playing with Alexander's spear and armour.

"Oh," Will said again. "Yes, I remember now." He looked at the two sheets of paper side by side, and chuckled. "This is more complicated than the story I tell about how they dated the painting to 1483," he said. "And that's saying something. So in summary, if this reference from Pocock is correct, this woman Semiramide wrote a letter in which she made an oblique reference to Botticelli's Mars and Venus."

Cooper smiled broadly. "Almost what we might call the beginnings of some *evidence*, if we could unearth that reference and prove it to be true," he said.

Will looked at him blankly for a moment and then began to understand what the old man intended.

"You want *me* to follow it up?" he said. "I can't do that. I know there was all that business last year but that's not what I do for a living. I'm a painter, and I only just heard about this woman. I don't know anything about her."

"Semiramide."

"Yes, her. I wouldn't stand a chance. I can't even speak Italian."

He realised the mistake as soon as the words had left his mouth.

"*Parlo correntemente l'italiano*," Alessa said sweetly, "and I also studied classical Italian as part of my doctorate."

"There we are then," Will said, folding his arms. "*You* are the perfect person to follow it up."

"I just thought it would be good for someone to work together with Alessa," the professor said mildly. "Two heads are better than one for this sort of thing, and as you can see, I'm bound by this wheelchair." He waved a hand at himself and went on. "I thought you'd be a good candidate because you demonstrated your investigative capabilities last year with that whole thing about Mars and Venus. And to be honest, I thought you'd like to find out the truth."

Will kept his arms folded. He felt stubbornly resistant, as if he were unexpectedly being backed into a corner.

"I see all that, but my whole way of life is being a painter," he said. "I know it sounds weird, but it's like a compulsion. If I don't paint for a few days I get edgy."

"It wouldn't be continuous," the professor said persuasively. "Just a helping hand here and there. Perhaps you could just think about it."

Alessa leaned forward.

"It would be exciting if we discovered a secret that no-one else knows!" she said with a sparkle in her eye, and Will wavered for a moment. She had such an animated face and he would love to capture it in paint. Then he remembered his resolve not to get involved with Alessa when he was trying to revitalise his relationship with Lucy, and he shook his head ruefully.

"I just can't," he said simply, and after that there was an awkward silence.

When he left them he felt guilty, but he wasn't going to go off on some wild goose chase with the beautiful Alessa and that was that. To be honest, he didn't trust himself.

Alessa did not stand at the door to wave him goodbye, but glared at him and closed the door behind him none too gently as he departed. For the entire ride back to Cambridge he turned it over in his mind, but felt sure he had done the right thing. He parked the Bonnie in the garage down the side of his old studio building, and walked back up the path to the front, fumbling for his door key. The studio was an ugly building which had once been a ball-bearing factory. He found his key and let himself in. The postman had been and he picked up a clutch of letters and junk mail. When he went up the stairs to his cluttered studio, he found a note on the table.

"Cats fed. Let us know when you are back. Hope all well with Lucy. Anna and George xxx"

As if on cue, Beauty came padding across the floor to him and meowed. He picked her up and crooned to her, scratching behind her ears, one of which was bent from some ancient feline fracas. After making a fuss of her he put her down on the chair and looked around for Beast, who was in his favourite place, stretched out on a chair beside the spiral wrought-iron staircase which led up to the roof. Will made a fuss of Beast as well and then went into the kitchen and filled the kettle.

While the kettle was boiling he turned up the heating a notch and then walked over to his easel, sweeping his long black hair out of his eyes and looking thoughtfully at the canvas. It was a painting of his model Sandy in a white dress, wearing a red scarf over her hair, drop-dead gorgeous in the back of a limousine. The window was down and she was leaning out coquettishly. Reflected in the gleaming black paintwork of the car were the lenses of the paparazzi, and behind the lenses were the grotesque distorted heads of wolves. He planned to call it 'Little Red Riding Hood'.

His mind was slowly clearing from the morning's frustration. After a while he slipped on his favourite painting apron, picked up a flat brush, loaded it with black mixed from ultramarine and burnt umber, and began to touch in reflections of a photographer's camera in the paintwork of the limo. When the kettle clicked, he did not notice.

7

Everything about Florence seems to be coloured with a mild violet, like diluted wine.

HENRY JAMES, Letter 1869

April 1482, Florence

Botticelli was making the short walk to the house of his friend Amerigo Vespucci in Borgo Ognissanti, as he had received an invitation the previous day to discuss a commission.

He was wearing silk-embroidered green hose and a very fine dark-blue doublet, with a light cloak thrown over the top. As a boy he had been apprenticed to the workshop of the master painter Fra Filippo Lippi, who had taught him a lesson about fashion.

"Sandro," Lippi had once said to him, "the world is full of painters who die without a florin in their pockets. You will be a great painter, but a patron wishes also to believe you are rich and successful, like himself. If that is how you appear to him, he will reach deep into his purse."

Botticelli had never forgotten the lesson. He didn't need to dress up for Amerigo, but it was a convention that he never broke.

A leather satchel of drawing materials was slung over his shoulder. He knew that a picture could best be described with a sketch. The Terce bell rang in the tower of the Convent of Ognissanti as he passed, making him remember when he had met the ill-fated Fra Martino there. Two years had passed but the old friar had never reappeared. Botticelli had not inquired further, for he remembered the blood in Fra Martino's bed, and the iron stink of his cell. He glanced left at the cypresses, which this morning were stirring lazily in a cool breeze. Two swifts arrowed out of the branches, disturbed by the Terce. The bell made him realise that he was tardy, but he wasn't concerned as he knew his friend was a late riser and would in all probability still be at breakfast.

Botticelli was feeling irritated, having had an argument with his brother that morning.

"You do nothing all day but paint," Giovanni had said, somehow believing that dealing shares in the public debt was real work but painting pictures was not. Botticelli would never understand how he and his rotund older brother could be so different. How could numbers in a ledger be more real than paint on a panel? His brother had no passion, whereas he himself represented love and fear and lust in light and line. Why couldn't Giovanni see this? They had ended up shouting at each other.

Botticelli was just back from a sojourn in Rome, where he had been frescoing the walls of the pope's newly completed Sistine Chapel, working with Pietro Perugino and some other painters. Ghirlandaio had been there too. The commission had been arranged by Il Magnifico, who was trying to woo the papacy following a rift which had become a chasm in the wake of the Pazzi conspiracy and Il Magnifico's hanging of Archbishop Salviati. But as Botticelli and his team of young apprentices had been putting the finishing touches to his works, word had reached him of the death of his father Mariano, and he had returned immediately to Florence.

It was good to be back in his own city. He knew every inch of its walls and streets, and somehow the air seemed fresher, despite the stench of the fulling mills when the wind was in the wrong direction. Yet while Florence was a delight to him, sharing the house in via Nuova with Giovanni and his family was disagreeable, and more than once Botticelli had considered renting a house of his own, now that he had money. His father had died on the twentieth of February, and the funeral had already taken place by the time Botticelli arrived back in the city. Giovanni had implied that morning that it was somehow disrespectful that Botticelli had not been present for his father's funeral, even though it would have been impossible for him to return in time. It was another irritation.

He paused in the piazza and breathed deeply for a few moments to gather himself before walking on. It wasn't long before he came to the Vespucci palazzo, a big old mansion decorated with porticoes and white marble statues. It was set back from the street and Botticelli went in at the gates. Wisteria was in full bloom against the stonework, and potted citrus trees bore yellow lemons which perfectly complemented the purple wisteria blossoms. The house had belonged to Amerigo's father, but Ser Nastagio had gone to God, and Amerigo was finding his feet without the old man's commanding presence. Botticelli had noticed a similar change in the atmosphere of his own house following the departure of his own father. In fact, he realised with a sudden flash of insight, Giovanni would never have been so bold had his father been alive. It was as if he were competing with his brother to lead the household. Giovanni was oldest and therefore the heir apparent, but

Botticelli had become famous, receiving commissions from the nobility and religious orders of Florence. This had given him a confident and jocular air that he had never possessed as a child, and Giovanni resented it. He could no longer push his younger brother around.

He may be jealous of my success, Botticelli realised.

Perhaps he should talk to the Rucellai, from whom they rented the house in via Nuova, and move out in order to give Giovanni the dominance he yearned for. Or perhaps, he thought with a roll of his eyes, *Giovanni* should move out.

A servant welcomed him at the door of the palazzo and led him through the vaulted hallway hung with Flemish tapestries. They made their way to the large central courtyard where there was a garden of shrubs and flowers surrounding a round stone patio, accessed by a path from a great door at each quadrant. As expected, Amerigo was seated at the white marble garden table in the centre, eating breakfast. Two peacocks strutted about him on the patio but they were so tame that they ignored Botticelli as he passed them.

Amerigo stood up and they clasped wrists in a perfunctory fashion, patted each other on the back as old friends do, and then sat down together. Botticelli had removed his cloak and a hovering maidservant took it from him. She offered him breakfast. He gracefully accepted even though he had already eaten, for it would have been rude to watch Amerigo eat alone. He decided nevertheless to have very little. Though he was still fit, he was now thirty-seven and conscious that his doublets recently seemed tighter. He was therefore eating less, partly in vanity but partly in dread of ending up like Giovanni. His older brother had been nicknamed Botticello – the little barrel – for as long as the family could remember, and this sobriquet had migrated to Botticelli when in his youth he had briefly trained with Giovanni as a goldsmith. He didn't want it to become his destiny also.

He put the leather satchel down beside his chair in case it should be needed.

"Sandro!" Amerigo said. "I was so sorry to hear of your father's passing."

Botticelli thanked him, and for a few minutes they discussed the recent decease of their two fathers, and the changes caused in the households by their deaths.

"Turning to a less moribund topic," said Amerigo after a pause for contemplation, "Lorenzo sends his best wishes and regrets having seen you only briefly since your return from Rome."

"I will write to him. He probably wants an update on the papacy."

"And how is dear Sixtus?" Amerigo asked, with a sardonic note to his voice. "Are we yet friends?"

"The pope is obsessed with two things at the moment," Botticelli said, "and thankfully it seems to have pushed the unpleasantness of the Pazzi out of his head. He has conveniently forgotten that he stood by while the conspiracy gathered steam and Giuliano was murdered – and in a cathedral, no less."

"The Lord will not forget," Amerigo said with a grin. "But what are these obsessions of which you speak?"

"The first is his new chapel," Botticelli said, "which walls I have been frescoing together with Ghirlandaio. It's looking very fine. Even before we started they had painted the ceiling blue with gold stars, and now we have completed the walls. Do you know Perugino from Umbria? He is leading the project."

"I have met Pietro many times and commissioned more than a few works," Amerigo said. "On behalf of others, usually, though I believe we have one of his Adorations somewhere in the house." He leaned forward conspiratorially with a hand to the side of his mouth. "I don't think much of his work," he said in a low voice. "Too sentimental and he lacks the beauty of your characters, Sandro. But Ghirlandaio – now there is a good painter. You did a pendant with him a year ago, didn't you?"

"Two years ago in fact, in Ognissanti. Augustine and Jerome. But yes, I agree with you regarding Perugino. He could be very pedantic. Sometimes I used to go and hide for a while. Which brings me onto the pope's other obsession, which is the new Vatican Library. An excellent bolthole when Perugino wouldn't give me peace."

"Ha," Amerigo said in surprise and with a new tone of respect. "A library is always good. What is Sixtus collecting?"

"Every holy book in the world, it seems," Botticelli said. "I was permitted a tour and it is already vast, containing every book collected by the Vatican, and more arriving daily. There are also many maps," he added with a gleam in his eye.

"I should like to see it," Amerigo said thoughtfully. "You know I am keen on cartography, but there is too much white space on today's maps. I need a place to research."

"Perhaps you should charter a ship and go exploring yourself," Botticelli observed. "But the new library is certainly worth a visit, though they might not let you in. I gained entrance because I was their commissioned artist and told them I needed to reference ancient works to ensure my biblical depictions were correct. You might need to think of an excuse as well, for they are very protective of it."

"I should become a cardinal," Amerigo said with a smile. "But in all seriousness I shall think on it. Thank you."

He bit into a pastry and took a mouthful of wine to wash it down.

"Now let me tell you a story, which is why I asked you here this fine morning." He gestured to the maidservant, who poured a glass of wine for Botticelli despite his protestations. Another servant put a dish of saffron-coloured sweets on the table. Amerigo took one and popped it into his mouth, then wiped the powdered sugar from his fingers with a cloth.

"The story begins with a young lady at a joust," Amerigo said with a sparkle in his eye, and Botticelli looked at him sharply, remembering an open bier.

"Simonetta?"

Amerigo shook his head.

"Not my dear departed cousin," he said, "but you are close. "Do you recall Simonetta's young niece, Semiramide? She was there to watch dear Giuliano on that happy day. She had been pledged to him once she came of age, you will recall. She must have been only eleven or twelve at the time."

"I remember the little girl well. Her mother commissioned me at that very joust to paint her daughter and her siblings, which subsequently I did. She was a sweet young thing, though with a fiery tongue if she thought she was being wrongly addressed."

"That would be her," Amerigo said with a grin.

"But then poor Giuliano was murdered."

"Exactly, and Il Magnifico swiftly made arrangements for a new betrothal so as not to lose the association between her family and the Medici. The Appiani are matrimonially linked to the Aragonese, I believe."

"I *do* remember," Botticelli said. "It was the talk of the court for a while. Semiramide is to marry Il Magnifico's nephew."

"Quite right," Amerigo said. "She is to marry Il Popolano."

Botticelli rolled his eyes.

"I know, first the Magnificent and now the Popular," Amerigo said with a grin. "The Medici know how to establish their brand. Il Popolano is now a young lord, nineteen years of age, and his *fidanzata* Semiramide is eighteen. They were to wed in May but Lucrezia's death has caused a delay."

Botticelli nodded gravely. Lucrezia Tornabuoni was Il Magnifico's mother, and she had gone to God only a few days previously at the end of March.

"It would be unseemly to marry when the poor lady has only just been interred."

"Yes," Amerigo said, sitting back and brushing pastry crumbs off the grey doublet he wore. "It seems we have had many deaths lately. First Ser Nastagio, and then your own father. Now poor Lucrezia, whom I liked very much. But back to the point, our young nobles are now to wed in July. Friday the nineteenth has been arranged and the invitations are soon to be despatched."

"And am I guessing correctly that a painting is desired?"

"Exactly," Amerigo said. "Il Magnifico asked me to talk to you. He has the idea of commissioning a wedding present for the bride and groom, and he specifically asked for you.

"I would be honoured," Botticelli said. "Does he have an idea for a subject, or would he like me to make suggestions?"

"He has proposed Pallas Athena, who you may recall guarded a sisterhood. His idea is to depict the young bride Semiramide as Pallas, endeavouring to control her wild future husband – Il Popolano – and stop his lascivious bachelor ways. A kind of taming of the beast."

"It is a good notion," Botticelli said thoughtfully, "though I wouldn't suggest depicting the young lord as a beast or it would appear derogatory. Let me think on it. Now tell me about the bride. I haven't seen her for so long and now she is grown. Is she attractive or plain?"

Amerigo laughed again. "Ever the straight-speaking Sandro," he said delightedly. "You're in luck, my friend, for she is in the bloom of youth and she is *bellissima*, so your brush need not lie."

Botticelli picked up his glass and Amerigo, sensing a decision, picked up his.

"Of course I will do it," the painter said. "It is an honour."

They raised their glasses and drank.

There is a complication," Amerigo went on, "which is why I asked you here at this ungodly hour."

"Hardly ungodly," Botticelli said. "But what's the complication?"

"I only learned of this myself yesterday. It seems that the young princess and her entourage are currently visiting Il Popolano so that the bride and groom can become acquainted. They are staying outside Florence in a Medici villa, and we would need to ride there today if you are to meet them both."

"Today?" Botticelli said in surprise. "But I am in the middle of a painting."

"The problem is not the young princess, but Il Popolano. He is to be an ambassador to France, with Il Magnifico as his mentor. If you are to meet him and receive his approval, it will need to be very quick. Politics is unpredictable so it could be a month before his return, and I imagine you would not wish to wait."

"I would certainly want no delay if I must deliver the painting before the union."

"Then will you come?"

Botticelli paused for a moment. "I will," he said. "But I must return to my workshop to get some materials. Where are we going?"

Amerigo looked sheepish. "A longish ride," he admitted. "The Villa Medici at Cafaggiolo. Do you know it?"

Botticelli stared at him. "That must be fifteen miles!"

"Perhaps a little more," Amerigo said apologetically. "But I will arrange good horses. I fear the road through the mountains won't sustain carriage wheels, and we must make haste. And I will bring some of my men at arms so that we don't encounter any trouble. I promise you that it will be worth it."

Botticelli gave him an old-fashioned look but eventually smiled.

"You old fox," he said, shaking his head. "I'd rather ride than be rattled in a carriage, for I know that road a little and it's not smooth. Is there anything else you forgot to mention? War, pestilence or plague, perhaps?"

"None of those things," Amerigo said with a grin. "Just wear something practical for the ride, or you will be sore." He slapped his rear to demonstrate. "And pack a chest. I'll have it collected and brought with mine, for we may be away for a few days."

Botticelli strode back to via Nuova with a spring in his step, ignoring the wool merchants who petitioned him to examine their wares. Despite the prospect of a gruelling ride, he felt excited. A commission for a Medici may lead to many more commissions. He could easily postpone working on his current painting and have his apprentices complete the background details during his absence, so it need suffer no delay. He arrived back at his workshop and began issuing swift directions to set things in motion. Then he went to his room, changed into comfortable riding wear and filled a chest with his finest clothes. As he worked his thoughts turned to the forthcoming painting, and he was reminded of the last time he had painted Pallas; seven years ago for Giuliano's banner, with the face of Simonetta Vespucci. He spotted a book of drawings he had recently acquired, frowned at it thoughtfully and then put it into the open chest. He remembered Simonetta on the day of the joust, so gay and then later at the palace, so sombre. He shook his head sorrowfully, eyes down. His gaze fell upon a silver box on top of a cabinet, inside which he kept his personal treasures. He opened the lid, moving things aside until he unearthed a silk handkerchief. He brought it out and unfolded it. The crimson stain upon it had turned brown with age.

8

The most difficult aspect of moving on is accepting that the other person already did.

FARAAZ KAZI

February, Cambridge

Will Bentley stopped painting at a quarter to four, his body aching. He boiled the kettle once more and this time made tea, then cleaned his brushes until four. He realised he didn't have anything in the house to eat so he stuffed a couple of bags into his coat pockets and walked down to a local supermarket ten minutes from the studio. He stocked up and lugged the heavy bags back to the house, once more thinking that he needed to get a car. When he got back he sautéed prawns with garlic and stirred them into a salad, adding a boiled egg but eschewing potatoes for fear that his weight would instantly rocket. He smiled to himself without humour. He must be getting old if he were putting on weight. He decided he would definitely start taking exercise. Then he sat with a book and a glass of wine in the chair by the spiral staircase to the roof, glancing up now and then to look at the painting of the girl in the limo that he was working on, frowning at some detail or thinking of an improvement.

He couldn't concentrate on the book so he placed it face down on the arm of his chair and went up the narrow staircase, pushing open the trapdoor at the top. As soon as the trapdoor creaked open the cold air hit him and he almost retreated, but decided to go on. He closed the trapdoor to preserve the heat in the studio below, then stood on the rooftop. He began to shiver almost immediately and wished he had grabbed his coat. His breath formed white plumes of condensation. Two years ago he had spent a lot of time and effort on this roof, modelling the safety border wall into a randomly rippling facade in the style of the main terrace of Gaudí's Parc Güell in Barcelona. His roof was the only homage to Gaudí in England that he knew of, and as a result had been the subject of newspaper stories, and had no doubt inspired some to visit the real Parc Güell and see the incomparable splendour of extraordinary mosaics first-hand. Now it was a place he came to for contemplation; a vantage point from which he could look out across Cambridge.

He looked out now. The sun was setting and cast a rose-madder glow onto exposed surfaces that made Cambridge seem as if it were blushing.

Beast had come out with him and wrapped himself around Will's legs, but Beauty had wisely stayed downstairs in the warmth of the studio. Will bent down and picked up the cat, which snuggled into the crook of his arm, fur fluffed up against the cold. It was twilight now and the lights were on in the windows, panelling the buildings with yellow oblongs. If you were inside it would already seem dark without.

His mind was a jumble of thoughts: Lucy in New York, where it would now be about lunchtime; Alessa's wheelchair-bound father in the pretty little cottage; Sandy and the fact that he should have called her but hadn't. Then he remembered that Anna had explicitly asked him to confirm his return so he called her to do so and thanked her for looking after the cats. She was in a rush because she was going out to her yoga class, so they didn't speak long before she had to go. He was dazzled by the bright phone in his hand for a moment, then turned off the screen so that the darkness could creep back. Down in the street below he heard heels tapping on the cobbles, and when he looked over the parapet wall he saw a man and a woman briefly before they disappeared around the corner. It was a Tuesday night and there wasn't much footfall going past the studio, though occasionally a car would cruise past, its headlights sweeping up the street like the rising lights on a theatre stage, then dimming again.

Will felt miserable because of the increasing distance in his relationship with Lucy, which had nothing to do with the physical distance between them. He decided to go for a walk to try and dispel his growing melancholy. He picked up Beast and went back down the narrow stairs, closing the trapdoor tightly behind him and settling the cat back into its favourite chair. Then he fetched his coat and scarf and went out into the crisp February evening.

He walked into town and stared into shining shop windows, watching Cambridge residents and the ever-present tourists flowing by in the reflections. The contrast between the quiet backwater around his studio and this glowing street in the city centre was palpable. He walked around aimlessly and ended up in the empty market next to St. Mary's, where a light snow began to flutter down onto the striped awnings, highlighted by the streetlamps. He enjoyed snow when he didn't have to ride the Bonnie in it, and he walked back slowly, following the line of the river once he reached it, passing the Fort St. George pub but not crossing its light-splashed perimeter.

When he got back he wondered what to do. It was lonely by himself and he could seek out company but knew that he would be company to no-one that night. After making coffee, he sat down in front of his computer and turned it on. He checked his email and answered one or two gallery requests needing action, but he knew what was in his mind and eventually he succumbed to temptation. A part of him had always known he would. He searched for 'Semiramide Appiano Frederick Pocock'.

He found the book reference almost immediately.

CHAPTER I (p 18)
12.   'Medici letter written by Semiramide Appiano…Lucian's tale of Alexander and Roxana…' Pocock, Frederick. The Classical Origin of Science Fiction, 1957.

He tried searching for the author's name alone. He got a number of genealogy references, such as a Frederick Pocock who died in Australia in 1956, followed by various sites offering contact details for dozens of people bearing this name. Next there were several Fred Pocock profiles on Facebook, one of which was a dog. He tried searching for the title of the book, but found that it was not on Amazon or coming up in other bookstores, for it was long out of print. However, there was a copy of it in the British Library. He wondered if it was that copy which had recently been digitised, as it might be the only surviving one in print, given that it was an old book on an obscure topic. He tried looking in the British Library's website and quickly found a page where you could search the catalogues and collections. After a minute or two more he had found the book itself, and discovered that it was possible to view the original in the British Library Reading Rooms, but you would have to pre-order it and would also need to be a registered Reader.

He sat for a while, pondering. He really shouldn't do what he wanted to do, which was to tell Alessa. He shook his head. It would be very stupid and in a way it would be a small betrayal of Lucy; an admission that their relationship wasn't working – that time and familiarity could not sustain the passion of those first few months.

He knitted his fingers together and rolled his thumbs, looking at his phone on the desk in front of him, propped against the computer screen stand. He could send her a text: surely that would be suitably innocuous? He picked up the phone and scrolled through recent calls. He didn't have her name in his contact list but he knew the number that was hers. He pressed the icon beside the number and brought up a menu offering him the possibility of sending a message, placing a call, opening a video conversation or sending an email. He sighed and looked at it for a long moment. What harm could come of it? It wasn't as if he were going to sleep with her – he would just be calling to talk about the quote.

"Well why not?" he said aloud, and pressed Call. There was a pause as the call did not immediately connect and he almost cancelled it. But as his finger hovered over the disconnect button she picked up and he hurriedly put the phone to his ear.

"Is that who I think it is?" she said in a guarded voice. A tingle went up his spine at her slight accent.

"Hello Alessa," he said. "It depends. If you think it's Will Bentley, then yes."

There was a silence for a moment and then she said in a slightly accusatory tone, "Why are you calling? I thought you didn't want to help."

He tried to put his tumbling thoughts in order to say the right thing. He was given a brief reprieve as she asked him to hang on a minute. She put her hand over the mouthpiece and called out to someone: "It's that Cambridge painter that did the talk yesterday and dad had breakfast with."

He supposed that her boyfriend was somewhere in the background and he felt embarrassed that he had made contact with her.

"I just wanted to paint and so I did," he said lamely when she said hello again. "I'm a painter, not an investigator."

"Well you really pissed me off," she said.

He smiled into the phone. She had pronounced it 'peessed' and somehow it was charming rather than aggressive.

"I know," he said. "But you and your father were coming on strong to persuade me to do something that I hadn't had a chance to think about, so I dug my heels in."

He didn't add all the background about Lucy and his fear of betrayal. Nor did he add that Lucy was in New York and he was feeling utterly miserable.

"So why are you calling?"

Now she had an imperious, slightly impatient tone, but he knew he deserved it.

"Because after I finished painting today, I went for a walk, and I found myself thinking about it all. So when I got back I tried a few searches and I found the reference from the Google Alert."

"Mm-hmm."

"Er, yes," he said awkwardly. "And I found out that there is a copy of the book in the British Library."

"Fancy that."

"Well I thought you'd be interested," he said, beginning to feel cross with her. She was the most infuriating woman.

"I already found out that there's a copy of the book in the British Library. This Pocock guy sounds like he went out of print decades ago, but they must have just reached that shelf, so they took it down and fed it through the scanner. They want to digitise the whole collection. Hang on a minute."

He heard her in the background. "Lucas, don't be so nosy! He's just calling about a Medici reference that dad found. It's all to do with who Botticelli's muse actually was. I'll tell you in a minute."

This time when she came back to him her voice was much warmer, although he suspected it was more to annoy her boyfriend than to be nice to him.

"Sorry Will," she said. "I keep getting interrupted. So what were you saying?"

He could hear a landline ringing somewhere in Alessa's background while he spoke.

"Well, I was looking it up," he said. "Apparently it's possible to view books in the British Library if you pre-book them. I expect they have to go and look along miles of shelving or something. Anyway, we could examine the actual book."

The landline had stopped ringing.

"And you think I might find out something more if I go and have a look at the original," she said. "I think so too. I wonder if – oh, for God's sake, hang on again!"

He heard her ask who it was but there was no reply he could discern, then presumably the landline phone was handed to her. Will waited patiently. There was another, longer pause and he began to grow impatient. Couldn't she finish one conversation at a time? Then there was a click and her call disconnected. He stared at his phone in irritation. She had just ended the call without a goodbye or anything! He waited five minutes for her to finish the other conversation and call him back, but his phone remained silent. When he called her back her phone went to voicemail, but he didn't leave a message, just shook his head and went to the fridge to get the wine. Suddenly he felt like finishing the bottle.

It wasn't until the next morning, when he was nursing another mild hangover, eating toast and listening to the local news, that the local radio station informed him of the death by heart attack of renowned Oxford historian Professor Humphrey Cooper. The old man had a brief mention because he had close connections with Cambridge University and had been a guest lecturer a few times. The announcer mentioned that his health had been suffering and that was it; an entire life and huge intellect summarized and dispatched in twenty-five seconds. It was humbling, really.

Will sat in his chair and stared into space for a while, thinking. He realized that the abrupt end to his call the night before had probably been someone notifying Alessa of her father's death; a neighbour or a carer perhaps. That would have been the landline call. He remembered how irritated he had felt when she had hung up, and felt guilty. He wondered whether to call her and express his regret, but it was awkward. They had not previously parted on the best of terms and then the phone call had terminated abruptly before they had made up. He didn't know her well enough to have any idea what to say to her, or even to justify why he would be calling. In the past when loved ones of friends had died, he would often paint them, but he didn't know her well enough to paint her deceased father and it would just come across as weird rather than a peace offering. She would be overcome with grief. The last thing she'd want would be a call from someone who had refused her father's last wish.

Will hoped the boyfriend – what was his name, Lucas? – would be sensitive and supportive. Somehow he imagined that might not be the case, although he didn't know the man and had glimpsed him only briefly in the pub. He had looked as if he might be rather smug. It was odd how some people ended up together, Will mused. He would never have placed Alessa with Lucas, and yet that instinct was based on the most fleeting of impressions, with no supporting facts.

He thought about the odd story that the Professor had recounted about the Medici woman. Semiramide, emphasis on the 'ra'. Now it would never be followed up, for there was no-one to do it and no reason to try. The old boy was dead, so the book would never be written, and it didn't matter who had inspired Botticelli half a millennium ago. Will still felt convinced that it must have been Simonetta Vespucci – why else would Botticelli get himself buried at the woman's feet?

The phone rang and he started, wondering if it were Alessa. What on earth would he say to her? What did you say when loved ones died? His own parents had died when he was still young and he hadn't much experience of how to handle these things. He could imagine in advance how clumsy he was going to sound. He grabbed up the phone, his heart beating faster.

"This is Will."

"Will! Sorry to call so early! Well I suppose it isn't early for you, but it's six in the morning here and I'm already showered. Woke up at two in the morning with my body clock saying I should get going."

He swallowed and took a moment to gather his thoughts.

"Hello Lucy," he finally said. "How's New York?"

"It's the same as ever. Skyscrapers and Uber. Are you okay? You sound funny."

"Do I? I'm fine, but something odd just happened. I met a chap after the talk in Oxford and had a chat, and I just heard on the radio that he's dropped dead of a heart attack."

"Oh *Will*, how horrible. Poor man. Was he young, old?"

"He was old and ill. An ageing professor in a wheelchair. Probably in his seventies I should think. Not that old these days though, and he certainly didn't look like he was about to peg out."

"How horrible," she said again. "Poor you."

"Yes."

They both paused for a moment.

"So you sound as if you're up with the lark," he said. "Are you going into the office today?"

"Yes, I'm going in early. The Chief Operating Officer wants to meet with me, so hopefully I'll get a raise once he realises how indispensable I am."

"I'm sure you will," he said, trying to make his voice sound warm when his heart wasn't in it.

"Yes," she said, sounding a little hesitant now as she picked up his mood. "Well, I'd better get on with it, I'm standing here dripping in a towel, with wet hair and one of those nasty hotel hairdryers to try and whip it into shape. I'll be back on Friday morning. I'm flying out on Thursday night, but it's the red eye so I'll end up sleeping most of Friday. We could get together on Saturday if you could handle coming down."

"That would be lovely," he said, meaning it, and after a few more minutes they said goodbye.

After he had put down the phone he felt angry with himself. He had just stumbled his way through a conversation with Lucy, and seemed not to be able to get the Italian girl out of his stupid head. He needed to make up his mind what he wanted.

Saturday was a long time coming and he finished the painting that he had been working on. At Lucy's request they met at the Sawyer's Hill entrance to Richmond Park, and her chosen meeting place surprised him because it wasn't far from her flat. He found a narrow parking bay into which he squeezed his Bonneville, and from there he walked up the road to the park entrance.

When he met her, she wouldn't meet his eyes. She was as beautiful as ever, with her long blonde hair lifted today and pinned, like an air hostess wanting to exude an air of professionalism. She was bundled up in her camel-coloured coat against the cold, and she had a purple scarf tucked in around the collar to stop cold air from getting in. She wore purple patent-leather gloves. Underneath the coat she wore a white sweater which just peeped through, with black trousers and black boots. She had said they should walk and talk but almost immediately she pulled him over to a park bench and sat down, looking at him earnestly. With a sudden awful realisation he had a premonition of what was coming. He felt stupid at his slowness.

"The thing is, Will, I've been offered a job running our investigative division in New York."

He looked at her, unable to form words.

"It's double the salary I'm on, and well – I've accepted it."

She took his hand and rubbed it with her gloved fingers.

"Which means that we need to part," she went on all in a rush. "I'm sure we can still be friends but we can't be in a relationship."

He still didn't say anything because he was choked and couldn't speak.

Eventually he said, "Right."

His voice sounded raspy.

"Well is that all you can say?" she asked a little peevishly. "The fact is we haven't been seeing each other much anyway what with you miles away from London, and now I'm moving to New York – well, it just can't work. I'm sorry, Will."

"So am I," he said. "I thought we had something good together."

He winced inwardly at how corny he sounded.

She was still rubbing his hand and looking into his eyes almost pleadingly, trying to make it all right.

"We *did* have something good together," she said. "But it was a sort of whirlwind romance after everything that happened. The fact is we're different. You're a bit of a rebel and I'm just *not*. I hate things to be out of place; you know I do. And I know sometimes I drive you mad simply by tidying up. It's silly things like that, not just that we live miles away from each other. And with me off to New York it would be a hundred times worse."

He nodded slowly, feeling slightly sick. It's one thing to worry that the other person doesn't love you, but another to have it clearly confirmed. And there was the strange way in which the Italian girl had been occupying his thoughts, making him feel like this was all his fault and that he had precipitated it.

"I know you're right," he said feebly. "But I thought if we hung on we'd work it out. Instead of which we haven't, really. We've just got further apart. I knew a girl once who described it like two trains on parallel tracks, and you're holding hands out of the window. Then the tracks begin to diverge and you can't hold on forever."

"Yes," Lucy said, turning the image over in her mind. "You try and be what the other person wants, but you can't quite do it. That's what we're like, and that's partly why I accepted the job. Because I don't think the tracks are going to converge."

"No," Will admitted sadly. "I don't think they are."

He looked into the eyes that he had so often painted and her beauty crushed him. He was the rebound from her boyfriend Sam, who had slept with her best friend, and before Sam from her husband, who had been murdered. It had all been very emotional, but now it was over and she was off. Like a ball hitting a wall and bouncing off, she was rocketing away into the blue.

She looked at him and now she had tears in her eyes.

"I'm sorry, Will," she said. "I didn't think you'd be so upset."

He smiled crookedly.

"I am always at the extremes," he said. "You know that. One minute I'm up and the next I'm down. I oscillate from high to low, and that's why I paint. I translate those feelings into brush strokes, but it isn't an easy ride. When are you going to New York?"

She took off a glove and wiped her eyes, carefully so as not to disturb the contact lenses that he knew she wore.

"I'm not off for another month because I've got to sort out the flat," she said. "Even then it's going to be a terrible rush. I'm going to rent the flat out and have someone else pay the mortgage, so I'll have to get an agent to handle all that. I'm taking Peaches with me and I have to get a carrier to ship over all my stuff like the piano and so on."

Peaches was her aloof white cat, and Will had sketched her once or twice.

"Then I have to find an apartment in New York and everything costs a fortune," Lucy went on, suddenly voluble. "It's going to be insane for a while but I thought I should just tell you now and not string you along. I spent the whole flight back thinking about it."

She paused and then added, "I hope we can still be friends."

"Sometimes the 'friends' thing works out," Will said. "There's just no way of knowing right now, but I hope so too."

There was nothing more to be said, so as if at a hidden signal they both stood up and faced each other. They hugged clumsily. She kissed him on the cheek and left him standing there, walking back the way they had come with a wisp of her blonde hair escaping its pins and blowing in the wind.

He watched her until she was out of sight and then he thrust his hands into the pockets of his leathers, feeling the keys of the Bonneville cold against the fingers of his right hand. He set off along the path beside Sawyer's Hill at a fast pace. He didn't know why he was so upset, but he was. Perhaps it was guilt at his mental betrayal, thinking about the Italian girl. He knew in his heart that he was just as complicit in this break-up, not the hard-done-by jilted lover, for he should have made more of an effort to come down to London and see Lucy. He also felt a genuine loss as he replayed images of her. His mind was such a jumble of confused thoughts and feelings that he genuinely didn't know what he thought or wanted. He just knew that he ached.

He walked for miles, veering right and taking the path through the middle of Pen Ponds, stamping on the puddles which were crusted with ice and avoiding occasional piles of horse dung. After a while he remembered about his resolution to start exercising and broke into a run, his boots crunching on the frozen paths. He lasted about a mile before he doubled over gasping, then carried on walking again when he had recovered his breath and the stitch in his side had eased. He knew he had only lasted that far because he didn't care about the pain and had been determined not to stop. He ended up all the way out at the edge of Wimbledon before finally he stood still and looked about him.

He had to think hard about how to get back to the Bonneville. He had no idea where he was and had to find his location with his phone. It was quite a distance back to the motorbike and by the time he got back to it he was shivering uncontrollably, and the light was fading.

His mind still played little scenes of Lucy: laughing at a dinner table in a smart restaurant whose name he had forgotten; posing for the painting that now hung on the wall of his bedroom; her hair whipping in his face on the drive back from the Isle of Wight last summer; making love in her bed and Peaches jumping up to see what they were doing.

The ride back to Cambridge took forever.

9

O Muse! the causes and the crimes relate;
What goddess was provok'd, and whence her hate;
For what offense the Queen of Heav'n began
To persecute so brave, so just a man.

VIRGIL, Aeneid, translated by Dryden

April 1482, Florence

They left the city through the Porta San Gallo to the north with two men-at-arms at the front of the party, followed by Vespucci and Botticelli, then two packhorses and four more armed men in the vanguard. There was no rule of law beyond the city walls and they didn't want to end up at the sharp end of a *cinquedea* blade for the sake of a casket of clothes.

They heard the Sext bell ringing noon from bell towers soon after they departed, and saw peasants in the fields stopping their work and gathering together to eat and rest. They passed Fiesole to the east after a few miles, clustered on its steep hill. The April sky was a patchwork of clouds. A heavy rain shower made them pull their cloaks about them, but it stopped as quickly as it had started and they rode on with the flanks of the horses and their wet cloaks steaming in the sun. The temperature warmed and there was a light breeze which slowly dried them. The horses snorted and stamped their feet, coquettish after the rain. Botticelli always liked the pungent smell of them and he patted his mare on the neck to calm her.

As they climbed into the hills they looked down at the city below and saw Brunelleschi's octagonal cathedral dome standing proudly above the lesser buildings. At one point as they rode, Botticelli caught a flash of light and imagined it must be a reflection from the copper ball containing holy relics at the dome's peak, put up as a crowning glory by his friend Verrocchio only a dozen or so years before. Florence was quite a sight, laid out in the level valley of the Arno and surrounded by walls and green fields and olive orchards, framed by mountains. The painter pursed his lips, nodded and made a slight bow to his city that no-one else saw.

Once they were out in the country they made good time, passing through the village of Montorsoli in a steady walk up to Pratolino, where they arrived mid-afternoon. There they paused a while to rest and water the horses, break some bread and drink a little wine. After that there was a steady drop down to Fontebuona and the horses found their rhythm after the long climb and trotted out briskly.

On the long road to Vaglia, still dropping steadily and watched by peasants working the fields, they passed at one point through a narrow pass and encountered a small group of scruffy individuals in the road. They looked as if they would raise a challenge, but were unmounted and backed off when Vespucci's black-clad men at arms drew their swords and held them with silent menace on arms stretched uppermost like lances. Botticelli was both nervous and impressed. He wasn't a brave man and now he appreciated his friend Amerigo's wisdom in bringing their guards. His mind teemed with colours and images; the bone-thin outlaws, the men-at-arms poised like scorpions waiting to strike, the hills covered with poplar trees and olives, and the distant terracotta roofs of occasional villas.

After more riding they entered the flat valley of the River Sieve and neared the town of Barberino di Mugello. It was only a couple of hours to sunset and Botticelli and Vespucci were weary after six hours in the saddle. The guards appeared unaffected by the journey. By the time the squat towers of the castle hove into view, Botticelli felt that his whole body was aching.

"Cafaggiolo," Vespucci said, pointing dramatically, and Botticelli nodded, almost too tired to speak. They had all sweated profusely in the relentless sun and Botticelli noticed that Vespucci's face was covered with fine dust thrown up from the trail. He presumed his own face wore a similar veil.

"I hope they have water in this castle," he said. "I need to wash."

"I have visited only once," Vespucci said. "It is a hunting lodge these days. It was changed by Michelozzo from a fortress into the curious castellated villa you see before you. It's quite charming though, and I'm sure they will have water for weary travellers. Have you ever been out to the Villa del Trebbio? It's like that."

"I went out to Trebbio once when the plague was in the city, and painted a fresco," Botticelli said. "They wanted me back but so far I have not made the journey. That is also quite a ride."

They went forward, the spring now gone from the horses' steps. The track had crested a small hill and the castle was below them. Built of pale yellow, almost white stone, it reared up from the flat valley with two towers, one at the front above the entrance and one set back. The rooves were of terracotta and the large building around the towers was surrounded by a courtyard and a moat. There was a drawbridge across the moat to the front gatehouse, still connected by chains to projecting timber gaffs so that it could be raised, though Botticelli wondered if it was ever hauled up these days. A second wall bordered the front of the villa, and there was a fountain beside which stood three tiny figures. To the left of the main villa was a long outbuilding, likely stables for the horses and kennels for the dogs.

They approached, went in by the stables and dismounted, stretching their backs and rubbing their legs to restore circulation. Grooms emerged and took the horses, and a male servant came out to lead them to the front entrance. A guard stood on each side of the drawbridge, clad in shining armour and topped with a helmet sporting a red feather plume. *True Medici style*, Botticelli thought approvingly. The guards bore tall halberds with polished blades, but swung them wide as the visitors approached to indicate that passage would be granted, for Vespucci had already sent ahead a rider to announce their impending arrival.

The servant nodded to the guards and led Vespucci and Botticelli without pause across the small drawbridge and into the gatehouse. Inside the dim interior Botticelli could see the timber drawbridge gaffs continuing on the inside of the wall, each bearing counterweights and connected to windlasses. He thought of his friend Leo, a brilliant protégée of old Verrocchio, and smiled. Leo would have been sketching these beams and cantilevers at the first opportunity, he knew. Indeed the drawbridge appeared still to be in working condition, and Botticelli wondered if they used it to prevent hill bandits from gaining ingress, such as those they had encountered on the journey. If so, perhaps they raised it more often than he had at first imagined.

Rooms had been prepared. They were able to wash and Botticelli's chest was brought up to his room. The servant unpacked his clothes and Botticelli dressed in fine raiment in anticipation of the forthcoming meeting with the Medici lord. When he was ready he followed the servant downstairs to a great library where they were to assemble. You could always be sure that any Medici household would have a great store of books. Vespucci was already there, and they awaited Lorenzo di Pierfrancesco de' Medici, while Botticelli unexpectedly felt a nervous flutter in his stomach despite his familiarity with the Florentine court.

Without fanfare and with no accompanying retinue, Lorenzo walked into the room clad in riding breeches and smelling of horses.

"Welcome to Cafaggiolo!" he said, with a ringing note to his voice as if this were the best treat he had had all day. He was better looking than Il Magnifico, though he was only about twenty and didn't have Il Magnifico's gravitas.

He walked over and took both Vespucci's hands in a familiar greeting.

"How are you, old friend?" he asked with a grin. "Still scratching a living with my uncle I see." He turned to Botticelli. "And you must be the master himself," he said, bowing. "I have seen some of your remarkable work. You are welcome."

Botticelli felt himself swelling up a little at the flattery and bowed in return.

"I am honoured to make your acquaintance, lord."

They clasped wrists and Lorenzo looked him in the eye.

"We shall be friends," he said solemnly. "I am sure of it."

Then he immediately let go and gestured to himself, laughing.

"But not until I wash off this mud! Cafaggiolo is a hunting lodge and I am still stinking from the hunt. Please allow me to change out of these clothes. Have you met my bride to be?"

"We have not yet had the pleasure, lord," Vespucci said.

"Ha! I shall see if she is available to entertain you," Lorenzo said. "Then we must eat, are you hungry? Yesterday we caught a fine pair of boar, so there's pork in the kitchen but no venison. Are you hungry?"

"We've been riding all afternoon," Botticelli said, "So I can't speak for Amerigo but I could probably polish off a boar or so."

Lorenzo grinned. "You shall have your chance," he said, and gestured to the servant.

"Look after them, Guccio, and don't leave them dry."

He gestured to their wine glasses. When he had sailed out of the room the library suddenly seemed calm again, as if it had momentarily been whirling like a wheel on its axis.

Botticelli caught Vespucci's eye and they both laughed.

"He's always like that," Vespucci said.

"He's quite a character."

Guccio appeared at their elbow with wine and refilled their glasses. The ensuing wait was prolonged but Vespucci found a whole corner of the library devoted to maps, including an oak table for laying them out, and a globe of the earth in the corner which could be rotated. At first Botticelli left him to it, wandering along the shelves and picking out works of interest to him, but eventually he gravitated towards the table where Vespucci had laid out a large map and they stood around it in animated conversation, discussing the unexplored areas. They were still doing so when the library doors were flung wide and a retinue of courtiers swept in, this time very grand and in complete contrast to the relaxed behaviour of the lord himself. Caught by surprise, Vespucci and Botticelli hurried over as the bride-to-be came in.

Semiramide wore a pale ivory gown embroidered with gold thread and yellow gems, and a simple gold necklace which complemented the pearls woven into her hair. Her skin was pale, her look regal and her demeanour elegant. She was eighteen years old and it shocked Botticelli that she was fully a woman. Without thought or logic he had visualised the little girl at Giuliano's joust. An image of Simonetta Vespucci came into his mind, who had been at the joust but now was with God. This young woman was

Simonetta's niece, and he could see a likeness. Suddenly he wished himself younger – at thirty-seven he felt positively ancient beside her.

For a moment he and Vespucci competed at how deeply they could bow.

"Gentlemen!" Semiramide said, coming forward. "Welcome to Cafaggiolo."

She turned first to Botticelli.

"Maestro Botticelli, I think? You painted me when I was a child, but I am sure you will not remember."

"On the contrary, I remember well," Botticelli said, coming up out of his bow. "We met at Giuliano's joust in Santa Croce, and then your mother asked me to paint you and your brothers. Is she well?"

"Alas, my mother passed last year," she said, making him wince inwardly at his crassness for asking the question without knowing the answer.

"I am sorry," he responded automatically.

"It was a short illness and she had lived well," Semiramide said. She sounded matter of fact about it, but Botticelli noted her inner sadness.

She blinked several times and inhaled deeply. Her eyes were brown. She held out a gloved hand, which he kissed. Then she turned to his companion, who stood a little awkwardly to the side.

Botticelli introduced him, grateful for the distraction.

"This is my dear friend and patron Amerigo Vespucci, my lady."

"The Vespucci name is well known indeed," Semiramide said graciously, offering her hand to Vespucci. Botticelli examined her with his frank artist's stare while her attention was on his friend. She had the smallest ears and a heart-shaped face, with high cheekbones and a long neck. Her hair was blonde with a touch of auburn, kept in place by tiny plaits in which the pearls nestled. Her hairline was not plucked high, in defiance of the fashion of the day, but her eyebrows were trimmed into thin lines which framed her eyes.

"Even in Piombino, five days off by carriage, the name of Vespucci is known," Semiramide went on, and this time it was Amerigo who glowed visibly in her presence. Botticelli saw that his friend had gone a little pink.

A servant handed Semiramide a glass of wine while another brought Botticelli and Vespucci their own glasses from the map table and topped them up. They all drank a toast. Semiramide had regained composure from her momentary sadness. She turned back to Botticelli and fixed him with a penetrating look.

"So, maestro!" she said. "Pallas Athena has been mentioned as the subject for a picture, but that is all I know. What are your thoughts?"

Botticelli was caught off guard.

"I hadn't realised that the subject had already been mentioned," he said.

"It has and I approve," she said simply. "But tell me your idea, if you yet know it. How will you do it?"

"First I thought of Camilla," Botticelli said, and felt he should explain the legend. "She was a princess described in Roman mythology, and she grew up in a forest, becoming a huntress."

"Yes, yes," Semiramide interrupted. "The daughter of Metabus, and a huntress is a good choice. And you moved to Pallas because she is a goddess." She arched an eyebrow. "Should I be flattered? Am I that goddess?"

Botticelli was surprised at her knowledge, then caught her eye on him and smiled.

"A goddess indeed, my lady," he said softly. "I do not wish to be impertinent, but I believe that Il Magnifico's notion was of Pallas taming a beast. You would be the goddess, and the beast would be your future husband."

She shook her head.

"No," she said. "The allegory is good, but my future husband cannot be represented as a beast."

"Exactly my thought," Botticelli said, moving to a table where he had placed the book of drawings that he had brought. He picked it up.

"As I considered the mythology of Pallas Athena, guarding her sisterhood of chaste nymphs from the perils of the world, I saw in it a parallel. The modesty of woman and the huntress combined, preventing her future husband from expressing his maleness to the sisterhood she protects. Il Magnifico had suggested a beast, but then I thought of a *centaur*: half man and half beast. I have brought some illustrations from antiquities for you to examine."

He opened the book of drawings to a page whereon there was an image of a centaur, with the head and torso of a man but the body of a horse.

Becoming suddenly bold, he added, "Thus Pallas ensures marital bliss."

She showed no shyness.

"How would you represent Il Popolano?" she asked.

"It is up to you both, but I am thinking that the centaur should not have the face of your future husband, as the centaur is still half beast. Instead he would have the face of a handsome young god, befitting company for the goddess Pallas. She would bear your face."

"Let's hope my face would not be too much of a burden for Pallas to bear," Semiramide said tartly. "But you already painted la bella Simonetta as Pallas for the joust."

Once again her gaze pierced him.

"Yes," he said, amazed that she had remembered when she had been so young. "But I would associate your Pallas closely to your lord through allegory."

She frowned, rocking her head slightly and looking up as if weighing the logic on a balance. After a minute she nodded.

"It could work," she said. "I like the idea of the centaur. It could be finely done. Tell me what allegory you would use."

She raised her glass and sipped wine from the Murano crystal, but before Botticelli could reply, Lorenzo di Pierfrancesco swept back into the room, this time clean and clad in a red doublet woven with jewels. He was scarcely recognizable from the huntsman they had met earlier.

"Ah!" he said. "You have met my bride!"

Semiramide, Botticelli noticed, immediately became less commanding and more demure in his presence.

"We have had that pleasure, sir," said Vespucci, who had been feeling rather left out as Botticelli and Semiramide had discussed the Pallas commission.

"Excellent," Lorenzo said. "But we must talk further while we eat, I am told. Dinner is prepared and the meat will be at its most succulent."

His manservant held out a tray and they placed their wine glasses on it, then Semiramide took Lorenzo's arm and the two visitors followed the lord and lady out.

The men were all hungry and they dug into the food immediately it was served, while Semiramide seemed to eat almost nothing but allowed them time to dine.

"We have been discussing the painting, my lord," Semiramide said when they began to slow down a little.

Lorenzo wiped his mouth.

"I'm sorry," he said. "Hunting gives me an appetite. What did you conclude?"

"Maestro Botticelli was explaining his ideas for composition," she said. "He proposes me as Pallas taming a beast. You would be the beast, lord," she added archly, and Lorenzo laughed, not in the least put out.

"A handsome beast I trust, maestro?" he said.

"I am thinking of a centaur," Botticelli said. "A mythical creature, half man and half horse."

"Forgive my ignorance but I am not sure I know the look of a centaur."

"I can show you something I brought with me, after our meal," Botticelli said. "I have an excellent book of drawings that I purchased from a Florentine agent, just as he was about to send it out to Mantova, of all places. I have sketched from it often and more than once made full paintings using it as a reference."

"And this book has drawings of centaurs?" Lorenzo asked.

Botticelli nodded.

"Very good drawings," he said respectfully. "The centaur usually has the upper body of a man, and it transforms below the waistline into that of a horse."

"The master proposes the face of a mythical god for the human head of the beast," Semiramide went on. And I as Pallas, taming the beast as I should tame you, my love!"

Lorenzo laughed again and took her hand, kissing it.

"The pleasure would be mine," he said to her, almost in an undertone so that Botticelli and Vespucci felt as if they were intruding on an intimate moment.

"I think I should entwine my fingers in your hair," Semiramide said to him in clear flirtation. "To convey the impending nuptial bliss, of course. What say you to that, dearest one?"

"I say that the touch of your sweet caress would be enough to begin the transformation of any beast into a man," Lorenzo replied gallantly. He grinned and added, "or any man into a beast." Now for the first time she did blush and tried to cover it by taking a draught of wine.

"I do like the idea of Pallas taming a centaur," she said after a pause. "But just as you arrived before dinner, maestro Botticelli was about to explain his ideas further."

"Yes," Botticelli said, stepping in quickly to help her. "But I caution you both that they are in no way fully formed. The centaur is the most challenging since he is unadorned, but I am thinking of some kind of a bow and quiver to represent the hunter, entering the forest or some kind of enclosure, to challenge Pallas with the intent of making off with one of the sisterhood she protects."

He paused and Lorenzo nodded enthusiastically.

"Excellent! And what of Semiramide?"

"Pallas would have the visage of your bride, if that may be permitted," Botticelli said, "and Pallas Athena may have symbols in abundance. For example, her dress could bear some kind of Medici motif, such as the six balls in a pattern."

"Or three interwoven diamond rings, perhaps," Semiramide said. "That also is a Medici motif and more fitting for a wedding."

Botticelli nodded, seeing it immediately in his mind's eye. She may be young but she was astute.

"Diamond rings would be fitting," Lorenzo agreed. "That was a symbol created by my grandfather. They would sit well on a wedding picture."

"Rings then," Semiramide said. "But how do we know this is Pallas? Is she to bear a lance as in the standard you did for Giuliano?"

There was a long pause as Botticelli considered. He needed to do something different, to move this away from Simonetta's Pallas. But he still needed to make classical allusions to Pallas that would be clear.

"She is a *guard*," he said quietly, almost to himself. An image came into his mind of the guards at the entrance to Cafaggiolo, and he had a sudden idea. He stood up spontaneously and held up his hand as if gripping an imaginary shaft.

"Not a lance, but a *halberd*," he said softly. "She is guarding her nymphs, so she should bear some kind of halberd fitting for a goddess. And olive, for that is the tree of Pallas Athena."

"So she bears a halberd, and a crown of olive leaves, perhaps," Semiramide suggested.

"More than just a crown," Botticelli said, extemporising. "She shall wear olive leaves as if they are a part of her, woven into her gown and held close by diamond rings. Pallas is the huntress who guards her sisterhood against the centaur, but she brings the olive branch of peace."

The others clapped to show their appreciation of this suggestion. Botticelli had drawn them all into his spell and they felt a part of the composition, each beginning to see it in their mind's eye.

"So the centaur has wandered in where he should not," Botticelli continued slowly. He ran his fingers through his own curls to sweep them back from his face.

He brings the myth to life, Semiramide thought, appraising the artist for a moment as a man. She shook her head as if to clear it, and he noticed.

"You disagree?"

"Not at all," she said, suddenly aware of the wine in her veins. She went a little pink as she had earlier, and knew he had noticed that too. She could keep nothing from the man. "I am just confused. When first we spoke you mentioned Camilla."

"Camilla?" Lorenzo said.

Vespucci felt embarrassed because he couldn't remember for the life of him who Camilla was. He cared more for maps than myth.

"Camilla was a virgin queen, according to Virgil," Botticelli said. "She was my first thought. For a wedding picture speaking of the triumph of chastity over lust and reason over brutishness, we could begin with Camilla, but there is a problem. She is not well known. Yet we have all heard of Minerva, yes? Or Pallas in the Greek? We know of Pallas, but Camilla is less familiar, and she has fewer allegorical symbols. This is why I moved to Pallas. She is the perfect huntress. She is strong, chaste and brave, and she tames the centaur so that he does not capture her nymphs with his lover's dart and carry them away."

There was a long silence as they thought about it.

"It's good," said Lorenzo at last. "Can you do it?"

"Oh yes," Botticelli said. "I can do it. But I will need to make some sketches of your bride to be, if I may be granted the honour?"

Lorenzo and Semiramide looked at each other, and Lorenzo opened his hands for a moment in a gesture indicating that it was up to her.

"If it is your will, my lord," Semiramide said demurely, and Botticelli almost smiled at the way she made the young Medici lord feel that he was in control.

"To Pallas and the centaur," Lorenzo said, and they raised their glasses and drank.

Botticelli rose as the dawn chorus was sounding in the gardens of the Castello, and ate in the same hall where they had dined the previous evening. Vespucci had also made an effort to rise at a reasonable hour since he was a guest in the Medici household, and joined the painter halfway through his meal. After eating they went for a walk around the grounds, because Botticelli said he needed to clear his mind and see the morning.

The Tuscan sun was already warming them as they wandered in the gardens behind the main building. There were vines growing in neat rows to the left, and an abundance of different vegetables that were beginning to gain in size, set into six large blocks bounded by neat paths and low hedges. Gardeners toiled among tidy rows of plants and tipped their wide-brimmed hats at the two gentlemen as they passed. Birds flitted in and out of the low hedges, and butterflies fluttered over the vegetables.

On each side at the rear of the garden there were two wide outhouses built with open stone walls and roofed with living vines. They contained tools and pots and working tables for the gardeners. In between these buildings there was a fountain from which a spring issued. The water gathered into a stone basin but by some aquatic cleverness, never overflowed. Botticelli and Vespucci held their hands in the stream and found it to be crystal clear and icy cold. Beyond the fountain was a white stone building with a cross on top, but the large oak door was locked. They made their way back to the castle.

The first thing that was apparent when they returned was that their host Lorenzo was leaving.

"My friends," he said regretfully, "Politics drags me away, as I knew it might. I ask that you forgive me, and stay as long as you wish. Maestro Botticelli, I would be pleased if you could begin the painting as soon as possible under the terms we discussed last evening."

Botticelli bowed and confirmed that he would start with sketches that very day if the lady was available. Semiramide herself then came out to see Lorenzo off, with a maid on each side of her for honour's sake. Lorenzo bowed to her graciously and held her hand for a moment, then without more ado mounted up and rode out of the gates. An impressive array of ten guards surrounded him, their pikes glinting in the sunlight. Semiramide waited until the riding party moved out of sight, then turned to Botticelli.

"Maestro, I will send my maid when I am ready for the drawings," she said. She turned to one of her maids; an older lady with a hatchet face who looked as if she had seen everything and no-one could pull the wool over her eyes.

"Caterina, please show the maestro to the main tower with the hunting tapestries, for the light is good there.

Botticelli bowed.

"Thank you my lady. I will gather my materials and then I am yours to command."

Semiramide disappeared in the direction of the dining hall. Vespucci made his excuses and headed off towards the library, where Botticelli suspected he intended to spend the entire day in the cartography corner. The painter went to his room and gathered up his leather satchel of charcoals and inks and a thick stock of paper. When he came down, Caterina was waiting. She gave him a look which would have withered fruit from the vine but led him through the house to a staircase. The tower was as light as promised and he set up his materials on a small table, then paced around the room inspecting the tapestries, while Caterina arranged the furniture and then seated herself in the corner.

Semiramide was taking her time and Botticelli found himself staring out of the windows. He was in a large central tower and the courtyards below seemed quite a drop. To the front was the narrower gatehouse tower which bisected the rolling hills he and Vespucci had ridden through. To the rear, the windows opened onto the main castle buildings and courtyards, beyond which were the gardens where he had strolled earlier with Vespucci.

Semiramide arrived after a further wait, but had the grace to apologise for her delay. She brought two ladies-in-waiting and they sat at the periphery of the room, leaning close to each other at times to whisper something. Semiramide arranged herself on the most comfortable chair in the room and Caterina fussed around her, repositioning the heavy folds of the pale green silk dress that she wore that morning.

"Please take no notice of me, my lady," Botticelli said. "I will pace around for a while and then draw some sketches, if you will permit it. I must look closely, and it will seem that I am staring impertinently, for which I ask your forgiveness and understanding in advance. At times I may take the liberty of asking you to incline your head differently."

She nodded.

"Should I try to remain still?"

"If you could do so, it would help."

"Then I will try. Pray continue."

He began pacing, and then sat down on a hard chair, using the back of another chair on which to rest his drawing board. He stared without turning away his head for a whole minute after taking his seat. She perceived his concentration. He looked almost angry, frowning at her as if evaluating whether she would do. It made her feel self-conscious. He noted each line and shape and angle of her, and then he began to draw swift, sure strokes on the paper, working with a stick of charcoal.

She was very aware of his intense look. She had never been sketched before like this, and it felt strangely intimate and embarrassing. She was fearful that she would blush and concentrated on keeping her breathing even in the hope that this would help. She wanted to see the drawing that he was developing but could not, and this irked her. She wanted to question him about it but he had asked her to remain still so she resisted the temptation. She simply sat unmoving, her skin beginning to turn a little pink under the strength of his gaze despite her resolve not to colour.

Meanwhile, Botticelli lost himself in drawing. She was like a princess out of a fable, he thought absently to himself as his hand flew. His charcoal snapped and fell on the floor but without looking he snatched up another piece from his wooden box and continued without pause. His finger became stained black where he rubbed and adjusted the page. After a few moments he stopped and moved his chair to a new position, replenished his paper and began again from a different angle. So it continued, with him moving slowly around her and capturing different images of her, each of which he tossed when finished onto the table behind him.

"I must see you so clearly that I can lay you down on the canvas," he said after a while. "That's the trick of it."

Did Il Popolano want *canvas*?" she asked. "I had retired when you discussed the final details."

"Yes," Botticelli said. "The choice is panel or canvas, but canvas is becoming much more popular these days. I had even thought of oils for the painting, as with the Dutch school, but I think with this picture we'll stay with tempera and put it on canvas. Canvas is easily portable, you see."

"But is it durable?" she asked.

"A good question, to which I can only say we strongly believe it so. Also, as a painter I can tell you that there is something special about canvas."

"And what is that?"

Before answering he frowned and then stood up and discarded the sketch he was doing, tearing it in two and sitting down again with a new sheet of paper.

"That one was irredeemably wrong," he explained, smiling at her quizzical expression, and continued to talk while he began the first bold strokes of a new drawing.

"Canvas, he went on," is like a living, breathing surface. As you apply the brush it flexes to your pressure – it reacts to the brush and the paint. It is a completely different sensation for the painter when compared to painting on panel."

She smiled but he admonished her not to smile, so she frowned and then *he* smiled and asked her please to adopt her previous straight expression.

After a while he paused so that she could stand up and move about. The ladies-in-waiting and Caterina gathered at the table and leafed through the drawings, chattering excitedly. He asked them to be careful, because the charcoal would smudge easily. Then a maid brought wine and they had some, though Botticelli declined as he wanted a clear head to draw. Semiramide stood in front of the table and looked at the drawings, and though she said nothing he could tell that she was pleased at the way he was bringing her to life on the paper.

When she sat down again he switched to pen and ink and asked her if she could adopt different expressions. She agreed to try and first he requested a look of sadness, and he drew her like that for a while. Then he asked her for a look of triumph and she couldn't think how to do it, so he demonstrated to her, looking up and ahead and proud, so that she giggled and earned a strict look from Caterina.

"Imagine that you have captured your centaur, and now you hold him by his hair," Botticelli said to her. He looked at Caterina directly, and asked her to come over to her mistress, which she did. He positioned her.

"Now the centaur is your prisoner," he continued to Semiramide, indicating Caterina to be the centaur and turning back to the princess. "You are the goddess herself, Pallas Athena, and the centaur is about to have his will with those chaste young nymphs you have guarded so well. But you are the huntress and you are now in control. Show me that look."

She smiled but then composed herself and tried to imagine the scene. Caterina could do nothing but comply, and he knew it. He managed to hold back a smile of his own.

"The centaur breathes heavily," Botticelli said quietly. "He has been running and his beastly flanks steam and quiver, but you have stilled him."

Semiramide tried to look her most bored and imperious and held out her hand, resting it on Caterina's head and entwining her fingers in the maid's hair. Botticelli laughed delightedly and Caterina shot him a look like a flight of daggers but did not resist. He sat down quickly in his chair, grabbed his board and paper, dipped his pen and began to sketch, refreshing his quill frequently.

Semiramide stood still and Caterina held her position too. When he had finished he nodded slowly and stood up, taking the paper and placing it on the table among the other sketches. The two women were released from the pose and Caterina straightened up crossly.

"Thank you," Botticelli said. "That was much better. The pen is working well."

Semiramide went to the table and looked at the picture on the table. It was extraordinary. He had captured a look almost of boredom on her face, as if imprisoning a lascivious centaur was something that she did every day and thought nothing of. And instead of Caterina, he had roughed in the face of an anguished young god, with his muscled torso fading at the groin into the body of a horse. Caterina came over and looked at the painting curiously, then eyed Botticelli with new respect.

"It is a fair likeness of you, mistress," she said, nodding grudgingly.

Semiramide looked at her face on the drawing and noted that he had made her prettier than she felt inside, but the picture was real – it was as if he had somehow captured a piece of her.

"It will do," she said, and when she looked at him, she found his eyes upon her so that she immediately had to look away.

10

In Xanadu did Kubla Khan
A stately pleasure dome decree:
Where Alph, the sacred river, ran
Through caverns measureless to man
Down to a sunless sea.

SAMUEL TAYLOR COLERIDGE, Kubla Khan

March, Cambridge

Will awoke in the chair in the studio with Beauty curled up on his lap. He was stiff from running the previous afternoon in Richmond Park, and hungover because when he had finally made it home after a freezing night ride back to Cambridge, he had finished off half a bottle of Haig Club that had been sitting around since Christmas. He felt bleary eyed, bad tempered and miserable. He sat up too fast and his head throbbed. Beauty opened one eye and gave him a baleful glare, then stood up, stuck her bottom in his face for a moment and hopped down disdainfully. He extracted himself from the chair, leaving a warm dent in it where he had been sleeping, and stumbled stiff legged into the kitchen where he put on the kettle, hearing it start up behind him as he headed for the shower. Sometime last night he had vowed that he would go running every morning to improve his fitness and lose some weight, but now this seemed like a ludicrous idea. He peeled off his sweaty clothes and stood under a jet of hot water for ten minutes, coming back to life in the steaming cascade. When he came out of the shower he wrapped a black towel around himself, towelled his hair dry and then padded barefoot into the kitchen to make coffee. He began to feel as if he might live after all. He got dressed in black jeans and a black shirt, not consciously choosing funereal colours but simply pulling out the first things he saw that would go together. He contemplated the contents of his fridge but it was spartan as he had planned to be in London. He decided to go out for breakfast, so he fed the cats and then pulled on a black leather jacket.

Stir Café was only a few minutes' walk away on the Chesterton Road. He looked at his watch and it had already been open almost an hour. The bells of St. Andrew's church were ringing out for the ten o'clock service as he walked and it cheered him – you couldn't be miserable forever when there was the sound of bells. He arrived at Stir and found it busy with rowers, fresh from practising on the River Cam. He didn't need to read the menu but ordered the brunch board and orange juice, then found a seat at the window. He decided he would order coffee later so that it would still be hot when he got to it – the coffee was too good to be allowed to get cold.

He kept having episodes of remembering Lucy and feeling miserable again. He already felt lonely, which was ridiculous but there it was. When he had eaten breakfast and supercharged himself with coffee he decided to visit his friends George and Anna. They were only five minutes away so he didn't call but just popped round, knowing that they tended to be early risers and would be up, even though it was a Sunday. He rang the bell and a dog began to bark furiously inside. Anna was a vet and the house had a big extension on one side containing her surgery. She ran the practice with two partners, but it was closed today except for emergencies.

Anna peeked close to the door glass to see who it was, then opened the door. She was wearing a white towelling robe. A Yorkshire terrier nosed around her legs and continued to bark until she commanded it sternly to be quiet. She fed it a treat from her pocket.

"Will, what a lovely surprise! I thought you were away. Come in and have a croissant. You need to have one to stop George being an absolute pig."

She called back into the house.

"George! It's Will, so stop eating all the croissants."

Will smiled at her as he followed her in, taking care not to let the terrier escape.

"You must be the only person in Cambridge with dog treats in your bath robe."

She glanced back at him and flashed him the grin which he so liked.

"I'm trying to train him but it's a bit of a hopeless task. This is Alphie, with a 'ph' according to his owner. After 'Alph the sacred river' because he peed a lot when he was a pup. Anyway, I'm just keeping him in the house because he had a small operation on a lump and he was miserable in the surgery, but he barks his brains out every time the doorbell goes."

Will bent down and patted Alphie, who had decided that he wasn't an enemy after all and rolled over to have his tummy tickled. He had a small, shaved area on one side and a neatly sewn-up incision where the lump had been removed.

"He's a big softy. Is he going to be all right?"

"Fingers crossed and we'll see. He's being collected at lunchtime and I was worried you might be the owner, with me still swanning around in a bath robe. Not very professional. Go and see George. I'm going to dive in the shower."

He could hear the last dying strains of The Archer's Omnibus as he went into the kitchen. Will never listened to The Archers by choice, but he had a sudden memory of walking down a street in a London suburb the previous summer and hearing it playing from more than one window.

George stood up and nodded to him. His brown curly hair was flecked with grey at the temples, marking out the slow but inexorable passage of time. He hadn't yet shaved. He wore new reading glasses which were black framed and somehow lent him an academic air. He held out a hand and Will shook it.

"How are you, Will? I thought you'd gone down to London."

"That was the plan," Will said, realising he was going to have to tell them about Lucy, even though he hadn't yet got it straight in his own head.

But George didn't pick up on it, just turned to the windowsill and clicked off the radio as the continuity announcer was enthusing about the forthcoming Food Programme.

"Croissant?" George continued, gesturing to the plate. "Tea or coffee?"

He was Will's oldest friend. They had first met at college and Will had been George's best man. His friend was a graphic designer and had his own small company. He had done all the posters for Will's most-recent exhibition, and he had cornered the market for stationery and graphic design work in several of Cambridge's art galleries as a result of Will exhibiting there.

"I couldn't eat another thing," Will said. "I've just had a Stir brunch."

"Aha, avocados," George said, putting on the kettle anyway. "Unusual but excellent idea. And good bread I seem to recall, though we only ate there once. I'm having more tea anyway. You sure?"

Will shook his head regretfully.

"Not right now. I just popped in as I was practically on your door-step." It suddenly occurred to him that he had not been pounced on by George and Anna's three children.

"Where are the kids?"

"Sarah's having a sleep-over because she was ten yesterday," George said. "She was very pleased with your box of paints by the way, and I promised her you'd give her a lesson, so I hope that's all right."

"Of course," Will said. He didn't have any children of his own so Sarah, William and Charlotte were like the children that he had never had. "I'm sorry I wasn't here. Did she have a good time?"

"I think so," George said. "We had eight little girls running riot around the house and it took us the whole evening to tidy up afterwards. That's why we're a bit late this morning."

He gestured at the kitchen, which was relatively tidy but bore signs of recent mayhem, such as a bunch of balloons in the corner and a Happy Birthday sign still stuck on the wall.

"And what about Wills and Charlotte? At the grandparents?"

"Got it in one," George said. "They went off before the party so that Sarah and her friends could be grown-up ten-year olds without having babies around. Anna's parents were delighted to have them so it all worked out."

They chatted and leafed through the Sunday papers, easy in each other's company, but Will didn't mention the break-up with Lucy as there never seemed to be the right moment. There was the sound of a hair dryer whirring upstairs and then Anna came down, pristine now in a yellow sweater and jeans.

"Good grief, there's a croissant left," she said, sitting down at the table and pouring herself a coffee. "Has George offered you something to eat, Will?"

He repeated the conversation about eating in Stir and she nodded.

"Nice place." She sipped her coffee and pulled a face. "Ugh, this is lukewarm."

She stood up and put the mug in the microwave, then hunted in the fridge and came back with a jar of fig preserve for the croissant. The microwave pinged and she recovered the now-steaming mug.

"So," she said, looking at Will. "You're supposed to be in London with Lucy for the weekend. Have I missed anything while I was in the shower? Did she come back from New York?"

The moment had come.

"Umm, she did come back, and I did go down to see her yesterday," Will said. "She's taking a job in New York, and well, to cut a long story short, we broke up."

George looked up in surprise from his paper, taking off his reading glasses.

"Really? You never mentioned it. What happened?"

Anna got up and came around to Will.

"How horrible," she said. "I thought you two were finally it, if you know what I mean." She gave him a hug and he hugged her back for a moment.

"So did I," he said ruefully. "But apparently not."

There was a short silence.

"Well go on then," George said, and he realised that they were both looking intently at him. "We want a blow-by-blow account."

Will laughed at the choice of language in the middle of his sudden embarrassment and revived misery.

"We didn't come to blows, exactly," he said. "I thought it was weird from the start because I was coming down to see her but she wanted to meet in Richmond Park. So I went along none the wiser and with my brain in neutral, wondering why on earth she wanted to meet me there. It's only ten minutes from her flat. Anyway I got there a bit late and she was waiting for me."

He went through the whole sorry tale and how he had walked and then ran in Richmond Park afterwards.

"You ran?" George said, incredulous. "How come?"

Will looked embarrassed again.

"I know," he said. "I'm putting on a few pounds so I thought I'd take up running. But I wasn't going to do it immediately or anything, it was just an idea. It would probably have taken me ages to get around to it, but then all this happened. And after she'd taken herself off I started walking and then after a bit I broke into a trot and just kind of ran right across the park. I think it was a kind of fight or flight mechanism. Flight after the fight, you see. Except of course we didn't fight. It was all very clinical. It just felt better to be running. I'm aching all over this morning, though."

"It probably did you a load of good," Anna said. "George ought to go running with you. He's getting a bit porky."

"I am certainly not," George said indignantly.

"You are, dearest," Anna said sweetly, poking him in the ribs so that he jerked violently.

"Well, I'm going to try to keep it up," Will said. "Now that I've made a start. I need to get some running shoes, though. I wasn't exactly dressed for running yesterday, so I've got sore feet. And a hangover, although it's nearly gone now."

"A hangover?" Anna said. "But I thought you biked down?"

"I did, and I biked back. But then I had a drink or three once I got home, and woke up this morning in the chair with an aching head."

"Oh, *Will*."

She reached across the table and rubbed his hand, tilting her head and pursing her lips.

Will's phone pinged with a message and he read it, then looked at their expectant faces with a downward-turned mouth. He held the phone across the table for them to read.

It was from Lucy.

Will, I am so sorry that it had to end. I've had a lovely last few months with you. I have left a few clothes in your wardrobe and in my drawer in your bedroom. Could you possibly put them in a parcel and post them to me?

"Fair enough, I suppose," he said. "I'd better go back and sort them out."

"How are you feeling about it all?" Anna said.

"Still a bit raw and horrible," Will said. "I don't think we were the perfect couple, if I'm totally honest, but you know me – I tend to hang in there and not think about it until something happens. I paint and paint and eventually they bugger off."

She nodded sympathetically. They *did* know this repeating pattern. Both she and George would have liked to see him with a partner. They saw how much he enjoyed spending time with their own children, but Will seemed unable to form long-term relationships and they despaired for him. Neither of them had privately thought Lucy was ideal, though they had never said so. It had been hard to warm to her. Anna in particular had found her very clinical – exactly the word Will had used earlier about the break-up in Richmond Park. Lucy and he had enjoyed a passionate romance following the drama of the previous summer, but it had never seemed like it would last forever, so it wasn't a huge surprise to Anna or George that the relationship had come to a close. They had found themselves in a similarly sympathetic position with Will a few times before, so this was nothing new.

Will's phone pinged again and he looked at it, but this time his face wore a note of surprise.

"Now I've got an invite to a funeral," he said, and they looked at him mystified.

"Lucy invited you to a funeral?" Anna asked, looking at him strangely.

"Not Lucy, someone you don't know," Will said. "It's another long story."

The doorbell rang at that moment and Alphie the terrier ran to the door barking, then started making little whines of pleasure as someone crooned to him through the closed door.

Anna grabbed a lead from the sideboard.

"That'll be the owner," she hissed. "Don't tell the funeral story until I get back."

There were five minutes of chaos while a man and a woman came in and Alphie went mad with delight. Anna took them through the inner door to the surgery to sort out the paperwork. She came back after ten minutes and switched the kettle on again.

"That woman is so over the top it's exhausting," she said, flopping down into a kitchen chair. "The husband's all right but she's kind of manic, like Alphie. I'm sure they infect each other with it. Anyway, sorry about that. Whose funeral are you going to? I hope you didn't tell it to George while I was sorting them out."

"Well, I'm not planning to *go* to the funeral," Will said. "In fact I'm quite surprised to get an invitation. I wonder if she invited me by mistake."

"She who?" George said.

"An Italian woman I met when I did that talk in Oxford on Monday last."

"But who died?" Anna asked. "Start from the beginning."

The kettle clicked and she got up to make tea, flourishing the kettle at Will, who nodded, ready for tea now.

"All right," he continued. "I did the lecture, and there was this girl who asked me a few tricky questions during it, and then she pinned me down afterwards and wanted me to meet her dad."

"Seems a bit sudden, meeting the parents," George said, and Will grinned.

"Very funny. Anyway, her dad turned out to be a professor writing a book about Botticelli. I saw him the next day and he–"

"–you stayed the night?" Anna interrupted.

"Well yes, in a hotel. It snowed on Monday if you recall and I didn't fancy skidding my way back to Cambridge. But I went to see this girl and her dad the next day."

"Uh huh," Anna said. "And does this girl have a name?"

"Alessa," Will said, and then caught the way they were both looking at him.

"Nothing happened," he said indignantly. "We just had a drink."

"Aha, you had a *drink*!" George said, looking significantly at Anna.

"And Lucy didn't know about this?" Anna asked, wondering if there was more to the break-up with Lucy than met the eye.

"There wasn't anything to know about," Will said in the same injured tone. "But no, she didn't."

"Okay," Anna said. "I was just wondering. So you had a drink with this girl Alessa and then visited her father. Where does the funeral come in?"

"That's the peculiar thing," Will said. "Very sad really. The old boy died, that night I think. I heard about it the next day on the radio. He'd had a heart attack. Mind you, he was in a wheelchair and didn't look at all well. I didn't think he was going to kick the bucket, though. I mean you don't, do you?"

"How horrid," Anna said. "And you'd only just met him. So I see now, his daughter has asked you to his funeral. What did he want to talk to you about?"

She handed Will a blue mug with a William Morris pattern on it. He tucked his long hair back and leaned over the cup, sipping the hot tea.

"That's the interesting thing," he said. "The old boy had this extraordinary idea that Botticelli had a different muse from the one everyone thought, and he wanted me to investigate it."

"And you said I'd be pleased to, as I am after all an amazing investigator and you should see what I got up to last summer," Anna said.

Will looked sheepish.

"Well no, I said I couldn't possibly," he admitted. "I said I was a painter and didn't have the time."

"Sounds pretty boring of you," George said. "Why don't you have a go? Honour the old boy's memory, sort of. Was he a nice chap?"

"Yes he was," Will said, remembering the old man in the wheelchair. "Very erudite."

"Alessa who?" Anna asked unexpectedly.

"Cooper. Alessa Cooper. He was Humphrey Cooper. Said I ought to call him Humph but I never did the whole time I was there. It just seemed too personal when I didn't know him. Then he went and died."

"Well why don't you follow it up?" George said again.

Anna was typing on her phone and after a few moments she turned the phone around so that Will could see the screen.

"Is that her?" she asked. "She's on Facebook."

Will turned a little pink.

"Actually yes," he said, knowing that Anna was noticing his change of colour.

"She's a Ph.D. student, apparently," Anna said, reading.

"Yes, although I think she may have finished it now, I'm not sure."

George craned his neck and looked at the picture, which Anna turned to him.

"Pretty," he observed. "Unusual surname for an Italian, though."

"Her mother was Italian," Will explained, and then thought that he shouldn't have done so. "I mean, she mentioned it in passing. Her dad was as English as they come."

"So," Anna said, ticking off points on her fingers. "You've met a smart lady who also happens to be gorgeous, her dying father's last wish was to send you off on another interesting adventure, meanwhile Lucy came back from the States and dumped you, but you're determined not to do anything about any of it."

Will started to laugh, shaking his head, and carried on laughing, wiping a tear out of his eye.

"Well, sort of."

"You couldn't make this up," George said, infected by Will's laughter and starting to laugh too, but Anna leaned forward and locked eyes with Will.

"Will," she said intensely. "If Alessa has invited you to her father's funeral, the least you can do is turn up. When is it?"

Will shook his head.

"It's on the twelfth, but there's no way I'm going," he said firmly. "I hardly knew the old chap."

Will arrived on the twelfth very late at St. Nicholas' Church in the centre of Islip, ruefully remembering Anna's indomitable powers of persuasion. The funeral was over and the cars had departed to the wake, which according to the text message he had received was in the professor's cottage. He left the Bonnie near the gate and walked over to the grave, which had already been filled in and was marked by a display of flowers. He bent down to read inscriptions on the bouquets: "HC, take care on the next journey. HP and Mads xxx"; "Humph, we'll miss you so much, love Venetia and Q"; and so on.

He stood up and looked around. It was a nice old church with a square tower. He went inside and met the vicar in the doorway, who asked him if he had come for the funeral and took Will's hands in his when he said he had. Will wasn't religious but warmed to the old man. The vicar pointed down the road vaguely and said that everybody had returned to the house. Will remembered where it was, and rather than putting his leathers back on for a five-minute trip he decided to walk. It was cold and he set off briskly. Once again he reminded himself that it was time to get a car – motorbikes were not ideal for February in England. He watched his breath cloud the air as he walked.

When he arrived he could hear the burble of voices from inside. The door was slightly ajar so he knocked and went in. The house was crowded and there was the usual post-funeral mixture of subdued melancholy and exuberant relief. As Will threaded his way through the assembly he came rapidly to the conclusion that the guests formed three distinct groups; local villagers who had known the professor, friends from the university who were rather bohemian, and family members. They had formed into cliques in each room and the house was crowded – Humphrey Cooper had been popular.

He found Alessa in the kitchen, dispensing drinks. Before she saw him, he took in her dark eyes and the tumble of long hair which curled from her jawline downwards. She had a dusting of freckles which he hadn't noticed in the Blenheim. She handed out a glass of white wine to a beautiful old lady who carried herself like a retired ballerina, then turned her attention to him. Alessa's eyebrows went up and her mouth opened in surprise and recognition.

"Thank you for coming!" she said. "I didn't think you would."

Her voice was taut, stretched thin with grief.

"Poor dear," the old ballerina lady said, laying a hand briefly on Alessa's arm and patting her before she departed.

"I'm so sorry about your father," Will said. "He seemed like a lovely man."

He examined her. Her mascara was uneven, so he suspected that she had cried at the church but hadn't had a moment to sort it out. Her face was as vivacious as he remembered. She was wearing a red dress, in contrast to his own dark suit and black tie.

"Well you certainly look the part," she said, tweaking his tie and pretending to straighten it. She had somehow managed to bend her mouth into both a rueful smile and a grimace. "I'm in red because this was papà's favourite dress and he didn't like black for funerals. He always used to wear a blue polka-dot bow tie when he attended them, in defiance of all the black."

"I'm sorry," Will said awkwardly. "I didn't know."

"No way you could have," she said, and flashed him the smile that he remembered from their evening in the pub, more open than a moment before. She had very white teeth. She asked what he wanted to drink and he opted for beer so that he could make it last. She popped the cap off a bottle of Peroni and gave it to him.

"Make yourself at home and I'll come and find you," she said. "There are sandwiches in the dining room, so help yourself. I just need to make sure everyone is fed and watered, but please don't vanish."

He found his way to the dining room, which had a fully extended table that was covered in plates of sandwiches. The room was more spacious than might be expected for the type of house. People chatted as they circled the table, grabbing food. Everyone seemed hungry. Perhaps they had all left in a hurry without breakfast, like him. The filmmaker woman was there – what on earth was her name? He had talked to her briefly after the presentation in Oxford. He remembered the crimson lipstick. She glanced up and caught his eye and smiled.

"Rachel Blake," she said as if somehow knowing his inner dilemma. "How are you?"

She caught his wary look and smiled more widely. "Don't worry, even I am not going to pounce on you about film-making when we're at a wake."

He grinned sheepishly.

"Then I'm all right," he said. "How come you're here, Rachel? Did you know the professor?"

"Not really," she said, "but I got to know Lucas when I chatted to him after your talk." She nudged the man beside her with his back to them, and he turned. Will had last seen him in the Blenheim pub from a distance.

"Lucas Flynn, he said, offering his hand. "I'm Alessa's fiancé." He had pale skin, high cheek bones, wavy black hair and an intense expression when he looked at you. His eyes were a vivid China blue and he was as Will remembered from the Blenheim – irritatingly good looking.

"Will Bentley," Will said, shaking Flynn's proffered hand. "I gave that talk about Botticelli and I think I saw you there. I did speak to someone named Flynn, actually, but he was an older man."

"That would have been my father, Sir Milton," Flynn said, looking around the room. "He's here somewhere."

"We had an interesting chat about the history of the Oxford terms," Will said, on his best behaviour and therefore omitting to mention that Flynn's father had been a pompous ass.

Lucas Flynn noticed that his own glass was empty and looked around again. He spotted a bottle of prosecco on the sideboard and grabbed it. He looked interrogatively at Will and waggled the bottle. Will smiled and shook his head, holding up his bottle of Peroni. Flynn turned his attention to Rachel and she held out her glass. There was something flirtatious about the woman, Will thought. She had a way of looking at you with the tiniest of smiles. She had turned it on him earlier and now she was focussing on Flynn, and he was lapping it up. He filled her glass but the prosecco frothed up and foamed out of the top.

"Oops, sorry!" he said, stepping back. Rachel's glass calmed and this time she tilted it as he finished topping it up. She smiled forgiveness.

"No harm done," she said.

"I *do* remember you now," Flynn said to Will, topping up his own glass with exaggerated care. "Didn't you have a long phone call with Alessa about Botticelli?"

He was beginning to speak a little loudly and Will realised he was already well oiled. Perhaps he'd had a glass or two before Will's arrival. One or two people turned as Flynn's voice reached them. Two young women about Alessa's age were standing by a bowl of fruit in the corner and Will saw one of them lean closer to the other and whisper something. They chuckled conspiratorially, and his brain recorded the moment like a photograph for a future painting. He wondered if they were Alessa's friends. They looked about her age. He saw the ballerina lady enter the dining room trailed by a tall red-faced man with a paunch hooked over the front band of his trousers. He had probably been slim and handsome when she had married him, but now he looked as if he had been levered into his dark suit with a shoehorn.

"Am I right?" Flynn asked with a certain relentlessness, bringing Will's attention back to him. "Chatting up the little lady?"

Will eyed his dark locks and clean-cut handsome face. He couldn't quite make out whether the man was trying to put him on the back foot or simply being friendly.

"Er, yes," he said, feeling uncomfortable. "We did have a brief chat about Botticelli." He decided to ignore the implication that he had been flirting with Alessa.

"I *know*," Lucas said, stretching out the word, and now Will definitely caught a note of condescension. He felt his hackles rise a little. Despite his good looks Alessa's fiancé was what his friend Lewis would call 'a bit of a dick'.

The man had already drained his glass again. He was certainly putting it away.

"I heard you both going on about Botticelli," Flynn went on. "I mean I heard *Alessa* of course, but I got the gist."

"I do love Botticelli," the ballerina lady said, joining their circle. "Primavera!"

She held a plate with a tiny quiche pie and two sticks of celery on it.

Her husband had no plate but had grabbed a prawn mayonnaise sandwich and was stuffing it into his mouth. He joined the circle too and spoke with his mouth full. He had a tiny pink spot of Marie Rose sauce on his upper lip, but no-one except Will had yet noticed.

"Priceless," the man barked, looking around the group. "Botticelli. Everyone loves the bloody pagans these days."

"You would know, Q," Flynn said, turning his condescension on the new circle member.

The red-faced man nodded at them all. "Quentin Hardy," he said. "Art dealer." He indicated the ballerina lady. "My wife," he said, without supplying a name.

"Venetia," the ballerina lady said, flashing a cold look in the direction of her boorish husband.

Lucas Flynn excused himself and disappeared, presumably on a wine quest.

"Mr Bentley is an expert on Botticelli and art forgery," Rachel said to the group, indicating Will.

"Bentley," said Quentin Hardy with a frown. "You that fellow that rode to the rescue when someone tried to pinch a Botticelli from the National?"

Cornered and unable to escape, Will was forced to admit that he was.

"Good Heavens," Venetia said in excitement. "You're practically a celebrity, you were on the news! I can't *believe* it was you!"

Before Will was obliged to explain the whole story, Alessa came into the dining room and all normal conversation was suspended as people murmured their condolences or rubbed her arm in sympathy. Will watched as the two girls in the corner immediately came over and gave her a hug, confirming his earlier theory. He overheard her ask them to give her a minute and then she turned away and joined his own group.

"Thank you all for coming," she said. "It's such a pity really, because papà would have loved to see you all and catch up."

"It's always the same with funerals," Venetia said. "You meet people you haven't seen for years and you want to catch up but it's such a sad occasion. It always makes me feel guilty if I enjoy myself."

"Well, don't!" Alessa said firmly. "You know papà would have wanted you all to have a lovely time and a good chat, so please do. I see you've all met Will Bentley," she added, gesturing to him and smiling her wide smile again.

Lucas Flynn came back with a fresh bottle of prosecco at the moment and heard her.

"We've met him but we haven't heard about his exploits," he said, re-entering the conversation. "I was just telling them you spent an age on the phone with him," he went on, drinking half his glass. "On about Botticelli's muse. Some deep secret or other."

Will noticed that Flynn's father had followed him in and stood listening. He pointedly avoided catching Sir Milton's eye lest he be overwhelmed with an irrepressible desire to punch it.

"His muse?" Sir Milton said. "What about his muse?"

"Lucas!" Alessa said warningly.

"I don't think we should really discuss it," Will said with embarrassment. "It was just a little something that Professor Cooper was chatting about." He attempted to change the subject. "I can't believe that he's no longer with us."

"Botticelli's muse," Lucas went on in a drawling voice as if Will hadn't spoken. "Not the same one as everyone thinks, according to Humph," he said. "Alessa knows all about it. I heard her talking with our bold adventurer here."

He raised his glass to Will in mock salute.

"Hmm," Sir Milton said with a resurgence of his previous pomposity. "Well, Botticelli's muse was Simonetta Vespucci. Not much of a story there."

"Ah, but that's where Humphrey would have said you were wrong, pops," Lucas chimed back in. Sir Milton frowned. He would probably prefer pater over pops, Will surmised.

Lucas flashed his handsome smile around the circle and winked, gesturing at Will and Alessa.

"According to *these two*, anyway!"

"Milton's quite right," Hardy said, stuffing another sandwich into his mouth. Venetia turned to say something to him but then paused and wiped away the dot of sauce from her husband's upper lip with her napkin. He looked irritated.

"Humph found some book about it and he was investigating," Lucas went on. "In fact," he added triumphantly as if it had only just occurred to him. "He called in an *investigator*!"

He indicated Will and all eyes turned back to him.

"Just a humble painter," Will said weakly. "But would you excuse me for a moment?" He left the room, unwilling to let the conversation carry on any further, and went and hid in the kitchen. After a couple of minutes Alessa came in, looking cross.

"I've shut him up," she said. "I do apologise. He has a bit too much to drink and then he gets garrulous and starts picking fights, like his father. I do wish he wouldn't."

"I didn't think you would want an open discussion about your father's ideas," Will explained. "So I ducked out as soon as I could."

"It nearly went that way," she said, "but I started thanking everyone for their beautiful flowers and everyone started talking about that instead. I certainly don't want Lucas going through papà's theory in public like that. And anyway, I want to follow up on it myself."

"Go to the British Library, you mean?"

"Well," she said. "I thought I might. Do you want to come or are you still terribly busy?"

"I'm sorely tempted," Will said, knowing that with such a statement he was now utterly committed. "But I shouldn't think your fiancé would think much of that."

"Then we shan't tell him!" Alessa said sweetly.

11

It was a meadow of fine grass, so deep a green that almost black it seemed, speckled with a thousand varieties of flowers, surrounded by green and vivid-orange trees and cedars, which, bearing both old and new fruits among blossoms, brought not only pleasant shade but also pleasing scent.

GIOVANNI BOCCACCIO, Decameron, 1353

10th July 1482, Florence

Pallas and the Centaur was finished, and had been delivered by Botticelli's workshop that morning to the Medici town palace in via Larga. Botticelli now stood in the bedchamber where it had been situated, with Il Popolano on his left and Amerigo Vespucci on his right. Semiramide was in attendance also, standing a little apart with Il Magnifico. Botticelli eyed her covertly. She seemed charged with excitement and anticipation.

The new painting was large at three and a half braccia in height, making it taller than a man. It was mounted over the doorway to an antechamber in the high-ceilinged room. It had been positioned there with much grunting and sweating by Botticelli's young workshop apprentices, for he did not trust ordinary workmen to erect the painting without damaging it.

At his request, his apprentices Biagio and Tommaso had hung a curtain of pale silk across the painting, and various courtiers had joined the Medici for the unveiling. Only Il Magnifico's wife Clarice was missing, as she was returning from Rome after conducting business on behalf of her husband. This was why Semiramide stood with Il Magnifico. When Botticelli looked at them he was reminded of the joust, when Simonetta had hung so prettily on Il Magnifico's arm in the way that her niece now did. The young woman had a growing resemblance to Simonetta.

"We are ready, my friends," Il Magnifico announced to the assemblage, and the buzz of conversation died to an expectant silence. At a nod from Botticelli, Tommaso twitched the ivory silk so that the impromptu curtain rippled down through the air, gathering in shining folds on the floor. There was applause from the assembled throng and Botticelli permitted himself a nod, knowing that the painting was good. He stood back as the Medici stepped forward and the courtiers clustered behind them, looking up at the picture.

Pallas and the Centaur was painted in egg tempera, so it was completely dry – he would not have veiled an *oil* painting finished only a few days previously for fear of smudging it, but this was safe enough. The picture had come together well. Pallas was clad in a diaphanous robe but Botticelli had covered it discreetly with the three-ring motif of Cosimo and wrapped Pallas around in olive branches, just as they had discussed at the dinner in Cafaggiolo. Where the transparent cloth fell across the green of her cloak, it let through an emerald iridescence.

Pallas bore Semiramide's face. She held a splendid golden halberd and twined her hand in the beast's hair just as Semiramide had suggested to her future husband back in the spring. The beast wore the face of a sad and chastened god, caught in the act of his intended flagrancy and thus tamed. He was a centaur; the body of the man changed into a horse whose legs were twisted in disorder as if suddenly arrested. The centaur held a bow which he had recently stretched, as indicated by the crooked middle finger of his left hand. The two figures stood out in dark relief.

In the lighter background scene a small ship sailed dreamlike on a lake, while close at hand the wall of a wooden palisade further confirmed Pallas Athena as the guardian of her nymphs. The ship was so tiny from their vantage point that it would likely not be spotted unless you knew it was there, but Botticelli knew that up close you would see figures on its deck, because he had put them there. It had a sail puffed out by the wind, a mast supporting rigging and a pennant fluttering backwards as the boat cleaved the water.

"It is a masterpiece," Lorenzo Il Popolano breathed, and then Il Magnifico began to clap, and suddenly the whole room was applauding again, more loudly this time having awaited Medici approval. Botticelli stood proud and red-faced at the same moment, and the imminent parting from a completed painting once more tugged at his heart.

Servants brought wine and the party grew more voluble. Botticelli found himself the centre of attention and shamelessly lapped it up. This was his element. Several commissions were proposed and Tommaso stood at his side taking notes so that arrangements for visits could be made at a later date. A young lady of eight or nine years held out her hand solemnly and congratulated Botticelli on his work.

"*Isabella d'Este di Mantova, il maestro Botticelli,*" said the servant behind her solemnly, and Botticelli kissed the young lady's hand as if she were fully grown.

"Delighted, madam!" he said with equal solemnity, and then something in her eye caught his and they both grinned at each other, dispensing with ceremony.

"Your Pallas Athene is beautiful," she said to him. "Is she modelled on Semiramide d'Appiano? She looks exactly like her. We are here for the wedding!"

"It *is* Semiramide," Botticelli said. It is a wedding gift, you see."

"Like Camilla from Virgil," the little girl said breathlessly, but then she frowned. "That is, I know there's a connection between Camilla and Pallas, but I can't quite remember what. I am studying Virgil, though. I like him very much."

"You like his *writing* very much," corrected the lady at her side, and then she smiled at Botticelli. "I am Eleanor," she explained. "Of Naples. I have the pleasure of being this precocious young lady's mother."

"What exactly *is* precocious, mamma?" Isabella said with a wide-eyed look. "Does it mean wise and beautiful?"

But before her mother could come up with a suitable reply, Botticelli's friend Leo appeared and Isabella immediately ran to him. He picked her up and swung her round before returning her breathless to the ground.

"How you've grown, little Bella," he said, and the young girl seemed to hang on his every word. He bowed to Isabella's mother, kissed her hand and then turned to Botticelli.

"A very fine picture indeed, my friend," he said. "You are the talk of Florence."

"Not quite," Botticelli said with a regretful smile. "I fear you are steadily upstaging me, but beware! There's life in the old dog yet."

"I'm certain of that," Leo agreed.

"Signor Leonardo has agreed to paint me," Isabella said dramatically. "He says I have only to name the time and the place, so I am biding my time until I am grown up and beautiful."

"I shall capture that enigmatic smile," Leonardo said, and Eleanor looked at him, obviously entranced. Leo had that effect, Botticelli knew.

"I'm sure you will make a very fine portrait," Botticelli said to the young lady, and then he turned as someone tapped him lightly on the shoulder. Lorenzo Il Popolano himself stood there, with Semiramide now on his arm. Botticelli had spoken to them both over lunch, but each time he saw Semiramide his eloquence deserted him and he became as gauche as a teenager.

Fortunately Lorenzo begged a moment with him, excused himself to Semiramide, and bore him away before Botticelli could make a fool of himself. They left Leonardo chatting brightly to Semiramide, Eleanor and the poised young lady who was destined to become Marchioness of Mantova.

Lorenzo steered Botticelli through the door beneath the painting of Pallas and the Centaur, then into another room and closed the door.

"My sleeping chamber and private meeting room!" he announced. "We should be able to get some peace and quiet in here."

There was a large bed and fine chairs set around an octagonal walnut table inlaid with black marquetry. Against one wall were tall cupboards. Lorenzo bid Botticelli to be seated at the table. The Medici lord had grabbed a bottle of wine during their retreat from the throng, and now he sat down beside the painter, refilling their glasses himself.

"A fine painting," Lorenzo said, raising his glass to Botticelli and looking at him closely. "So very fine that my thoughts turn to the notion of another. My bride is bringing a large dowry from her estates in Piombino, and I would like to acknowledge it with a gift to her which demonstrates Medici generosity."

"I would be honoured," Botticelli said. "Do you have an idea, a subject?"

"We were to have married in May, so something spring-like. New beginnings, love triumphs, gods and goddesses. You know the sort of thing."

He waved a hand airily.

"Except that Lucrezia's passing has moved the wedding to July," Botticelli observed pragmatically.

"No matter," Lorenzo said. "We should not reflect death's delay in a joyous painting of life and love."

The painter considered, then nodded.

"May is named for Maia," he remarked after a pause. "And Maia's son was Mercury. Perhaps I could cast you as Mercury, and we could have a wedding theme. Semiramide is easy. With a theme of love she surely must be Venus."

Lorenzo rocked his head to one side and then the other. Then he brought his eyes back to Botticelli and smiled, not in the least bit embarrassed at being cast as a god.

"Better than being half a horse! Mercury and Venus could work in the right setting. Where would you put them?"

"Should we discuss it with Semiramide? I recall she has...firm views."

Lorenzo grinned but shook his head.

"Firm indeed, but I want it to be a secret," he said, putting a finger to his nose. "I want her to see it for the first time when it is finished. Nay, when it is on the wall. That's why I smuggled you away, because no-one other than a servant will enter here unless invited."

"Then let us begin at the beginning," Botticelli said. "Where is the new painting to be sited?"

"In this same palace," Lorenzo said. "You saw the *lettuccio* in the room we were just in?"

"The pinewood settle with the inset *cassone*, on the wall opposite the long cupboards?"

"Yes. It is about five *braccia* in length and the room rises to a good height. I am thinking of a framed painting to fit the length of it. Perhaps a white frame to match the bed, or pinewood like the *lettuccio*."

Botticelli stood and used his outstretched arms against the wall to measure out the approximate size with his arms, starting from the edge of an armoire. He looked at the result.

"That will be...expensive, my lord," he said, reseating himself. "Five *braccia* is a goodly width."

"Almost the size of the Uccellos in the ballroom of the Palazzo," Lorenzo nodded. "I had one of my men measure it up. But I have seen your capabilities. Would a hundred gold florins suffice?"

Botticelli felt his face colour at the mention of such a large sum. "Again I am honoured at your trust in me," he said. He rubbed his chin and frowned thoughtfully. "So let's think – it would be a little above eye level. Do you have any more thoughts about the scene?"

"A spring meadow or a garden," Lorenzo said. "I am reading Decameron again and it is very good. There is a bit in the third book, right at the beginning if I remember. Let me look."

He sprang up and crossed the room to a desk on which several books and manuscripts lay. He picked up a book and brought it over. It was a very fine book and Botticelli looked at it enviously. He had read Decameron in the form of a tatty old manuscript with pages missing, but this was a bound book, clad in leather and with illuminated pages. Lorenzo leafed through it and found the right page. The third day in the ten-day period comprised an amusing story of promiscuity between a convent of nuns and their gardener. Lorenzo ran his finger down the page and then pointed.

"This part in the introduction," he said. "Somehow it struck a chord within me."

Botticelli took the book and held it carefully, knowing it to be valuable. He read aloud slowly, as if tasting the words on his tongue.

"It was a meadow of very fine grass and so green that it seemed almost black, painted with perhaps a thousand varieties of flowers, enclosed by the greenest and liveliest orange and citron trees, which, having the old fruits, the new ones and the flowers too, not only gave pleasant shade to the eyes but also a pleasant perfume."

He stopped and sat still, looking at nothing. At last he became aware again and looked back at Lorenzo.

"It's good," he said. "It's very good. I like the black grass and the carpet of flowers. And the orange grove like the garden of Venus." He fell silent again, and Lorenzo knew him well enough simply to wait. There was neither brush nor pigment but the master was at work.

"*You* are easy enough," Botticelli went on after a minute's silence. "I'll paint Boccaccio's citrus fruits in this garden of Venus; Medici mala. And bay laurels as symbols of Lorenzo." He grinned. "Yes, and golden flames on Mercury's garment to represent Santo Lorenzo."

Lorenzo grinned back. "A saint as well as a god!" he said. "And he could carry a caduceus as a messenger of the gods. Didn't Mercury bear one?"

"A herald's wand that can restore life," Botticelli agreed. "So here it could also represent healing. *Un medico* for a Medici. Now give me a moment to think about your bride as Venus."

The moment turned into fully five minutes in which he stood up and paced around Lorenzo's bedchamber, occasionally stopping, staring at the wall where he had marked out five *braccia*, and gesturing with his arms as if gauging the positions of invisible figures.

"All right," he said at last. "This is a wedding gift to your lady, so Venus must indeed bear Semiramide's face and she shall represent love and marriage rather than lust. Indeed, I shall make her with child as an auspicious omen of your fruitful loins, which will add to her beauty. But this casts her in the role of matron, the *madonna*."

He grimaced, shaking his head slowly.

"The trouble is that Semiramide is a young woman and we must honour her youth and gracefulness. She won't want only to be perceived as a married woman with child. She is— what, seventeen?"

"Eighteen."

"We can all be sensitive about age."

"When we are young we want to be older," Lorenzo pointed out. "I myself still have another three weeks until my nineteenth year and I am very tired of pompous old lords calling me 'young man'."

Botticelli felt embarrassed. He had forgotten how young Lorenzo was. The lord seemed older than his years, perhaps because of his position and the many experiences he had already had.

"I must warn you that some old gentlemen never let up," he said gravely. "They still call me 'young man' even though I am approaching forty. Such condescension is a way of seeking dominance." Then he grinned self-deprecatingly. "Mind you, I am beginning to like it."

Lorenzo returned his smile and leapt up nimbly to fill their glasses.

"Perhaps you're right about Semiramide," he nodded. "There's more mystery in womanhood than in all the rest of nature. I never have any idea what she is going to say or think, but that's part of the magic."

Botticelli stood up and paced some more, and Lorenzo waited with barely contained impatience until at last the painter pointed a finger in the air and exclaimed that he had a possible solution.

"What if I were to include the *three Graces*? I am thinking of Capella's *De Nuptiis*. The marriage of Mercury with Philology, in which Venus attends as the protector of Hymen, god of marriage and a relative of the Graces. Semiramide as a young unmarried woman would be one of the Graces, struck by cupid's dart at the very moment that her eyes rest on Mercury in the garden."

He looked expectedly at his lord and patron, but Lorenzo mouth was turned down.

"I did like *Venus*," he said plaintively.

"Yes, yes," Botticelli said impatiently, forgetting entirely that he was talking with his lord and patron. "We include her *twice*. As one of the Graces we see the moment she is taken by love, and as Venus we see what follows. We capture different moments in time, before the wedding as a nymph, and after the wedding as a madonna."

Lorenzo looked at him sideways for a long moment and then nodded slowly.

"The moment she is taken by love and what follows," he repeated. "I like it."

"It is very romantic," Botticelli said. "Just as a wedding present should be. And in the Graces I shall work as much magic as these fingers can muster." He held up his hands and wiggled his fingers for a moment, then knitted his fingers together and rotated his thumbs. After a moment he raised his forefingers and rested his nose on them. He sat for a moment staring at the patterned surface of the walnut table, but then stood and paced again.

"The Graces must be beauty and youth personified," he went on. "Clad in virginal white robes, with long tresses of hair. All men shall desire them."

He caught sight of Lorenzo with his head tilted slightly, unsure of this.

"Every young woman wants to be desired, lord. But only you shall wed her, and so the painting will compliment *her* for beauty, and *you* for choosing her!"

In his enthusiasm he clapped the Medici lord on the shoulder and snatched up his glass, spilling a few drops.

"Trust me," he said. "It will be *perfect*!"

Infected by his enthusiasm Lorenzo stood, and they raised their glasses aloft before draining them.

Botticelli discarded his empty glass and faced the wall where his imaginary painting was laid out. He began to count on his fingers, pointing at invisible figures as he did so. "One, Mercury, two, Venus, three, four and five, the Graces. And Cupid, but he flies above and is too small to count." He shook his head, his mouth turned down. "Not enough for such a large picture," he said. "Venus is on her own. We need more figures in the garden."

"Well, we talked of spring," Lorenzo said. "What about Flora, all in green?"

Botticelli clapped his hands at once and looking delightedly at Lorenzo.

"Flora is perfect! The goddess of flowers who brings in the spring. She shall cast petals on the ground. Not green though," he said, shaking his head as if commanded by an inner voice. "Can't have her in green, she wouldn't stand out, but she could be all in white and covered in flowers."

A wicked expression crossed his features.

"I'll paint her smiling!"

"Smiling?" said Lorenzo, shocked at this breach of artistic etiquette.

"Why not smiling? She brings the spring!" Botticelli said, remembering Leonardo's earlier pronouncement that he would capture Isabella's smile. He waved his arm dramatically high and then fluttering his fingers as if casting down petals. "And the wind must take the petals and blow them in the garden, so I'll add Zephyr, exhaling a gentle spring breeze." He raised his arms wide and blew out his cheeks.

"Well that's up to seven, or eight with Cupid," Lorenzo said. "Does it seem right?"

Botticelli nodded slowly. "I *think* so," he said. "Let me think some more and do some sketches. "We may yet need another for a painting this wide. He went back to the blank wall where he had done his measurements and frowned at it, then gestured with his hands to imaginary figures.

"Mercury, the three Graces, Venus in the centre, then Flora, and Zephyr on the right, swooping from the trees just as a breeze should. Before and after, so perhaps we need – wait! I have it! We'll have *Chloris*."

"Er…"

"Chloris! She was abducted as a nymph by Zephyr and transformed into Flora. She's a young and virginal version of Flora, being pounced upon by Zephyr, and the older Flora is the result. Again we have before and after."

There was a long silence and then Lorenzo held out his hand, and Botticelli clasped it, looking triumphant.

"Sandro, I *think* it's wonderful, but go and make me sketches. You may be able to imagine it on the wall beside an armoire filled with my underclothes, but I need something on paper."

"I shall begin at once," Botticelli said, standing up. "Give me a week and I will call upon you again."

Lorenzo stood up. "I'll be here," he said. "And bring that rogue Vespucci with you. We shall all share a glass together. Go now."

Botticelli set his mouth in a serious shape and nodded once. They looked into each other's eyes.

"It will be great," Lorenzo said after a few seconds.

"It will," Botticelli agreed, and then again, pointing his finger like a baton in the air. "It *will*."

Without a bow or even a backward glance he stalked out the way he had come, and left Lorenzo shaking his head and laughing at the wit and cheek of the man.

As Botticelli strode through the door into the main room he almost cannoned into Semiramide, and brought himself to an abrupt halt.

"Forgive me, my lady," he said, colouring up.

"Maestro Botticelli," she said, pinning him with her intense look. "What exactly have you been discussing with my future husband without me? Another painting, perhaps?"

"My lady, I can say nothing at all," he said, "except to say that tonight your face may haunt my dreams."

Then with the shortest of bows and a magnificent flourish of his cloak, he swept out of the room.

It was her turn to blush.

12

I have owed you this letter for a very long time - but my fingers have avoided the pencil as though it were an old and poisoned tool.

JOHN STEINBECK, 1968

March, London

The British Library in London is located at 96 Euston Road, a few minutes' walk from St. Pancras railway station, which rises behind it in vertiginous spiked towers like a gothic fairy castle. Alessa and Will travelled into London on Tuesday morning by train from their respective cities and met in the Library entrance hall in front of the staircase at ten in the morning. As a student studying the Italian Renaissance, Alessa had long been a Reader, and had reserved a copy of Frederick Pocock's book to be accessed in the Humanities Reading Room. In contrast Will had never been to the British Library before, but at Alessa's insistence he had registered online as a reader.

"Otherwise you'll have to sit in the cafe and wait for me."

Alessa took their coats down to the cloakroom while Will went to the Reader Registration room, showed his proof of address and signature and got photographed for his first-ever Reader Pass. When he got it he felt rather proud. Alessa was waiting for him, wearing a red top and standing out in the crowd. He flourished his pass with a grin. They had an easy camaraderie together.

"Congratulations," she said, "you are officially a swot! Let's go; it's this way."

She led him around to Humanities, threading between desks of seated students. In the middle was a vast glassed-in stack of library shelves which went down two floors when you leaned over the balcony, but went up far above their heads to the ceiling above. Will counted six floors.

"The Library has four hundred miles of shelves, apparently," Alessa said in a low voice.

They found the Humanities room, showed their passes to the door staff and went in. Alessa leaned closer to him.

"They'll ask for our desk number," she said very quietly, "so we need to go and find somewhere with no-one close because we're not supposed to make any noise."

Will nodded and followed her. They went right over to the other side and found a quiet spot.

She put on a pair of white cotton gloves.

"Wait here," she murmured, noting the desk number and disappearing. After a few minutes she came back from the Issue desk with a dark blue book. It looked worn and the outer spine was a little damaged. It had a white index number on it.

"Is that it, Pocock's actual book?"

"It is, and we were right, it recently went forward for digitisation, so that's why it popped up as an alert."

She showed him the spine of the book and he looked expectantly at it.

"Wow, it really is. Do I need to wear gloves?"

"Not for this book, but I can't break the habit after all this time. We would have to have them for old manuscripts and incunabula, but this book is dated 1957 and the lady at the desk just handed it to me like this."

"Incunabula?"

"Early printed books. I mean *very* early, printed before 1501."

"Really? I thought printed books were only a couple of hundred years old."

She shook her head.

"Gutenberg invented the printing press in the first half of the fifteenth century. By the end of the Quattrocento there would have been millions of books in circulation."

"Jesus."

"Yes indeed," she winked. "Lots of them would have been bibles. But anyway, no gloves. We just have to be careful with it."

"No pens allowed," Will said, remembering the conditions of use he had signed earlier.

"Exactly."

He himself had a small sketchbook which he usually carried with him, and a 5B pencil but no pen. She produced her own notebook and a pencil from her bag. They examined the dark-blue book. The title was embossed on the front cover in white letters: 'The Classical Origin of Science Fiction'. In black letters at the bottom, 'Frederick Pocock'. It was odd to see the real thing. She opened the book at random and brought it up to her nose, inhaling.

"I love the smell of old books, kind of baked in history." She caught his expression and giggled a little with embarrassment. "You think I'm bonkers."

He leaned in and smelled the book too.

"A bit, but I know what you mean. There was a painter called Robert Lenkiewicz who had an extraordinary collection of old books, and he used to say they had been burned with time."

She smiled.

"I like that."

Will let Alessa handle the book, since she was the professional. He brought out the printout with the reference that had started their expedition, smoothed it flat and put it on the desk before them. It read:

CHAPTER I *(p 18)*
12.   *'Medici letter written by Semiramide Appiano…Lucian's tale of Alexander and Roxana…' Pocock, Frederick. The Classical Origin of Science Fiction, 1957.*

Alessa opened the book carefully and went to page 18, then began to read with Will reading over her shoulder. Her dark hair brushed his face and smelled faintly of coconut. He had to resist burying his face in it, which made him laugh at the thought of what she would do if he surrendered to the impulse. She swung around and gave him a questioning look.

"Tension!" he said feebly. "Carry on."

She turned back to the page and almost immediately said, "Oh my God!" and put her finger on the start of a section.

Some scholars[11] today hypothesize that Lucian's works declined in favour and were rediscovered only in their remarkable entirety as a portent of the future – a series of scientific fictions parodying authors such as Homer. However, this author has personally witnessed an original letter authored by Semiramide, wife of Lorenzo di Pierfrancesco de' Medici, in which she makes explicit mention[12] of Lucian's account of Alexander and Roxana's nuptials, thought to be inspiration for Botticelli's painting of Mars and Venus. Lucian states the following, which connoisseurs of Botticelli's painting (acquired by London's National Gallery in 1874) may find familiar:

It must have been a very wonderful picture, I think I hear someone say, to make the High Steward give his daughter to a stranger. Well, I have seen it—it is now in Italy—, so I can tell you. A fair chamber, with the bridal bed in it; Roxana seated—and a great beauty she is—with downcast eyes, troubled by the presence of Alexander, who is standing. Several smiling Loves; one stands behind Roxana, pulling away the veil on her head to show her to Alexander; another obsequiously draws off her sandal, suggesting bed-time; a third has hold of Alexander's mantle, and is dragging him with all his might towards Roxana. The King is offering her a garland, and by him as supporter and groom's-man is Hephaestion, holding a lighted torch and leaning on a very lovely boy; this is Hymenaeus, I conjecture, for there are no letters to show. On the other side of the picture, more Loves playing among Alexander's armour; two are carrying his spear, as porters do a heavy beam; two more grasp the handles of the shield, tugging it along with another reclining on it, playing king, I suppose; and then another has got into the breast-plate, which lies hollow part upwards…

From this anecdote we have irrefutable evidence that the Medici were familiar with Lucian in the late Quattrocento, even if this be not proof of familiarity with scientific satires such as Lucian's 'A True Story'. We see also that Botticelli, a master painter of that era, was familiar with Lucian. Following the evidence in this introduction, let us turn our attention in Chapter II to science fiction.

"So far so good," Alessa said. She licked her bottom lip in concentration. "Let's find citation 12."

She turned to the back where there were several pages of citations. Unfortunately citation 12 said exactly what they already knew and nothing more. There was no copy of the letter itself, simply a reference to it as they had seen on page 18.

"A dead end," Will said. "Interesting to read that bit about Alexander and Roxana, though. The bit about the Loves getting into the breastplate is spot on for the Mars and Venus picture, except they call them satyrs these days. I've seen mention of it but I've never seen the actual source."

"How bloody irritating, though!" Alessa whispered crossly. "I wonder if Pocock wrote anything else."

She turned to the front of the book and checked, but there was no list of other books by the author. There was just the frontispiece which proclaimed that the book was Copyright, 1957 by Frederick C Pocock. It had been printed in Honiton, Devon.

"I wonder if he's got any heirs," Will said suddenly. "They might still have his stuff. Look him up."

She got out her phone, selected the search engine and typed: Frederick C Pocock Honiton Devon.

Monochrome images of beribboned military officers appeared, but while the names were a mixture of Frederick and Pocock, never the twain seemed to align.

Alessa tried again: "Frederick Pocock" Honiton Devon.

No joy.

She tried: "Frederick Clifford Pocock" Honiton Devon.

Nothing useful.

"Clifford?"

"Papà's brother was Clifford," she said. "I thought I'd try it. "What other English names begin with C?"

"Er, Charles? Christopher?" He paused and thought. "Claude, Conrad?"

She tried: "Frederick Charles Pocock" Honiton Devon.

The first entry this time was a PDF file containing a list of memorial headstones. They selected it and searched for Pocock, finding the following entry:

Name: Ethel Margaret Pocock (1934 - 2012)
Inscription: IN LOVING MEMORY OF MY DEAR WIFE, ETHEL MARGARET POCOCK, WHO PASSED AWAY MAR. 12TH 2012, AGED 78 YEARS.
Plot: Cross on double tapered plinth with raised edging. NW corner, St. Michaels, Honiton, Devon
Reservation: Frederick Charles Pocock (1932-)

"It could have been him," Will said. "Frederick C Pocock. I bet Charles was a common name then."

"Yes, but don't you see?" she said excitedly. "He *wasn't dead* in 2012, he just had a plot reservation to be buried with his wife.

Will counted up the decades on his fingers. "Well it's not impossible that he could still be with us. He'd be pretty ancient, though."

Alessa went into the BT online phonebook and selected Find a Person. The page appeared and she entered Pocock in Honiton (Devon).

There was a single entry: Mr F.C Pocock, Abbott's Rest Cottage, Combe View, Combe Raleigh, Honiton, followed by a postcode and a telephone number.

"We could call him," Will said in realisation, and they looked at each other solemnly.

"I think we should go and see him," Alessa said. "You get better results by going to the source. We might scare him to death if we call him."

They thought about it in silence for a moment.

"I do see what you mean," Will said. "But maybe we should call him anyway and then go and see him if he's still alive and is the right one. It's a long way to go if he turns out to be the wrong Pocock."

She nodded.

Once they had returned the book and were outside and away from the study desks clustered around the cafe, Alessa called the number. They had decided that she would be less threatening to an old man than a male voice.

Someone duly answered and she had an animated conversation with him for a few minutes, then hung up, a look of excitement on her face.

"He's definitely the author of the book!" she said. "He doesn't mind if we visit him this afternoon. I think he was flattered that anyone had ever even *heard* of his book."

"This afternoon? Well it's gone eleven already. If we're going to get down to Honiton today we'd better be ever so quick. Where's the cloakroom?"

She shot downstairs and grabbed their coats while he checked a rail app.

"If we can make it to Waterloo in time, we could get the 12:20 to Honiton," he said, and they both headed for the stairs. "But it's ten minutes' walk back to King's Cross so we'd better get a move on."

"Let's *run!*" she said over her shoulder, and suddenly she was off, threading through the tourists, and he found himself jogging in the wake of this wonderfully impulsive woman.

They managed to get the 12:20 with three minutes to spare and arrived in Honiton at a quarter past three. While on the train they had checked ahead for ways to reach their destination without a car, and now they walked briskly up to the High Street. It was a sunny day with a cutting wind so they were glad of their coats as they stood outside the job centre and awaited the number 20 bus. It was only a short ride to Combe Raleigh but it took them another half an hour to find Abbott's Rest Cottage, which turned out to be the middle of a row of three thatched cottages set directly on the road. There was a black Land Rover Discovery parked outside with a child's car seat strapped in the rear. They walked up to the door and knocked. A woman in her thirties opened it, with a pleasant but no-nonsense air about her.

"Yes?"

"My name's Alessa Cooper and this is my colleague Will Bentley," Alessa said. "I called ahead to Mr. Pocock. Is this the right address?"

The woman looked at them with narrowed eyes.

"My grandfather lives here," she admitted. "Frederick Pocock. But he's very old and mustn't be unduly excited. Can you tell me what this is about? And do you have some kind of identification?"

"Yes of course," Alessa said. "I know it's very peculiar." She was reaching for her purse. "Here we are, this is my Reader's Pass for the British Library." She turned to Will expectantly and he found his wallet and extracted his own shiny new Reader's Pass. While the woman inspected the photo IDs, Alessa went on quickly: "We were looking up a quote in a book called The Origin of Science Fiction, written by your grandfather," she explained. "And we were completely stuck because the quote didn't tell us anything more than we already knew."

"So we were about to give up," Will went on, flashing a rueful smile at the lady in the doorway, "and then we suddenly wondered if Mr Pocock was still around. And when we looked him up we found much to our delight that he is."

"How did you find this address?" the woman asked, still obviously not completely satisfied. "I'm sorry to ask a lot of questions but it's a bit odd that you've come all this way down from London."

"We just looked him up in the phone book and there he was," Will explained.

"I know it sounds a bit mad," Alessa said. "You must think we're bonkers, but we just came on the spur of the moment after we'd phoned to make sure we had the right Mr Pocock. I'm a student writing about the Italian renaissance, and my friend Will here is helping me. Honestly, we are very normal and ordinary! We just hoped that we could have a few minutes with Mr Pocock to ask him a few questions about his book."

"You look a bit older than your average student," the woman said, still apparently suspicious.

"That's because I'm doing further study to be a Doctor of Philosophy," Alessa said, reaching into her pocket. "I already have a first-class degree in classics from Oxford and a masters." She found her student identification and held it out for the woman to see.

"A *doctor*," the woman repeated, wavering in her resolve for the first time.

"Is it the researcher who called, Margaret?" came a voice from inside.

"Yes, granddad," the woman in the doorway called and then turned back to them.

"Well, all right then," she said. "You don't look like scammers but there are so many terrible stories these days I wanted to be careful, so I stayed on when grandad told me you were coming."

"I would have done exactly the same," Will said with his most infectious smile, and at last she smiled back. He and Alessa were invited into the house and they entered a bright kitchen which had an Aga in the corner, and copper pans decorating the walls. There was an old man seated at the kitchen table, but when he saw them he stood up and they could see that he was still sprightly.

"Alessa Cooper?" he said. "The researcher? I am Frederick Pocock. And I presume this is the colleague that you mentioned?"

They shook hands, finding the old man's grip surprisingly firm.

"I'm Margaret Riley," the woman said, and they shook hands with her too. She offered them tea and put a kettle on the hot ring of the Aga when they gratefully accepted.

"Come into the study and we can talk," Frederick Pocock said, opening another door and passing through. They followed him past the stairs into a warm book-lined study with a large cherrywood desk and a fire burning in the hearth. Arranged before the fire were an old sofa and an armchair of matching floral design. Pocock gestured to the sofa and they sat down while he fussed about at one of the bookshelves. The fire glowed with hot coals and was a pleasure after their brisk walk up from the bus stop in the fading light of the March afternoon. When he came back and sat down they saw that he had his book with him. It was a copy identical to the one they had viewed in the Humanities 1 Reading Room that morning, though in better condition.

"I think this is what you were asking about," he said, almost apologetically.

"That's the one," Alessa said. "I can't tell you how happy we were to find that you were still here in Honiton. We looked you up in the phonebook just on the off chance, and there you were! There's a particular reference in your book that we were hoping you might be able to tell us more about. May I find it? I will be very careful with your copy."

"Yes of course," Pocock said, and held it out. Will saw her hand move instinctively towards her bag for a moment before she stopped it. No need for gloves. She took the book and located the reference on page 18, then held it out to him, her finger marking the place. There was a pause while he patted his pullover pockets and then finally found his reading glasses on the table beside him.

He looked at the reference to Semiramide, his lips moving silently as he read the words. Then he sat back and smiled.

"The Medici letter," he said. "Oh yes, I remember that very well. I don't suppose it will matter now, but I have a small confession to make."

Margaret Riley appeared at that moment with a tray bearing traditional bone-china tea-cups, teapot, milk jug, sugar pot and a plate of biscuits. A curl of steam escaped from the spout of the teapot.

"Let's leave it a minute or so to brew," Pocock said. "Take a seat, Margaret. Now then, let me tell you the story of the Medici letter. My goodness, I haven't told this tale for a very long time."

He leaned forward and so did they. Margaret Riley sat in the desk chair.

"I must have been in my early twenties," Pocock began slowly and crisply, addressing Alessa. "It was just before the Suez crisis and I was studying classics up at Oxford, just like you my dear. That summer I decided to go to Rome to conduct some research I needed for my thesis, but I stopped off at Florence. I'd never been, you see, and my college roommate convinced me that I should. He lent me Edward Forster's Room with a View – you know it? – and then I was hooked. It turned out he was quite sneaky because he wanted me to go and look something up for him while I was there. He was lazy as could be, but he had deep pockets – family money – so he offered me some cash if I would do it."

"Sounds like a good bargain," Will said, "as you wanted to go anyway."

"It was," Pocock nodded. "I would have done it for nothing, actually, but this chap's offer was a decent sum in those days and well worth having. I didn't have rich parents so I hitchhiked all the way down to Italy, you see."

"Quite an adventure," Alessa said, fascinated.

"It was," Pocock agreed. "I could tell some stories about that journey too. Anyway, my roommate Douglas was supposed to be studying Lorenzo de' Medici, which was a typical subject suggested by the tutor in those days if one didn't have an original thought in one's head."

He looked apologetic.

"Sorry to be so scathing, but Douglas didn't. Anyway, he wanted me to find some examples of Medici household accounts – I forget why, but he gave me the details he needed and I was to photograph them for him. The one good thing I did have was a camera, you see. An Agfa Isolette that my father had given me. Douglas gave me some money, bought me a couple of films and said I should try my best but he would understand if I were unsuccessful and I could keep the cash."

"Did you have to go to the Medici Archive?" Alessa asked. "The MAP project?"

Pocock frowned.

"I don't know what that is," he said, shaking his head. "These were early letters in the Florentine State Archive and it was in the Uffizi, where they've got all the paintings now. Anyway, I almost didn't get admitted but fortunately being up at Oxford got me through the door. There wasn't much security in those days."

"So what happened next?" Will prompted.

"They sent me to a dusty old room," Pocock said. "Following this doddery old chap."

He smiled ruefully.

"Now I'm a doddery old chap. Anyway, this room was big but it seemed smaller because it was stuffed with filing cabinets and boxes. In the corner I remember there were all these wooden pigeonholes crammed with letters. Hundreds and hundreds of them, and the old man led me over to them. I remember thinking he might die any moment but he was probably only in his sixties. I can see him to this day in my mind's eye. He was bent over and had a white moustache that was stained nicotine yellow. And he shuffled along, you know. Anyway, having got me to the right spot he waved his arm at all these wooden pigeonholes as if presenting the crown jewels to me, and just left me to it.

"As you can imagine, I had no idea where to start, or how the letters were classified, if they had even been organised at all. So I just had to dive in, and I was cursing Douglas I can tell you. I felt duty bound to earn my few pounds but I'm quite sure he wouldn't have taken the trouble I did. I ended up being there the whole day, and the funny thing was, they forgot all about me."

"What did you find?" Alessa asked, but he wasn't to be hurried.

"Well, I took a few sample letters out and looked at them. Carefully you know; they were extremely old, but I was used to handling old manuscripts. After a while I worked out that they had been organised in blocks, such as tax collection, letters from Lorenzo to his wife or his father; you know. One of the sections was household accounts for the various palaces, so I settled in and found they were organised more or less chronologically in a whole line of pigeonholes. Too many to count. Douglas had asked me to aim for 1480 to 1492, but I didn't know what I was looking for so I just started sifting through to see what I could turn up."

"Lorenzo the Magnificent died in 1492," Alessa said. "So there wouldn't have been any point in looking after that."

"Yes, I have since found that out," Pocock nodded, "although I was an empty-headed student at the time and had no idea. I wasn't covering the Medici at all, you see. I was covering the ancient Romans and had an interest in Lucian. It was fortunate that I spoke Italian, as my *own* research sources were all in Latin."

Margaret poured the tea and they all had a cup.

"How come you speak Italian?" Will said.

"Grandfather speaks seven languages," Margaret said proudly. "He's a polyglot."

"That's incredible," Alessa said with real admiration. "I speak four but my French isn't fluent, and I thought *I* was good. What do you speak?"

"English, Latin, Italian, French, German, Spanish and Portuguese. Oh and a fair bit of Russian, which I'm learning now," Pocock said. "Bit of an obsession of mine, learning a language. It helps keep the Alzheimer's at bay, apparently."

Will drank tea and shook his head in amazement. Even his schoolboy French was awful. He opened his sketchbook, grabbed his pencil and started to sketch the old man, whose entire attention was on Alessa.

"So there I was," Pocock continued, "having no idea what to look for, just picking out a few letters and reading them, and if they seemed to have interesting things in them, then I would lay them out flat and take a picture. They were a little hard to read so I didn't want to copy them out, you see. You get the eye for reading old manuscripts after a while, but it was laborious trying to make any sense of them. I decided to use up both Douglas's films and then he would be delighted. In a way I wanted to impress him, you see. And to prove to him that I knew how to do research and had earned my fee. I had to take both sides of the page so that I had the name of the recipient. I must admit they were fascinating letters, as well. Some very boring, but then you'd find something fascinating, like an order for cinnamon and ginger, or a bolt of red cloth, or chapel candles."

"Yes, I've seen some of them myself," Alessa nodded. "They bring it all to life."

"They do," Pocock agreed. He paused for breath and drained his teacup, then topped it up from the pot.

"I had finished the second film and put in a new one of my own, as I was finished and I was intending to go out and take some snaps around Florence. Be a tourist, you know. Then I found a letter which was still sealed."

"Sealed with wax?"

"Yes, most of the letters had originally been sealed, you see, but they had all been opened. Then I found this one and the seal was intact. It had an imprint of the Medici balls in the seal, as if from a ring. It was stuffed into the back of one of the pigeonholes and I only saw it because I had taken out a bunch of letters to look through."

"And this was the Semiramide letter?" Alessa said, leaning forward excitedly. "My goodness, whatever did you do?"

"Well, I looked at it, you know. It was addressed to Pierfrancesco di Lorenzo de' Medici. I know it's odd but I can still see it in my mind's eye. It was all yellowed with age but the ink was clear and black and the seal was black too. You could clearly see the Medici balls in it. They used to fold letters into four and seal them, so it was about this size."

He held up his hands to make a rectangle about a hand in height and a couple of inches wide.

"Quite stiff paper; expensive stuff. It bore the date of 1523, so it was in completely the wrong place because everything else in that pigeonhole was dated 1485. I turned it over in my hands and realised that this must be a different Lorenzo, not the Magnificent but another one."

"It sounds like Il Popolano's son with that date," Alessa breathed. "Pierfrancesco the Younger as we would now call him."

"Yes, I found that out afterwards too, when I was looking it up on my own account. But here is the confession," he added, looking sheepish. "I know I shouldn't have done, but it was intriguing, so I carefully peeled away the seal and opened the letter. It came away easily enough because it was so old."

"The British Library would have kittens," Will grinned, looking up from his sketch, and Pocock flashed him a smile.

"They certainly would. So of course I started to read the letter, which was from Semiramide, the wife of Pierfrancesco as you say, and written to her son. You can imagine my sudden excitement when I saw Lucian's name on the page, when there I was, studying him.

"You were writing about him even then?" Alessa asked.

"Yes, for my thesis. The book came later, but I did mention the letter in my thesis too. It's just that my thesis won't have made it to the British Library, I'm afraid."

"And what did the letter say? You mentioned Lucian's account of the story about Alexander and Roxana's marriage. Can you remember anything else?"

"I can't remember the details, but there was enough to see that it was all very mysterious," Pocock said. "She was trying to tell him about another letter which was some kind of secret, but she was being very circumspect. It was over sixty years ago so I can't remember what she actually said."

They looked disappointed but he smiled at Alessa as he finished his second cup of tea and gave her a sideways look.

"And," Alessa prompted, "is that it?"

"Well, I did think it would be useful for my research, and I had a brand-new film loaded into my trusty old Agfa, so I took photographs of the letter."

There was a stunned silence at this announcement, and Will lifted his pencil from the page.

"I don't suppose…?" Alessa prompted, not needing to finish the sentence.

"I think I may have it somewhere," Pocock nodded. He stood up, his knees cracking. "Let me look."

He hummed as he hunted along the shelves. Margaret Pocock was checking the time on the mantelpiece clock.

"I'm going to have to go soon," she said awkwardly. "I'm very sorry because this is so interesting and I've never heard this story before from granddad, but I have to pick my son up at six and I don't really want to leave you here."

Of course," Alessa said. "Perhaps just a few more minutes?"

Margaret Riley nodded.

"I'll gather up," she said, and went out.

Alessa and Will sat in an agony of waiting while Frederick Pocock looked along the shelves.

"No sign of it," the old man said regretfully," but at that moment spied what he was looking for and bent down to extract it from a low shelf. He brought it back to them and sat down. It was an old photo album and on the front was a paper label saying 'Firenze 1956' which had been taped on but was now peeling off.

"This is the one," he said, and swung it open. The very first entry was a photograph of an old letter's outside face. You could see a brown mark where the seal had been. The next page showed the letter itself, facing a picture of a river between two tall columns on the right-hand side. The letter was first in the album because it had been first in the new film. However, the print was only about three inches by five and it wasn't possible to make out the words.

"It's too small to read," Alessa said, enormously disappointed.

"But how did you read the quote from it," Will asked, looking at the small black and white print.

"Ah yes," Pocock said apologetically. "I used the college's darkroom and made eight by ten prints, but I'm afraid I haven't got them anymore. They were destroyed in a fire in the 1980s when I was living in London for a year. But tell me, why are *you* so interested in this letter?"

"We are following up on an idea my father had," Alessa said in a very despondent voice. "He had an idea that Botticelli might have had Semiramide as a muse, so we're trying to find evidence of it and this is the only connection we've seen. Do you mind if I take a picture?" We might be able to blow it up."

"Of course," Pocock assented, and she took several pictures with her phone.

"I don't think it's going to be any good," she said gloomily, pinching out the photos on her phone to make them bigger. They're blurred."

"I'm so sorry," Pocock said, looking almost as crestfallen as her. "The quality of commercially made prints wasn't very good in those days."

Margaret Riley came back in and stood in the doorway.

"I do have to go," she said, and they stood up. Will tore the page out of his sketchbook and handed it to Pocock.

"A small memento of our visit," he said, and Pocock stared at it.

"I didn't realise you were an artist," he said. "This is very good. I shall have to find a frame for it."

Margaret came over and looked. Despite being in a hurry she also admired the sketch of her grandfather. Then there was a flurry of hand-shaking and Margaret offered to drop them off in Honiton.

"Well, if it wouldn't be too much trouble that would be great," Will said. "We were going to walk back to the bus stop."

She looked at her watch.

"You'd have to wait for the last one at half six. I'll drop you near the station because I'm going past, but we'll have to go right now or I'll be late and the nursery gets cross."

They thanked Pocock once again and hurried out, feeling depressed to have got so near but to have missed the prize. There was no traffic at all. They climbed in, Alessa in the front and Will next to the child seat in the rear. Margaret Riley started the Land Rover and did a three-point turn, but just as she was about to drive away Frederick Pocock appeared in the doorway of the cottage, waving an envelope at them. He came over to the car and Alessa buzzed down the window.

"Sorry," he said apologetically. "But in the back of the album were the negatives, so I took out the first strip and here it is. You might be able to get something from it. Post it back to me once you've finished with it, Miss Cooper."

He handed the envelope to Alessa, who took it and thanked him profusely, promising to return it. Margaret waved and called another goodbye, then they lurched off up the road, leaving the old man standing outside his cottage door, one hand raised in salute. Alessa peeked into the envelope and extracted a strip of celluloid film, holding it carefully by the edges. She held it up to the white upholstery of the roof and could see that the first two frames looked like the letter, and the third was the shot of a river with buildings on the other side.

"That must be the Arno," she said. "It's right by the Uffizi. This is the right strip!"

Margaret gave her a congratulatory smile from the driving seat as she put the negative back into the envelope. Will put his hand on Alessa's shoulder for a moment and squeezed. She turned round and flashed him a smile.

"All we need now is a dark room," she said, her face at its most animated. Her brown eyes sparkled.

"My friend George is a graphic designer," Will said. "I know he used to have a dark room, but I'm not sure if he has anymore."

"If he does then we'll have to get it out of mothballs!" she said, the last word sounding like 'mouthballs'. Her long dark hair swung in curls on her shoulders when she turned back to the front, so that Will's thoughts were more about her than their prize.

13

For she doth make my veins and pulses tremble.

DANTE ALIGHIERI

12th August 1483, Florence

It was a baking August and Botticelli was working in his studio workshop in his house in via Nuova, when there was a sudden flurry of activity at the door and Biagio came in looking agitated. Botticelli frowned. Was his neighbour causing more trouble? Was there a new tax collection?

"What is it?" he asked testily, paintbrush poised.

"It's the Lord Lorenzo di Pierfrancesco de' Medici, maestro. In person, here and now," Biagio stammered.

Botticelli stopped in surprise and straightened up.

"Here? Then let him in, Biagio," he said and put his brush wet end up in a stone jar that he reserved for this purpose. Oil paint was unlike egg tempera in that it could be left for a few hours without drying out. It was completely changing the way he and his workshop apprentices worked, because several brushes could be waiting at once with different colours. He was wiping his hand on a rag when his friend and patron strode in, and he cast down the rag on the table and managed a bow.

"Welcome, my lord," he said. "It is an honour to greet you here."

Lorenzo did not seem to notice that the workshop was any less grand than his palaces, striding forward and clasping Botticelli's wrist in welcome.

"Good to see you," he said, and looked him up and down. "So this is your working attire! I suppose you couldn't paint in the fine cloth I normally see you in."

"It wouldn't last long if I did so," Botticelli said, a little embarrassed.

"Anyway, I had an idea so I walked down from via Larga with a pair of guards who are standing outside. Should we bring them in, do you think?"

Let's invite them in by all means," Botticelli said. "There is occasionally a passing drunkard from via San Paolino who causes trouble, but not until after dark. Besides, this heat has sent everyone inside who doesn't have to be out in the sun. Speaking of heat, I have some cold ale in the cellar. Or there is wine."

Lorenzo chose ale and Botticelli called to a twelve-year-old apprentice called Matteo who was newly arrived from Verona. He was ostensibly grinding pigments on the stone table at the side of the workshop but actually was goggling at the finely dressed Medici lord.

"Matteo! Ask Francesca to bring ale for us. Then find Giorgio and tell him the master wishes him to invite in the lord's men-at-arms and offer them something from the kitchen."

Lorenzo looked around the workshop, which was a long room and somewhat chaotic, with many finished and unfinished panels clustered against the walls, and various tables and benches bearing pots of painting materials, such as bright dishes of pigment, rolls of canvas cloth, glass bottles of solvents, oils, brushes and knives. There was a strong smell of wet paint and spirit. Several easels were erected, varying in size, and apprentices worked in front of them on panels or canvases, painting in backgrounds and clothing, most standing but some sitting. Botticelli bid the lord sit at a table to the side and Francesca appeared with a jug of ale, closely followed by her seventeen-year old sister Smeralda, the younger daughter of his brother Giovanni, named after her grandmother. Smeralda was demure and kept her eyes averted despite Lorenzo's interested examination. She was to be married in three weeks to the owner of one of the cloth mills beside the river. Francesca was just turned fourteen but was saucy and giggled when Lorenzo smiled at her, then hurried away when Botticelli pretended to glare at her and turned to pout in the doorway until he stood up threateningly.

He shook his head after her despairingly.

"You'll have trouble with that one," Lorenzo said with a grin, looking after the girl, who had a narrow waist but already showed the rounded hips and breasts of womanhood.

"It will be a miracle if we can get her into a decent marriage before there is a child," Botticelli said. "She is my brother Giovanni's daughter and he and his wife watch her like a hawk, but they cannot be there at every moment. It is only a matter of time."

He slid the board of cheese across to Lorenzo, who took his own knife from his belt and pared off a sliver. They drank some ale and Botticelli sat forward expectantly.

"What brings you to my humble and inadequate table, lord?"

Lorenzo stared into his tankard of ale for a long moment, and grimaced.

"Almost a year has passed since my marriage, but my wife is not with child."

He held the painter's gaze. For once Botticelli didn't know what to say, so he said nothing. Lorenzo remained silent also after this pronouncement.

"A child will come when God wills it," Botticelli said after a pause, feeling a need to fill the silence.

"Yes," Lorenzo said as if trying to convince himself. Botticelli suddenly saw the young man as he was, only twenty and unsure what to do. He was comfortable conversing with kings, but remained an impatient youth in matters of the heart. "I fear she may be barren," he added worriedly.

Botticelli's mouth twitched. It was generally believed that the man's seed must be planted in the woman to grow, but it had not occurred to the young man that *he* might be the problem, and certainly the painter was not going to suggest it to a Medici lord, even though he were a friend.

"Is there a potion that could be used to…enrich her?" Botticelli asked.

Lorenzo pursed his lips. "I have consulted with the guild of doctors and pharmacists and with surgeons of the long robe. I have even spoken with nuns. All advise that potions such as essence of the poppy may ease the heart but do not encourage childbirth."

"Does she…" Botticelli leaned in conspiratorially and looked around before he continued in a lower voice. "Forgive me lord. Does she bleed?"

"Once a month," Lorenzo nodded. "A goodly amount which should balance her humours, according to my doctors."

Botticelli had no idea what to suggest next. He was a painter and knew something of muscular anatomy, but nothing of the functions of the organs.

"I have spoken to Leonardo about it," Lorenzo went on in an equally low voice. "You know that he has gained much knowledge of the human body?"

"From his dissection of cadavers," Botticelli nodded, trying to suppress his distaste. Leonardo di ser Piero da Vinci was his friend but the man's extraordinary mind had led him to explorations that would make Botticelli empty his stomach on the tiles. "Did he have any suggestions?"

"None," Lorenzo said rather stiffly. "He believes the man's seed passes up a channel from the woman's cleft into her body, where the baby then grows as blossom on a tree becomes an apple. He told me this and then asked me if I thought my own cock was working as it should. That man! If I wasn't his patron I'd have him executed."

Botticelli couldn't help it – he laughed and one or two of his apprentices stopped what they were doing and looked at the two seated figures curiously. Lorenzo had the grace to chuckle in return.

"Paint on, paint on," Botticelli called out to his charges, waving his hand as if shooing them away. "I shall be around for inspection after Nones and I want to see *progress*." He turned back to Lorenzo. "They'd sooner gossip than paint, especially with you here."

"I had thought," Lorenzo said, "that your Primavera painting would bring us fertility, but it hasn't."

Botticelli considered. He didn't like the idea of his paintings being responsible or otherwise for Medici heirs. It was a dangerous association. Lorenzo picked up his tankard and drained it gloomily. Botticelli drank a little and then topped up the lord's ale from the jug, though his own tankard was not yet half finished. He knew that if he drank too much there would be no more painting that day. They each cut more cheese.

"Primavera depicts the spring and fertility," he said solemnly. "But perhaps there is not enough *intimacy*. It shows the moment of love's beginning through cupid's dart, not the act of love itself."

"This is potent stuff," Lorenzo said, looking into his ale tankard. He put it back on the table without drinking more. "What you say is right. Perhaps I need a painting of the act of love itself, for the *camera*."

Botticelli shook his head. "It would be unsubtle, even for the bedroom," he said. "You may have political discourse there. But I could capture the moment *after* love's act, when one is sated. It should be Venus, of course, as goddess of love, though she should be fully clothed, as Semiramide is now your wife."

"And Mercury again?"

Botticelli put his knuckles under his chin and rested his head as he thought.

"Mars," he said. "You would be Mars, sleeping after your passionate dalliance with the goddess of love." He waved a hand. "Just like the Roman myth."

"But she was betrothed to Vulcan."

"She was, but she made love to Mars and their daughter Harmonia ensued."

"I don't want a daughter, I want an heir."

Botticelli gave his friend an old-fashioned look over the ale tankard.

"I can paint a scene of passion," he said," but I cannot influence the gender of your child."

Lorenzo grinned.

"All right then, but I need it quickly. How fast can you do it?"

Botticelli opened his hands and pulled a face.

"It will take time," he said. "We haven't even decided upon the size or finalised the design. Then a panel must be prepared, and the successive layers have to dry so that the painting has a firm base. What size are you contemplating?"

With Lorenzo it would be uncouth to ask about money. The Medici lord had never disappointed him in that regard. Primavera had earned him his highest price ever, and many other commissions from rich Florentine merchants and from the Church had come to him as a result of it.

Lorenzo looked around the workshop and espied two large white panels that leaned against the wall near him.

"That will do perfectly," he said. "Use one of those!"

Botticelli looked at the two poplar panels, which were identical in size and about the height of a man."

"Those are indeed ready," he agreed. "But they are a matching set. A diptych for the left and right side of the altar in San Barnaba."

"San Barnaba? For the Augustinian canons, I presume. Hmm."

Lorenzo pulled his lip and then looked back at Botticelli.

"What if you painted a central picture to go over the altar instead? That would keep them happy."

"They have particularly requested a diptych. They want balance on either side of the altar."

"No matter," Lorenzo said, waving his hand dismissively. "You can talk them out of it. Just tell them that a diptych would dominate the altar too much, but a central painting would draw the eye to the table of the Lord rather than distract from it."

"I don't know…" Botticelli said.

Lorenzo stood up and walked over to the two panels. He hefted one experimentally and found it a strong piece of wood which was perfectly smooth and already prepared with gesso.

"This will be just right," he said again. As if to demonstrate he picked up the panel, rotated it slowly and lowered it onto its side. He rested it on the cloth which had been placed on the floor to protect the edges. He straightened up, stepped to one side and pointed at the perfect white surface.

"Mars lies spent, while the seed flowers within Venus and she contemplates motherhood."

Botticelli stood up and walked over to the panel. He looked at it, considered the proposition and decided that he liked it. The panel on its side *was* the perfect size and shape. He began to think about how to position the recumbent figures.

"I would need to make drawings of you and your wife," he said, thinking of the delightful Semiramide and the notion of again spending many hours drawing her. It was considerably more appealing than the San Barnaba diptych and he thought he probably *could* convince the canons that a single central picture would do more for the glory of God. He would have to think of something to put on the other panel but that need not be immediate.

Lorenzo said, "We are at via Larga and available, but you'll have to be quick to capture me as I am to be dispatched as our ambassador to Paris."

"Ah, I believe the coronation of Charles VIII approaches?"

Lorenzo sighed and rolled his eyes.

"He is but a child of thirteen years but Florence must pay homage to the boy king or France will side with Naples or Venice against us. My brother and I don't always see eye to eye with Il Magnifico as you know, but he is remarkably astute when it comes to politics. Can you make sketches of me in the next two days?"

Botticelli shook his head and chuckled.

"You are as impatient as ever, lord," he said, "but I will do it."

Before leaving the workshop, Lorenzo had invited Botticelli to stay as his guest at the palace while he made his sketches. The master had readily agreed to this, for one did not decline the hospitality of the Medici. Accordingly he had packed a casket and Matteo gathered together sketching materials according to his instructions.

Early next morning, all these goods were assembled on a hand cart and his man Giorgio wheeled the cart while Botticelli led the way, wearing his finest cloak and sporting a bit of a swagger. They made their way along the riverfront to the Ponte alla Carraia and then turned left into the city, avoiding the carriages and carts that gave the old stone bridge its name. They picked their way through the throng of busy merchants and glimpsed the tall cathedral dome to their right whenever they reached street intersections. They kept an eye out for cutpurses but Giorgio was a large man and had a short temper when crossed. He wore a knife on his belt and a taciturn expression, his eyes roving in every direction. Men of low character retreated when they saw him.

Despite the hawkers in the Piazza di Santa Maria Novella, which for one moment threatened to overcome even Giorgio, they made it to the other side without incident apart from Giorgio boxing the ears of an over-zealous tradesman. The new marble façade of the basilica glowed in the morning light. Botticelli eyed the church balefully, for a frescoed lunette depicting the nativity adorned its walls, painted by his own workshop while he had been busy in Rome, and he despised it for its poor depiction of the stable animals.

It took half an hour to reach the palace, though it would have been much less without the cart. When they arrived, Botticelli was admitted immediately into an anteroom and servants efficiently emptied the cart for him. Giorgio was dismissed by his master and returned to the workshop.

Lorenzo came and greeted him briefly soon after his arrival, but the lord was busy preparing his retinue for the journey to Paris which would set out the next day. He disappeared again immediately, having arranged that they would meet properly after lunch. There was no sign of Semiramide. Botticelli was led by a maid to a huge bedroom on the upper floor, richly decorated with fine gilt furniture and tapestries depicting hunting scenes.

The master was fed a hearty lunch and could have slept after, but kept himself awake so that he could attend his lord and patron. By mid-afternoon he was beginning to despair of getting any time with the Medici lord. Finally Lorenzo appeared and at first was uncharacteristically impatient, but after a few sketches in different positions he relaxed, lulled by the concentrated silence and the scratching of charcoal on paper. Every half an hour or so his manservant would appear with yet another request requiring his attention, while Botticelli did his best to capture the essence of the man and ignore the distractions. Fortunately he had his own intensity when drawing and was able to proceed. His hand moved swiftly across the paper and reproduced lines and shapes and curves and angles, capturing the likeness of the man. After two hours he had captured several different poses of Lorenzo's head, and they had to stop so that Lorenzo could attend a meeting. The sketches would be sufficient, Botticelli decided. He already had a picture in his mind's eye of how the finished painting would depict Lorenzo as the great god Mars. He would do the body later, using an apprentice if required to establish the right perspective, and being generous with the anatomy of the muscles in order to compliment his patron.

The next day Lorenzo bid Botticelli an early farewell and his group departed, leaving the master to wonder when Semiramide would make an appearance. While he waited he wasted no time but developed many different layouts for the two figures that he would paint. He ended up with a design in which Semiramide, as Venus, would sit and look out of the picture to one side. He would then arrange Lorenzo, as Mars, on his back with his head thrown back, sleeping after the act of love, and he had the perfect sketch to use for this. He began considering the story, and a smile played on his lips as he sketched in a wasp's nest to illustrate the deepness of the god's sleep, then a conch shell after a story about Pan that his friend Poliziano had told him. He began to sketch in satyrs playing with the god's armour, with horns and goat's legs like little echoes of Pan, depicting a story he liked from Lucian's writings that described a painting now lost in antiquity.

He covered the floor of his *camera* with drawings and before he was aware of the time, the light from the windows was fading and he was forced to stop. He got to his feet and stretched, his neck cracking when he twisted his head from side to side. He rubbed his knees, then stretched back his head and massaged his face, rubbing his eyes with his fingertips.

For the first time in hours he remembered that Semiramide hadn't made an appearance, and a frown creased his brow. His mind was relaxed after drawing but his body ached a little – he was in his late thirties and no longer a young man. He ran his fingers through his hair. He didn't know why Semiramide kept coming unbidden to his thoughts. She was young of course, with the blessings of God for her looks as well as her youth. He was still in good shape but he wasn't twenty. He feared she must mock him behind his back for his age and his presumptuous remarks. True, young women married men of his age, but usually for money or title and it was *she* who had both, not he. He had only his experience. He knew he could paint, but he'd be a fool if he thought that would attract her. And besides, she was married to a Medici lord so her virtue could never be his.

He wished he didn't spend all his life lusting after women he couldn't have. He had a romantic ideal about women in which he put them on a pedestal. To him they possessed a sort of magic, like perfect goddesses rather than flesh and blood. It had been exactly the same with Simonetta, God rest her soul. Utterly unattainable despite his private obsession. He had tried whores but though they gave him temporary relief, there was only a momentary pleasure in those encounters; they bore no magic. He had lain with one of his pretty apprentice boys but experienced little joy from the young man's touch. He had even lain with a married lady from the Medici court, but that was years ago and he wouldn't dare repeat such an escapade now. He would never take a wife, for he feared it might make women seem unexceptional, and that would destroy his art.

He picked up his drawings from the floor, feeling his back creaking, and arranged them on the table in a careful pile, trying not to rub the papers together for fear of smudging the charcoal. In his workshop he would have had an apprentice fix them in a bath of gum, but he couldn't do this in via Larga.

He paced up and down his palatial bedroom and then remembered his last encounter with Semiramide, his heart sinking a little more. He had not even begun Primavera at the time but had just met with Lorenzo – now her husband and his friend, he reminded himself grimly. He had been excited after the meeting with his patron and had made an impertinent remark to Semiramide about her being in his dreams or some such nonsense. She had flushed with embarrassment. He felt his own face colour now at the memory of her perfect pink skin, and the tiny threads of hair that had escaped her jewelled braids. The next day he had reflected that he had probably angered her, and then when Primavera had been unveiled she had stayed away. They'd said she had a fever and remained indisposed; an easy way to avoid an unwished-for encounter with the fool, Botticelli.

He shook his head and sighed, still pacing. It was getting dark in the room.

"God's bones!" he said to himself. Would she even come at all? Lorenzo had promised she would, but Lorenzo was already on the road to Paris and she may simply decline. Botticelli could then do nothing but return to his workshop and attempt the painting with no new drawings. He brightened a little as he remembered that he still had his previous sketches of her, done in Cafaggiolo. He could likely work from those if she refused to meet him.

There was a knock on the door and his heart almost leapt out of his mouth, but it was only a manservant summoning him to dinner. He realised that he had not changed and he waved away the servant, saying that he would be along in a few minutes. He stripped off his working tunic and put on a cream silk shirt with puffed upper sleeves and more buttons at the cuff than he had time for. Over the top he put on his best black doublet. Then he battled with the buttons, smoothed himself down, ran a hand through his hair and went downstairs.

Semiramide watched from a high tall window as her husband rode out. He looked every inch a leader and she knew she had done well enough for a political marriage. Her father had assured her the Medici lord was handsome and he had not spoken false. Her childhood love of another young boy in her own court now seemed a foolish, far-away fantasy. Yet she frowned after Lorenzo, despite this. Did she love him? It was hard to say. He was charming and pleasant, but so often his mind was on Medici politics and in that she counted for nothing. Shouldn't there be something more? She felt piqued by it. She loathed the way Florentine women were simply expected to make male heirs. Why couldn't he treat her as Il Magnifico treated his own wife, Clarice Orsini? *She* was allowed to represent her husband in Rome, by the grace of God, and yet it seemed that Il Popolano would never entrust Semiramide with such a responsibility. She was someone to talk with and make love to, but then he'd be gone on a political errand and she'd be left behind.

She amended this thought: not always, to be fair. Sometimes he would make wonderful romantic gestures and steal away her heart, but then like today he would set off to Paris with a perfunctory kiss on her brow as if his thoughts were already in the French court of the boy king. Now she was expected to meet the Maestro Botticelli without him, though he would only hint at the details of the painting.

How different was Botticelli! Whereas to Lorenzo she was a plaything and a child-bearer, the maestro seemed to peel off her skin and see what lay beneath. Even now at the thought of it a tingle of anticipation rippled up her spine. Was his attention just lust, like the lascivious lords who eyed her surreptitiously in passages or peasants that watched her riding by? It seemed more. He asked her opinion, which she found flattering. He would discuss politics or art or religion with her – he didn't hold back on any topic. He must be twice her age and yet he had a presence about him, and no fat belly like many of his rich compatriots. And humour – he made little jokes that made her giggle; he employed witty badinage. Sometimes he seemed to toy with her and challenge her, but never disrespectfully. Hardly ever, she amended. She remembered what he had said to her after he and Lorenzo had planned Primavera without her. *Tonight your face may haunt my dreams.*

How *dare* he say such a thing? And yet she had done nothing, said nothing of it. And when the much-talked-about Primavera was to be unveiled she had claimed that she could not attend due to Eve's curse. Her maidservant had brought her unneeded blood moss and she had remained in bed, hiding from Maestro Botticelli and his penetrating look. But next day she had arisen so early that it was barely light, surprising maids only just awake while she padded in silk slippers along palace passages, until in the right room she had stood in awe in front of Primavera, seeing in each painted female her own face. The man must have God or the devil in his fingers to paint like that.

After breakfast the next morning, Botticelli followed a manservant to a high room in the Medici palace, there to find Semiramide with her stern-faced maidservant Caterina. He swept into a deep bow immediately, immensely relieved after a night in which he had slept little for fear that she would refuse to meet with him.

"My lady," he said. "I am deeply honoured that you have found the time to see me."

"Maestro Botticelli," she said. "It is a pleasure to see you again. I am sorry that I was unable to attend the unveiling of Primavera, upon which I have since looked many times with fondness."

Her words were formal but her voice was warm and his relief was evident.

"Thank you, my lady. I tried to capture you many times in the painting, but sometimes you eluded me."

"If I permit you to draw me again, perhaps you could remain awake for a time afterwards?"

He looked confused and she had him.

"For fear of troubled dreams," she added, smiling sweetly.

He turned puce and bowed his head.

"I shall do so, my lady."

"Very good," she said, and smiled at Caterina, who was looking mystified. "Now to business. Where would you like to draw me: in front of the window so that you have sufficient light? I seem to remember you saying in Cafaggiolo that good light is essential."

His colour was returning to normal but all his movements radiated obsequiousness.

"That would be perfect," he agreed. She suspected that he would have agreed if she had suggested standing on her head.

Botticelli fussed around busily to get over his embarrassment. The young manservant who had led him to the room was still standing to attention in the background with a box of drawing materials. At the master's request he placed them on a low table, then almost bolted out of the door when Caterina shooed him away with an impatient wave of her hand.

Botticelli picked up the low table and placed it before the window, then arranged cushions for Semiramide to lean upon. She was wearing an understated white silk dress which he felt would be ideal for the scene, though he might embellish it later with some red or gold ribbon. Her hair was braided but unusually she had left curled strands hanging down to either side of her face in a style that he hadn't seen.

He showed her how he wanted her to arrange herself and she did so, leaning on the cushions but remaining upright, looking to her left. Botticelli extracted some materials, then pulled out a clean sheet of paper, put it on the low table and kneeled before it, resting himself on one of the pink and gold brocaded cushions that festooned the room. He looked at her for a long moment without speaking and then frowned.

"Do you have a favourite piece of jewellery, my lady?" he asked. "It would help to add context. "Perhaps a brooch or some other ornament?"

She thought about this and saw that it made sense.

"Caterina, bring my pearl brooch with the sapphire," she said. "We will await your return."

"Yes milady."

Caterina left the room and the two of them were alone. She sat there calmly.

"How do you want me to look, Maestro Botticelli? Or may I call you Sandro? I have noticed that both my husband and Amerigo Vespucci refer to you as Sandro."

"My lady, I would be honoured," Botticelli said, not daring in return to suggest that he call her Semiramide.

"Very good, then Sandro it shall be," she said primly, but then she caught his eye and smiled impishly, so that he almost blew out his cheeks before he checked himself. God's Bones, he was a puppet before this woman!

"Very well my lady. Let us consider your expression in the painting. Your mood is to be reflective. Imagine that you are looking far away but you see nothing. Your thoughts are in your mind's eye, not what you see before you in the field where you sit with your lord."

"And he is to be…indisposed," she said, eying him still with an echo of that smile. "My husband explained a little of the theme to me, but he was…ambiguous. For a Medici banker he is surprisingly shy on some topics, but I understand that he believes the painting may encourage the birth of a child."

"Yes my lady," Botticelli said. "He hopes that by painting a future as he wants it, God will honour you with children."

"May it be so. That is of course presuming that God makes a study of your paintings, Sandro."

He looked embarrassed again but recovered quickly this time.

"God sees all things, my lady."

She nodded at his swift riposte.

Caterina returned and knelt beside her mistress, offering the brooch that she had requested. Semiramide remained still while Caterina unclasped the brooch and pinned it to her dress in the centre of her bodice.

"It is a beautiful piece," Botticelli said when it was in place. She looked down at it. It had eight pearls in a circle and a fat round orange sapphire as a centrepiece. The sapphire was very unusual – she had seen no other such stone in the court.

"It is my favourite," she said. "And it is appropriate, because my husband gave it to me on the day of our marriage."

"It is an excellent choice. I will make a separate drawing of it later on, if I may. But now let us begin. Please don't face towards me but look over this way." He gestured with his right hand and her eyes shifted. "Yes, like that. Find something upon which to affix your eyes."

"May I blink?"

He laughed and Caterina gave him a withering look from her seat a few feet away.

"You may blink, my lady, and you may move if you need to, but it is a little easier if you do not. I am going to begin by drawing your head, so you may move your arms as you wish, but I would be honoured if you could try to keep your head in the same position. You are not a still life, and later I will sketch you in movement, but for now I am interested in the fall of light and shadow, which is unpredictable and treacherous."

They began, and the familiar scratch of charcoal started up in the quiet room. She remembered that sound from Cafaggiolo. As soon as he began to draw, he became her master rather than she his mistress. She wanted to talk with him but he had asked her to be silent and she should honour his request. It was excruciating that he was drawing with the paper flat on the table, so she could perfectly well have seen it develop before her eyes, except that he had bid her not to look in his direction.

She tried to look serene. She had no desire to look plain in a painting by Sandro Botticelli. Her mouth was dry and she wished she had taken a cup of wine before beginning, even though it was morning, for it would have calmed her nerves. She had an itch on her leg but she couldn't scratch it, even discreetly, so she had to sit there tantalised until it went away. She wondered how the drawing was progressing. She felt Caterina's eyes upon her back and knew the old nurse would initially be over-protective, but would relax after a while as long as Botticelli behaved himself.

A small smile dressed her lips at the thought of Caterina's stern look, and she felt rather than saw Botticelli's disapproval. She rearranged her face into calm serenity once more. What had he wanted? A far-away look. What then should she think of? Of babies, perhaps, of little girls clinging to her dress as she had seen others do, of little boys calling her 'mamma'.

"Very good, my lady," he said after what seemed an interminable period. "You may rest."

For a moment she continued to hold the pose but then unwound and looked at him.

"I'm stiff!" she said. "Who would have thought that being still could be so tiring?"

"That's just what my apprentices say," Botticelli agreed. "They often do double duty as models."

Semiramide stood up and looked at her old maid.

"Caterina, do we have some water or a little wine?"

"It's early for wine, milady," Caterina said, and Botticelli noticed that Semiramide did not argue with her but complied immediately. "I have water freshly drawn from the well which is still cool."

They drank some water and then Semiramide seated herself again. Botticelli was keen for her to resume her original position.

"You're too far back," he said, frowning. "Sit up a minute." He came forward and plumped the red cushions back into shape. "Now lean back on them," he commanded, forgetting that she was a lady and that he should not order her about with such impunity. He shook his head. "Still too far back, try resting your weight on your elbow, here."

He indicated a spot on the cushion and she sat up, taking her weight on her arm.

"Good," he nodded, looking at her appraisingly. "Now push your lower foot back behind you so that it is lost in the folds of your dress. Perfect!"

She was wearing little gold slippers on her feet and now just one was visible.

"My lady, may I ask that you remove your slipper?" he asked humbly. "I do not think that a goddess would be wearing a slipper."

"Please do it," Semiramide said, indicating her foot with her head while trying to hold the pose in which she had been arranged. He started forward but Caterina cleared her throat noisily and he stepped back as if he had been slapped. Caterina knelt by her mistress's foot and removed the slipper, catching Botticelli with a glower as she did so. When she turned her back he caught Semiramide's eye, and she raised her eyebrows and smiled in a way which could only be described as flirtatious.

He swallowed and licked his lips without meaning to. He tried to focus not on the woman but on the painting that was to be, and looked once more at Semiramide.

He imagined how the lines of her body would complement the figure of Lorenzo as Mars. She was resting her hand on her lap.

"Please move this hand down, my lady," he said, pointing to it. "Just rest it on your leg about there." He indicated a position and she complied. He stepped back and looked.

"Yes," he nodded, and ranged his eyes across her in that penetrating way he had, so that she felt as if she were naked before him. "Stretch out your foot straight. Yes, *exactly* like that. Now hold the position for as long as you can. You may move your head but nothing else."

Again she marvelled at how quickly he forgot himself and ordered her about in a peremptory fashion when he was working. He had taken a fresh sheet of paper, expensive though she knew it to be, and again his hand with its stick of charcoal began to glide swiftly across it, sometimes stopping to rub the surface as if to smooth a gradient or blend a curve. This time he drew for a very long time and she was desperate to move by the time he at last said that she may do so. She exhaled, stretched her head from side to side and flexed her shoulders up and down.

"I am worn out from doing nothing," she said, getting to her feet and walking up and down. "Caterina, for the love of God can we not have a little wine?"

This time Caterina went to the back of the room and returned with two glasses of wine.

"Please take my glass for yourself, Caterina," Botticelli said, "if your mistress will permit. Give me another but half with water, for I shall not be able to draw if my brain is addled."

Caterina looked enquiringly at Semiramide, who nodded permission. She put Botticelli's untouched glass on a table beside her own chair and poured another glass for him, filling it to the halfway point and then topping it up with water as one would for a child.

He bowed his head graciously to her as he took the glass and then raised it to the two women.

"A good morning," he said to Semiramide. "There is more to be done in the details but please take some exercise first. I know it is hard to pose for so long and I thank you very much."

They all drank some wine and then Semiramide and Caterina went over and looked curiously at his drawings on the floor. The first picture was a tonal drawing of his subject's head, ending at the neck, with eyes that looked distant and thoughtful, a mouth that was unsmiling and matter-of-fact, and braided hair that stood out against a dark blocked-in charcoal background. The second picture was of Semiramide on the cushions, catching all the curves of her shape but leaving her head only roughly sketched-in, with no face or detail apart from a few lines hinting at hair.

"You have lost none of your skill, Sandro," Semiramide said with a smile. "This first one even looks a little like me."

He chuckled, knowing she was teasing him.

"It was hard to do justice but I tried," he said, daring an expression of his former charm.

They went down to lunch, for more time had passed than he had expected and it was the appointed hour. Botticelli realised that he was hungry and ate heartily but fast, eager to get back and begin again. When they returned he took some time to arrange Semiramide and then spent time on detailed drawings; her outstretched foot, the pearl brooch, each of her hands, the braids of her hair; and then some time on the folds of her dress, capturing the fall of the cloth. Then he drew her head again, at a slightly different angle this time, making her neck a little longer so that she looked particularly elegant. Caterina had fallen asleep in her chair, lulled by the wine and the quiet room. She snored very quietly and Semiramide and Botticelli exchanged looks, smiling.

"She's not used to drinking wine," Semiramide whispered. "You have corrupted my old nurse, Sandro Botticelli!"

He grimaced in mock horror, placing a hand on his heart.

"I am so sorry, my lady," he said.

But he was not.

He was unhappy with his sketch of her foot, which he said was very important to get right, so he moved in closer for a second attempt. She was tempted to wiggle her toes at him. She too felt the effect of the wine and being drawn was pleasingly intimate.

"Is it in the right position?" she asked, indicating her foot.

He tilted his head, frowning. "Almost," he said. "Stretch it out a little more, no…twist it up a little more."

He looked at Caterina but she was fast asleep.

"Just move it," Semiramide said, and he looked at her for a moment before stepping forward and kneeling. Her mouth was dry again. He took her foot in his warm fingers and moved it just a little. His touch sent a shiver of anticipation up her body, but he released her and sat back in his place on the cushions. He began to draw her foot.

Botticelli was finding it hard to concentrate. He had to draw Semiramide's foot twice because he made such a mess of the first one, being unable to think of anything but the warmth of her soft skin. Then he abandoned the pen for charcoal and somehow he translated his passion into lines and shades which captured her foot in beautiful, almost erotic detail, as a love goddess's foot should look. It wasn't yet a painting, but he knew how the painting would look.

He didn't really need any more drawings but he was still inflamed and asked to draw her head again. She immediately agreed, then stretched her foot and her leg out as a cat stretches itself, bending her foot from side to side at the ankle. When she was ready she assumed what she believed to be the correct position for her head.

"How is that?"

"Almost right. Lift your chin a little and twist your head."

"Just move it," she said again, and this time she marvelled at her own daring. She was conscious that she could hear the quiet snores of Caterina behind her.

He approached, took her face gently in his hands and adjusted the position of her head. The tips of his fingers touched the nape of her neck and sent a tingle of pleasure into her scalp and all the way down her back. He knelt like that for a moment, just looking at her, and she thought he was going to kiss her, and she thought she would let him. Then with a particularly loud snort Caterina awoke, causing him to leap back as if stung. The old maid was blinking and stretching.

Semiramide licked her lips and moved her eyes to look at him, raising an eyebrow. Then the merest hint of a smile touched her lips.

"Ready?"

14

The Moving Finger writes; and, having writ,
Moves on: nor all thy Piety nor Wit
Shall lure it back to cancel half a Line
Nor all thy Tears wash out a Word of it.

Translated by EDWARD FITZGERALD, The Rubáiyát of Omar Khayyám

March, Cambridge

Will and Alessa arrived in London just after nine that evening, both feeling exhausted after the long day. Will had phoned George from the train and found out that he still had a darkroom set up in his loft.

"That's to say, I *have* it but I never use it," George had said. "Everything's digital these days so we'll have to move a ton of storage boxes. Can't you get this mysterious work done somewhere else?"

"I did have a look," Will said, "You can get negatives processed commercially but I'm nervous about handing this negative over to anyone. I did find a photographic club, but you have to be a member and then of course you have to wait your turn. It could be a few days before we get in there. And besides, you can meet my friend Alessa."

"Oh, go on then," George said, giving in at the prospect of meeting the girl that Anna had found on Facebook. "It'll be a pleasant break from the brochure I'm working on."

Will disconnected and gave Alessa the thumbs up.

"We have a darkroom," he said happily.

They parted at Waterloo station because Alessa needed to go back and get a change of clothes. While Will had been talking to George, she had found out that trains from Oxford to Cambridge were problematic because you had to go into London and out again. She had no car. However, there was a direct coach service and she thought she could get up to Cambridge by noon the next day. She made him promise that he wouldn't start without her. When they were ready to part company it was an awkward moment, but then Alessa gave Will a hug.

"Quite a day!" she said, then kissed him on the cheek and was gone. He stood there for a moment, watching her dash for her platform before he followed, a soppy smile on his face.

George swilled the photo paper in the bath of developer and after a few seconds the ghostly image started to come up. They had already done a test exposure, covering a further strip of the paper every 10 seconds, and they had opted for 35 seconds, which was how long this paper had been exposed. Even in the red light they could make out handwriting. They had a second print with only a few lines on it, which Alessa said was probably the other side of the original letter, bearing the address.

George removed the two sheets and put them into the fixer, swilling them about for a few seconds before restoring the ordinary light and extinguishing the red bulb. He moved the prints into a third tray containing water, agitated them, and then for good measure went to the corner sink and ran them under the tap to ensure all the chemicals were gone. Will and Alessa were practically breathing down his neck so that he almost collided with them when he turned.

"Give the genius some space!" he said. "I now need to dry the prints using the technically advanced method of paper towels followed by Anna's hairdryer. Not what Ilford would recommend but it'll do for now."

After a further fifteen minutes, George had dried the prints to his satisfaction and they all went down to the kitchen where there was plenty of light. Anna was working next door in the surgery but she had a steady stream of people with ill dogs and cats, so she could not leave them. Will and Alessa had promised to visit her before they left.

George handed the prints to Alessa and she took them carefully, holding them by the edges as if they were ancient manuscripts, which in a way they were. She sat down at the kitchen table and laid the prints side by side, studying them carefully.

"It is definitely a letter," she said, pointing to the sheet which had just four short lines on it. "It's going to be hard to read because the calligraphy was so different. George, do you have a magnifying glass, and a notebook or something? I need to write it out in Italian first and then translate it. You two should probably go away and do something else because I've done this before and it's going to take a while."

George found Alessa a black and red wire-bound notebook and tore out the first three used pages, crumpling them up and putting them in the unlit fireplace.

"That was just rubbish," he said. "You can have this."

After it became evident that an instant translation wasn't going to be forthcoming, George went up to his office and carried on with the gallery brochure he was creating, and Will paced around the sitting room, finally taking down a huge book of photographs by Terence Donovan, and leafing through black-and-white images of Sophia Loren, Norman Wisdom, Pamela Stephenson and advertisements for Terylene.

George went out at three to pick up the children from school, and shortly afterwards Anna came in from the surgery, having despatched her last customer. She found Alessa frowning over the notebook, which was now filled with several pages of scribbles and crossed-out notations. They introduced themselves to each other and Alessa explained what she had been doing.

"It's about as far as I can get," she said. "I need to spend some more time on it and I need my textbooks, but I think it's reasonable. Where are the men?"

"Will's pacing up and down the sitting room looking anguished," Anna said. "And George must have gone to pick up the kids. Have either of them thought of making you a drink or giving you anything to eat?"

"Well no," Alessa said with a smile. "Some coffee would be good."

"Coffee we have in abundance," Anna said, fetching a mug. "Do you want a crumpet or some cheese? Or I've got rainbow cup-cakes that the children haven't yet scoffed, but the icing is a rather virulent colour."

"Just coffee for now. I'm too pent up. I need to read this through." Will came into the kitchen, saw the two women and asked Alessa immediately, "Have you done it?"

Alessa nodded and picked up the notebook, turning to the page on which she had written out her final clean copy and holding it up for him to see. She was excited. She tossed back her dark curls and assumed the pose of a teacher reading something out to her class. He decided that very soon he needed to draw those curls, and the elfin face they framed.

Anna put a cup of coffee on the table beside Alessa and offered her milk and sugar.

"Just black, thank you," Alessa said. She picked up the first photographic print which had a few lines of writing on it. "This is the address on the outside of the letter," she explained. "They would have folded it into four and then if it was a private letter, they sealed it with wax. You can see where the seal was, look."

She held up the photographed sheet and a blemish was evident above the four lines of the letter's address. She put down the photograph, then waved the other photographic sheet.

"And this is the letter, on the other side. It would have been folded inwards so that only the recipient could read it unless someone else broke the seal. The interesting thing is that Frederick Pocock told us yesterday that *he* was the first one to break the seal, which means this letter was never read by the recipient." She turned to Anna. "Mr Pocock is the old man who gave us the negative of these prints."

"Yes, but what's in the letter?" Will said, unable to contain his impatience. "What does it say?"

She picked up her translation. "It was very hard to read," she said. "Most old manuscripts are written by people with a clear hand, but this was written by Semiramide herself when she was near to death. And of course, handwriting in quattrocento Italy was very different to today. That's why it took me ages. Frederick Pocock must have been a brilliant student to have read enough to recognise what it was, there and then."

She began to read her own neat handwriting.

Pier Francesco di Lorenzo dei Medici,
By Hand of Giuseppe Bronzino de' Rossi, Lawyer
From His Mother's Hand

I write at my desk on this second day of March 1523, and I beseech you by God to forgive what I told you last evening. You will honour my memory if you heed these words, for if you read them now I am with God. The doctors say that He may have charity but I read doubt in their eyes. Their intentions are well meant, but I feel a hard lump in my flesh, I bleed where I should not, and I am so very tired.

You left in fury before I could say what I must tell you, so I am writing this letter and will pass it to Giuseppe Bronzino, with instructions to place it in your hands when I am dead. You were always capricious, but be not so now.

When you visited me yestereve I was half insensible with milk of the poppy, but I took none this morning so my head is clear, though my body feels as though it might twist into a knot with the pain.

So to business, my beloved son. There is evidence of what I told you that must be destroyed.

You will remember the allegory of love's triumph over war, after Lucian, painted on my spalliera. It depicts the Greek tale concerning Alexander and Roxana, and you know its history. The brooch you see there is by my hand as I write. I will place it in a box for safe-keeping and instruct Giuseppe to hand it to you with this letter. Take it to a secret place and examine it very closely. Act alone and send no messengers.

Thus you will confer dignity on your loving mother and I shall rest in peace.

Semiramide d'Appiano

Alessa looked up. "That's it," she said. She was slightly pale.

"My God," Will said, sitting down heavily in a kitchen chair. "It's the real thing. You can hear her voice across the centuries. You can imagine her pen scratching on the paper."

She squeezed his hand.

"It's an odd letter," Will said. "May I read your translation again myself?"

She handed the notebook to him and he scanned through it, his lips pursed.

"I wonder why she signed off so formally, not 'mamma' or whatever."

"It was the fashion then," Alessa said. "Relationships were more formal."

"All right. So she was near the end of her life, and she told her son something from her death bed that made him furious. He went off in a rage and she wrote this down to make sure she sent him on the track of whatever it was."

"And she gave it to her lawyer to make sure that her son would get it," Anna said.

"Yes. She didn't think he was going to visit her again before she passed away. He must have been a mean-spirited character."

"Sounds like she had cancer," Anna said. "A hard lump in her flesh could be a tumour, and she might have been passing blood. She's rather circumspect about that, but then she would be."

Alessa shook her head, grimacing.

"It's so sad. All those centuries ago, she was an old lady and she'd had a horrible row with her son. Then he wouldn't even come to see her when she was dying."

"People can be very cruel," Will said.

They all sat in silence for a moment and contemplated the situation that the letter had brought to life like a window into history.

"She wanted her son to find this evidence, whatever it was," Will mused.

"Sadly we'll never know," Alessa said. "I puzzled over that for a bit but I'm sure I've got it right. She mentions 'evidence' but not a hint of what it is."

"And what is all that bit at the end about Alexander?" Anna said. "I got completely lost with that."

"It's a reference to Botticelli's Mars and Venus painting," Will said. "Alexander and Roxana is a direct reference. What's more, we didn't ever know for sure before that the painting was based on that story. This letter is the first direct proof of it!"

"It's very significant," Alessa said. "I've been puzzling for ages about a good direction for my thesis, and this is the focus I needed. That's why I wanted to follow it up, because I felt papà might have come up with something, but I could never have dreamed it would be this good."

"*Is* it good?" Will asked in surprise.

"Oh yes," she said emphatically. "Semiramide, the wife of Lorenzo di Pierfrancesco de' Medici, a man who by this time was dead, if I'm not mistaken, makes a direct reference to the painting on her *spalliera*. That's a kind of chest that might have been used to store linen. Anyway, it's thought that the Mars and Venus panel was originally on just such a chest. And the little satyrs in the painting are straight out of this tale about Alexander and Roxana, so this is very exciting. I could make it the crowning glory of a new theory about the artwork."

"And what about this brooch she mentions?" Anna said.

"Good point," said Will. He looked around and spotted a tablet computer. "Can I find a picture of the painting? I'll show you what I think she's referring to. It's a bit sad but I practically know the painting off by heart."

Anna picked up the tablet, propped it on its stand and turned it on. Will found a picture of Botticelli's *Mars and Venus*.

"Here we are," he said, pointing. On the screen was the pearl brooch on Venus's white dress, resting between her breasts as if pinning her hair braids together. It had eight pearls and a round stone in the middle that might have been red or orange. Anna looked at the screen.

"You're right, that must be the one," she said, picking up Alessa's translation of the letter and searching the last paragraph, her lips moving unconsciously as she read.

"Yes, and that's totally amazing if you think about it," Alessa said excitedly. "Because it proves that it was *her* brooch. She says she has it right there by her hand. So it's *her* brooch and she was wearing it. That means that *she* is Venus in the picture and papà was right. And it also means that all those people who think that Venus is Simonetta Vespucci are completely wrong. They just can't see it!"

Will smiled.

"The invisible muse," he murmured absently, and then looked at Alessa. "I got heckled by some girl in the audience recently who said the same thing."

"Well I was right," she said with a grin. "Or papà was right, at least."

"It's rather a good legacy for him," Will said. "Even though he's gone, to be proved right like that. You must write it up."

"Wild horses wouldn't stop me," Alessa said, and turned to Anna. "Thank you for helping us!"

"Well I didn't do a thing," Anna said. "But I do feel rather excited I must admit. "I've got to go up to the school, though. George has just texted me to remind me that it's Parents Evening and we both forgot. You're very welcome to stay but I need to get over there and provide George with some moral support. He sounds a bit desperate and he's got Charlotte and William and Sarah hanging around causing mayhem. Our three little angels," she added, seeing Alessa's look of confusion.

Will and Alessa left Anna to sort out her children, with instructions to thank George, and they walked back to Will's studio. On the way, Alessa's fiancé called her and she ended up on the phone for most of the walk, making

Will feel embarrassed that he had somehow until this moment avoided thinking too much about the handsome Lucas Flynn and his sardonic expression.

"I can't stay long," Alessa said, pulling a face when she got off the phone. "That was Lucas and he's getting grumpy."

"About what?"

"About *you*, Mr Bentley," she said, fixing him with a stern look but then smiling. "He's getting cross that every time he asks where I am it turns out I'm with you. He's started referring to you as 'that artist'. He's getting jealous! I need to get back and mollify him."

"That's okay. Have you known him for a long time?"

"A few years. He's very clever. Papà knew his father and we met at a college party. He proposed three months ago and I said yes."

"Congratulations," Will said, not feeling at all congratulatory. "When's the big day?"

"Not until next year. You wouldn't believe how much organising there is to do for a wedding."

"I'm sure," he said, remembering his own aborted engagement some years previously. He didn't want to go through all that again – too many bad memories. "Well anyway, look across the street. We have almost arrived at the Bentley residence."

He gestured at the studio and she looked at it. It wasn't a good first impression. It looked like an interior designer shop stuck on an ugly black building.

"Not very posh I'm afraid," he said, feeling embarrassed as he examined it through the eyes of another. "It was once a ball-bearing factory."

It had a large glass window and there was a sign which said "Will Bentley, Painter" over the top. As they approached, she saw in the window a single painting. It was a refugee family sitting on the green House of Commons benches, invisible to the politicians all around them who were baying with laughter at some joke. There was something about the expressions on the children's dirty faces that brought a lump to Alessa's throat. She looked at Will but he hadn't noticed her reaction; he was patting his pockets for his key.

He unlocked the studio door, which had a surprisingly sturdy locking system. They went in and she followed him up the stairs, noticing an old-fashioned line drawing of a hand pointing upwards with a snake twirled round its finger. It was deliciously warm after the cold March evening outside. At the top there was a door and then a small vestibule. He went through and they emerged immediately into a huge studio which was splendidly chaotic. It was full of hundreds of paintings, stacked around the edges of the walls. There were various easels and tables covered with pots of brushes and half-squeezed paint tubes. There was a heady smell of oil paint and turps in the air. There was a large window and an open doorway through which she could see a kitchen and a corridor. A black spiral staircase wound its way up to the roof.

"Wow!" she said, looking around. "This is amazing!"

He looked pleased.

"It's rather a mess."

"It's a good mess," she said. "What a wonderful place to paint. I had no idea you were so prolific." She gestured around. "There are loads of paintings here."

"I do sell them, so a lot of these are the ones that didn't make it, or that I'm so fond of that I hang onto them."

She started to walk around and inspect the studio more closely.

He went into the kitchen and called, "Tea, coffee, wine?"

"Black coffee," she said absently, and then louder so that he could hear: "Black coffee please!"

She was looking at the large painting on the easel, which depicted a young starlet in a red cape leaning from the window of a black limousine, and photographers reflected in the shiny paintwork of the vehicle, like wolves cornering their prey. It was unsettling. She started wandering around the walls, crouching down and looking at the stacked paintings, lifting them away from each other so that she could see the ones behind. She was inspecting a half-completed painting of a clove orange, in which every projecting clove was a human head, when a cat rubbed itself against her and made her jump.

She reached down and stroked it. It meowed in appreciation and rubbed its head against her knee.

"What's the cat's name?" she called.

Will appeared in the doorway with the coffee.

"That's Beauty," he said. "She's friendly but very lazy. "And somewhere there's a black tom called Beast, probably parked on my bed making it all hairy, because he has *no* manners."

He said this last with a very serious expression that made her laugh. They sat down together on a sofa and he handed her a steaming mug.

"Today is turning out to be very special," she said. "This letter from Semiramide is the most amazing thing. I feel like we've uncovered a clue to treasure, a sort of historical gold. I wonder if the original letter is still in the archive."

"It should be there somewhere," Will said. "Unless it got lost or something. "Pocock said he put it back among all the household accounts and there were loads of them, so it might not have been noticed."

"The Medici kept meticulous records," Alessa said. "They were bankers, after all. They understood the importance of proper accounts. So it could just be there somewhere and it hasn't got digitised yet. That means I need to find it fast and stake my claim before some other beastly scholar gets his hands on the loot."

She looked so alarmed at the possibility of someone else getting there first that he laughed.

"Finish your coffee first."

They opened the notebook with the photographs of the letter and Alessa's translation. She looked through it again and frowned.

"I wonder what happened to Semiramide's brooch," she said. "Up until now it was just a brooch in a famous painting. Botticelli might have invented it, or it could have been made of paste and plucked from a bowl of trinkets in his studio. But now we know different. We know that it was a real Medici jewel. We know it belonged to the actual lady who sat for him as Venus, whose face we see in so many of his other pictures. We know she was Semiramide and that her husband must surely have commissioned Mars and Venus. When you think about it, we know a whole bunch of things that we didn't know before."

"*And* we know that she was probably his muse, just like your father suggested," Will went on. "That's significant because just about everyone, including me until I met you, thought that his muse was Simonetta Vespucci."

"La Bella Simonetta," Alessa said, nodding. "But even before papà's theory I always thought that was odd, like I said in the pub the other day. She died of tuberculosis, and seven or eight years later he was painting her in Mars and Venus. What's he supposed to have done, painted her perfect memory in his mind's eye?"

She rolled her eyes.

"Well he probably could," Will said. "We're talking about Botticelli, after all. But I'm only arguing to be contrary. Artist's muses tend to be the living, breathing type."

"With tits," Alessa added, making him grin at her pronunciation: 'teats'.

"With heaving bodices," he agreed with a smile. "That's how it was with Picasso, anyway. Although nobody knows about Botticelli. He may well have been homosexual. He never married, and there's no record of him living with a woman or fathering a child."

"Maybe so," Alessa said. "But he didn't paint women that looked like men, the way Michelangelo did. Men's bodies with boobs stuck on. Botticelli's women look very feminine."

Will used his hand like a weighing scale.

"His boy angels look very feminine too," he observed.

She shrugged and smiled, conceding the point. They sat in companionable silence, sipping coffee.

"I'm still wondering about the brooch," Alessa said after a bit.

"Perhaps her husband gave it to her. A birthday present or a wedding gift."

"And he was Medici," Alessa went on, following his train of thought. "So it would have been expensive. You can tell that. Imagine a gemstone that big surrounded by a ring of pearls, probably set in gold."

"I wonder what the stone is," Will mused. "It could be a ruby, like Lightbown says."

"Lightbown?"

Will pretended to be taken aback.

"You mean there's something you don't know?"

"Oh, very funny."

"Ronald Lightbown. He wrote *the* definitive work on Botticelli," Will said, leaping up and going over to the bookcase. He hauled out a large and heavy book and plunked it down on the low table next to the sofa.

"This bloke. He reckons it's a ruby. I only know because I've been earning a second living talking to people about last year's adventures, and I had to read up about it. The paint may have faded but it's not very rubylike. It's got bits of orange in it."

She lifted the volume with difficulty.

"My Gawd, Lightbown *must* be good. I'm practically getting a hernia picking up his book."

She started to flip through it.

"I can't even think of any orange stones," she pondered. "Oh wait, yes I can. What about topaz. Isn't that orange?"

"I think so," Will said, crossing over to his computer and moving the mouse to awaken the screen. He brought up images of topaz stones. "That could be it. Here's an oval cut, look."

He looked at the prices from jewellers.

"It's not very expensive, though. I shouldn't think a Medici would give his wife a topaz."

"It might have been expensive then. But whatever stone it was we'll never know," she said. "Unless of course we found the brooch."

He laughed and shook his head regretfully.

"Unfortunately it was more than five centuries ago."

"It *was* an expensive brooch, though. People wouldn't just chuck it out."

They both thought about this and Alessa looked him in the eye.

"We could have a look on the internet."

He stood up and offered her the computer chair, which was on wheels.

"Be my guest. Are you any good with computers?"

"I have a degree in computer science," she said.

"Really?!"

"Nope, that was a complete lie. I am *quite* good, though." She flashed him a wicked grin. "I've spent years being a swot."

He laughed sheepishly. She typed and brought up a picture of Botticelli's Mars and Venus painting, then zoomed up on the brooch which festooned Venus's breast.

"Here it is. So we're looking for an eight-pearl brooch with a round stone in the middle. And the top two pearls are a bit smaller, see?"

She pointed and Will leaned in to look. He smelled her scent and had a sudden memory of the Royal Blenheim, where he had first talked properly to her.

"They *are* smaller," he said thoughtfully, "but I think he just wanted it to look tilted back, because she's leaning back on her elbows, and her chest is sloping because of her breasts."

"OK then, so eight pearls of the same size. I see what you mean about the colour of the stone in the middle. It's hard to tell."

"It could be deep crimson, but it could be orange. Most likely a ruby, though. It feels like a criminal offense to disagree with Lightbown."

"It's a shame we're not in London," she said. "We could go and look at the real thing."

"Even if we did, the paint could just have faded or changed colour over the centuries."

She began to type in search phrases.

Brooch. Pearl ruby brooch. Eight pearl ruby brooch.

There were lots of pearl brooches but all the wrong shape: butterflies, insects, square pins, star shapes.

Eight pearl topaz brooch. Eight pearl orange brooch.

More wrongly shaped brooches, this time featuring lots of amber.

Medici brooch. Vintage Medici pearl and ruby brooch. Semiramide brooch.

More pages appeared to scroll through but there was nothing the slightest bit similar. She tried other combinations of words but got no closer.

"Hopeless," she said in frustration. "I wonder if an image search would work better."

She spent some minutes finding the highest resolution picture of Semiramide that she could, and then snipped out just the brooch and saved it as an image. This time she searched by image and uploaded the picture of the snipped-out brooch. The search engine suggested that it was a snowflake but she deleted that and typed in 'brooch'.

The screen filled with pictures of brooches, and this time they were much more like the one they were looking for.

"What about that one," Will said, pointing at a Virgin Mary and child with four little children ranged around her, and a brown building with a tower in the background. Alessa opened it and they could see a brooch in the painting, but it had only seven pearls.

"It's a bit of a cluttered picture," Alessa said, and frowned at the description.

"Russian, anonymous artist, in Saint Petersburg."

"You wouldn't paint seven pearls if you meant eight," Will pointed out. "See what else turns up."

Something turned up immediately. Alessa continued scrolling and they both gasped in recognition.

"That could actually be it, on the turban of this woman," Will said.

They enlarged the picture. It was a Titian painting of Isabella d'Este, a formidable woman and fashion icon of her era. She had been Marchioness of Mantova from 1490. They looked her up, although Alessa already knew many of the details. Isabella had been an important political leader and influencer of the renaissance.

"This is interesting," Alessa said. "Apparently she met lots of humanist artists and scholars, so she could have crossed paths with Botticelli. She could have known the Medici. And she was born in 1474, so let's see, if Mars and Venus was painted in the early 1480s, she would have been a child."

"A young girl, but already betrothed at the age of six," Will said, pointing to a line on the screen. "She would have been a young princess, in today's terms."

"She could have got the brooch somehow," Alessa said, rather optimistically.

"Yeah, but look," Will said gloomily, pointing. "Get it a bit bigger if you can. Yes, this time it's got the eight pearls, but the centre stone is square, not round."

She pursed her lips.

"Maybe the stone was replaced, or maybe old Titian was distracted by her beauty."

Will looked at her and solemnly quoted:
"While Titian was mixing rose madder,
His model reclined on a ladder.
Her position to Titian suggested coition,
So he went up the ladder and had 'er."

She giggled, but then they examined Titian's painting of Isabella d'Este's brooch and grimaced at each other.

"It just isn't the right one," Alessa said. "Very close, though."

Her phone buzzed and she looked at it. "I *do* have to go," she said, grimacing. "Lucas is asking what time my train arrives and I'm not even on it yet. We should keep looking, we might get lucky. Call me or I'll call you. No, on second thoughts I'll just call you."

He called her a taxi and a silver Mercedes arrived in a few minutes. With a kiss on his cheek she was gone, bound for the station and Lucas. He watched the taxi disappear around the corner, and then shook his head in irritation. He closed the door and locked it, then went back up to the warm studio. Beauty nuzzled his legs as he came through the door. He bent down and picked her up, stroking her.

"Fuck Lucas," he said to the cat, and Beauty began to purr.

It was late by the time Alessa got back to Oxford and Lucas picked her up at the station. She kissed him warmly to dispel his suspicions and they went back to his flat, which was the upstairs of a house with a shared garden in Summertown. They ordered an Indian takeaway, drank a bottle of white wine and went to bed at half-past midnight.

Alessa woke at 4:15AM with Lucas asleep beside her. She looked at his dark straight hair falling onto the pillow and felt guilty that she had been spending so much time with Will. It wasn't fair on Lucas, and he had a perfect right to be cross about it. And he had been a bit cross, though less so than she had been expecting. There was something about him that she couldn't quite identify and a couple of times she had asked him if everything was all right and he'd reassured her that it was. She had put it down to jealousy. It wasn't a nice characteristic, but she had given him every reason to be jealous, so she couldn't be cross with him about it. In a way it was flattering. And the next day –in just a few hours – he was going off to Venice for a conference. She shook her head on the pillow and stared up at the ceiling.

She tossed and turned for half an hour, trying to get back to sleep but finding her mind too active. She thought about Will's studio, and imagined him painting while the two black cats prowled about the place. She thought about the brooch they had sought but not found. She picked up her phone and checked the news, but there was nothing of interest. After another quarter of an hour she slid out of bed, quietly in order not to wake Lucas. She padded into the sitting room and sat down in front of her laptop. She woke it up and frowned at the waiting screen. Then she went back to the bedroom and peered through the door. Lucas was still fast asleep.

She slumped down again in front of her computer. She often woke like this, her mind buzzing. She would fret about her teaching, or the thesis which was currently stalled. She felt excited about Semiramide's letter. She knew it was going to enable her to finish her thesis, and she wished her father could have seen it. She would have to get a signed affidavit from Frederick Pocock, in case he passed away and she found herself with no proof. She thought of reproducing Semiramide's letter as an image of evidence in her manuscript, and basked in imagined glory for a moment.

She opened up her browser, found the picture of Mars and Venus again, and snipped out the brooch, this time taking more care. She ran another image search and quickly found the same images as before. She modified the search so that the image was accompanied by the words 'eight pearl brooch' and started to scroll again, watching page after page fill with new images.

Still nothing.

She remembered about the picture of Isabella d'Este, wearing a sort of turban headdress which was called a Balzo and had been all the fashion in late renaissance Italy. She started a new image search, because the search engine had an annoying tendency to forget that it was doing an image search at all. She typed *'spilla'* – the Italian word for 'brooch' – then added 'Isabella d'Este' and started to scroll again.

She saw it immediately.

The exact brooch.

It was an eight-pearl brooch with a round orange stone in the centre, lying on a piece of black velvet. Her mouth went dry. She clicked on the image and read: '*Una spilla di perle e zaffiri arancione, proprietà di Isabelle d'Este, Marchesa di Mantova, 1540, Museo di Palazzo Ducale, Mantova*'. A brooch of pearl and orange sapphire, owned by Isabella d'Este, Marchioness of Mantova.

Orange *sapphire*, she muttered to herself. Not ruby or topaz.

She looked up orange sapphires, which she had never heard of, imagining that sapphires were only ever blue, and found beautiful cut stones. A large sapphire would be expensive, and an orange sapphire perhaps more so. It would be a gift worthy of a Medici.

She looked at her watch, wondering if she could call Will, but it was only half past five in the morning and he probably wouldn't take too kindly to get a call from her. It was frustrating as she very much wanted to tell him what she had found out. Also, if Lucas found her on the phone to Will when he woke up, he would be mad at her. She decided to text Will so that he could look at it when he woke up. She picked up her phone and dropped the link to the page onto it, then typed a message: '*Will, I think I found the brooch! Take a look. I'm sure it's the one that Semiramide was referring to, and it could prove she was his muse. We absolutely have to find it and examine it! It's in a Museum in Mantova. It was the one owned by Isabella d'Este so I don't know why Titian painted it wrong. Alessa xx*'.

She typed in his name and it came up in contacts. She sent the message and then sat back, imagining him receiving it. Then she wondered if she should have added the kisses, but she always added kisses to everybody, and anyway it was too late now.

Suddenly worried that Lucas might have an early alarm because he was catching a flight to Venice, she crept back into the bedroom and slid into bed. He was still fast asleep, and now that she had solved the puzzle, against all expectations, she felt heavy-eyed. In ten minutes she was in a deep asleep.

Lucas wasn't asleep. He was lying with his eyes closed, but he was awake. He had awoken earlier, somehow sensing in his sleep that Alessa's warm body was no longer beside him. He had got up and peered through the door, seeing her on the computer, intent on something with her back to him. He had crept back to bed.

When she was fast asleep and her breathing was even, he turned over and lay looking up at the ceiling, his own mind in turmoil. The conference was an important one and he was speaking at it. But he had a secret and he couldn't tell Alessa. He was excited about the days to come. She had been spending all her time with that artist anyway, so he didn't exactly feel guilty.

He decided to get a glass of water and slid out of bed quietly, just as she had done. She didn't wake. He went into the kitchen, poured water into a glass and drank. Then he went over to her computer, which had gone to sleep. Next to it was Alessa's phone.

15

The Birth of Venus delights the eye and the imagination by the smooth caress of its lines and colours.

RONALD LIGHTBOWN, Botticelli – Life and Work

24th March 1486, Florence

"Sandro, your painting has worked its magic with the gods," Lorenzo said with a smile.

He and Semiramide stood next to the painting of Mars and Venus that Botticelli had completed two years previously. A toddler stood on wobbly legs next to Lorenzo, holding his hand. He beamed at her proudly. Her head was a mass of pretty curls, though she was not beautiful for she'd had the misfortune of inheriting her father's nose. She twisted out of his grip and was off between the assembled lords and ladies, threading her unsteady way through a sea of legs clad in breeches and bright silk dresses. The ladies cooed and the gentlemen smiled. A harassed nurse pursued the small but determined figure. Botticelli had met the little girl a few times – she was Laudomia, the firstborn of Lorenzo and Semiramide.

"And this is Ginevra," Semiramide said proudly, leaning into the cot next to her where a baby was fast asleep, her eyes squeezed tight shut against the hubbub of the room.

"How old is little Ginevra?" Botticelli said, leaning over the crib and looking at the tiny hands, thrown up as if in surprise to either side of the baby's face. She was prettier than her older sister, as if she had taken her looks from her mother and not her father.

"Twenty-three weeks," Semiramide said, unconsciously smoothing down the front of her dress. Botticelli would never forget the moments of flirtation when he had drawn her for the Venus picture, but there was now no hint of coquetry in Semiramide – it was as if it had never happened, and he was obliged to forget it, though sometimes the memory would plague his dreams.

He looked up and found Semiramide's eye upon him. He reddened guiltily at his secret thoughts, as if she could see inside his head.

"I suggested to my husband that we ask you here today," Semiramide said to him. She turned and took her husband's arm. "Lorenzo?"

"Ah yes," Lorenzo said with a slightly rueful smile. "As you can see, we have the two most adorable young ladies in the state of Florence, but there is a small problem."

He gave the smallest of self-deprecating shrugs, opening his hands and spreading his arms.

"We have no heir."

Botticelli grimaced sympathetically. A male child was needed to continue the Medici line.

"I understand," he said cautiously, "but I cannot make paintings which order the Creator's dice."

"Perhaps another painting would hasten another birth," Semiramide said.

"I'm sure it may," Botticelli said gravely, though privately he was sure that babies were the work of people and God, not of paint. But if Semiramide should think otherwise, who was he to disagree and perhaps put in jeopardy his chance of seeing her again?

"We were imagining something to do with birth and creation," Lorenzo said. "The birth of a god, perhaps."

Botticelli stood and looked at Mars and Venus in the painting before him, and said nothing for almost a minute. Then he looked up.

"The birth of the Christ child?" he said. He looked at Semiramide. "With you, my lady, as the likeness of the Madonna?"

Lorenzo shook his head.

"No. The Medici do not elevate themselves," he said. "We prefer subtlety. We don't wish to liken ourselves to God himself."

"Of course," Botticelli said quickly. "Then we should think on some moment from mythology."

He frowned and began to pace up and down. His thoughts turned again to Mars, born of Juno. The god of war would be a suitable heir, magicked from Juno's belly by the touch of the goddess Flora, at least according to Ovid.

"The birth of a god," he said, nodding slowly, but then thought of an objection. He needed to put Semiramide into the painting if he were to see her again. It would be odd to paint her as Juno when she had already been painted as Venus. He grimaced in exasperation. He could do the birth of Venus but how on earth could he make that the story of a male heir?

"Let me give it some thought," he extemporised. "Do you have an idea in mind?"

"None at all," Lorenzo said with a grin, and raised his glass. "My toil these days is of politics and money, Sandro." He took a draught of wine. "I leave the design department to you."

Botticelli looked thoughtful.

"There is a moment that Angelo has written of," he said, referring to Poliziano's poetry. "The birth of Venus herself, or rather, the moment at which she is blown by Zephyr and an Aura to alight on the shore. Venus brings love into the world, and her birth echoes the idea of a birth for you."

"I hope, maestro, that you do not propose to depict me unclothed," Semiramide said, giving him a look that seemed to dissect him.

Where was that flirtation now?

"My lady," he said hastily," I would not wish to be impertinent, and yet…" He moulded the air with his hands as if describing shapes in his mind's eye. "Venus herself must necessarily be unclothed at her birth," he went on firmly. "She must be unadorned by jewels and her hair must be unbraided as nature intended. I would of course cover her modesty."

"You would cover her modesty with what?" Semiramide said icily.

"Er, well I would use a branch of myrtle or some such," Botticelli said in desperation.

"A branch of myrtle when she has just emerged from the sea?"

He shook his head in exasperation.

"Well I don't know, I must think on it. A Venus *Pudica* pose, perhaps, where she demurely conceals her modesty with her hand."

"Perhaps you could change her face," Lorenzo suggested, perceiving his wife's glowering expression.

Botticelli turned to his patron. "I could, my lord, but if I am to associate the birth with the mother…" he bowed briefly to Semiramide, "…then I should not depict someone else."

Lorenzo nodded slowly while Semiramide continued to look stony-faced.

"Why can't I wear a robe?" she asked. "I mean Venus. Why can't *she* wear a robe?"

"She *could* be clothed," Botticelli said, "but in every tale I have ever read, she emerges unclothed from the sea, as do we all from the mother's womb."

"So we do, but as babes and not full-grown," Semiramide said. "Some artistic license is needed. Talk to Angelo, but if she is to be unclothed, she should not bear my face unchanged or the ladies of the court will laugh behind my back, and the gentlemen…well I cannot even think how the gentlemen will react, but it will not be gentlemanly. Do you understand my meaning, Maestro Botticelli?"

"It is clear, my lady. But if I may make one other point? A painting such as this should be hung in a private bedchamber, above the marital bed, to inspire the intended procreation. It need not ever be seen by the court."

She pursed her lips at this, but then nodded slowly after a moment of reflection.

"That's true," she agreed, turning to her husband. "Could we arrange for it to be on private display only?"

Lorenzo nodded fervently.

"Of course, my love. This room would be too crowded if we put up another large work. We could hang it in the main bedchamber at Cafaggiolo and no-one from the court would ever see it. I could even have it excluded from the inventories if you wish, or described vaguely. And we could have bright colours and gold to enliven that dull room in the villa."

"On canvas, perhaps?" Botticelli suggested, keen to do a large canvas painting. The picture was beginning to take shape in his mind. "That would be more fitting for a villa, and lighter to transport."

"Canvas would be satisfactory," Lorenzo said. "Provided that it lasts. Does it wear out?"

"We don't yet know for sure, lord," Botticelli said. "But it seems extremely durable. The size might be a problem, though. How big should it be?"

Lorenzo spread his arms wide.

"Big," he said simply. "Maybe five braccia, like Primavera." He smiled. "We have to draw the attention of the gods if we are to be honoured with a boy to carry on the line."

Botticelli nodded, pleased to remember the price that he had received for Primavera and looking forward to the prospect of something similar. Most of all, they seemed to be accepting his proposal for a secular painting of Venus, rather than yet another Madonna and Child. That was a quiet triumph.

"It shall be my best work," he said quietly. "And for that size, I will look into the possibility of joining two canvases with a wooden brace. Failing that we will revert to panel, but I am thinking that canvas would be better if we are to transport it to Cafaggiolo. I cannot," he added apologetically, "paint it *in* Cafaggiolo, as I am these days in too much demand from my workshop here in Florence, and I must keep a close eye on my apprentices lest their work be of inferior quality."

"I understand," said Lorenzo. Neither man brought up the subject of Semiramide posing for Botticelli, even though she would without question have to be fully clothed. Botticelli decided that he would raise that topic later, when Semiramide had cooled down, not wanting the whole idea to be rebuffed if he dared to mention it now.

Later, when they were going into dinner and Lorenzo had Botticelli on his own for a moment, the Medici lord grasped him by the elbow. They stopped and Lorenzo leaned in to speak in an undertone.

"We are agreed that the painting will not be on public display, Sandro," he said. "It will be for our private contemplation, so I give you leave to fully unclothe this goddess. Make her sensual as only your brush can do. Semiramide may be shocked but she has passion. She must be stirred by the painting, for I need an heir. She will not object if you create what I hope for."

Botticelli looked at him solemnly.

"I understand and obey, lord," he said. He turned away as he felt his ears begin to redden at the thought of painting an unclothed Semiramide, even though he would have to do it from his imagination.

A month after this commission, Jacopo Saltarelli was sulking in the maestro's workshop in via Nuova. He was the artist's model that Biagio had drafted in for capturing the difficult position of Venus that Botticelli was aiming for. Botticelli himself was already in a bad mood, because Semiramide had declined point blank to be drawn by him.

"You will have to do your best to make me beautiful from your previous sketches," she had said icily. "I certainly do not intend to pose for this painting, even in my thickest cloak."

"I understand, my lady," he had said, but though he had remonstrated, she had stood firm and no drawing session had been forthcoming. He had never expected that she would remove any item of clothing, nor would he have dared ask, but it was still very annoying because he needed to capture her in the pose and he would have preferred to make more sketches. He also wanted the chance to be with her; perhaps even the opportunity to repeat that magical moment when she had bid him touch her and they had almost kissed. Perhaps she remembered that moment too, and feared it.

Instead he had Saltarelli, whom Biagio had recruited on the word of Leonardo, and he was regretting it. It was uncommon to get female nude models as it was considered improper, yet he was all too familiar with the dangers of using a male model to depict the female anatomy. Apart from the obvious differences of breasts and genitalia, a woman's hips were wider than a man's and her shoulders narrower. Her waist was narrower too, and she was more flesh than bone; curves rather than angles. He wasn't going to paint Venus, the epitome of feminine pulchritude, as a boy with no cock and two puddings on his chest for breasts. He wanted men to be excited by this painting and women to be jealous.

For an hour now he had been trying to get Saltarelli to stand in the correct position.

"Venus is just stepping out onto the shore," he had explained. "She is in movement. That is why you can't simply stand on one leg, because you'll be supporting your weight upright. She is not upright. She is in mid step."

"If she isn't upright, why doesn't she fall over," Saltarelli said, still sulky.

"She doesn't fall over because she is moving," Botticelli explained yet again. "That is why I have given you the wall to lean against, so that you can align yourself in the position that I need."

"It's cold," protested Saltarelli plaintively. "The wall's cold."

"It's not cold," Botticelli said forcefully. "You just don't seem to be able to understand any instruction."

They tried for a further fifteen minutes, but the truth was that Botticelli felt uninspired by the man. Saltarelli could never stand in for Semiramide – it was like using a beetle as a substitute for a butterfly. Saltarelli was in more or less the right position now, and Botticelli had made a sketch or two, but it was coming out all wrong and that made him cross with himself, and angry with Saltarelli as a result.

"It's not working," he said after a while further, shaking his head irritably. "Put your clothes back on. Biagio will pay you for today but I won't be using you again."

"What?" Saltarelli said, his voice now ugly. "I was hired for two weeks by your apprentice."

"Well you're no good," Botticelli said bluntly. "That's not my fault."

"I'm good enough for Leonardo," Saltarelli said bluntly. "Perhaps you just can't draw."

"Out!" roared Botticelli, now genuinely angry at being unfavourably compared with Leonardo, which was too close to the bone. "Biagio!" he yelled. "Pay this man and show him the door."

16

Yon light is not day-light, I know it, I:
It is some meteor that the sun exhales,
To be to thee this night a torch-bearer,
And light thee on thy way to Mantua:
Therefore stay yet; thou need'st not to be gone.

WILLIAM SHAKESPEARE, Romeo and Juliet

March, Cambridge

"Hello?"
Her voice was sleepy. Will had waited until eight before calling Alessa but she had not picked up. He had called again at ten past nine and this time she did so, but her voice was drugged with sleep.

"Alessa? It's Will. I got your message."

She groaned.

"You must have risen with the lark. You didn't have to call me in the middle of the night."

"It's not night. It's after nine."

"Oh." There was a long pause. "Let me call you back in a minute."

The line clicked off and he felt frustrated that he had only got so few words out of her.

While he was waiting he switched on the kettle but then paced up and down the studio and forgot that he had done so. He kept staring at his phone as if somehow he might have missed a call. He checked for the third time that the sound wasn't muted. Then he opened the message from Alessa that had arrived in the early hours of the morning and read it again.

'*Will, I think I found the brooch! Take a look. I'm sure it's the one that Semiramide was referring to, and it could prove she was his muse. We absolutely have to find it and examine it! It's in a Museum in Mantova. It was the one owned by Isabella d'Este so I don't know why Titian painted it wrong. Alessa xx'*

The first thing he noticed was not the content of the message, but that she had ended with kisses. Which was foolish, he knew. Everyone ends messages with kisses, all the time. He sat down in front of the computer and selected the link she had sent. The screen lit up with pictures of brooches. He started to scroll down and almost immediately saw the brooch. It had a round orange stone ringed by eight pearls. It looked identical to the brooch in Botticelli's painting.

He clicked on the image and read the inscription, just as Alessa had done in the early hours of that morning.

"Ha!" he said aloud, but just then his phone began to ring and he almost dropped it even though he had been expecting the call.

"You found it?" Alessa asked, her voice now properly awake.

"Orange sapphire," he breathed, reading off the screen. "Not a ruby at all."

"Exactly!" she said. "Not a ruby, and not a topaz either. I'm not much of a jewellery expert but I should think a big sapphire costs plenty of money."

"Worthy of a Medici," Will said. "I didn't even know they came in orange. I thought they came in blue or blue."

"Me too but apparently not. And it belonged to Isabella d'Este, who was around at the same time as Botticelli. It can't be a coincidence."

"It seems unlikely, and this one is identical to the one in the painting. The only weird thing is that Titian painted it differently in his portrait of Isabella on that turban hat thing she's wearing."

"The Balzo headdress," Alessa said.

"Whatever. The stone is square and definitely not orange. I've just brought it up on the screen now. It looks red or purple."

"Maybe there were two similar pearl brooches, but we'll never know now because it's five hundred years ago. The fact is, we've found the real brooch even if it's different to how Titian painted it."

She sounded a little impatient and a thought occurred to him.

"By the way, I'm sorry I rang so early," he said. "I presume your fiancé isn't very happy with me calling first thing. Tell him I'm sorry."

He didn't feel sorry at all. Actually he felt glad.

"I would, but Lucas isn't here," she said. "He's gone to a conference, in Venice of all places."

"He went to Venice and he didn't take you?"

"I know," she said regretfully. "It's a bloody cheek! He's been told it's all work and they aren't allowed to bring partners or spouses in case everyone slopes off in the evenings rather than 'networking'. It just means they all get pissed together in the hotel bar. But I couldn't have gone anyway, I'm teaching today and I couldn't just nip off to Venice even if I had the money. I must admit I was jealous when he told me, though."

"Was he all right when you got in last night?" Will asked, and then immediately regretted what had come out of his mouth. "I mean, it's none of my business, so feel free to say so."

"It's none of your business," she said, but then laughed. "He was okay. He was a bit cross I've been spending so much time chasing clues with you, but I told him about Botticelli's muse and he got quite interested. Asked me all sorts of questions."

Something else that she had said stuck in his head.

"So you're teaching today," he said. "Are you teaching tomorrow?"

"No, it's Saturday tomorrow," she said, enunciating slowly as if explaining to a child.

"Oh yeah," he said sheepishly. "So how would you feel about flying to Mantova? And is that the same as Mantua? I vaguely think it is."

She laughed.

"Yes, Mantua is the English translation. I'd love to go to Mantova Will, but you don't seem to understand student life! I am completely skint until I get my father's inheritance. The solicitors are taking their own sweet time, and I lecture as part of my D. Phil but the university pays me about fourpence. So I will have to politely decline your brilliant idea."

"The law's delay, the insolence of office," Will said. "Well I can pay for both of us if you like. We ought to go and see the brooch now that we've got this far."

"I couldn't possibly," she protested. "It would be like a thousand pounds or something at this short notice."

"I just sold a painting for fifteen. It's not a problem."

"You mean fifteen thousand pounds? Oh my Gawd, I should be marrying you and not Lucas! All right then, but only on one condition. I'll pay you back as soon as the estate money comes in."

They landed in Verona at eleven the next morning. It was dry and sunny and warmer than London, even in March. And it was noisy. There seemed to be a babble of voices compared with London; tourists starting the season early, perhaps. They purchased tickets and got on the Aerobus into the city, arriving soon at Porta Nuova, the railway station.

"This is so amazing," Alessa said, who was brimming with excitement and enthusiasm to be back in what she persisted in calling her 'second country of birth'. "I can't believe we just decided to come and now we're here. I can't believe you got tickets!"

"We're out of season so it was easy."

At the station they had an espresso at the *Bistrot Porta Nuova*, then had to gulp it down when they looked up train times to Mantova and found the next one was leaving at the bottom of the hour. Arming themselves with extraordinarily cheap train tickets from the automated machine, they hurried as fast as they could with wheeled suitcases along the under-platform corridor, mounted the stairs to platform 11 and threw themselves onto the train with three minutes to spare, collapsing on opposite seats gasping and laughing.

Will was having difficulty taking his eyes off Alessa. She had tied up her brown curls into a bunch at the back and every time she caught his eyes she grinned that wide smile. He looked out of the window at the passing fields and farms. It was quite different to an English landscape. He thought how he'd like to spend a day out there with a full palette and a stretch of canvas to paint on. At one point they went past a walled cemetery which was bathed in a yellow glow of sunlight, as if God had sent down a shaft of light to illuminate the cream-coloured stones marking the departure gate from Earth to Heaven. There was a brief flurry of rain for a few minutes, running in lines on the windows, but when they got out of the train at Mantova the platforms were already dry and it might not have rained for weeks.

They waited for the crowd to get ahead of them, as they were trundling suitcases. It was one fifteen in the afternoon.

"We made it," Will said, gesturing at the large station sign next to him. "And I've never seen you look so happy, or felt so excited myself for that matter."

"I haven't been to Italy for ages," she said. "And I only went to Verona once when I was a little girl with papà and mamma, so I don't remember it. And we never came here, to Mantova. And what's more, we're on an adventure!"

She hugged him spontaneously.

"Thank you," she said. "Now let's get into town and see if we can find old Isabella's brooch."

"Semiramide's brooch," he said, holding up crossed fingers. "We hope."

There was a single taxi in front of the station so they climbed into it and went to their hotel in *via Accademia*, admiring the view across a lake on the way. The concierge expressed surprise when it emerged that they were booked into two rooms, which was embarrassing, and Alessa smiled shyly at Will before explaining in fast Italian that they were colleagues. They dumped their suitcases and reconvened downstairs after ten minutes. They picked up a small tourist map from the concierge, on which he marked a cross to show their location.

Once outside they paused to get their bearings, but then they had to go only a few metres, passing through a tall archway, to bring them into the corner of the *Piazza Sordello*. The *Palazzo Ducale's* arched walkway stretched along the entire eastern side of the huge, cobbled square. In the far distance was the huge baroque façade of San Pietro's cathedral.

They bought tickets and audio guides to the entire palace, then went into the gift shop and found the best guidebook available. The palace was huge. It comprised a complex of over five hundred rooms, joined by corridors and courtyards and gardens and cloisters, and it had been standing for over six centuries. Built and renewed and abandoned and sacked and rebuilt, the palace was the beating heart of Mantova. It was most famous as the residence of the Gonzaga family, into which the young Isabella d'Este had been betrothed at the tender age of ten.

It was clear as soon as they started to explore that the palace was a maze. The passageways twisted and rooms flowed into more rooms, making it almost impossible to identify where they were. The free Visit Information leaflet did little to help, providing more of a bird's-eye view than an actual map of the complex. They knew that the room they needed was in the *Corte Vecchia*, but there was also the *Corte Nuova*, and the *Castello di San Giorgio* containing the famed *Camera degli Sposi*: in short, it was a full day's visit or more for any tourist.

In the Old Court were Isabella D'Este's old apartments. Somewhere near her studio was a tiny secret garden, adjacent to which they should find the room they sought containing the personal possessions she had left behind at her death. But it wasn't easy because there was so much to see. As a result of the confusing map and the beautiful things on display, they made their way somewhat slowly towards Isabella's *studiolo*.

"We're getting warm," Alessa said when they entered an anteroom and came upon a copy of Titian's portrait of Isabella. By now it was very familiar to them. They stood and admired it critically for a moment.

"Definitely a square purple jewel," Will said, pointing to the pearl brooch on Isabella's headdress. They looked at each other and shrugged, while Will realised that he had unconsciously picked up Alessa's habit of shrugging and echoed it back to her.

"I'll tell you one thing I found out last night about this portrait while you were booking plane tickets," Alessa said. "How old would you say she is?"

Will looked critically at the portrait.

"Quite young. No more than twenty."

"Exactly!" she said triumphantly. "Well it turns out she was sixty-two at the time!"

"Sixty-two?" Will repeated incredulously, looking at the pretty young woman in the picture. "In that case old Titian painted a *very* flattering portrait of her."

"Yes, and she was rather plain by all accounts," Alessa said. "So if he changed her age so dramatically, he might have changed the brooch as well."

The study and the accompanying *grotta* were somewhat disappointing for the lack of paintings, but impressive for their original ceilings. Much of Isabella's art collection seemed to have gone to the Hermitage in Saint Petersburg, or the Kunsthistorisches Museum in Vienna, including Titian's original portrait of her. Nevertheless, many of her everyday possessions remained in her home city. The *grotta* had marquetry panels concealing cupboards, made from briar-root, olive, maple, cherry, pear and durmast.

They had an almost Chinese quality about them and Will took pictures with his phone.

Beyond the *studiolo* and the *grotta* lay the Secret Garden, nestled between the tall buildings. It was a tiny oasis of green tranquillity amidst the cream stone walls, with low hedges, topiary and pots.

"Isabella built this garden in 1522," Will said, reading from an information plaque.

"Yes, but where is *our* little room?" Alessa said, wrinkling her brow. She walked over to the corner but it emerged into a cloister and a larger garden. She came back. "We must have overshot."

She returned towards the corridor leading to Isabella's apartments and he followed. They saw a small anteroom they had missed, leading to another room beyond. Its terracotta floor was marked by squares of light from the windows, patterned with octagon shapes cast by the leading in the window frames. One of the museum guides was sitting on a chair beside the inner room's door, typing into her mobile phone. There was a grey wooden barrier drawn across the doorway of the anteroom, and incongruously there was red and white *Polizia* tape criss-crossing the doorway behind the seated young guide.

"Is this the room with Isabella D'Este's personal possessions?" Alessa called to the young woman in Italian. She looked up from her phone.

"*Oggi la stanza è chiusa. C'è stato uno scasso,*" she said. She was about twenty and looked sulky, as if she had been given the most boring job in the world and knew it.

Will stared at her uncomprehending and Alessa frowned.

"That's weird, there's been a break-in and the room's closed," Alessa explained in an undertone to Will. "Let me talk to her, but go and loiter in that cloister for a bit so that she doesn't feel intimidated. You look as if you're about to yell at her."

"What?" Will began, but she gave him a warning look so he went back in the direction of the Secret Garden and the cloister beyond. As he left he heard Alessa begin a conversation in Italian with the young woman.

The sunlight in the adjacent garden beyond the cloister was brighter than it had been earlier, and it warmed Will's neck. He put on his sunglasses, then took them off and dusted them before putting them on again, screwing up his eyes against the bright glare of the afternoon light. The garden square within the cloister was another oasis, like the Secret Garden, but larger and manicured by a hidden platoon of gardeners. There were gravel paths surrounding a central lawn, framed by a perfectly straight box hedge. Round topiary bushes like huge beehives were dotted across the lawns, and young trees cast shadows on them. Cream stone walls with shuttered windows overlooked this tranquil scene.

It was cool in the cloister behind Will, so he stood at the edge of the garden, where it was warmer and very pleasant for March.

He still scarcely believed that they had come all this way only to find that a petty thief had ruined their mission. He leaned against the wall feeling anger and frustration, his arms folded. He looked back over his shoulder to the doorway into the Secret Garden, but there was no sign of Alessa. It was a further ten minutes before she emerged and came over to him, unaccustomedly gloomy of countenance.

"The girl was very bored so she was happy to gossip," she said. "I've got the whole story but you aren't going to believe it. *I* don't believe it."

"Try me."

"Okay, well her name is Sofia. She says that one of the cabinets in that room was broken into yesterday, so the room has been closed by the police while they investigate. And guess what was stolen from the glass cabinet."

He gave her an odd look.

"Go on, guess," she insisted grimly, and he shook his head once as if loosing a thought from it.

"It can't have been the brooch," he said. "No-one knows about it except us."

"It *was* the brooch," she said. "Sofia says it was a round orange sapphire brooch with a ring of pearls, which had belonged to the Marchioness Isabella and was found in her possessions when she died. It was *our* bloody brooch. Take a look at this."

She showed him three photographs on her phone; one of a room full of glass cases, one closer of a glass case cover on the floor, and one very close of the black velvet inside the opened case, showing neatly labelled items of jewellery, a handheld Venetian mirror, a silver comb and brush, a set of pearl-ended hair pins arranged like a fan, and a pair of black slippers which had survived the centuries least well. Each item was labelled with a white hand-written card in a spidery but perfectly legible hand.

"I thought you said the room was closed off?"

"It was, but I chatted Sofia up and she let me have a quick look."

She pointed to the space where the brooch had been, its label still in place. Will sat back in stunned silence.

"You're right, I don't believe it," he said at last, shaking his head. "We only started looking for it two days ago and now it's been nicked after sitting around for five hundred years. What's the chance of that?"

"No chance at all," she said. He took her hand and rubbed it.

"We must be the unluckiest people in the world."

She stood up abruptly, putting her hand on his shoulder.

"Let's get out of here," she said, looking down at him. "It's early, but I think I need a drink."

Thirty minutes later they had extricated themselves from the museum and were sitting glumly at a blue-painted table outside a small café. The waiter had just bought them a bottle of Lambrusco Mantovano. He opened it and offered the cork to Alessa, who sniffed it and smiled at him, saying something in Italian so that he nodded and smiled back, pleased with whatever she had said. All the tables around them were full and there was a hubbub of conversation. They leaned across the table when they were alone so they could talk in confidence.

"So what on earth's going on?" Will said as an opener.

She shrugged.

"I don't know," she said, clinking his glass perfunctorily and then taking a long draught of wine.

"Tell me exactly what the girl said again."

Alessa gathered her thoughts.

"Sofia told me that she didn't find the break in herself but she heard all about it from the other staff. One of her colleagues went into the room this morning for a routine check of the thermostats and humidifier. The first thing he saw was that the glass box had been lifted right off one of the displays and placed on the ground."

"Can they just do that? Aren't they locked?"

"She says they are but with a fairly feeble little lock which holds the glass on with a black wire strap. All you need is a pair of wire cutters to snip a strap at each corner, and you're in. That's what the perpetrator did."

"And the alarm never went off?"

"No alarm on the case, apparently."

"Great."

"Yeah. So the young man who found all this called his boss on the radio and she came along to see. When they looked at the display, they could see that there appeared to be just one thing missing. Our brooch was gone, and they knew it was that because the label was still there and the velvet had a couple of holes where it had been pinned."

"Which is peculiar, because if I robbed a case of jewels I wouldn't just pinch one thing, I'd sweep the whole lot into my bag of loot."

"Me too," she nodded.

"That girl Sofia certainly obliged you with all the details."

"Like I say, she's totally bored. I think she was glad to talk about it, and I was terribly nice. I told her I was a Ph.D. student because no-one's ever heard of a D.Phil., and it turned out she's a student too, reading Art History. Anyway, I just kept asking questions like I was nosy and she told me everything. But she did mention one particularly interesting fact. They've got CCTV of the theft and it's going to be on local TV tonight. We ought to watch it. The six o'clock news, she reckons."

Will glanced at his watch and saw it was after five.

"Well, we'd better drink up and get back then," he said.

They drained their glasses and Will left money pinned with the bill under the ashtray. Alessa took a photo of the receipt, determined to pay him back for her half when she could. Then they recorked the bottle and hurried back to the hotel, convening in Alessa's room.

Alessa took the remote and fiddled with the channels, using the information card to find the local channel they were looking for. When they were ready they sat down next to each other on the end of the double bed, staring at the screen.

"We ought to record it," Will said suddenly, getting out his phone, and she nodded, taking out hers. They started recording, one at normal speed and one in slow motion to grab as much of the scene as possible.

Will spoke no more than a smattering of Italian so Alessa translated a little as the news began. Then she leaned forward.

"This is it," she said excitedly. "Blah, blah, break in at the *Palazzo Ducale* yesterday. Discovered this morning by museum officials when they opened up." There was footage of the outside of the museum, which was already familiar to them because they had only been through that very entrance a few hours previously. "Blah, blah, priceless stuff, Studio of Isabella D'Este collection. No picture of the brooch that was stolen yet but oh my God, they're going to run the CCTV footage."

She stopped talking and they both held their phones steady. The screen filled with darkness apart from an incrementing timestamp on the bottom left of the screen, then the lights came on and a hooded figure moved into view, making for one of the glass cabinets.

Alessa was staring intently at the screen.

The figure fiddled at the corners of the glass case and then lifted the top up and off, placing it on the floor.

"Ha," Alessa said frowning, "Lucas has got a coat like that. I wonder if we can trace who makes them."

The hooded figure leaned over the opened case, unhooked the brooch and stowed it away, then moved back out of the frame and was gone. It took only half a minute from start to finish. The news reader came back on, said a few words with a very serious face, and then an advert break started, so they stopped recording and sat back, looking at each other.

"That was weird," Alessa said.

"What?" he said, but she shook her head absently.

"Body language. Let's play it back again."

They both watched the video on Will's phone, which was poor quality because he had been taking in the whole TV screen.

"Very weird," Alessa said.

"What?" Will said again, laughing despite the seriousness of the moment. He got two glasses from the minibar and poured them more wine.

"I don't want to say because it sounds too stupid," Alessa said.

She picked up her own phone and played the video again, this time in slo-mo. She used the slider to skid through the video until the thief leaned over the cabinet, then stopped it.

"There," she said, her voice husky. She took a screen photo and carefully zoomed in on Isabella D'Este's Venetian hand mirror, in which the face of the thief could now be seen, framed by the hood.

Will frowned at the image and tilted his head at it, his lips pursed.

"Is that…?"

"Yes it is," she spat, like a volcano about to erupt. "My beloved fiancé. It is Lucas!"

17

How many times for having too much hope,
Since first I found myself a slave of Love,
A flood have I then shed of bitter tears.

LORENZO DE' MEDICI, Lyrics XVII Sestina I

25th March 1486, via Nuova, Florence

Botticelli awoke from an erotic dream about Semiramide. He was bathed in sweat and twisted up in the bedclothes. The details of the dream were gone but he was left with a fleeting echo of her; hair unbraided, legs straddling his body, riding him. Half-awake he let his imagination fly, and her nipples were brushing his lips as he arched his back and slid into her. He caressed her body like a brush on a living canvas, and drank in her quizzical smile and the touch of her hair on his face.

But to his waking frustration, her face somehow eluded him, and he lay still for a moment, trying to capture it. She was beautiful, but so much more. She was clever, learned, witty and strong-willed. All this essence was reflected in her face. She knew what she wanted and her self-assurance made her special. He flung aside the bedclothes in a swift movement and leapt out of the bed as if suddenly it had become too hot to contain him. Little ripples crossed his skin and he shivered in the darkness as he stood motionless for a moment, his breath uneven, his heart thumping. Then he ran lightly down the stairs and strode into his studio, still breathing deeply. He felt as if the air might crackle and lightning set the heavens aflame. He stood mercurial, in his element.

Moonlight shafted in and cast silver on the studio walls. There was a smell of wax from the snuffed-out candles. He found what he was looking for in the back storeroom – the second panel, matching his Mars and Venus painting exactly in size. It had been intended for an altar diptych but had never been used. He carried the panel into the main workshop and set it up in the place where he worked, looking at it. After a minute or so he rotated the panel so that it was standing on end. Then he lit an oil lamp, picked up red chalk and began to execute swift, sure strokes on the smooth white surface.

He would find her face.

The painting took him forty-three nights.

In the days he was tired and short-tempered, but something drove him on, and on the sixth of December it was finished. After each session he carried the panel back into the storeroom and put it in a dark corner, covered with an old cloth so that none of the young apprentices ever saw it. He had used egg tempera so it dried fast after each session.

He left the painting for a few days after it was finished, and then one night he awoke again after *that* dream. He went down to the storeroom, brought out the shrouded picture and lit two lamps, one on either side of it. Then with a flourish he twitched off the muslin shroud and stood staring at what he had wrought.

He had her face now; he had all of her.

She stood almost naked, covered only in places by a translucent veil of gauze. She faced the left side of the picture, her face angled up and out with her head thrown back, her mouth a little open and the tip of her tongue just glimpsed. It was unmistakably Semiramide. The arm furthest from the viewer was raised, her hand tangled in her unbraided hair. Her breasts were full and nipples erect, and between them hung a thin gold chain bearing the pearl and sapphire brooch she had worn for the Mars and Venus sittings. Beneath her breasts were the subtle curves of four ribs, then her navel, beneath which her skin blended into a perfect mons Venus. Her nearest arm was hooked backwards over the shoulder of the figure behind her – *his* shoulder, for he had painted himself pressed against her back, his bare chest exposed, one hand curving around from behind to her navel, and the other resting on her hip, his fingers curled possessively around her inner thigh. His own face looked out of the picture, just as deliberately insolent as he had painted himself in his Adoration of the Magi a decade before. The background was painted in earthy brown *terra d'ombra bruciata* and the skin faded into dark at the edges, so that both figures in the painting seemed to glow.

The painter and his muse, he thought. He hated what he had done, and he loved it.

It was on the tenth night after the painting was finished that he was caught.

Biagio sat with his friend in a local hostelry. He was a blunt-faced young man who could not have looked less like an artist if he tried. He looked like a fulling-mill worker or perhaps a carter; thick-necked and bulky, with a small chin and wide jowls that made him seem square-headed. His fingers had the thickness of sausages and he habitually wore a dark apron. It was only the smears of colour on the apron that betrayed his trade. He was short and wide and had an air of slight astonishment about him, but he was also friendly, disarming and good-natured. When the Master and the other apprentices had tricked him by sticking paper hoods on his painting of angels, he had first been silent in supernatural awe, but when he realised the trick, he had laughed with such infectious delight that they all ended up convulsed in fits together. No-one could dislike Biagio.

With him at a small table beside the bar sat his best friend Tommaso, who was a thin, long-haired, intelligent youth with pointed features and a beard and moustache that gave him a Christ-like visage. He had an intense expression which could quickly break into a smile. Girls found him intriguing. Of the two he was the cleverer one, but Biagio could sometimes surprise him with observations about people that he had not himself perceived, and Biagio's sausage-like fingers belied his skill with a brush.

The two young men were each drinking ale, and Saltarelli had recognised one of them as apprentices in Botticelli's workshop when they had first come into the hostelry. Saltarelli himself was seated in a shadowy corner by the dark window, with a cup of red wine in front of him. They had arrived after him and they had not noticed him, for why should they? He had only attended the workshop for a couple of days. Biagio might remember him, for the apprentice had as good as thrown him out when the Master had been displeased with him, but Biagio's face was turned away from him, so he would need to crane his neck around to spot the figure in the shadows. The man with Biagio would not know him.

Saltarelli did not have the classical round-featured Greek looks of a painter's model. He was clean-shaven and had unusually pale skin and a high forehead, but his hair was already thinning and his face seemed too narrow. He was thin lipped and his mouth seemed always set in a sardonic smile. His chin was pointed and bore a dark stubble that would quickly become a beard had he not shaved every day. His cheekbones were high and his ears small. His expression could be most likened to one of cunning. Women were discomfited by him, for somehow they perceived his contempt for them.

As soon as Saltarelli saw Biagio he was reminded of his humiliation by Maestro Botticelli – a man who had disdained his skills at modelling and then thrown him out. He would very much like to hurt Botticelli, to punish him for the wrong he had done, but he didn't know how. As he sat there in the gloom and men grew steadily drunk around him, it occurred to him that

Botticelli's business was painting, and he could most hurt the pompous fool in his purse. He imagined breaking into the workshop and slashing the paintings with the wickedly sharp dagger that he kept in his sleeve sheath; throwing ink on the pristine panels; smudging wet oil paintings with a cloth.

Revenge would be sweet.

He watched Biagio and his companion, who were settling in with a second ale apiece. The other man's name was 'Tommaso': he knew this because a young woman had called out to the man in recognition and had then sat in his lap for several minutes like a little whore. Saltarelli's thoughts flowed on. He knew Biagio slept at the workshop, in the side room with small beds where all the apprentices slept, for he had slept in there himself for one night. There had been loud snoring from two of the young men, and another had been so tall in stature that his feet had stuck out beyond the bottom of his bed.

Saltarelli contemplated Biagio and Tommaso across the room from him. A different young woman had sat down on the stool beside Tommaso, and she was engaging him in conversation while he gave her an interested look. Biagio was looking down at his drink, sheepish and a little embarrassed, as if he didn't know what to do with himself. On the night Saltarelli had slept at the workshop, he had seen Biagio go out for the evening with two others, and he remembered that they had left the door unlocked until their return. Perhaps it was unlocked now? After a moment's more contemplation, Saltarelli picked up his cup and drained it, then shuffled his way out through the crowd of revellers with his face averted from the two young men.

The May evening had cooled after a hot day so he pulled his cloak about himself, turning his face from the candlelit windows of the hostelry, hearing the ribald laughter from inside. He set off walking swiftly. Via Nuova wasn't far and he arrived in a few minutes. There was no-one in the street but an orange cat, who glared at him for making such a lot of noise when there was rat-catching to be done. Saltarelli looked up and down furtively, then listened at the door to Botticelli's workshop. There was no sound. He tried the latch and sure enough the door swung open easily, making no noise. His heart was beating wildly. It was dark inside but for a single candle. The key was in the lock on the inside, and there was a hefty wooden bar that would be slotted into iron brackets, but which now stood on its end beside the door. He closed the door noiselessly behind him and looked for a hiding place. On the table beside the candle a kind housekeeper had left half a loaf of bread and a hunk of cheese. He was hungry and his mouth watered at the sight but he didn't touch the food. Instead he slunk into the darkened cloakroom and buried himself in a corner, concealing himself behind boxes which bore a stack of aprons and folded cloths. He pulled a dark cloth towards him, shrank into the shadows behind it, and waited. There was no light and he was completely invisible.

After an hour he heard Biagio and Tommaso return, locking the door behind them and barring it. They went rather noisily to bed but Saltarelli didn't move. He wondered where the Master himself slept. Upstairs, perhaps? He'd like to find him and stick him with the sleeve dagger, but he wasn't foolhardy enough for that. He could hear the drone of distant snores that were familiar from the night he had stayed in the workshop.

He rested his head back against the wall and after a short while he fell asleep himself. He awoke sometime later with a start, fearful and having no idea of the time except for the feeling that it was far from dawn. He pushed off the cloth and stood up, listening for any sound. The cracking of his own knees sounded unnaturally loud. What should he do? He didn't feel at all brave now that he was here. He decided he would exact some damage without making noise and then leave quietly. They would have to clean up the mess and start the work again. They would be late with their commissions and their clients would be displeased. Biagio might be dismissed for leaving the door unlocked and it would serve him right for manhandling Saltarelli.

Saltarelli entered the main workshop like a ghost. It was lit by silver moonlight. He looked around for a tool to do damage, but saw none. He withdrew his own knife, which was his pride and joy with its keen iron blade and ivory handle. It had been a gift to him from a nobleman at the court. He lifted a cloth covering a large canvas painting and saw a half-finished Annunciation, in which the Archangel Gabriel knelt before the Virgin Mary, about to tell her that soon she would become the mother of Christ. He raised his knife to cut the canvas but then froze, suddenly afraid, with the point of the blade an inch from the painted surface. He had seen the guttering light of candles in the far storeroom. Candles would not be left alight for fear of fire, yet surely no-one was up at this hour.

It occurred to him that the main entrance door was locked and barred, preventing a quick exit. He returned to the door swiftly and felt for the locking bar in the near darkness, lifting it out of its brackets with hardly a sound. With great care he placed it to one side. Then he twisted the key in the lock and opened the door a crack. With an enormous effort he avoided the impulse to make his escape, for if he left now he would have achieved nothing.

Leaving the door ajar he padded back into the workshop and moved wraithlike through it, taking care not to collide with anything in the shadows, heading for the guttering light at the back. He reached the far door and peered slowly and carefully around the frame.

Maestro Botticelli stood with his back to the door, his nightclothes pooled around his feet. He was standing stock still in front of a painting, staring at it. Saltarelli looked at the painting and frowned, but then his mouth fell open as he realised what he was looking at. It was an erotic painting of Botticelli with a woman – both figures all but naked – and the woman was Semiramide de' Medici, wife of Lorenzo. Saltarelli almost laughed out loud and clutched his mouth, stifling any sound. The great Maestro had painted the wife of a Medici *in flagrante* with himself. Wait until her husband heard of this! It was more precious than any damage Saltarelli might inflict on the paintings in the workshop. Saltarelli couldn't take his eyes off the scene. He clutched the door for a better look but to his horror it moved and creaked loudly. Botticelli started guiltily at the noise and turned. Saltarelli threw himself back and too late remembered the series of brush-filled jugs behind him. He crashed into them and they cascaded in all directions. He slipped down onto one knee and his knife flew from his hand, then he heard Botticelli cry out a challenge in a hoarse voice. The man was almost upon him but there was still a chance he hadn't seen him in the gloom. Saltarelli took to his heels and ran, barging his way through the tables and easels, tugging loose objects off surfaces and hurling them behind him. He reached the main door, snatched it open and flung himself through it. Then he surrendered to the instinct of flight and ran as if all the demons of hell were behind him. He didn't stop running until he had four streets and many twists and turns between him and the workshop. Then he doubled over gasping. But as he slowly caught his breath he began to chuckle, like a ticking sound under his breath.

He would make the pompous Maestro suffer now.

Botticelli was terrified. He had been in the middle of drinking in the sight of his love when someone had interrupted him. At first he had imagined it must be an apprentice or one of his brother's household, but then he realised it was an intruder. He had seized up his nightclothes and run naked into the workshop in time to see the man ploughing a path through the easels to the front door. He hadn't been able to identify the perpetrator. He stood and stared helplessly, then tugged on his nightclothes in a panic. Tears began to run down his cheeks as he contemplated his predicament. Had the man seen the painting? To paint himself naked with a Medici wife was a sure path to the hangman's noose. He looked at the sleeping quarters of the apprentices but the snoring continued unabated. He went to the door and peered out nervously, but there was no sign of the intruder. He locked and barred the door, angry that it had been open, then went back to the storeroom and covered his secret painting with a muslin cloth. He felt utterly miserable. The painting, rather than being his private contemplation, had become a tether leading him to the gallows. He had to get rid of it, but where? He could not bring himself to destroy it. It was his love for Semiramide personified, in the only way that he could ever have her, and now he felt debased, for someone else had stolen his most private thoughts.

All at once a solution came into his mind. He went to his bedchamber and dressed quickly, putting on dark clothes and a hooded cloak. Then he went to the storeroom, wrapped the painting up thoroughly and tied the muslin cloth in place with black ribbon. It was the middle of the night when he opened the front door, and the sky was black with stars. He saw no movement apart from a ginger cat who eyed him quizzically. The panel was bulky under his arm but bearable. He peered up and down the street but all was quiet, so he set off in the direction of the river. He was back in fifteen minutes, breathing a sigh of relief. When he had once more locked and barred the door behind him, he began for the first time to feel some sense of relief and his beating heart finally began to calm.

It was dawn and Jacopo Saltarelli sat in his room at the small desk, but he wasn't tired. He took down a piece of his best paper, then used a dagger as a penknife to sharpen a new quill. He took out a pot of ink and uncorked it, then dipped the quill, shook off the excess ink, and began to write the address with a steady hand:

Lorenzo di Pierfrancesco dei' Medici, on a private matter concerning an artist.
For delivery by the Bearer.

He paused for a moment and composed the letter in his mind's eye, then began to write steadily.

It is my sad duty to inform you of the obscenity that I have just witnessed in the workshop of Maestro Botticelli. It involves the mother of your children...

Interlude

She heavily raised her sloe-black eyes
And murmured back in softest wise,
"One more thing and the charms you prize
Are yours henceforth for aye."

THOMAS HARDY, The Sacrilege

March, early morning Verona to Venice Express

Lucas was wondering how he had ever got himself into this. It was Rachel, of course, Rachel from start to finish. She was studying her phone now on the seat opposite, and he watched her for a few minutes, unable to believe that she was so cheerful. She had even found a moment to renew her lipstick. Now and then she would look up and offer him that smile, full of promise. He felt very tired from being up all night. He closed his eyes and shook his head in dismay, then guiltily opened them to see if she had noticed. She had not. She was engrossed in something on her phone. He closed his eyes again and went back through how he had arrived here.

It had begun in Oxford, in the assembly room after the lecture from that artist fellow in St. Ebbe's. Rachel had come up to him and given him an intense, sardonic stare and asked him if he was with the college. He had introduced himself and she had admired the fact that he was a doctor and a lecturer. She had asked him if he could find her a glass of red wine. When he had returned with two glasses, she had moved into a quiet corner and he had gone over to join her.

From the very start she had flirted with him and he had enjoyed the sensation. She had arched eyebrows which gave her a slightly quizzical look, full red lips and a gold ring in her left nostril. Her hair was mid-brown and combed into an untidy bob which had a single blonde streak at the front. Somehow she seemed to dominate the conversation, directing it where she wanted, but he liked that too. She had wanted to know if he were familiar with the artist who had just delivered the lecture about forgery, and he had confessed that he was not. She had told him her name was Rachel Blake and that she was a documentary film maker. She had said she was looking for a new story, and she had leaned in conspiratorially as she told him this, so that he had been offered a view of a black brassiere through the loose neck of her cotton blouse. For a moment her breath had been hot on his ear, and he had unexpectedly felt his groin tingle at this sudden intimacy. Then she'd leaned away again and it was as if she were playing him, like a fisherman tiring out a big fish on a line. They had carried on talking. Lucas knew some filmmakers at Oxford Brookes University, and it turned out that she knew them too. She had invited him to a party later that evening, but he had said he could not because he was meeting his fiancée for a drink.

"No," she had said matter-of-factly. "Come with me. Tell her you have a meeting."

He remembered just how she had smiled as she had said this, and she had then told him where and when to meet her. Somehow he had found himself unable to refuse, as if she had already bewitched him. He'd had a row with Alessa in the Blenheim and then he'd gone after Rachel, telling Alessa that he had forgotten that he had to meet someone about his research, but refusing to go into details, and behaving as if she were jealous when she objected. At the party, Rachel had questioned him for hours regarding all aspects of university life, and later in the bathroom she had locked the door and pushed him down onto his knees with her hands on his shoulders. She had raised her skirt to her waist and he had found that she was not wearing any knickers. She had twisted her fingers into his hair and had pulled his face into the cleft of her legs, grinding his face against her sex so that her delightful scent filled his nostrils. Then with a giggle she had stepped back, dropped her skirt and flounced out of the bathroom, leaving him on his knees, half-erect and dumbfounded. When he had recovered himself and stumbled out to look for her, she had left the party. The hostess had grinned as if she were somehow complicit. She had handed him Rachel's business card, but though he had immediately called her mobile number, he had got only voicemail that night.

She had kept him waiting but the next day she'd finally answered her phone, and after that they'd enjoyed a number of clandestine meetings, some in his and Alessa's own bed, during which he had become steadily more obsessed with her. He would do anything to please her. She called him her little boy and would allow him sexual intimacies, but never permitted him the complete act of making love to her.

Alessa had been distracted with that artist fellow and at first Lucas had been jealous until he realised that it perfectly suited his own need to be with

Rachel. When he had told Rachel about the impending conference in Venice, she had said that he must take her as well, as he had half-known that she would. So he had bought her a ticket, and she had promised him that in return he could have all of her when they were in Venice.

That's why he had been unable to sleep on the night before his flight, when Alessa had got back late from the artist's studio in Cambridge. He imagined that she must be sleeping with – what was his name? – Will. But Lucas didn't care anymore. All he could think about was Rachel.

On that fateful night he had lain awake while pretending to sleep. Alessa had got up, but then returned and fallen into an exhausted sleep, which he knew was genuine by the sound of her breathing. He had risen and gone into the other room, thinking that a Scotch might settle his nerves and help him follow her example. But then he had seen her phone next to the computer and keyed in her PIN on impulse. He had read her text to the artist: *'Will, I think I found the brooch! Take a look. I'm sure it's the one that Semiramide was referring to, and it could prove she was his muse. We absolutely have to find it and examine it! It's in a Museum in Mantova. It was the one owned by Isabella d'Este so I don't know why Titian painted it wrong. Alessa xx'*

He had felt vindicated by the kisses that she had added to her message. He'd known Alessa must be on intimate terms with the artist. It made him feel better that he and Alessa were both cheating, but unreasonably angry that he was being cheated on. He had copied Alessa's message to his own phone and sent it to Rachel, knowing that she would be intrigued and wanting to please her.

The message had made an impact on Rachel. At the airport she had questioned him about all the details and then linked it to the story of Botticelli's muse which had come out at old Humphrey Cooper's wake. That had been clever: he had forgotten about that and yet Rachel had remembered it immediately and made the connection.

Then the difficulty had begun. Rachel had discovered that Mantova was not far from Venice; only two or three hours away by train. To his immense horror she had insisted that they must go and look at the brooch first, before Alessa and the artist fellow got there. He had imagined he would be enjoying Rachel's carnal delights while his conference droned on about art education in the first-floor ballroom, but instead he had found himself chasing after a brooch which he knew nothing about, following Rachel's instinct that it would turn into a good story. When he had continued to resist prior to their departure, she had pushed him down onto the bed and loosened his trousers, and he could still remember every delicious moment of what had come next. She had promised him that on their return she would make it a night to remember. It had been enough to make him agree to go.

It had got worse once they'd found the brooch. They'd arrived with only an hour to go before the museum closed, and only located the brooch in its glass case just before closing time. Before they had entered the room, Rachel had pulled up the hood of his coat, then held his ears and kissed him, telling him that they were on a secret mission and mustn't be seen by any cameras. Confused but bowled over by her, he had gone along with it. And then once they had found the brooch she had dropped another bombshell – that he should stay behind once the museum closed, and steal the brooch so that they could examine it and see what all the fuss was about. They could post it back, she had said, so it wouldn't really be stealing.

Somehow he had found himself concealed in a cramped utility cupboard, standing in near darkness amidst bleach-smelling mops, while Rachel had left the museum with the other tourists. Clutched in his sweaty hand was a pair of nail clippers that Rachel had given him. While examining the brooch in the glass cabinet, she had discretely used the clippers to snip through the black strap of one of the locks, so he had no excuse that the cabinet would be locked and impenetrable. It was almost as if she had planned that he should steal the brooch all along.

He had felt very scared, but he didn't want to let Rachel down on this one last request, so he waited quite some time in the darkness, and eventually stumbled out into the half-lighted room, making sure that his hood was up as she had instructed. There was no-one about and the museum was silent. Each snip of the remaining three cabinet locks had sounded like a gunshot, but no-one had come to investigate, and he had lifted the top off the cabinet and grabbed the brooch, wrapping it into his handkerchief where it nestled right now in his jacket pocket. He had escaped through a window and dropped a few feet into an outside garden courtyard, from which he had been able to walk into the main piazza. His fear had disappeared and become replaced with euphoria. Rachel had met him and kissed him at the corner of the square and they had walked briskly through the streets back to the station, where they had made their escape on the first train out in the morning to Verona and thence to Venice.

He put his hand into his pocket now, as he sat opposite Rachel on the express train and the fields and hedgerows sped by outside the windows. The rocking motion of the train was making him feel very sleepy. He felt the lump of the brooch in its handkerchief wrapping, and felt a mad mixture of fear and pride that he had done what she had asked. She looked up again and smiled at him, and he smiled back, his thoughts drifting in delightful anticipation to their bed in the Venetian hotel, and what awaited him there under her expert fingers. It had been worth it.

18

Show me a liar, and I will show thee a thief.

GEORGE HERBERT, Jacula Prudentum (1651)

March, Mantova

Will was sitting on the end of Alessa's bed wondering what to do. The local news had finished and she had abruptly disappeared into her bathroom about twenty minutes ago. She didn't come out so after a few more minutes he got up to leave, tapping on the bathroom door on his way out.

"Alessa?" he said. "Are you OK?"

"Not really," came her voice through the door.

"Right. Well, I'll be in my room, so if you want to talk about anything then come and knock."

She didn't answer and he left her room and went back to his own. He was totally mystified about the sudden unexpected appearance of her boyfriend in the museum video excerpt. He couldn't for the life of him think how it had come to be. He opened his minibar, extracted a miniature of Scotch and poured it into the tumbler provided. His room had no balcony but there was a wide shuttered window and he opened the shutters and looked out. It was dark now and via Accademia was uninspiring; no tables out and just a slow-moving car or two. He made a sudden decision to go back to the pretty little café on the corner of Piazza Sordello where they had drunk wine after they had discovered that the brooch had been stolen. He messaged where he would be to Alessa, and then picked up his old brown bowler hat, which in a crazy moment he had decided to bring with him. It was the hat he liked to wear when he went out for a drink. It made him look a little ridiculous but he didn't mind that. He put his jacket back on and wrapped a scarf tightly around his neck, for though it was Italy it was only March and it was cool. Just as he was about to leave the room he remembered the Scotch, so he drained the glass, feeling the golden liquid burn his throat as it went down. Then he left, twisting the old-fashioned key on the lock, and was just passing Alessa's room when her door opened abruptly and she stood there looking at him. Her face was streaked with tears.

"I heard your door," she said. "Wait for me downstairs for five minutes."

She closed her door without waiting for his reply and he did as she had asked. He had a sudden tender memory of the first time he had properly met her, in the Blenheim pub in Oxford after she had argued with Lucas. She'd had the same red-rimmed eyes then, and had gone to the Ladies to clean up.

He handed in his key to reception and sat in an armchair to wait. She took fifteen minutes rather than five, but she had cleaned up and looked beautiful. She wore a red woollen fleece which he had last seen in Devon when they had visited Frederick Pocock. She was still distracted and forgot to hand in her key until he touched her arm and pointed to the reception desk. Then they left the hotel and walked around the corner, passing underneath the arch into the piazza.

"I want to kill Lucas slowly," she said matter-of-factly, and then flashed him a weak smile. "But I need something to eat first."

They were hungry and located a small restaurant that smelled good and had people in it. There were three tables outside and a couple occupied one of them, but Alessa shivered.

"Let's be warm," she said, so they went inside. It was almost exactly eight as they sat down. The first ten minutes were occupied with ordering food and a bottle of Rosso Saline from Lake Garda, but then the wine came almost immediately so they had to wait for it to be poured. When the waitress had departed they looked at each other for a long moment, and then held up their glasses and clinked.

As she drank he realised that she was left-handed. "No engagement ring any longer," he observed, his heart doing a private little dance.

She smiled and grimaced at the same time – a twisted-lips smile.

"It's in my purse," she said. "I'm going to give it back to him. While I was in the bathroom I came to the conclusion that he's an absolute liar, and I don't want to marry a liar."

Will didn't know what to say.

At last he said, "How on earth could he even have *known* about the brooch?"

"I thought about that," she said, "and there is a way. We figured out the brooch on Thursday night, and I texted you. He left the next morning for his conference in Venice, so he must have read my phone text that I sent you."

Will considered this.

"The timing makes sense, except that I can't think *why* he would do it.

Could he even have got hold of your phone?"

"Absolutely. It was lying on the table next to my computer after I found the brooch picture. We know each other's PINs so he could just have woken up the phone while I was asleep and had a look."

"But why would he?"

"Who knows? Perhaps he was jealous of you and being nosy. But that's the other thing I've been thinking about. I think he's got another woman."

He stared at her.

"Then he must be insane," he said.

She smiled for the first time and toasted him.

"Thank you. The thing was that he didn't seem to mind me going off with you all the time and it was out of character. I was pleasantly surprised as he's usually quite jealous."

"Well, that doesn't mean he's got someone else."

"No, but the other day in his flat I noticed the strangest thing. We were in bed and I turned over to go to sleep and the pillow smelled of perfume. But it wasn't *my* perfume. I wear *Prada Tendre* and it's quite distinctive. This wasn't it."

"What did you do?"

"I didn't do anything," she admitted. "I suppose I convinced myself that I must be imagining it. It was just a smell, so it would have been hard to make a big deal out of it. On reflection, I think I chickened out of making a fuss."

He sipped some wine and looked at her. He wanted to believe that she was right, because he wanted Lucas to be gone and there to be no chance of him coming back, but he was cautious. He didn't want to rush to any conclusion and then have her forgive Lucas and go back to him.

"There's another thing I forgot to mention," she said. "Remember Sofia in the Palazzo Ducale? The security girl? She said they had this same guy – Lucas, as we now know – on a different security camera earlier in the afternoon, but they still couldn't see his face as it was turned away. They matched him up because of the coat, but here's the important bit I forgot to mention because it didn't seem important at the time. Sofia said he was with a *woman.*"

"Ha," Will said. "It starts to sound like too much of a coincidence."

Olives and cheese and salami arrived at their table on a wooden platter, and they tucked in, realising they were both very hungry. There was some thinly sliced pickled onion in a little pot, sweet and purple, which melted in the mouth.

"Any idea what this woman looked like?" Will said when they had demolished half the platter.

"Sofia didn't say," Alessa said. "But think about what we now know. We know his bed smelled of another woman's perfume. We know that he has come to Venice, ostensibly for a conference about art education, and that he told me I couldn't come because partners weren't invited. We know someone wearing his coat was seen on camera with a woman, and that he then stole the brooch that he must have read about in my text to you."

"What I still don't understand is why he would steal the brooch," Will mused. "It's as if he's following the same story as us, but he can't be, because he doesn't know anything about it."

"I don't know either," she said frowning. "That's the peculiar part. Lucas is self-centred but not a thief. It's completely out of character. I wonder if his dad put him up to it. Milton's an evil old sod."

"I did talk to his old man," Will said with feeling, remembering the discussion about the Hilary Term after his presentation at St. Ebbe's. "Milton Flynn certainly struck me as pompous, but why would he care about a brooch?"

"Only that Milton is an academic too and was probably interested in the idea of Botticelli having a different muse. When my text message connected the brooch to the muse, I imagine he'd be interested. Remember the muse story came out at papà's wake, and both Lucas and his dad were there. Maybe Milton was interested enough to ask his son to find out anything he could."

"Perhaps," Will said, "but the timing is tight, and there's another possibility. Maybe this mysterious woman persuaded him to do it. If you think about it, we would have been well and truly stuck if the museum had ignored your scholarship and refused to let you examine the brooch. Maybe they just decided to pinch it."

She rocked her head, weighing options.

"Could be," she agreed. "They may have thought there was no way to examine the brooch unless they could actually get hold of it. You wouldn't learn anything from peering at it through the glass."

"That makes sense. So he goes to the conference and brings the woman, whoever she is, for a bit of–."

He stopped awkwardly.

"A bit of the other," Alessa said grimly. "He leaves me behind and brings this other girl here to fuck her preety little brains out."

He smiled at her pronunciation and she picked up the bottle and refilled their glasses.

"And then," Will said, warming to his theme, "just before he leaves England he gets the message about the brooch and he tells mystery woman. And they decide to go and check out the brooch."

He rubbed his lower lip.

"Except they're in Venice," he finished. "Isn't that miles away?"

She grimaced and fished her phone out of her bag.

"Actually it's not all that far," she said. "I reckon you could come by train like we did. Let me look."

She busied herself while the waitress came and removed the empty platter. Alessa looked up after a minute or two.

"Venice to Verona is about an hour, and Verona to here took us about an hour. Or you can go via Monselice. I think they could have come by train, done the deed and gone back to Venice in a day, no problem."

The waitress brought their next dishes: pumpkin tortellini for Alessa and polenta with fish for Will. For a few minutes they said little and tucked in.

"So he's probably back in Venice with our brooch," Will went on after a while, and grinned suddenly. "Maybe we should steal it back. He wouldn't expect that."

She looked at him, her eyes sparkling.

"That's a crazy idea!" she said. "But I love it!"

Will looked suddenly embarrassed: he still needed to tell Alessa about his chequered history, and she might get up and walk away. He took a deep breath.

"There's something I haven't told you," he began awkwardly. "I was convicted for forgery and went to prison for a short while. I didn't commit the forgery, by the way, but no-one ever believes me. I only mention it now because prison is a great place to learn how to steal things."

"I already know that," Alessa said, casting him a slow look over the top of her glass which was unquestionably flirtatious. "I checked up on you and there was this article on the internet about your shady past. I'm not sure I should even be talking to you."

"But you do need a burglar," Will pointed out, wiggling his eyebrows at her. "Do you happen to know where he's staying?"

"Funnily enough," she said dryly, "he usually tells me but this time he 'forgot'. I only know that he's somewhere in Venice, and there are hundreds of hotels there."

"You said it was something to do with art education. Do you know anybody else that's going?"

Alessa frowned in thought.

"Actually I do. His friend Ralph was going, and I go running with Ralph's wife sometimes. I have her number."

Alessa mentioning running reminded Will that he had resolved to do the same. He hadn't done well so far. He didn't even have the fancy shoes.

She opened her phone contacts, oblivious to his sudden private guilt, and searched for a name.

"Right here!" she said triumphantly. "And it's only 7:30 in England. Hold on."

She called the number and was about to hang up when her friend answered. The conversation carried on for several minutes.

"Sorry," she said when she had hung up. "I had to chat and just mention it at the end so it didn't look odd. He's staying in the Hotel Grande di Visconti, and it's a weekend conference on art history in education. So he ought to be out of the room during the day tomorrow."

Alessa searched for the hotel name and then held up her phone to show him.

"Quite a big place, and located on a canal. It says it's ten minutes' walk from St. Mark's Square."

"Well it's too late to go tonight," Will said. "But we could go first thing in the morning and case the joint."

The morning didn't start well. They arrived at Mantova railway station at half-past five in the morning in order to catch the 5:40 to Venice, and then realised that it was a Sunday. The first train didn't leave for an hour.

"Let's go and find some coffee," Will said, rubbing sleep out of his eyes.

"We won't find any," Alessa said. "It's Sunday, remember? All sensible Italian people are still in bed."

They sat in the waiting room and found they had a good phone signal, so they looked up the Art History in Education conference and found it advertised online, with a reference to the location as the Grande di Visconti. Alessa phoned the hotel.

"I've just arrived at the airport and I'm running late," she explained in Italian. "I'm attending the conference on Art History. Is it taking place at the hotel?"

There was a pause while the man asked her to wait because he was night security and the day reception didn't start for another half an hour.

"Yes madam, it will be located in the Filippo Maria Conference Room on our first floor. But you don't need to worry, it only starts at nine, so you have plenty of time to get from Marco Polo. When you arrive you can go straight up the stairs and the registration table will be on your left."

She thanked him and disconnected, then updated Will.

"So we know where he'll be," she said. "But there's this bloody fucking woman to think of, if she really is with him."

He grinned at her.

"Yes, so we'll have to call to make sure neither of them is in the room. And you're going to have to keep out of sight because if you see her you might kill her, and if he sees *you* then the cat's out of the bag."

"True, but he knows what you look like as well."

"He's only ever met me once, but you're right. I don't know what to do about that right now, but it might be the least of our problems."

"Like how the hell are we going to get into his room?" Alessa said.

Will looked sheepish.

"I did once spend an entire afternoon chatting to a guy who was a lock expert," he said.

"What kind of a lock expert?" she asked with narrowed eyes.

"Rather a special kind," Will admitted. "He didn't use keys."

She giggled.

"So I've got a few ideas," he went on, "but it depends what kind of room locks it's got. You'd be surprised what you can do with a plasticised Fast

Food Menu. Apparently it's got just the right amount of stiffness to stick in the door jamb and pop the latch."

"What if it's got super-secure locks and we can't get in?"

"I was thinking of abseiling off the roof and then cutting a large circular hole in his window with a laser. That's what they do in the movies."

She giggled again.

"Failing that we need a spare key. Really what we need is his passport to flash at the front desk, but then I'd have to get a haircut and a new face to go with it."

"Sounds complicated," she said, frowning. She took out her purse and hunted in it, coming up with a business card. "Would this be any good? He gave it to me when we first met, and I kept it."

He took it from her and found it was Lucas Flynn's business card.

"It might," he said, but then looked serious.

"There's a snag, though."

"They'd say, 'Room Number, Signor Flynn?' and you'd not know it and then they'd call the *Polizia*."

"Yeah, that's the snag. I could hang around outside his room in a towel and then call reception and say I locked myself out. That's a winner, apparently, but my friend told me it's not great for a fast getaway, legging it down the road barefoot in a towel."

"You're not inspiring me with confidence," she said. And there's the snag again, as well."

"Yep, which room to hang around outside."

They pondered for a while in glum silence. The waiting room in Mantova railway station was warm and completely quiet. No-one else was stupid enough to arrive this early for the first train connecting to Venezia via Monselice. With some coffee it would have been tolerable, but there was none.

"I suppose I could ring him up and chat to him," Alessa said. "And then ask him what room he's in."

"Why would you do that, though? Ask him his room number, I mean?"

"I have no idea," she sighed.

"Does he speak Italian?" Will said suddenly.

She looked at him.

"No. Just a bit of French. Languages aren't his strong point, actually. He says everyone should just speak English."

Will looked at his watch and saw that it was just turned six.

"He's probably still in his room," he said. "Let me try something. What's the number of the hotel again?"

She gave it to him and he called the hotel. This time a female voice answered. Evidently she'd just started her shift."

"Good morning," Will said briskly. "Do you speak English?"

"Of course, sir," she said. "How can I help?"

"I'm sorry to call so early, but could you please put me through to my son's room? He's staying at your hotel, Doctor Lucas Flynn. He's expecting my call. I'm afraid I don't know the room number."

"Not a problem sir," she said, and without preamble the line began to ring. He put the phone on speaker. Alessa flashed a look of alarm at him but he held a finger to his lips.

A sleepy male voice answered and Alessa gestured violently at the phone, miming "that's him!."

"Signor Flynn, this is Antonio on the front desk," Will said in a passable imitation of an Italian speaking English.

"Yes?" Lucas said. "Do you know what time it is?"

"I'm sorry to call so early, Signor Flynn, but we have had a complaint from the room next to you," Will continued, winking at Alessa.

"A what? A complaint?"

"A complaint that you are making a lot of noise," Will said in a grave tone. "Loud music. Is it possible you could respect our quiet hours until seven, sir? It is Sunday morning."

"I'm not making any noise at all," Lucas said, his voice rising. "Not a bloody sound. I was fast asleep until you called."

"That is very strange, one moment sir. This is Signor Flynn of Room 102?"

"This *isn't* Room 102, it's 207," came Lucas's testy voice.

"Oh. In that case my deepest apologies, sir," Will said, now sounding very apologetic. I think I have the wrong gentleman."

"For God's sake. Can't you check before you ring people up in the middle of the night? It's still dark outside!"

"I am extremely sorry, sir. I will send you a bottle of Prosecco with the compliments of the management for your inconvenience."

"I should bloody well think so too," Lucas yelled bad-temperedly, and slammed down the phone.

Will and Alessa sat for a moment grinning stupidly at each other, then he raised his palm slowly and she high fived him.

"Room 207. Not bad going, Mr Burglar," she said.

He grinned. "Now we just need to get in it when he and his female friend have departed," he said.

They arrived at Venezia Santa Lucia station at twenty past nine. The sun was bright though the day was still cold.

"I'm not stealing anything until I get a large cup of coffee inside me," Alessa said, taking him by the arm. They had not had enough time at Monselice to look for a coffee shop, even if there had been one open.

They went in a place called the Relax & Caffé and had hot ciabatta rolls filled with salami and cheese, together with apple juice and coffee. Will quietly pocketed the plasticised menu, earning an old-fashioned look from Alessa. When they had eaten they felt warmer. They took vaporetto number one to Rialto Mercato, which was the nearest stop to the Grande di Visconti, and Will bought a black-and-white baseball cap from a tourist stall which said "I heart Venice" on it. He also purchased a black hoodie top which said *'Per Rialto, Per S. Marco'* on the front in yellow letters. To top it off he acquired a pair of mirrored sunglasses.

After a few minutes he and Alessa found the hotel, which overlooked a quiet backwater canal. It was built of red stone and looked as ancient and imposing as its name suggested.

Alessa looked around nervously.

"I feel like I've got a huge flashing red light on my head which says ALESSA IS HERE," she said worriedly, tilting her head down and stopping at the corner.

"You do need to disappear," Will said, looking around, but not really wanting her to go. "He might walk past us at any moment."

"I'll go and find somewhere to drink more coffee," Alessa said. "What's the plan?"

"There is no plan," Will confessed. "I'm making it up as I go along."

Now that they had arrived he was not feeling at all confident about the outcome. What had seemed so easy after the triumph of obtaining the room number now seemed ridiculous and impossible. He could end up in an Italian court, and the English authorities would nod sagely and say 'lock him up, he's got previous'. He looked at his watch. It was coming up to eleven in the morning.

"Lucas ought to be at his conference, so now's the time," he said. "Just so long as he and the Unknown Woman aren't, you know, in the room. Anyway, you get going. How about we meet back in that station café? There's no point in hanging around here where he and Unknown Woman might come along."

"OK then," she said absently. She was looking for something in her purse, then she took his hand and put her engagement ring in it, folding his fingers around it.

"Leave it in his room if you get the chance," she said, and then she turned abruptly before he could say anything and hurried away. She was crying.

He looked at the ring for a moment and then slipped it into his pocket, blowing out his cheeks. This whole situation wasn't a lark anymore. He called the hotel and asked for Dr Flynn in 207, preparing to hang up if anyone answered, but there was no reply and it went to voicemail. He hung up before the bleep.

Time to get on with it, though he didn't know what he was going to do.

The menu crackled in his pocket and suddenly he wondered if he was insane even to be attempting this. Then he shook his head. Lucas had stolen the brooch. Everything would be lost if he backed out now, and Lucas would win. He wasn't going to surrender without a fight.

The Grande di Visconti had an impressive main entrance with three marble steps and columns framing either side, opening onto a small piazza. The canal flowed languidly off to one side, with balconied windows overlooking it. There was a metal plate beside the entrance doors proclaiming the hotel's name and bearing four proud gold stars. This looked like a hotel that would have good security.

To one side of the main entrance was Ristorante Visconti, where guests dined. It had tables and chairs outside and one well-wrapped couple even sat at an outside table drinking espresso from tiny cups. The other tables were set for breakfast by an optimistic staff and napkins flapped in the breeze, each weighed down with cutlery. The restaurant entrance looked the most promising possibility so he moved towards it, slipping through the glass doors. It was busy inside with a crowd of people taking breakfast. Waiters and waitresses moved swiftly about, taking orders or carrying laden trays. No-one took the slightest notice of him so he made his way to the glass doors at the back. They opened into the hotel foyer.

In the foyer he looked towards the reception desk, where three couples waited in the check-out queue with wheeled suitcases beside them. None of the men were Lucas, and two of the couples had children, one of whom was pretending to be an aeroplane and another, a teenage girl, was arguing loudly in French with her mother, who looked a little harassed by the altercation. Various people sat or stood around the large foyer, staring at their phones. There was a small gift shop to one side and a woman stood looking at scarves.

Will was just wandering how to get upstairs to room 207 without detection when he had an outstanding piece of luck. A couple who had checked out were heading for the door when the man realised he hadn't handed in their disposable key cards. He turned and looked at the desk queue, then flipped the key cards into a rubbish bin before leaving.

Will snatched a free newspaper from a pile on the counter beside him, folded it in two as if it had been read, and walked swiftly towards the bin. His heart was beating hard enough to burst out of his chest. He paused beside the bin and glanced around. No-one was looking his way. He made a show of studying the newspaper for a moment. He could see both white plastic room key cards. They had yoghurt or something on them. He folded the newspaper up and placed it carefully into the bin, pushing it down and taking the two key cards as he did so. Then he straightened up and walked casually back across the foyer, feeling as if klaxons were about to sound.

Nothing happened.

The teenager was still arguing with her mother, and two men in light coats had joined the check-out queue, glancing at their watches and looking irritated at the delay. People still studied their phones. Will held the cards without looking at them and headed for the toilets. Inside a stall he took out the cards and examined them. They were pale grey with red calligraphic writing on them saying Hotel Grande di Visconti. There was a magnetic strip along the back of each, and nothing else. He wiped away the yoghurt with a piece of toilet paper, then pocketed the stolen key cards and emerged to wash his hands.

So far, so good.

He had not one but two room keys, albeit for the wrong room, which presumably had just been deactivated since the couple had checked out. He took a coin from his pocket and used it to scratch up and down the two card stripes a few times, hoping they would now give an error reading.

When he emerged into the foyer the check-out queue had cleared. He went over to the reception desk, his heart in his mouth. If it all went wrong, he was pretty sure he could take to his heels and be gone before anyone could stop him, but then all would be lost. The young woman behind the desk was pretty and had dark hair which she had bound up in a tight bun. She bore a gold badge which said Grande di Visconti on it and in large letters beneath, 'Hanna'.

"Checking out?" she said to him with a professional smile. She had an East-European accent.

He took off his sunglasses and smiled back, full wattage.

"Hello," he said. Could you give me a second room key? Mine is working fine but my wife's does not work. I'm Dr Lucas Flynn. I'm attending the Art History conference upstairs."

"Room number, sir?" she said.

"207," he said, taking Lucas's business card off a stack of his own business cards and placing it on the desk in front of her. She leaned forward and looked at it, then took the key card from him.

"I'm sorry about that, sir," she said, dropping the key card into a box beside her without even checking it. She took a new card, typed on her keyboard for a moment and then swiped it. She smiled at him and held out the card.

"If your wife has any more trouble please let us know," she said. "Is there anything else I can help you with today?"

"No, that's perfect, thank you," he said, his throat dry. He smiled at her and took the key card, then picked up his business card and turned to go.

"Dr Flynn?"

He turned back slowly, trying to remain casual. She was holding out a piece of paper to him.

"Could you take a moment to fill in our customer survey?" she asked. "It is just two questions."

"I certainly will," he said, smiling at her and then pointedly looking at her badge. "It's Hanna, isn't it? *Excellent* service."

She beamed at him and he nodded, then walked away.

He decided that he was *definitely* too old for this sort of thing. But he also felt excitement thrill through his veins.

He replaced the mirror sunglasses and went up the staircase that led to the first floor. He turned right rather than left, spotting a bored girl at the registration table outside the conference room, who was also looking down at her phone. He pressed the call button of the lift and the doors opened immediately. The lift was key-card operated so he swiped his new card and pressed the button for the next floor. The doors closed and he breathed a sigh of relief. A minute later he was outside 207. Two doors down from 207 was a small doorless room with an ice-dispensing machine in it. Suddenly alarmed that Lucas or the Unknown Woman might be in their room, he rapped smartly on the door of 207 and then sprinted for the ice-room door. He waited but there was no sound of an opening door down the corridor. He peeped cautiously out, feeling like an idiot.

This was it. He was about to break the law in a foreign country. He slipped on latex gloves he had bought in a *farmacia*, then took out the key card, went back to 207 and held it to the lock. It bleeped, a green LED came on and he heard the latch whirr back. He turned the handle and went in.

The room was empty. That was the first relief. It was large and had an ensuite bathroom off to one side. There were sliding doors which led to a balcony overlooking the canal. There was a white rug on the wooden floor and the double bed had an ornate headboard edged with gold. There was a Turner print over the bed in an ornate gold frame. The bed had already been made by the room staff and cream cushions on top of the bedspread were edged with gold. The bedspread and the drapes were all in burnt sienna, and there was a wooden desk, two easy chairs in matching sienna, and some kind of a chest on which a suitcase rested.

Will checked that the bathroom was empty, then crossed quickly to the balcony doors and unlatched them, sliding one open. A pleasant breeze filled the room and he ducked out onto the balcony, looking left and right. The balconies for each room were separated by a white-painted metal barrier which was spiked to prevent climbing. The lazy waters of the canal drifted by two floors below, and there was a flagpole set on the bank bearing a fluttering Italian flag. No-one was in sight on any of the balconies. No doubt they were all out enjoying Venice.

He went back inside and looked around the room. He had no idea where to start the hunt so he just opened the first drawer and went quickly through it, finding socks, underpants, ties, vests, and two belts.

No brooch.

The drawer next to it contained lady's underwear and he felt uncomfortable going through it. He searched through the other drawers swiftly and found blouses, shirts, scarves, jerseys, but no brooch. He opened a cupboard but found only a minibar. Nothing helpful there. The bathroom yielded nothing but toothpaste, two electric toothbrushes, a razor and two sponge bags. One sponge bag obviously belonged to Lucas and was empty apart from a pair of nail clippers and a set of cufflinks. The other was full to bursting with deodorants, perfume and make up.

No brooch.

Will began to despair and re-entered the main room. He had already been in 207 for ten minutes and they might come back at any moment. He had a sudden thought and threw the deadbolt on the door, so that at least they couldn't walk in on him. Then he spotted the wardrobe and realised he had stupidly overlooked it. He opened the double doors. There was a jacket and two pairs of trousers, two dresses, several more blouses and a woman's coat. In the bottom of the wardrobe were a pair of black high-heels and a pair of brown brogues.

No brooch, but he noticed that the room-safe door was closed. He rattled it and found it locked. He tried pressing Lock and then six zeroes, which apparently opened many room safes in America, but the Italian hoteliers had been careful and had reprogrammed the default secret code for opening the safe. He rattled the door again as if willing it to open, but it remained obstinately shut.

He thought for a moment and then snatched out his phone. He ran out to the balcony so as not to be heard if anyone was outside the door, calling Alessa as he went. She picked up almost immediately.

"Will?" she said. "Where are you?"

"I'm in the room, he said in a whisper. "And I need to be quick. The room safe is locked and I can't get into it. Do you know Lucas's PIN? You said you did."

"It's his birthday backwards," she said crisply, and he thanked God for her swift understanding. "Which is 8th January, so his PIN ought to be 1080."

"Thanks!" he said. "Got to go, I'll call you back."

He hurried back into the room and knelt down at the safe, typing 1080. The safe bleeped and said Error.

He swore under his breath. He tried 0801 and got an error. Maybe they had used Unknown Woman's PIN. He was going to have to call Alessa back, and he was running out of time. Every moment that he spent in there he was more likely to get caught. They'd stop him at the airport and...no.

He needed to focus.

He stopped his wildly skittering thoughts and breathed deeply. He read the instructions on the safe. *Enter a number between four and six digits and press Lock. To open, enter the same number code.*

Maybe Lucas had been paranoid and had entered six digits. Will tried 108010 and got the error bleep. He hoped the safe didn't have a lock-out if you entered the wrong code too many times. He racked his brains. Lucas looked to be about the same age as Alessa, and she was twenty-eight, Will knew. He calculated a possible year of birth, reversed the whole thing and tried again. Three error bleeps. He shook his head. He was fishing in the dark. He tried the next year along and there was the sweet sound of the locking bars moving back. The door popped open a centimetre and triumphantly he swung it open.

There was a dark-blue jewellery box inside,. He took it out, his hand shaking a little, and opened it. A familiar eight-pearl brooch nestled inside, with an orange sapphire glowing in the centre. A brooch he immediately recognised from the painted gown of Botticelli's Venus. A brooch which had somehow passed on to Isabella d'Este from Semiramide d'Appiano over half a millennium ago. A brooch which he now held in his hand.

He looked at it in awe.

19

Love quickens the heart, but betrayal stills it.

ANONYMOUS

13th May 1486, Villa di Castello, Florence

It was midday on Saturday when Jacopo Saltarelli reached the gates of the Villa di Castello. The May day had started warm and the sun had burned all morning in a cloudless sky. He had walked from the centre of Florence for the best part of two hours, so he was very hot. He had started at the Medici palace in via Larga, only to be told that he should take his letter to the Villa di Castello, where Lorenzo di Pierfrancesco de' Medici was in residence. They had warned him that naturally he would not be able to speak directly to the great lord, but would have to deliver his letter to the door. The footmen at via Larga had offered to add his letter to other mail being delivered to Castello, but he had declined. He didn't want to risk it being lost. With no horse of his own and no coach travelling the road from which he might beg a lift, he had walked.

He was tired after being up all night but proud of his letter. It would destroy Maestro Botticelli and he would have his revenge for the way in which he had been mistreated. However, on the long road across the fields he had convinced himself that perhaps it would be better if he did not deliver the letter in person to Lorenzo. After all, the lord might fly into a rage and blame him, the messenger. The safer path would be to deliver his bombshell and then depart. His only disappointment was that he would not be present when Maestro Botticelli was exposed. He wondered if he might loiter in via Nuova for the next day or so, where the pompous painter had his workshop, in the hope of seeing an arrest take place. There might be a public hanging for such a crime, though Saltarelli doubted the Medici lord would take this course. He would not wish to dishonour his wife. Nevertheless, Saltarelli had no doubt that Botticelli would be toppled from his pinnacle. At the very least he would lose all future Medici commissions. More likely, he would be quietly put to death, for one did not make an enemy of the Medici. They might not formally rule but they had a commanding influence with the ruling Signoria's guild members. The sudden disappearance of the painter would lead to regretful shrugs but no retribution.

Saltarelli suddenly wondered if he should have left his letter unsigned. He felt momentarily alarmed as he walked the dusty road. Yet he had committed no crime, he reasoned, except to witness an act that the Medici lord would find despicable.

He inspected himself as he arrived in the vicinity of the Villa. He had runnels of sweat down each side of his nose. He had a small pebble in his left boot. His boots was covered in a thin veil of white powder and when he beat at his clothes, dust puffed off his doublet and hose. He had toiled up a shallow hill to approach the villa, and he was a little out of breath. He tidied himself up as best as he could and then walked up to the gates, where he presented himself to two pike-bearing gate guards. They crossed their pikes before the gateway as he approached.

"I bear a letter for the lord Lorenzo de' Medici," he proclaimed, with more confidence than he felt. He held out the letter so that they could see it, but kept a firm grip.

The door guards eyed his dusty clothes. They marked him as a man of no importance, which anyway was obvious since he had arrived on foot.

"Hand it over," said the taller of them, but Saltarelli shook his head firmly.

"It says I am to deliver it personally," he said, pointing to the instruction which he had penned himself that morning. The door guard squinted at the writing of the letter but it was clear that he couldn't read. Certainly the letter had writing on it and an important-looking red seal on the back. He relented and raised his pike, and the other man copied him.

"All right then, present it inside," the guard capitulated, pointing to the main doors. "If they let you in."

Saltarelli tucked the letter back inside his doublet. He crunched up the loose stone path to the main doors, which were set in the exact centre of the building. Here he went through the same rigmarole again with the two door guards, and was eventually admitted, following one of them up the steps and through the huge doors. There he had to stand and wait while someone else was called. The wide hall opened into an inner courtyard, across which busy people walked on their errands. There were white marble statues in the courtyard, but when he moved a step closer to look, the door guard halted him with an admonishing finger and a shake of his head. In the entrance hall there were doors to adjoining rooms on both sides, and tapestries on the interior walls which were probably each worth more than Saltarelli's entire house. People went about their business, ignoring him. The hall had a pleasant smell, like incense, and it was tiled. The sunlight flooded into its darker interior from the courtyard. The door guard kept an eye on Saltarelli, making sure he stayed put.

While Saltarelli shifted uncomfortably from one foot to the other in the wide hall, Semiramide's old nurse Caterina passed across the courtyard, and for some reason he caught her eye. She stepped closer and frowned, squinting in the sunlight, then switched direction to enter the entrance hall. He didn't notice her. He appeared to be trying surreptitiously to wipe the dust off one boot with the other. She had seen the man before in via Larga in the company of Leonardo da Vinci, dressed in much finer clothes. The young maids had been giggling together over something about him. He was a cocksure individual, she knew, and she was surprised that Maestro Leonardo entertained his company. What was his name? *Saltarelli*, she remembered.

Antonio, the head footman, went up to the man while she hovered just inside the door, and a conversation ensued. The man was getting red in the face but Antonio was firm over whatever they were arguing about. In the end Saltarelli sulkily handed over a letter. Antonio took it by the corner and frowned at the man with evident distaste. He flicked a finger at the door guard and the man took Saltarelli by the arm and marched him out. Caterina wondered briefly what it was all about, but it was none of her business so she went on her way. She was carrying Semiramide's finest blue silk cloak, which had a loose hem needing repair. She went up the stairs, her knees creaking, and paused halfway up, out of breath. She didn't hear Antonio on the dark servants' stair until he rounded the corner and they collided. The folded cloak slipped from her arms and she lost her balance, sitting back down on the stair with a bump and a sudden exhalation of breath.

"Master Antonio, have a care," she said sharply, feeling cross although she was to blame for standing in the way.

"Mistress Caterina, forgive me," he said, always courteous to her. He helped her to her feet, gathering up the shining silk cloak. She found she had landed squarely on the letter he had dropped. She plucked it off the stair, reading the address.

For the great lord Lorenzo de' Medici, on a private matter concerning an artist. For delivery in person.

She handed it to Antonio, still a little piqued.

"What does that weasel Saltarelli want with letters to his lordship?"

Antonio smiled.

"A weasel he is," he said. "Certainly I didn't like what the evil rascal was implying."

"And what was that, pray?"

"He wouldn't say exactly, just bade me give the letter to his lordship. I didn't tell him that the lord is away for two days, for the man's a liar in his throat and it's none of his damned business. Oh, pardon my tongue, Mistress

Caterina."

"How odd," she said with a frown. "And who is this artist, I wonder?"

"I did get that out of him," Antonio said. "I threatened to burn his letter if he didn't tell me. It is apparently a reference to the Maestro Botticelli."

"Surely you wouldn't burn a letter addressed to the lord," Caterina said, shocked.

"Of course not," Antonio said with a smile. "But he didn't know that."

He tipped his red cap to her and went on his way. She carried on up the stairs after him and handed over the cloak to the maids for sewing, then returned to her mistress, deep in thought. Something wasn't right. She knew that the mistress had a soft spot for Sandro Botticelli. He was charming, and Caterina had seen the way they sometimes looked at each other.

The mistress sat reading in a shaft of sunlight in the *studiolo* next to her bedchamber. Semiramide had a separate study and bedchamber from Lorenzo, for his bedchamber was often used for political meetings. Her daughters, Laudomia and Ginevra, were at her feet. Laudomia sat with her young nurse, playing a game of winding wool between fingers. Little Ginevra was only seven months and was fast asleep in a soft basket, swaddled in warm blankets. Caterina had nursed Semiramide from birth, but the old nurse was getting older now and didn't have the energy to deal with a toddler. Laudomia was giggling because the young nurse Isabetta, herself not yet seventeen, was distracting the little girl from the wool by pulling funny faces; crossing her eyes, sticking out her tongue and tucking in her top lip so that she looked like a rabbit. She was then pretending to be a hungry rabbit who thought that Laudomia looked like a particularly tasty morsel.

"A word, mistress?" Caterina said.

Semiramide looked up as Caterina indicated Isabetta with her eyes, and looked quizzically at her old nurse. However, she reacted quickly.

"Isabetta, Laudomia hasn't been out today," she said to the young nurse. "Take her for a walk in the gardens. You can leave Ginevra here with Caterina and me for a while. Laudomia, you must wear your hat that papà gave you."

Laudomia pouted and frowned crossly. She had been enjoying playing with Isabetta, who was funny and not as serious as her mummy. But Semiramide tickled her and she started giggling again and rolled over onto her back. When she and Isabetta had departed, Semiramide looked enquiringly at Caterina.

"I'm sorry mistress," Caterina said. "It's probably nothing, but I thought you should know. "Do you remember that Jacopo Saltarelli who goes around with Maestro Leonardo from time to time? He's just delivered a letter to your husband and Antonio took it to his lordship's study. Something about Maestro Botticelli."

Semiramide frowned.

"I do remember him," she said. "I didn't like his unctuous ways. What does the letter say?"

"I don't know, mistress," Caterina said. "It's sealed."

Semiramide glanced at Ginevra but she was still fast asleep. She stood up.

"Show me," she said, and went off to Lorenzo's chamber, trailed by Caterina. The letter was lying in the silver tray on Lorenzo's writing desk, together with some household accounts. Semiramide picked it up and turned it over.

"I hope Saltarelli's not up to mischief," she said, looking at the address. She shook her head absently, then turned the letter over and inspected the seal. Unlike her own letters, where her personal seal of the Medici balls was imprinted in the wax, this had not been stamped with a design. Wax had simply been dripped onto the edge of the folded paper to seal it.

"I have some more of that wax," Caterina said noncommittally.

Semiramide looked at her.

"Go and fetch it then," she said after a long moment. "Let's make sure the horrid little man isn't making trouble. I wouldn't put it past him to invent some lie."

Caterina curtsied and went off to find the sealing wax, locating it in what she called her oddments drawer. She returned to the chamber but was shocked at the sight of her mistress. Semiramide was sitting on Lorenzo's bed looking ashen, as if the blood had been drained out of her. The opened letter lay on the floor where it had slipped from her fingers.

"Whatever is it, mistress?" Caterina said in distress, sitting down next to the young woman and taking her hands tenderly.

"Read it," Semiramide said, wiping away her tears. "It must surely be a lie, but it's a wicked lie and you know how gullible men are."

Caterina looked at her with a troubled face, then bent down and picked up the discarded letter, her back creaking. She began to read to herself, her lips silently shaping the words.

...obscenity...mother of your children...collecting belongings from Maestro Botticelli's workshop...all asleep...chanced upon the Maestro...a painting of your own wife unclothed...every private detail evident...his own hands holding her body...insolence...touching himself in front of the painting...my duty to inform you...

Caterina's throat felt dry and for a moment she could not trust herself to speak. She sat down beside her mistress without being invited, her legs feeling as if they might give way. The two women remained dumbly side by side. She took Semiramide's hand.

The scene in Botticelli's workshop had been described in careful detail by Saltarelli and Caterina had no doubt that it was real. She turned her head and caught Semiramide's eyes, no longer mistress and servant for a moment but just two women with a terrible secret.

"Do you think he'll believe it?" Semiramide asked, but Caterina could tell that she herself believed it, despite her denial.

"It has the ring of truth," Caterina said gravely. "It would be an unlikely thing to invent, even for that man."

Tears were sliding unheeded down Semiramide's cheeks.

"But I have never given the Maestro the slightest encouragement," she said indignantly. "He is not of my station. How could he *do* such a thing? It's not just insolence, it's complete madness. Did he think he wouldn't be discovered?"

Yet she remembered moments. She had let him adjust the position of her foot when Caterina had fallen asleep, and then she had let him move her *head*! He had cupped her face with his warm hands and she knew he had almost kissed her, and she knew she would have let him. There was something intoxicating about the man, and she realised she had never admitted it to herself until now. She felt ashamed by her self-denial. His words after the unveiling of Pallas and the Centaur were etched into her brain: 'Tonight your face may haunt my dreams'.

"When a man wants a woman," Caterina said, "he stops being guided by this," she tapped her temple, "and starts being guided by this." She clutched her crotch roughly as if adjusting an imaginary cock. Semiramide squeezed her lips together and then they both burst out laughing.

"It's not funny," Semiramide said, wiping away her tears. "What on earth am I going to do?"

Caterina looked at the beautiful face of her young mistress and a cold fury began to boil up inside her at what Saltarelli had done.

"Maestro Botticelli should never have used his skill to insult you," she said. "But Jacopo Saltarelli is exploiting his lustful weakness. He must have been slighted by the Maestro to wish him such harm."

"But what should I *do*," Semiramide said again, her voice now hopeless.

A desperate plan began to take shape in Caterina' mind.

"First we must write a replacement letter filled with nonsense," she said.

She sat down at Semiramide's writing desk and took a blank sheet of letter paper, then dipped a quill. "I must do it, for the lord won't recognise my hand."

With Saltarelli's letter beside her she began to write the address, copying his hand as best as she could, and duplicating the words exactly. Then she turned over the sheet and looked into space while she thought for a moment.

"What will you write?" Semiramide asked, and Caterina dipped the quill.

"I'll admire the master for his great wisdom, and give him a letter with nothing at all of import in it, just ingratiating rubbish. I'll mention how good the master is to support the great Maestro Botticelli. We need a letter in case Antonio mentions the delivery to the master. Let me think on it, now. Go to, and turn away Isabetta if she returns."

She wrote for a while and then dusted sand on the ink to dry it. Semiramide returned and read it, careful not to smudge it. It was the sort of toadying letter that Lorenzo received every day from one merchant or another. She nodded approvingly.

Caterina took the now-dry letter and folded it twice in the manner of Saltarelli's original, then took a lighted candle and melted wax to make a new seal. Semiramide took the replacement letter and inspected it, then nodded again and went back into her husband's study, putting the replacement letter onto the silver tray.

"The master must never know of the original," Caterina said when she came back.

She pointed to the fireplace and handed Saltarelli's letter to her mistress. After a moment's hesitation, Semiramide walked over and put the letter into the grate, then lit it with the candle. It ignited immediately and curled up, the wax seal flaring with a sound like a purring cat, then burning brightly. Once the letter was consumed she took up a poker and stirred the ashes into dust, then stood up.

"That's the easy part," Caterina said grimly. "Now you must go to Maestro Botticelli and have him destroy the painting. Your honour and his life depend on it, for if the master hears of this he'll feel betrayed and it will never leave him."

Semiramide looked at her dumbly.

"But how can I do that?" she said plaintively. "It is so shameful."

"We must go together to the city in disguise," Caterina continued. "You must wear servant's garb and borrow my hooded cloak. You must cover your face. I'll get horses from the stable and tell them I am on an errand. There's no time to be lost. It will be dangerous but we have no choice. We can't take a carriage or the servants will talk, so you take a short sword and I'll have a dagger. If anyone tries to stop us, we'll stick them."

Semiramide looked at her, eyes wide. She had never seen her old nurse like this.

"You will accompany me to see Maestro Botticelli?"

Caterina looked back at her grimly, then came to a resolution after a long pause.

"No," she said. "I shall ride with you, but you must confront Maestro Botticelli while I have words with Jacopo Saltarelli."

The women set a good pace on the horses. At one point a pair of men tried to flag them down, but they ploughed on and the men had to jump aside as the horses bore down upon them without sign of slowing. Caterina was matter of fact about it but Semiramide was both frightened and excited, utterly outside her normal element.

Once they had entered the city gates they found a modest inn and purchased a room for the night. It was already late afternoon and they needed a base. When it got dark the city gates would shut. They did not want to ride back at night as it would be even more dangerous for two unaccompanied women. Caterina went out and made inquiries, returning at dusk with the addresses of both Maestro Botticelli in via Nuova, and Jacopo Saltarelli in the east of the city. They decided that they should not go out yet, because it was still early and there were many people on the streets. They were hungry, so they had the innkeeper serve a supper in their room, getting top service with the help of Semiramide's purse. They waited until dusk at nine, an hour after vespers bells had sounded across the city, then donned their cloaks. Semiramide covered her face as before. They crept down the back stairs, emerging into the back yard of the inn amidst chickens pecking in the dirt. The rear gate exited onto a dingy street but they were heading in different directions. Caterina had lectured Semiramide again and again as if she were still a child: remember where she was, keep her eyes peeled, keep her hand on her short sword inside her cloak, and stick anyone who tried to accost her. Semiramide, normally so confident and imperious, took her old nurse's counsel without argument. This wasn't her world. The two women hugged each other, and Caterina grasped Semiramide's hand for a moment.

"Be safe," she whispered, as one would say to another when the plague was rising.

Then she was gone, her dark cloak blending into the dusk.

Semiramide was suddenly alone and fearful at the back gate of the inn. She began to walk quickly, using an effort of will to stop herself from breaking into a run. Her servant's clothes were rough on her skin and she was unaccustomed to the feel of them. Caterina had warned her to avoid dark alleys as much as she could, so she headed for the larger streets where candle and oil lamplight from the shop windows spilled out. She jumped at every shadow. More than once she glanced around for her retinue and felt shocked at finding no-one at all. She reached the main street and found with relief that plenty of people were still abroad. A musician was even playing a fiddle, and he gave her a look of amazement when she tossed him a coin of her usual denomination. Too late she remembered that she wasn't a lady in her current dress, and hurried away. Slowly she calmed down as she walked, and her heart eased. Much to her astonishment she found that she was ignored: nobody glanced her way, and no beggars approached her seeking alms. A bright three-quarter moon added light, so she could see where she was going. She recognised the street and set off towards the river, the stench of the fulling mills making her wrinkle her nose. The dark cloth over her face left only her eyes exposed. It was unusual and gave her the appearance of a Moor. Only the lightness of her skin gave her away, but that couldn't easily be perceived in the gloom.

When she reached the river she turned right and headed towards the Convent of Ognissanti. Via Nuova was just before the church on the right, Caterina had said. Sure enough she found the street, which was lit only by moonlight, and turned into it apprehensively. She walked up it, her heart beginning to thud again, but all at once she saw the workshop she sought. It was a tall old house on the corner of via Nuova with via Palazzuolo, and above the door was a hanging Guild sign bearing a picture of an artist's palette. It squeaked as it flexed in the evening breeze. The windows at the front were already shuttered, as was the custom after nightfall, but above the door was a wooden board on which was painted '*Bottega di Botticelli*'. The door was of stout oak, studded with iron bolts which spoke of inner defences.

Now that she had arrived she didn't know what to do. Should she knock, should she go in? How should she ask for him? How could she attract his attention alone? She made a decision and, glancing around, rapped on the door with the hilt of her short sword, then concealed it again in her cloak.

The door swung open and a long-haired, good-looking fellow stood there. He was slim and sported a pointed beard and curled moustaches, though he looked younger than she. A journeyman from the workshop, perhaps.

"I have a message for Maestro Botticelli from my mistress," Semiramide said, remembering to coarsen her accent.

"Who's your mistress?" the young man asked rather cheekily, looking her up and down.

"I would speak with the master on it," Semiramide said, with her customary penetrating look. "You will take me to him."

Something in her tone caused the cockiness to drop from his manner, and he stepped back.

"Better come in then, signora," he said.

Semiramide was led into a hall lit by a solitary oil lamp, and after a minute the lad returned with the maestro himself, much to her relief.

"Good evening, madam," Botticelli said formally, his customary charm mixed with surprise at this incongruously masked visitor. But as he approached she saw a shock of recognition flood his face and he faltered in his passage, words forming and then freezing unspoken on his lips. After a moment he turned and nodded at the lad, who stood uncertainly in a doorway which presumably led to the main workshop.

"Leave us, Tommaso," he said. "I would speak with this visitor alone."

Tommaso sensed the sudden change in atmosphere and left without further discussion.

Botticelli came closer and stood uncertainly before her, looking over his shoulder to ensure that they were unheard. She noticed even in the dim light from the oil lamp that he was flushed.

"My lady," he said, looking as if he might burst into tears. "*You* are here."

"Obviously," Semiramide said, pushing down the cloth so that she her face was exposed beneath the hood of her cloak. He stepped back at the sight of her as if slapped. She softened at his pleading look and didn't immediately unleash the bitter recrimination that she had planned.

They stood facing each other, his hands dry-washing at his chest as if in the act of cleaning them of sin.

"Whatever have you done?" she said quietly, looking into his eyes. "Jacopo Saltarelli sent a letter to my husband telling of a painting."

He looked horrified.

"A...a painting?"

"An *obscenity*," she said, feeling her own face blush. "In which you bring dishonour to me and my family."

She saw the Adam's apple on his neck bob in and out as he swallowed.

"It was *Saltarelli*," he said in realization, remembering the intruder storming out of his workshop, and a knife that had been found next day bearing the initial 'S'. "I am dead," he groaned in despair. "Where is his lordship?"

She continued to glare at him and he wrung his hands in anguish.

"By great fortune my lord is away," she said coldly. "He has not seen Saltarelli's poisonous letter. But I have read every detail of it. How *could* you do this?"

He was shaking his head.

"It was foolishness. I had to have something of you." He dropped his eyes from hers. "I am sorry."

Now it was she who was having difficult speaking, her throat dry. She cleared her throat.

"Show it to me," she demanded, her voice raspy.

"Oh no, you cannot possibly see it," Botticelli said, shaking his head. "I am too ashamed."

"You *will* show me," she ordered. "Where is it?"

She looked past him towards the workshop and stepped around him as if she were going in search of the painting.

"It isn't here," he said urgently, taking her arm. "After Saltarelli caught me, I hid it."

"Well, where is it?" she said again, raising her voice so that he put a finger to his lips, looking over his shoulder in alarm, conscious of the apprentices not far away in their room.

"Quietly," he said, dropping his voice to a whisper. "It is in the church of Ognissanti."

"You have taken an obscene painting of me into the *holy church of All Saints?*" she said enunciating each word in a furious whisper. "I can only hope it is well concealed. Take me to it this instant." She felt the short sword against her side. She would slash the painting to ribbons and be done with it.

She saw his shoulders drop as he capitulated. She felt scared that he had given in. He bade her wait and disappeared into the main body of the house. When he returned after a few minutes he was carrying a large key.

"For Ognissanti," he said. "Please cover your face again my lady, and follow me."

He collected his own cloak and tossed it round his shoulders. Then he selected a stout stick from a wooden stand and they stepped into the street, closing the door quietly behind them. He locked his door and turned to her.

Her masked figure seemed small and vulnerable in the shadowy street. He wanted to take her hand or put his arm around her in protection, but he resisted the impulse.

They did not enter Ognissanti through the front doors which faced the river Arno. There was a narrow alley between the houses, off to the right from via Nuova, and Botticelli turned into it, motioning her to follow him. They were unobserved. They went through a small gate in a long wall, crossed a small orchard and came up to a large, locked door. Carved into the stone arch of the door was a Latin inscription: '*AD HONOREM SANCTORVM OMNIVM*'. Botticelli produced his key and unlocked the door. The huge church was two centuries old, built by the Umiliati, and the large key looked ancient to Semiramide.

"I painted a fresco of St. Augustine in Ognissanti," Botticelli said in an undertone. "About six years ago. I had my own key because the friars were in and out of prayer. They will be abed now for they rise in the night for the glory of God, but we must be very quiet."

They entered the church which adjoined the larger Convent of Ognissanti, and Botticelli locked the door behind them. Now that they were so close, Semiramide was both terrified and fascinated at what she was about to see. She vowed that once he had unveiled the painting's hiding place she would send him away and then destroy it.

The tall building was cool inside. Candles burned and she could see a vaulted roof far above. She had been in Ognissanti before by day, but it looked different at night. She expected it to seem eerie but it did not; instead there was a profound atmosphere of silence and peace.

Botticelli turned and addressed her in a low voice, making one last plea.

"We should not do this, my lady."

She refused to relent. This was what she had come for.

"Take me to it," she repeated firmly and he nodded in reluctant acquiescence, his face a mask of embarrassment and regret.

"Then follow me. The painting is hidden in the choir."

He led her towards the upper end of the nave. No-one was there, for vespers prayers were long finished. On the front wall which enclosed the choir were two frescos, to the left and right of the doorway. He stopped in front of the left-hand painting.

"St. Augustine in his cell, when he had his vision of St. Jerome's passing," he said, and bowed his head for a moment as if in silent prayer.

Semiramide pushed down the cloth from her face, which was damp from her breath. He was struck by her beauty. She cast back her hood and looked at the painting, then at the painting of St. Jerome on the right of the doorway.

"You did this painting, and Ghirlandaio did that one, I understand?" she said, her voice imperial.

"Yes my lady. It was a contest."

"It is remarkable," Semiramide conceded, forgetting for a moment to be angry, but then immediately remembering and turning to him.

"Never mind that. Where is the *obscenity* hidden?"

He looked around the deserted nave and then spoke very quietly. "When I painted this fresco, an Umiliati friar ordered both paintings. The friar told me a secret that must remain unspoken. There was a hiding place behind this painting, and he wanted me to conceal something in it."

"What thing?"

"Nothing evil. The order of the Umiliati was founded by San Giovanni da Meda in the twelfth century, and they possessed his sacred relics. Behind the painting the reliquary sits, and only I know it."

"You and the friar," she corrected, but he shook his head.

"Just me, and now you. When I finished the painting I was ready to return my key, but the friar disappeared and they would never say what happened to him. I went to his cell but found blood in his bed straw. I believe he was murdered by someone seeking the sacred bones of the saint."

"What did you do?" she asked, distracted from her primary goal for a moment by the gruesome account.

"What could I do? I checked in the alcove behind the painting and there were the bones, so I shut them away again. I believe I am the only man on earth who knows it, and I can tell no-one for fear of losing my own life in turn."

"Then this is your hiding place," she said, understanding. "But cannot anyone open the alcove?"

"No, my lady," Botticelli said. "Fra Martino – that was my poor friar – devised a hidden clockwork mechanism." He pointed up at the painted clock above and to the right of St. Augustine's head. "You see the clock of the hours? This I used to indicate the time of Jerome's death, on the twenty-fourth hour, using notation to show that as the moment of sunset."

"And St. Jerome died at sunset," Semiramide said, engaging in his narrative despite herself. "So the painting tells us that the moment captured is that of the vision. But how is that related to a clockwork mechanism?"

"I will show you," Botticelli said, once more remembering what was about to be exposed and feeling horrified, though perhaps also a little excited. He looked at her, with her hood thrown back and her hair flowing free, not in its usual braids and jewels due to her disguise. Her arms were folded across her breasts as if in defence.

She was quite lovely.

She returned his look, and found herself as usual affected by the odd magnetism that he had. What on earth was it? She didn't feel this, even for her husband.

"Well get on with it," she said, trying to conceal her feelings. She felt hot and nervous. A tingle passed down her spine. It was as though she were a tightly strung bow, on which a deep and long note might at any moment be played.

He took a small stool from a nearby confessional, placed it at the bottom of the painting and stood on it. Then he reached up to the painted clockface and pressed five numbers on it, saying them aloud.

"Two, fourteen, twenty-two, nine, one."

She watched.

There was a click and the fresco moved a finger's width, revealing that it was a hinged stone door. She looked at it in fascination. Botticelli hopped down from the stool and returned it to its proper place. Then he swung open the heavy panel on its oiled hinges, revealing an alcove behind. She could see a brass-bound reliquary chest decorated with jewels. Behind the chest, leaning against the stone of the wall, there was a large panel, perhaps two braccia high, swathed in cloth.

She reached into her cloak and put her hand on the hilt of her sword. Short it may be, but it was razor sharp.

"Bring it out," she said in her most dangerous voice, and he could do nothing but obey. First he lifted out the chest and placed it to one side, then gripped the large panel and brought it out, leaning it against the frame of the alcove. She took out the short sword and he looked at it dumbly, realizing her intention.

"Remove the cloth and then retire down the nave," she ordered peremptorily.

"My lady…" he pleaded.

"*Do it*, Sandro."

Struck by her sudden use of his first name, he obeyed.

He unlaced the ribbon holding on the muslin covering, slid the cover off the painting, and stepped back beside her to take one last look.

Her sword clattered to the ground.

The painting was beautiful and erotic. He had captured her perfectly, naked but for a diaphanous cloth that twisted here and there. She blushed hotly, realizing that he had painted the detail of her most private parts, in a flagrant breach of artistic convention. She didn't know how he could have rendered her naked body so accurately in paint when he had only ever seen her fully clothed. It was quite clearly her, and to her shame she felt herself becoming aroused. Her nipples were erect in the painting, and he had even reproduced her favourite sapphire and pearl brooch, hanging between her bare breasts. He was painted naked behind her, also perfectly recognizable, his darker skin in perfect contrast against the creams and pinks of her own flesh, his muscles firm. His hand rested on her thigh in the picture, pressing in the skin slightly. They were, indisputably, performing the act of love. And the awful thing was, she felt herself becoming wet at the sight of it.

"Why?" she asked, her voice coming out a croak.

"Because you have become my muse," he said helplessly, looking at the painting he had thought he would never see again. "Because I cannot stop thinking about you, though I can never have you. Because I am foolishly in love with you."

She turned to him and he saw that there were tears in her eyes.

He reached with a thumb and, with the softest touch, wiped away first one tear, and then the other. She didn't stop him. She gripped his arm and held it for a moment with shaking fingers. Unable to resist, he put his thumb to his mouth and tasted the salt of her tears.

"I'm so sorry," he said simply. "It has been…difficult."

For a moment she stared at him, uncertain whether she might slap him. Then she stepped in close, tilted up her face and kissed him gently, tasting her tears on his lips. Their mouths broke apart as if they had accidentally collided, but then they kissed again, this time with longer and deeper need. They looked into each other's eyes for several seconds in silent anticipation, then he slid his hands around her waist and pulled her body to his. She wet her lips with her tongue. He could feel the warm softness of her breasts against his chest, and some detached part of him gloried in the line of her long neck. Then they merged their mouths together and were tugging at each other's cloaks. He felt the sweet tip of her tongue melt on his. In a comical moment she had to unhook the leather scabbard of her short sword and put it to one side. Then their cloaks pooled onto the floor and he grabbed a stack of altar cloths from a nearby table and shook them loose to form a cushion of white, rippling linen. In moments he had found her breasts beneath her coarse servants' clothes and she felt his warm hands caressing her stiffening nipples. Then they were sinking to their knees, peeling off layers of clothing and moulding together into one, their hands on each other, cocooned in white cloth. Her body was as soft as he had imagined, all rounded shapes and voluptuous curves. She smelled of rose oil. To her his body was hard and male, tight and muscular, and without a cap his curls framed his head like an angel in one of his pictures.

"You are adorable," he whispered, his breath hot in her ear.

They blended together in the deserted church before the painting which had started it all, their hands everywhere, until at last she felt him pushing and he slid into her. Then they rocked and thrust as one until her back arched and she cried out, while he shuddered and unloaded heat into the heart of her.

Caterina disappeared into the dusk quickly once she left the mistress. She was afraid for herself but she was horrified at the idea of leaving the mistress on her own in the city at night. Mistress she might be, but Caterina still thought of her as her own child. Yet she had no choice, and she made her way across the town towards the street where Saltarelli lived. When she got there the house was dark, and she was uncertain whether she had the right one. She counted again; it was the third house from the main street and had a white door, she had been told. She had even gone beyond it to where the shadows were deeper, and confirmed that there were no more white doors. It wasn't yet late and she wondered if Saltarelli were out, but there was only one way to find out. She beat on the door with her fist and waited. There was no answer so she picked up a stone, used it to beat some more and waited again. She was about to give up in despair when she heard sounds from within, then Saltarelli's angry voice called out.

"I'm sleeping. Who's hammering down my door at this hour?"

"Signor Saltarelli," she said in an urgent whisper, her mouth to the door, her voice obsequious. "My mistress would speak with you."

"Your mistress? Who up God's arse is your mistress?"

"Semiramide, the madonna and spouse of Lord Lorenzo di Pierfrancesco. She promises that it will be to your advantage. I implore you to open the door, signor!"

There was an exclamation from inside, then the sound of bolts being drawn back and the door creaked open.

"The wife of the lord?" he asked, rubbing sleep out of his eyes. He had been in a deep sleep, having retired early after walking all the way back from the Castello, and now he was struggling to wake up. However, the name of the woman's mistress had sent a dart of excitement coursing through his veins, shocking him into wakefulness.

"The wife of the lord, yes sir," Caterina said. "She would speak with you. She says you will find it very much to your advantage."

He looked the ugly old woman up and down with his customary arrogance.

"Well, where is she?"

He craned his neck, looking beyond the old woman but seeing no other figure in the gloom.

Caterina looked over her shoulder, a picture of nervousness.

"Forgive me sir, I am affrighted," she said, with a quaver in her voice. "She awaits you and I am to bring you to her, for she must not be seen. Put on your clothes sir, and you must hurry." She glanced over her shoulder again as if checking that her mistress was not in earshot. "She brings a purse of gold, sir. Will you attend or shall I tell her that you refuse?"

Saltarelli looked at her, his eyes narrowed and his head tilted, his lips pursing into a half-smile. The game had changed! The lord's wife had somehow intercepted his letter and she was quaking with fear. She was a pretty thing. Perhaps he'd let her pay him and then make her suck his cock before he agreed to say no more.

"Wait," he said curtly, and turned back into the house. After a minute or so he emerged, tucking in his shirt. His cloak hung loose and flapping around him as he walked.

"Very well," he said. "Take me to your mistress."

"Very good, sir," Caterina said, curtseying, and then she turned. "It's not far."

She hurried into the dark, gesturing with a hand, and he strode after her.

After half a minute she turned into an alley on the left.

"Well where is she?" he asked the old woman again with irritation. She stopped and turned with a finger to her lips.

"Very quiet now," she said in a whisper, and pointed behind him. "Here is my mistress!"

He turned and peered into the dark but could see no-one. As he strained his eyes to see, the most excruciating pain he had ever experienced lanced through him and he looked down, unable even to open his mouth to cry out. A dagger had been plunged into his side and he watched as a hand twisted it deep in his vitals. He staggered and fell down on one knee. He could see a hot wave of blood welling out of him, but his mind was unaccountably confused. Some detached part of him realised that the old woman had stabbed him. He would *kill* the old bitch! He tried to reach for his own knife but then remembered that he had lost it in Botticelli's workshop. The dagger withdrew from his body, leaving his cloak soaked in blood, but then he felt the wicked point at his throat and the sharp blade plunged into his neck again and again. He tried to shout but the air gurgled from a hole in his neck, blowing red bubbles of blood. He collapsed onto the ground of the alley, his blood pooling in the dirt, and saw the old woman bending over him, her face grim and determined. His fingers still twitched reflexively at his cloak.

His heart faltered, then ceased beating. The sardonic look slowly smoothed out of his features and his jaw sagged open. His head slumped to one side. His bowels opened, releasing a sudden stench. Blood gathered around his head, black in the darkness but glistening. His sightless eyes mirrored the moonlight.

Caterina watched him die with a mixture of horror and satisfaction. It had been much like sticking a pig. She knew she should feel remorse but she did not. She was disgusted with what she had done, but satisfied that he could not cast down the young mistress she had loved since the cradle. She looked up and down the dark alley but no-one was around.

She found a purse on a leather cord inside his cloak, and used her dagger to cut it away from him. Then she departed, leaving him lying in the dirt in a pool of his own blood, his eyes still open, his purse stolen as if by a cutpurse. On her way back to the inn she passed beside the Arno and went down to the silver water's edge, flinging the purse far out. It filled with water and sank swiftly. Then she cleaned her dagger and washed spots of blood away which had landed on her cloak. She made her way back to the inn but the mistress had not yet returned. She had a large gulp of brandy from the flask they had brought, but though her nerves calmed the mistress still did not come back. Filled with worry she sat up and waited for her, eventually falling asleep in the chair beside the bed.

20

Remember tonight. For it is the beginning of always

DANTE ALIGHERI

March, Venice

Having recovered the stolen pearl and sapphire brooch, Will Bentley had tucked the jewellery box into his pocket, tidied up Lucas' hotel room and attempted to leave unobserved.

It was then that his luck had changed.

He had almost got caught by Rachel, the filmmaker he had met in Oxford, who was evidently the woman sharing a room with Lucas. Her return to the room as he was leaving had forced him to retreat and hide in the only place available – the balcony. He was stuck there, and about to be spotted by Rachel.

He looked around wildly, then suddenly grinned as he saw an opportunity. He patted his pocket to make sure the brooch was secure, then stepped up onto the balcony balustrade and launched himself into space.

After a gut-wrenching moment he grabbed the top of the flagpole he had aimed for and locked his arms and legs around it, willing it to support his weight. It wobbled dangerously but held. His latex-gloved hands had a tight grip. His heart was thudding fit to burst out of his chest. He slithered down the pole and landed like a cat on the ground, looking around. No-one was gesticulating or shouting. He glanced up but Rachel had not come out onto the balcony. Realising that she might do so at any moment, he gathered himself and walked away, rounding the corner undetected.

Once out of sight, he spent a minute leaning against the wall and catching his breath. Then he discarded the gloves and caught the next vaporetto back to Venezia Santa Lucia. He sat in a seat on the open deck at the rear of the boat, feeling increasingly elated as the beautiful buildings and striped poles of the Canal Grande slid past him. He had texted Alessa and she was waiting outside the Relax & Caffé holding two takeaway coffee cups. The café was now crowded. It was almost two o'clock and tourists were eating lunch.

She was staring into the crowd and when she saw him she looked enormously relieved.

"My Gawd, I've been sitting here like a nervous wreck waiting for you," she said, holding out one of the cups and looking expectantly at him. "Well?"

He took the cup and tapped his pocket.

"All's well, but let's get out of here. I feel like if I see a policeman they'll tackle me to the ground and search my pockets."

"There's nowhere to sit in there anyway," she said, indicating the café over her shoulder, "and the next Mantova train leaves at ten past."

They got on the train, which this time was going via Verona and was so busy that they couldn't inspect the brooch, especially since it had been on the news and might instantly be recognised. While the fields rolled by, he leaned close and quietly told her how he had got into Lucas's hotel room.

"Rachel Blake!" she repeated when he got to the part where he saw Rachel and she almost caught him in the room. "That woman has been making eyes at him ever since she turned up at your talk, and she probably thought I didn't notice. I bet it was her perfume I could smell on his sheets. Whatever did you do when she turned up? Did you get out of the room or find somewhere to hide?"

He told her and she burst out laughing, making others in the carriage smile at her. She leaned in and lowered her voice to a whisper.

"You leapt off the balcony and shinned down a flagpole? You're a crazy boy!"

She took his hand and squeezed it.

"And did you manage to leave my engagement ring in the room?"

"I left it in the safe so that he'll find it when he opens it. Except I thought I'd win us a bit of time for our getaway, so I typed in a different safe combination. He'll have to get hotel security to open it up."

"Can they even do that?"

"Oh yes. They have a master combination, because if guests locked away their wallet and then forgot the code, they'd have a good excuse not to pay the bill."

Alessa giggled. "I wish I could be there. He'll think he typed the wrong combination. He might even think that Rachel has changed it, and she'll think he's changed it. It's priceless! So eventually he'll get the security man up there and the guy will open it and they'll both have kittens when they realise that the brooch has gone."

"Yes, and he'll have to explain the engagement ring to Rachel, and she'll probably think he's lying through his teeth and two-timing her."

"Perhaps he'll think *she's* nicked the brooch," Alessa went on, "but he won't be able to understand how your ring got there."

"And then he'll call you; that's the only bad thing. You could block him."

"Block him?" she said, her voice rising again until she realised and lowered it. "Block him? I *want* him to call me so that I can tell him how I never want to see him again. Block him! I'm going to rip his heart out."

He tried not to smile and said nothing.

They had an hour's wait in Verona and didn't get back to Mantova until after five. Someone got off the train before them and took the only waiting taxi, so they angled left and walked through the streets to the hotel.

They met in Alessa's room. The minibar had two miniature bottles of Prosecco and Will opened them both. Then they sat down at the glass-topped breakfast table beside the window. Will brought out the jewellery box from his pocket and placed it in the centre of the table between them.

"You open it," he said.

She carefully popped open the lid and they looked at the brooch nestled in its bed of cotton wool. It was one of those special moments, like the first time you see the Leaning Tower of Pisa and its reality messes with your brain.

"My Gawd," she said in a whisper. "È vero."

Spontaneously they lifted their glasses and toasted each other.

"To crime," Will said solemnly.

They drank and then Will reached for the brooch but she slapped his hand away.

"Don't you dare touch that without gloves," she said. In fact, let me do it."

"Are you thinking about fingerprints and DNA?"

"Of course not, silly. Acid on your fingers! This brooch is over five hundred years old so we don't want to damage it. This is Semiramide's *actual brooch*."

Just voicing the words brought a catch to her throat. She stood up and went to her bag, hunting through it until she found the white cotton gloves that he had last seen her wear in the British Library. She also extracted a jeweller's loupe. She slipped on the gloves and then picked up the brooch reverently, shaking her head in disbelief.

The brooch had a silver setting for the orange sapphire and the eight pearls, and it was immaculate – unmistakeably the one that Botticelli had painted on the breast of Venus in the Mars and Venus picture. The back was a plain silver disc with a clasp pin and a simple hook. The silver was tarnished and could have done with a good polish.

"Nothing on the back of it," she said with disappointment, looking at it through the jeweller's loupe. She took off a glove and tapped the back with her nail.

"It could be hollow, I suppose."

"We need a knife," Will said, patting his pockets absently as if he might find one.

They sat and thought.

"I've got a nail file," Alessa said suddenly. She replaced the brooch in its bed of cotton and went into her bathroom. He stood up and followed her, excited. When she saw him in the mirror she turned and blushed a little but he didn't know why. She flourished a metal nail file and then went back to the table and sat down, picking up the brooch. There was a thin gap all around the back disc.

"This is terrible," she said. "I can't believe I'm doing this." Then she inserted the pointed end of the nail file and levered outwards. The silver back of the brooch resisted but suddenly flipped off and tinkled onto the table. A piece of parchment was packed tightly into the back of the brooch, folded and sitting on top of the setting holding the stone and pearls. Using the point of the nail file she very carefully eased out the sliver of parchment, and it fell onto the table. It was a creamy yellow colour, as if it had been singed a little.

"Burned with time," Will said, and she remembered he had mentioned that before – some painter had said it but she couldn't remember who.

She very carefully placed the brooch and its backing disc back into the cotton wool for protection.

"It might fall to bits if I try to unfold it," she said, looking at the fragment of parchment.

"Maybe so, but we didn't come all this way not to try."

She grimaced but nodded. Then with the point of her gloved forefinger she held the parchment in place and carefully opened out the fold. The parchment did not break. She realised she had been holding her breath and let it out in a sigh. With extreme care she opened a second fold and they saw spidery black writing. There was a short line, then two longer lines, and finally an exaggeratedly curled "S" with a dot on each side of it.

Alessa said, "Based on the Frederick Pocock letter, this must be a private note from Semiramide to her son, Pierfrancesco the Younger."

"All of the Medici seem to be called Lorenzo or Pierfrancesco."

"Yes, or Cosimo. When they carried on the Medici lines they kept repeating the names through the generations. It's very confusing. Anyway, let me read this."

She leaned close and used the loupe to magnify the writing.

"The first bit says it was written on the 26th day of February 1523. I'm pretty sure she died that year, but let me check."

She got her laptop, started it up and typed rapidly into it.

"According to this she died on 9th March 1523, so this note was just a few days before she passed away, and a week before the Pocock letter, which if I remember rightly was 2nd March. I would say it's her handwriting, though the letters are quite wobbly. She must have been very frail. She was fifty-nine when she died."

"Fifty-nine isn't old."

"Not now, but it was a good age to reach then. Remember, they didn't have modern medicine, and they had the plague going round, not to mention wars with France and skirmishes with other Italian states. A lot of them didn't make it out of infancy."

"All right then," he said. "So she wanted to tell him something secret before she died. What does she have to say?"

She frowned and studied it.

"You'll have to give me a minute. It isn't like reading today's Italian, remember. It's just like the Pocock letter, with different usage and funny old words. It will take me time to get my eye tuned in."

Feeling useless, he brought her notebook and she started working on the two lines of spidery black script. While she fretted over the lines, he took out his phone and took several close-ups of the brooch with its disassembled back, then added pictures of the note when she was finished with it.

"OK, I think I've got it," she said after a few minutes, sounding troubled. "But it's very cryptic."

She adopted a reading-out voice.

"Look where your father hunted. Stand under the bell and find the mark of my ring where you feared to lie."

He looked at her and grimaced.

"That's cryptic all right. He could have hunted anywhere in Italy."

She frowned in thought and typed the text into her computer in its original Italian. Nothing meaningful emerged so she tried again in English.

"I'm getting references to signet rings," she said. "Which would make sense as she says the mark of her ring."

"Look up signet rings and see what it says."

"Well I know what a signet ring is. It was originally used for putting your seal on something." She caught his sideways look. "Oh all right then, hang on."

She typed.

"Huh, lots of shopping opportunities for signet rings. 'Express your individuality!' Let's try good old Wikipedia." She typed again.

"Kenya, American books, racing dinghies, a 1950's Kodak camera. 'Signet' is a popular word. OK, here we are. Wikipedia says the engraved mark leaves a raised impression when the ring is pressed onto soft sealing wax. They have been used since ancient times as the personal seal of an individual."

"This is fairly ancient times, I'd say," Will said. "And I'm thinking about sitting in Frederick Pocock's kitchen. He said the letter he found had an imprint of the Medici balls in the seal, as if from a ring."

She looked at him, impressed.

"Well remembered," she said. "We know that was Semiramide's letter, so we know that her seal was the Medici balls, which would make absolute sense."

They looked at each other, realizing they didn't know where to go next.

"Let's talk through what we know," Will said. "We know that Semiramide's son, Pierfrancesco the Younger, was afraid to lie down under some bell somewhere. Maybe he thought the bell would drop on him. And we know that if we can find that bell and look underneath it, we'll find a symbol of the Medici balls left there somehow by Semiramide."

"It's weirder than that," she said. "It doesn't mean lie as in lie down. *Mentire*. It means lie as in tell untruths. A place where he was afraid to tell untruths."

He blew his cheeks out.

"Deep."

"*Under the bell*," Alessa murmured, as if thinking out loud.

She typed 'bell locations' and got references to bookshops, Taco Bell and lots of articles about electric bells. She tried 'Renaissance Italy bell locations' and read down the list.

"Well, apart from books by people with the surname 'Bell', of which there seem to be loads, bells come up mostly in bell towers."

"Like in a church."

"Yes, a church or anywhere else with a bell that could be rung. A monastery, for example. It must be a fixed bell, not a handbell, or she couldn't be sure it would still be there. Anywhere with a bell tower where they would have rung the hours, which was everywhere. They didn't yet have a lot of accurate clocks. I once had to write 5,000 words on renaissance timekeeping, so I know. They had spring-driven movements but they didn't figure out pendulum clocks until the mid-seventeenth century."

"So they rang bells, like a church clock, to tell people what the time was?"

"Yes, or had clockwork mechanisms to ring the hour mechanically. We might be looking under the bell in a bell tower." She grimaced. "Unfortunately there are quite a few bell towers in Florence."

They looked at each other gloomily.

"Are you hungry?" Will said suddenly. "I'm starving. Why don't we go out and get something to eat and you can bring your laptop and we'll keep on trying to work this out."

"I could do with something inside me," she nodded.

He wiggled his eyebrows at her and she punched him on the arm.

She made him wait while she tidied herself up. When she came downstairs she had on a polka-dot red dress and red heels. He had never seen her in this outfit before and she looked stunning. She tossed a light coat over her shoulders. He had changed too and now he wore a black collarless shirt, black trousers and a grey jacket. As he followed her out of the door, her perfume lingered in her wake. They walked from via Accademia to Piazza Sordello and caught a cab to a seafood restaurant that they had found on the web. It was expensive but Will said they should enjoy what was probably their last night in the sleeping-beauty city of Mantova. She smiled when he said that.

When they were ensconced amid a sea of pristine white tablecloths and the bow-tied waiter had brought them menus, they pored over them for a while and then chose exactly the same: mussels followed by grilled tuna, with a Friulano white wine because Alessa said it would be a good match with the fish. The waiter lit a candle at their table and, noticing that they were speaking in English, asked if they were enjoying the romance of Mantova.

"Oh, we're just doing a study project together," Will said gallantly, and Alessa looked a little shy. When the waiter smiled and left they sat for a moment in the subdued lighting of the restaurant and didn't know quite what to say.

"This is very nice," Alessa said at last.

"You do look lovely," Will said. "And I didn't bring a scrap of decent paper with me. Remind me to draw you the second I can make a proper job of it."

She smiled and looked shy again. Then her phone vibrated on the tablecloth and she looked at it before pressing the red telephone button to reject the call.

"Lucas calling," she explained. "But just now, I'll let him stew for a while."

He laughed, and then the mussels came and they spent some time working through them. When they had finished and had each had a glass of wine, Alessa whispered, "this place is so smart that I can't bring myself to open a laptop."

She gestured at the room, which she was facing. He had his back to it so he turned around and took in the other diners, the immaculate waiters and the gold-framed oil paintings on the walls. He turned back and nodded.

"I know what you mean, but at least we can talk. Can you remember what Semiramide said in her note? A glass and a half of white wine seems to have erased it from my brain."

"I've got it written on a piece of paper from when I was working it out," Alessa said. She looked around guiltily and then opened the laptop for a moment, releasing the paper from where it had been pinned against the keyboard. She hurriedly shut the lid again before the screen lit up.

"Here it is," she said, smoothing out the paper on the tablecloth. "It says *'Look where your father hunted. Stand under the bell and find the mark of my ring where you feared to lie.*"

"Right. And we've partly worked out the second part. She's talking about her signet ring which had an impression of the Medici balls, and we are going to find that mark somewhere near where her son was afraid of telling untruths, under a bell."

"Maybe in a bell tower," Alessa added. "That being a good place for bells."

Will topped up their glasses.

"We need a place where his father hunted," Will said. "And his father was Lorenzo, right?"

"His father was Lorenzo di Pierfrancesco dei Medici, known as Il Popolano. So his grandfather's name skipped a generation to him."

"Where did his dad go hunting? That's the question."

"I don't have any idea," she said. "And Semiramide says 'hunted', which makes me think Pierfrancesco was a boy when his dad went hunting."

"How old was he when this note was written?"

"I worked that out earlier. In 1523 he would have been thirty-six, but his father died when he was sixteen so he would have been a boy or at most a young man. In fact he died himself when he was only thirty-eight, so he only lasted a couple of years after his mother. She would have been heartbroken if she'd known."

"My God, he died when he was only thirty-eight? What did he die of?"

But she didn't know and then the tuna arrived and they were busy eating for the next while.

"This is utterly gorgeous," Will said between mouthfuls. "I think I'm going to have to emigrate to Italy."

"Thank you for bringing me," she said, and put her hand on his for a moment. It was warm and her touch sent a thrill through him. Then she retrieved her hand and confessed that she couldn't possibly manage any dessert, even though there was tiramisu and gelato. He agreed and they ordered coffee. The manager of the restaurant came over to their table and poured them each a glass of Limoncello on the house, which was very agreeable. He left the bottle with them.

While they were sipping *cappuccini* and nibbling tiny biscuits provided on a silver salver, two adjacent tables finished up and departed. One had been a voluble foursome and the noise level dropped considerably once they had left. Alessa looked around surreptitiously.

"I reckon I could look something up now," she said very quietly. "We've got space around us and the waiter won't be back for a bit. You wanted to know what poor old Pierfrancesco died of?"

She opened her laptop and it lit up. She looked around guiltily and turned the brightness down to minimum, keeping the machine on the seat beside her so that it was concealed from the casual observer.

"No mention of what he died of. It just says where he died – oh my God!"

Her voice had suddenly taken on an urgent note.

"What?"

"He died at Cafaggiolo in 1525."

"OK, where's that?"

"Well, Cafaggiolo is one of the Medici castles outside Florence, but I think I've read about Cafaggiolo. '*Faggio*' is a beech tree. Hold on."

Her fingers flew over the keys and then she sat back triumphantly, tilting her screen back so he could read from it.

Etymologically speaking, the word cafaggiolo has particularly ancient origins: the Longobards used it to refer to a wooded area. As the vulgar tongue developed, the word cafagium was used to indicate a beechwood, and the word cafaggiolus subsequently took on the meaning of a hunting estate.

"It sounds spot on," he said.

"Exactly! It says the Villa Medicea di Cafaggiolo is a villa situated near the Tuscan town of Barberino di Mugello in the valley of the River Sieve, some 25 kilometres north of Florence." She read on silently and then paraphrased. "Il Magnifico owned it but the Pope seized loads of his assets and he was short on funds, so he borrowed from his younger cousins and wards, *Lorenzo di Pierfrancesco* and his brother Giovanni. It all got a bit nasty and he ended up transferring Cafaggiolo to them in part payment. So Semiramide's husband, Pierfrancesco the Younger's *father*, owned the villa. I bet they lived there a lot because it was in the Tuscan countryside outside Florence. The rich families used to decamp from the cities any time there was a sign of the plague, so the children could have spent quite a bit of time growing up there."

"His father would probably have hunted there. Is it still around or has it been bulldozed and replaced with high-rise flats?"

"It's a UNESCO world heritage site," she said, reading her laptop screen. "So they can't knock it down. Oh *merda!*"

"What?" he said, catching the sudden consternation in her voice.

"It says here that Cafaggiolo originally had *two* towers but the larger one was demolished in the nineteenth century. I wonder if that was our bell tower. Look at this."

She held up her phone sideways and he looked at a lunette painted by Gustav Utens in 1599, just three-quarters of a century after the note had been concealed by Semiramide in her brooch. The picture showed a huge white-walled, terracotta-roofed villa with two towers, one at the front over the gate, and a much larger one in the middle.

"So I presume this smaller front one is the remaining tower," Will said. "Does it say if it has a bell? We need a belltower."

She was silent for a while as she read the article, but then blew out her lips. She shook her head at him.

"No mention of a bell. We're still in with a fair chance though, because they would usually put the bell in the gate tower, which is this one at the front that is still standing. The taller one in the middle would have had a commanding view of the garden, which was regarded as an integral part of the house. Water was scarce so only the rich could afford green lawns because they needed irrigation. The front tower had a drawbridge, look. The men at arms would have occupied the gate tower because they guarded the inner courtyard, and they'd ring the bell if there was an attack."

"And Cafaggiolo is still standing today."

"Yes, that's what I'm saying."

She showed him a modern photograph of the front of a terracotta building which was clearly the same place. It looked old and unkempt, but three windows were evident in the top of the front tower, exactly as had been painted by Utens.

"Well there we are then," Will said. "All we have to do is get to the top of the tower, find the secret hiding place beneath the bell, and make off with the loot."

She grinned and closed the laptop.

"We've solved it, Will!" she said triumphantly. "Semiramide meant that her son should go to Cafaggiolo, where they would have frequently stayed, find the bell which is in a place where he was afraid of telling untruths – that part is still very weird – and look for her seal, which as we know is the Medici balls."

She ceremoniously topped up their empty Limoncello glasses and they toasted and drank. Then they paid up and decided to walk back because it was a warm evening and they were full of wine. Life felt good.

"Are you going to be OK walking in heels?" Will asked, eying her lovely but impractical footwear.

"Will, I have Italian blood," she said, bowing to him. "I was born in good shoes!"

Somewhere along the line as they walked through the quietening Mantova streets, their hands touched and then clasped. They held hands for the rest of the way back to the hotel, not saying much, just enjoying the feeling of each other's touch. They let go each other's hands when they reached the hotel and collected their room keys. They reached her door first and she turned to him in a slightly awkward moment.

"I think I owe you a goodnight kiss," he said, and they flowed naturally together after a second's pause, his hand on the warm nape of her neck, her breasts pressed against his chest. Their lips touched and then their mouths were upon each other. He felt her tongue on his in a gorgeous moment. They stood in her doorway for what seemed a very long time, just kissing, and then with a sudden urgency she found her key and opened the door and they fell through it together.

"Babies?" he asked awkwardly.

"No babies," she said. "It's fine, just give me a minute." She disappeared into the bathroom and he didn't know what to do, so he took off his clothes and climbed into her bed, hoping that he wasn't being presumptuous. But she emerged wearing only red knickers and climbed onto the bed, leaned over him and kissed him. Her nipples brushed his bare chest.

They did not get a great deal of sleep.

It felt very different when they woke up together; warm and comfortable. It was ten o'clock because they had been awake most of the night, talking and making love. They showered and checked out and left their luggage with the concierge while they had an early lunch out. It was Sunday but there were plenty of places open for tourists.

"What we need to do now is to stop thinking about last night and be practical," Alessa said.

He shook his head.

"I can't."

"You can. And we've got to return the brooch to the museum," she said. "Otherwise we're just as bad as Lucas the Liar and the Bloody Fucking Woman."

He grinned.

"But we mustn't get caught doing it," he added. "Or they'll think that it was us that stole it rather than Lucas and the BFW."

They carefully wiped down the brooch and box to remove any possibility of fingerprints, then tucked it into a paper bag with a note in block capitals addressed to Museum Security. Will pointed out that he was the burglar and should return the stolen goods. He put on the black Venetian hoodie with the hood up, and the mirror sunglasses that he had bought in Venice, then disappeared towards the Palazzo. He came back after half an hour to the small bar where they had agreed to meet, and she looked up expectantly.

"That was quick! How did it go?"

He leaned over and kissed her on the lips before sitting down.

"It was fine. I tucked it inside the information desk when the attendant's back was turned. She's probably found it by now. Then I got rid of the hoodie, so we're all set."

"And those horrible sunglasses I hope?"

He nodded. "I stamped on them and it was quite satisfying."

She gripped his hand for a moment with a new intimacy.

"Perfect! Now while you were gone I've been trying to find out everything I can about the Villa Medicea di Cafaggiolo, but it's been quite difficult because there are conflicting stories."

"What did you find?"

"It used to be open for tours, but then it was bought by some rich family and it's supposedly being renovated and turned into a resort. Lots of people are up in arms about it because it's a UNESCO heritage site. Anyway, that was all announced a while ago and it doesn't seem to have reopened yet. They seem to have weddings, and they used to have wine tours but I'm not sure if they still do. I've come to the conclusion that we actually need to go there and check it out, because the internet is being pathetic."

"Is there a number to call?"

"Yes, and I've tried calling it, but it just goes to a message saying it's closed, with no explanation as to why."

He looked at his watch and saw that it was almost two o'clock.

"Well, we could go to Florence for the night and hire a car to get out there tomorrow."

"We could. It's possible to get there from Florence by bus but a car would be easier."

They collected their luggage and took the train to Florence. Alessa booked them a hotel from the train, then checked the news headlines and looked up happily.

"Apparently the brooch stolen from the Palazzo Ducale has mysteriously turned up!" she said. "It's in perfect condition and even came in its own presentation box. Police think it may have been stolen by someone as a prank. The museum says it will be improving its security procedures and in the meantime the brooch will be kept safely under lock and key."

"Thank heavens for that," Will said. "There are all sorts of thieves about."

21

A mighty flame follows a tiny spark.

DANTE ALIGHERI

14th May 1486, Villa di Castello, Florence

Semiramide and Caterina arrived back at Castello in the early morning and attached themselves to tradespeople delivering food. Semiramide was back in her bedchamber before her normal time of waking, and Caterina swiftly disposed of their soiled servant's clothes. She ordered Semiramide's young maid to fill a bath for her mistress, using hot water from the kitchens. Semiramide soaked for an hour and almost dozed off in the bath, for she had not had any sleep.

Il Popolano returned to the Villa late that afternoon, and his wife awaited him, now clean, rested and sweet-smelling, with Laudomia and Ginevra by her side. Isabetta and Caterina spirited away the children for bedtime shortly after their father had greeted them. Semiramide wore her most attractive dress to dinner in honour of her husband's homecoming, and her hair was braided with glittering jewels. Her glances in his direction were beguiling. When they went to bed she left the door to her bedchamber open while she let down her hair. She was wearing an ivory silk shift which revealed the fair skin of her back. When he visited her, he found that she smelled of rose petals and seemed more desirable to him than she had ever done. They had a night like new lovers, in which she gave herself to him no fewer than three times before they were both spent, and slept the sleep of the exhausted.

"I don't think we need Maestro Botticelli after all," he whispered to her when they lay together afterwards. Her heart skipped a beat before she realised that he was referring to the maestro's paintings designed to encourage childbirth.

A month later she missed her bleed and knew she was with child.

At the beginning of March 1487, Semiramide gave birth to her son and heir, Pierfrancesco di Lorenzo di Pierfrancesco de' Medici, who would in time become known as Pierfrancesco the Younger. He was an unusually bonny child, with lots of hair, unburdened with the characteristic Medici hooked and flattened nose. This was attributed to the beauty of his mother, for Semiramide by that time was a radiant young woman of twenty-three years. It was said that her political marriage had matured into one of love, for she seemed ever-more devoted to Il Popolano and rarely left his side.

It was when the baby Pierfrancesco was six months old that the Medici held a grand ball, thrown by Il Popolano to show off his son and heir to the lords and ladies of Florence. It took place in the Medici Palace in via Larga at the end of summer 1487. The September temperatures were beginning to recede a little from the peak of August, but lords still sweated freely in their embroidered velvet doublets and ladies in layered silk dresses tried in vain to fan away their perspiration, complaining with each other crossly that Il Popolano had not waited for the more temperate month of October to hold his ball. But Il Popolano wanted the date to be six months after the birth, so invitations went out to aristocrats and the Signoria and Guild leaders, both within Florence and beyond, for the second day of September.

Botticelli was once again invited as an honoured guest, along with many of the other painters of the day, including his friendly rival Domenico Ghirlandaio, who was three years his junior but somehow seemed older. Poliziano was there of course, now well established through his wit and erudition as court poet and bosom friend of the Medici. Verrocchio turned up, though he only just made it for he was off to Venice to open a workshop there. He was over fifty and Botticelli privately thought age was taking its toll, for he walked with the aid of a stick and seemed in pain. Verrocchio introduced the assembled group of artists to his protégé Lorenzo di Credi, whom he announced would run his Florentine workshop until his return. Leonardo di ser Piero da Vinci had apprenticed in Verrocchio's workshop but was not at the ball, for he had been in Milan for the last five years and visited Florence less often than he and his friends there would have liked.

A band of musicians had viols on the leg and on the arm, but the true entertainment was the singers who would come later. Until then, people were occupied with the business of food. They paid scant attention to the players. There was a long top table at which the Medici and their families were seated. Il Magnifico was there despite his recent disagreements with Lorenzo Il Popolano and his brother, surrounded as always by an admiring group, his power and charisma attracting acolytes like iron to a lodestone. It would be inconceivable to hold a celebration of a Medici birth without him, although his poor health was beginning to plague him more and more. Il Popolano was in the centre of the top table, with Semiramide to his left and his younger brother Giovanni to his right. Numerous other tables were placed around the great ballroom, both large and small, so that the assembled multitude could stand or be seated as they wished. There was a loud buzz of conversation as people exchanged court gossip, flirted with each other, brokered deals, wagered money and exchanged a hundred conversations. The volume of the crowd rose above the music, almost drowning it out.

The Vespucci family was present in force and Amerigo came over to see Botticelli, who was seated alone at a corner table and seemed to him uncharacteristically quiet.

"What's the matter with you, my friend?" he asked, slumping down into an upholstered chair beside Botticelli and carefully positioning his wine glass before him on the table. "You're normally prowling through the crowd reminding them of your greatness and picking up commissions. I've never seen you so modest! And not only that, I hear you've been overcome with religious fervour of late."

Botticelli smiled sheepishly at his friend. It was true that he had worked more for the Church than the Medici in the last months. He'd had no contact with Semiramide since Ognissanti, when his wildest dream had come true and they had made love in a sudden outburst of passion. On that night she had then gathered herself together and departed without him, cloaked and hooded. If he looked at the top table he could see her at this very instant, for the Medici table was elevated for all to see.

It was excruciating for him to look at her, yet since that wonderful and fateful night he had experienced endless agonies of fear and guilt. He regarded Lorenzo Il Popolano as his friend as well as his patron, and yet he had cuckolded the man. Not only had he coveted the man's wife, he had committed adultery with her and thus broken not one but two of the Lord God's Commandments. He felt as if he needed to send a message to God, a confession of his guilt and a plea for forgiveness, but he did not know how. He had a dozen times resolved to confess to Lorenzo, but a dozen times had failed in this resolution. He was not brave enough, nor did he want a dagger awaiting him in a dark alley.

A dagger in an alley made him think of Saltarelli.

On that fateful night when he had been caught with his secret painting, he had been terrified that the unknown intruder would tell all. The very next evening, Semiramide had told him about the letter from Saltarelli. After she had left Ognissanti and he had walked home in a pleasant daze, it had suddenly occurred to him that Saltarelli might write another letter, and another, until one reached Il Popolano. He had stumbled into bed in the early morning, terrified and depressed.

The next morning he had awoken late after the wild night, still filled with both ecstasy and anguish. He had stumbled downstairs to his workshop, earning curious looks from the apprentices due to his dishevelled appearance. He had immediately learned that Biagio had found a knife under a workshop bench, and someone had recognized it to be Saltarelli's. A boy had been despatched to return the knife to its owner. On hearing this, Botticelli had retired to his bedchamber feigning sickness, where he had sat on his bed with his head in his hands, certain that his secret would soon be out.

But the wheel of fate had turned.

Biagio had come back with a dramatic tale that Saltarelli's body had been found in an alley close to his house, murdered by cutpurses. A guilty well of relief had washed over Botticelli at this news, and he had given silent thanks to the wicked ruffians who had committed the deadly deed. It never occurred to him that he might be in any way connected.

In self-retribution, Botticelli had abandoned his pagan subjects and now all his serious work depicted sacred moments from the Christian faith. He was becoming more aware of Savonarola, the priest who preached against profligacy and challenged the humanist ideals of the Medici family.

"So what is it?" Amerigo repeated, interrupting his train of thought. "You've been despondent for months, don't deny it. You've abandoned visionary works in favour of altarpieces. I never see you at the court. People are saying you've lost your touch but I don't believe it for a moment. What's going on?"

Botticelli smiled weakly again. This was a tale he could never tell, even to his most excellent friend.

"I have seen the light and I am focused on doing the Lord's bidding," he said feebly.

Amerigo scoffed and drank a quaff of wine.

"Your Rites of Spring captured the beauty of the world," he observed sagely, "and I don't think the Lord could disapprove of that. But if you won't tell me, Sandro, I can't force it out of you. What are you painting at the moment?"

Before Botticelli could tell him, there was a blast of trumpets and the crowd fell silent. Il Popolano was standing in the middle of the top table with a glass in his hand, and Semiramide sat beside him, looking up at her husband with evident adoration. Her loving expression cut Botticelli like a blade.

"My Lords, Ladies, Gentlemen and Others," Il Popolano began, to general laughter from the inebriated throng.

"Love, according to Petrarch, is the crowning grace of humanity, the holiest right of the soul, and the golden link which binds us to duty and truth. And it is because of the fruits of love that I welcome you here, on the day when my son and heir Pierfrancesco reaches his sixth month."

There were loud cheers and applause from the assemblage.

"He remains strong," Lorenzo went on, "and joins his sisters Laudomia and Ginevra. Thankfully he has the grace of his mother rather than his father." There was a polite titter from his audience. He smiled down at

Semiramide, who held the baby in her arms but handed him to Lorenzo on cue. Lorenzo held up the small sleeping boy and the crowd cheered and applauded some more before he returned the child to his wife and lifted his glass. He put a finger to his lips and the crowd quietened.

"Never wake sleeping children!" he said *sotto voce*. "And now I ask you all to stand, and to join me in a glass to celebrate."

Those seated got to their feet, although a few ancient lords were already asleep and were politely ignored. When everyone awake was standing with charged goblets at the ready, Lorenzo raised his glass and announced, "To Pierfrancesco di Lorenzo di Pierfrancesco de' Medici. May he be strong, wise and happy."

Everybody drank a toast and applauded loudly until Lorenzo sat down again. As soon as he was seated, others followed suit and the sound of conversation redoubled. Botticelli suddenly found he was still standing, like an island in a sea of people. Lorenzo was bouncing Laudomia on his knee, who was clearly unhappy that her baby brother had all the attention and not her. But it was Semiramide to whom Botticelli's attention was drawn, because her eyes suddenly caught him like arrow shafts streaking across the talking heads. There was an instant of recognition in her face before she turned away. Botticelli sat down again heavily, next to Amerigo who was already seated, and looked at his old friend with studied attention.

"So what have *you* been doing?" he asked Amerigo, and he listened with apparent attentiveness as Amerigo described how Il Popolano was becoming increasingly unhappy with his business agent in Sevilla, one Tomasso Capponi, and was considering sending Vespucci on a voyage to find a replacement. There could be much trade in it, but also the opportunity for Amerigo to advance his interest in cartography. He would, he told Botticelli, have a chance to explore inconsistencies in Toscanelli's famed map of the world.

Lorenzo and Semiramide began to tour the tables to show off the young Medici heir. The little one remained quiet but attentive throughout this entire noisy experience. Semiramide held him close in her arms while a young servant called Isabetta carried little Ginevra behind her. Laudomia held her father's hand, yawning but determined to stay awake. Semiramide's old servant, Caterina, accompanied them, glaring at anyone who got too close. Amerigo and Botticelli were in such close conversation that they never noticed the approaching entourage until suddenly the crowd parted and it was upon them.

"Maestro Botticelli," Lorenzo said warmly. "We have not seen enough of you these past months! And Amerigo! I hope you've been telling the maestro of your plans?"

Vespucci and Botticelli both leapt to their feet and bowed deeply.

"Maestro Botticelli," Semiramide said, inclining her head to him with an enigmatic smile. "And Amerigo, who I am delighted to see, for I need you to procure me a cap for Pierfrancesco. Something in grey velvet with a tassel, like the one you showed me."

"The one I found for my nephew? It would be my greatest pleasure," Amerigo said gallantly, bowing again.

"For little Bartolommeo, yes."

Botticelli looked at her but her eyes were fixed firmly on Amerigo. He had made love to this woman on the floor of a convent, yet she was steadfastly ignoring him and discussing hats for babies.

"Me present too?" Laudomia said indignantly, and Amerigo inclined his head to the little girl with a smile. "Why, you shall have a silver comb to put through the tresses of your beautiful hair," he said, and her face broke into a beaming smile.

"I understand you've moved more to Christian themes," Lorenzo said easily to Botticelli. "Perhaps we should discuss a commission for one of our family chapels?"

"It would be my pleasure," Botticelli said, bowing again even though this was an offer he would not pursue. The crowd began to press closer at this point for an opportunity to talk to Il Popolano, who like all famous men in a crowd knew that the trick was to keep moving. Accordingly the entourage moved on, and Botticelli felt both relief and heartache. Amerigo got up with their empty wine glasses, seeking a maid to refill them. While he was gone Botticelli was surprised to find old Caterina suddenly by his side, leaning close.

"The mistress would speak with you later, so don't leave early," she said in an undertone, and then she divined something from his expression. "And it'll be just talk, mind," she added tartly. "I'll find you, so await me."

She turned and was gone, leaving him astonished. Normally he would have felt piqued to be treated in this way, but her words made him suspect that the old woman somehow knew what had happened in Ognissanti. His mouth turned dry. He wondered if anyone else knew.

"You look like you've seen a ghost," Amerigo said cheerfully, returning with two charged goblets and placing them with exaggerated care on the table. He slumped once more into his seat. "Now where was I?"

It was midnight and carriages were collecting the rich and powerful. Botticelli would normally have slipped away by now, but he had remained at Caterina's bidding. Amerigo had disappeared to the jakes about an hour ago, and must have become distracted for he had never returned. Botticelli sat alone in an alcove. Lorenzo was leaving the top table looking pleased and a little drunk. He would sleep soundly tonight, Botticelli thought. Semiramide had long since departed with the little ones and her maids, but now Caterina appeared from the shadows, caught his eye and beckoned to him with an inclined head. She didn't approach him or speak. She passed down the side of the great ballroom and he followed at a distance. They went along a corridor past the jakes, which stank like a freshly turned midden. He saw the staircase which he had watched Simonetta Vespucci ascend more than a decade previously. Then they came upon a velvet drape concealing a narrow servants' stairway. Caterina glanced back to make sure he was following, then disappeared up the stairway. He looked around. No-one was watching so he went after her. The old lady was already at the top of the staircase, breathing a little heavily, and she beckoned him again, this time with her hand. They passed along corridors lined with closed doors, then up another narrow stair. He caught up with her.

"Where are we going?" he asked Caterina in a whisper.

"Here," Caterina said shortly and opened a door. He went in and Semiramide sat on a chair before a window with drawn drapes.

"This is Caterina's room," Semiramide said. "She has kindly lent it to us so we can talk. I have things to say to you, Maestro Botticelli."

"I am honoured, my lady," Botticelli said, echoing her formality.

"Very well then. Caterina, leave us. I will look for you in my own bedchamber when the Maestro and I have talked."

"You are sure you wish to be alone, mistress?" Caterina said with a warning note in her voice.

Semiramide smiled wearily.

"Don't worry," she said. "This won't take long."

Caterina continued to look disapproving but she went out and closed the door quietly. Semiramide went to it and twisted the key.

"So that we shall not be disturbed," she said.

"We have not spoken since Ognissanti," Botticelli said, his throat dry. "I don't know what is in your mind."

"Then I will tell you," Semiramide said in a firm voice. "What is in my mind is that we must never speak again, at least not in private."

"But you are my *muse*, madam," Botticelli said hopelessly, shaking his head. "I love you."

"Do not say such things," she said sternly. "Even to think such thoughts is to invite our downfall. Would you have that?"

He shook his head again dumbly.

"Then swear to me," she said. "Swear to me on your honour that you will never reveal our secret."

She waited, with that imperious look in her eye that he knew so very well.

"All right," he said weakly.

"Swear it."

"I do so swear before the Lord God as my witness," he said formally.

"I hear your oath," she said. "And I too so swear that I shall never speak of it. My servant Caterina knows but she will go to her grave with sealed lips."

Botticelli felt terribly sad.

"I had hoped…" he said, but didn't finish his sentence.

"There *is* no hope," she said. "For if there were hope at all for you and me, we would threaten the life of our child."

He stared at her.

"What...?"

"Did you not notice the face of my sleeping babe, Sandro?" she said gently and stood, coming to him now and taking his arm. "he is not of Medici stock, despite his name. Now do you see?"

He looked at her and he *did* see with sudden appalling clarity. The babe was no Medici heir at all.

"How can you be so sure?" he said weakly. "Babies look the same."

"You of all people know that to be untrue," she reproofed him gently. "But if you want confirmation, he has a *naevus* just here." She indicated a place on her abdomen, and blushed a little. "As do you."

He looked at her and nodded slowly. His father had borne the same birthmark, though they had never spoken of it, for some would name it the devil's mark. He put his hand on hers and there were tears in his eyes. She did not take her hand away.

"We have a child, you and I," he said in awe.

"We do, but we will lose him if either of us ever speaks of it. You would be hanged, I would be cast out as an adulteress, and our bastard son would lose his name. *That* is why we had to swear."

Tears ran down his cheeks.

"I shall love you always," he said, "but I understand. I won't let slip that you're my muse."

"Try not even to mention my name," she said, looking alarmed. "We cannot meet except by chance, for we must protect the life of our son." She was quiet for a few moments as she deliberated.

"Perhaps you could name Simonetta for your muse."

"Simonetta Vespucci?"

"Yes, my beautiful aunt. I adored her, you know. I was broken-hearted when she died. She played with me when I was a little girl, and she was very kind."

"Everyone already thinks La Bella Simonetta *is* my muse," Botticelli said, "But they never think to ask me to confirm or deny it." He raised a finger as if to hold a thought. "I could ask to be buried at her feet. She lies in Ognissanti."

"That would be clever of you," Semiramide said.

He smiled ruefully.

"She *was* my muse before you," he admitted. "It would work."

"Then I have your word on it?" she asked.

He assented.

"Very well then. Leave after me, but wait a few minutes. If you are seen, pretend to be drunk and hunting the jakes, but be gone as quickly as you can."

She took her hand away and went to the door, but then hesitated and came back.

"Thank you for our beautiful boy," she said. "Know this, that I loved you too."

She reached up to his face and kissed him once on the lips, then fled swiftly to the door and was gone.

22

He that is without sin among you, let him first cast a stone at her.

CHRISTIAN BIBLE, King James Version, 1611

March, Villa di Cafaggiolo outside Florence

Will and Alessa checked out of their hotel in Florence on Monday, rented a black Audi and made the forty-minute drive up *strada statale* 65 to the Villa di Cafaggiolo. Alessa drove and they didn't talk much because they were both tired, having again spent little time sleeping. Will watched her as she drove and now and then she would catch his eyes on her and smile. Once she popped her eyebrows and he had to resist the urge to ask her to pull over.

"It's coming up soon," he said, looking at his phone. "Round the next bend."

They emerged from fields and trees to see buildings on the right, fronted by a forest of signs announcing that they had arrived in the village of Cafaggiolo and they were now in the municipality of Barberino di Mugello; a *comune* twinned with Betton in Brittany. More signs warned that they shouldn't toot their horn, that the speed limit was 50 kilometres per hour, and that speed cameras awaited those ignoring this decree. Alessa carried on with all the other drivers, none of whom slowed; in fact the road straightened and everyone speeded up.

A collection of large buildings appeared at first to terminate the road, but then the traffic swung round a sharp bend to the right. As they approached they could see that almost every wall of the Villa di Cafaggiolo was covered by scaffolding, which in turn was swathed in white fabric.

"Restoration underway," Alessa remarked.

She followed the traffic around the bend and they could immediately see the villa on their left, beyond wide lawns and partially hidden by two huge cedars.

"There's our tower!" Will pointed, and they saw it flash into view for a moment before it disappeared behind a thick hedge.

"If it *is* our tower. I hope Semiramide's message wasn't in the tower they knocked down. And we don't know that Cafaggiolo is even the right place."

"I'm sure it is," Will said. "All that stuff about a hunting estate was true, and Semiramide mentioned hunting."

They passed some buildings and Alessa pulled into the opening of a small track to the right, just before a sign marking the end of Cafaggiolo. She swung back onto the highway the way they had come and drove back slowly past the front of the villa.

"It looks like one of those wrapped buildings," she said.

"Like Christo," he nodded. "The bloke who wrapped up the Reichstag in Berlin."

Alessa slowed still further and pulled into a layby before wrought-iron gates. The driver behind sounded his horn energetically, clearly not having noted the ban on horn tooting.

They climbed out of the car, stretching. It was a warm day for March. Beyond the gates an access road passed beside a long building which had once been stables, then curved round to the front of the villa. There were six parked cars. By standing to the left of the gates they could see the tower emerging behind the nearest cedar. Their hands touched and then clasped.

"It's weird to be here," Will said.

Alessa squeezed his hand but then let it go to fetch the bottle of water from the car. When she returned he was looking up at the wall of the crumbling edifice which fronted the highway. There was a huge curved white spike high on the wall.

"I read about that on the train," he said. "You'll never guess what it is."

"It looks like a huge tusk."

"It does, but it's actually a whale's jawbone, and they reckon Leonardo da Vinci might have found it. There's an article in his notes about finding a fossilised whale skeleton in a crystal cave. This could have been the creature's jawbone. After all, he had close ties with the Medici, and Il Popolano was fond of him."

She stared at the bone.

"How peculiar. A sea creature miles from the sea. But I guess if we go back far enough, all this could have been under the sea."

"That's what they think, but here's the real reason why it stuck in my mind. Do you remember that painting of the villa we were looking at?"

"The one by Utens?"

"Yes, the lunette," he said, outlining a semicircle with his hands. Well, the whale bone was in it."

She shook her head.

"That painting was too small for anyone to see a whale bone."

"That's what I thought," Will said, "but if you look closely at the Utens, it's up on the stable wall. They had a close-up so you could see."

He pointed along the access road before them.

"In the painting, it's up on the wall just along there."

"Ha."

They stared for a few moments.

"Come on then," Alessa said, returning to the car. "Let's see if we can talk our way in and get up the tower."

The wrought-iron gates were shut, but another access road wound in between the buildings. They drove round the back of the long building. There was an automatic barrier but it didn't open, so they reversed and parked on grass at the rear of the whale-bone building. When Alessa killed the engine there was just the sound of birdsong and the swooshing sound of cars on the highway. They climbed out and looked around. Like all great estates the villa was slightly elevated and the Tuscan fields rolled away before them. There was a bedraggled willow and the buildings needed painting.

"It certainly does need a refresh," Will remarked.

"Let's do what we worked out," she said. "I'm a scholar from Oxford studying the Medici, with a focus on Renaissance campanology."

"Okay, though I still can't see why you'd be writing about bells."

"Time-keeping," she said. "It was a big challenge then, so they had a system of bells to announce the hours. *Prime, terce, sext, nones.* I'll blind them with my academic brilliance."

She wiggled her eyebrows at him and he grinned.

They walked past the barrier towards more parked cars and a couple of white builders' vans. There were several tall, closed doors which didn't look as if they were used. In the corner the building angled left and there was a tall archway. They walked beneath it and found an open door.

There was a woman of about forty sitting at a desk and she glanced up with an irritable expression when they entered. She had on a dark blue business suit which looked a couple of sizes too small for her. She wore glasses with light-blue frames, and too much blue eye shadow. She had long nails and she was in the middle of painting them blue. The woman was obsessed with blue, Will decided. The smell of nail varnish filled the room. The woman looked embarrassed to be caught painting her nails.

"*Ciao,*" Alessa said with her friendliest smile and began a rapid conversation in Italian, but Will could tell almost immediately from the tone of voice and the body language that it wasn't going well. He tried to look charming and affable. The woman was shaking her head now, and gesturing with her hands. Will could tell that Alessa's smile was in danger of slipping, but the whole exchange was in Italian so he stood dumbly by, thinking that he needed to learn the language.

The blue woman gave an exasperated sigh and picked up a black walkie-talkie from her desk, holding it carefully because of her wet nails. She pressed a button with exaggerated care and spoke into it.

"She's calling the site manager," Alessa said in an undertone with her back to the woman. "She's a beetch."

Will smiled toothily at the woman over Alessa's shoulder and nodded to her. The woman put down the radio and said something to Alessa.

"The site manager is coming," Alessa said to Will in English, then nodded and thanked the woman, who waved them away with a 'whatever' gesture, audibly tutted and picked up her bottle of nail varnish.

They stood just outside the door while they waited, remaining in sight of the receptionist so that she wouldn't assume they had departed. There was a breeze blowing through the archway and the air was mercifully free of acetone.

"That seemed difficult," Will said quietly, and Alessa rolled her eyes.

"Horrible woman," she said through gritted teeth. "But I had to be nice."

The site manager turned up after ten minutes. He was also about forty and wore a blue suit. Maybe he was the receptionist's husband. Maybe she chose his suits for him when she was buying hers. Certainly he could be her husband – he had a similarly truculent expression. His hair was long but thin on top, and he had a cadaverous look as if he had once been a drug addict, maybe last Tuesday. He stared at Alessa's breasts the whole time she talked to him. Will felt the site manager would look considerably better with a flattened nose. The conversation went on for a minute or two and then the man was shaking his head even more vigorously than the receptionist. Will didn't speak Italian but he did recognize the word *'impossibile'*, which was uttered several times. Then the man turned and marched away, saying "no, no-no-no no-no no-no no" over his shoulder, in case they didn't get the idea.

Will looked at Alessa.

"So that would be no, then?"

She marched away herself through the archway and he had to hurry to catch up with her.

"Apparently the place belongs to some rich foreigner and it would be more than the site manager's life is worth to let us in. He's never heard of Oxford University! They rent the place out for weddings and there's one happening today and we have to go immediately or he'll call the police and report us for trespass."

"He actually said that?"

"Uh-huh."

"Wow, and there was me thinking that all Italian people are charming."

They got back to the car, which had caught the sun and was hot inside. The air conditioning roared when Alessa started the engine.

"A wedding," Will said thoughtfully, and pointed. "Is that what the sign says?"

There was a white poster beside the automatic barrier, and she squinted at it.

"*Parcheggio per la festa di matrimonio.* Yes, Antonio Ossani is marrying Sofia Toscani today. Not here though, in a church, but the reception is here, starting at four."

He tilted his head at her.

"Maybe we could gate crash the wedding."

"Have you seen yourself, Will? Or me, for that matter. We don't exactly look like wedding guests."

"Right now we don't, but it's only half an hour back to Florence. We could get spruced up and come back here around nine when everyone's drunk a few glasses of booze."

"There is no *way* I can spruce up for a wedding. I haven't anything to wear. And what about you? Is there a suit in that suitcase?"

"There are shops," Will said blandly.

It was dark when they arrived back from Florence. They pulled the black rental into the access road and this time the automatic barrier was raised. They had tied white ribbons around their wing mirrors so that they looked like wedding guests, but there was no-one to check – all the genuine guests had arrived hours ago. They parked at the end of a long line of cars and got out. Will was wearing a black tuxedo with a white wing-collar shirt and a white bow tie. His hair was heavily gelled and drawn back into a pony-tail. He wore shiny black patent-leather shoes and a white silk scarf.

Alessa was in a better mood than she had been after the encounter earlier that day. She collected a new gold-lamé clutch bag from the floor well and locked the car, putting the keys into the small bag. She was wearing a long burgundy dress and had matching burgundy nails and lipstick. Her dark hair was pulled back tightly but then it burst into a cluster of curls. She took Will's arm and grinned.

"All right then, just this once I'll admit you were right," she said. "Now we need to get in without getting stopped by those ghastly blue people."

"I suggest we sneak in," Will said, "as sneakily as we know how to sneak."

They walked past the archway they had entered before and went around the building until they came to another entrance. There was a wide inner courtyard and music was coming from double doors on the opposite side. Tables were set out in the courtyard and wedding guests were sitting or standing in groups. The sound of their voices and laughter reverberated off the courtyard walls. There was a diehard knot of smokers and vapers standing outside the double doors, drinking and chatting. As Will and Alessa approached they could see the interior room, in which people were dancing.

Neither the azure receptionist nor the site manager were to be seen. There were two white-jacketed security men at a table beside the double doors, but someone had given them a drink and they had loosened their ties. Will and Alessa grabbed empty glasses from a table and passed through the doors, crossing the threshold without challenge.

The music was coming from a band comprising two guitar players, a pianist, a percussionist and a violinist. A female singer with pink hair had the microphone and the audience was clapping to the beat and her swaying voice. She was good and there was a drunk and happy mood. Further to the back of the large room, people were leaning close to each other and talking loudly to make themselves heard. Will could make no sense of the fast Italian, but Alessa's eyes sparkled. These were *her* people, and it was as if the hubbub made her resonate. Waitresses and waiters weaved expertly through the crowd with canapés and fizzing glasses. Will and Alessa dumped their empty glasses and grabbed two drinks for camouflage, then worked their way through the crowd. After a few minutes they reached the doors on the far side of the room and went through them into a wide corridor with a white-tiled floor and a beamed ceiling. There were wide arches which served no purpose other than decoration. There were more tables there and the lights were low. Couples kissed in corners. Will and Alessa moved on casually and no-one took any notice of them, apart from casting one or two flirtatious glances in their direction.

They didn't know in what direction the tower lay.

"We need to find a window," Will hissed in her ear, "so we can get our bearings."

They found one on the right and peered through it. All they could see was scaffolding and white cloth. They looked at each other, grimaced and moved on. A window on the other side of the corridor proved more useful. It was partly obscured but in the distance they could make out passing headlights.

"That must be the highway," Alessa said.

"Which means that the tower should be this way." He pointed where the corridor forked left. They checked but they were unobserved. Alessa's high heels clicked on the tiles so she slipped out of them and held them in her hand. She seemed suddenly small beside him. At the end of the corridor there was a door and a wide staircase. The door was locked.

"Towers go up," Alessa said quietly, so they went up the staircase as quietly as they could. They could still hear the distant party music but now it was muted. The upstairs corridor smelled of fresh paint, as if it had not been open for long. In one room with open doors they could see tools and workbenches. They passed a spiral staircase and the corridor beyond opened out into a gallery which looked down on the entrance hall. There was nobody down in the hall, which was full of builders' materials.

"This must be the base of the tower," Alessa said, whispering because it was clear that a normal voice would carry.

They backtracked a few yards and headed up the spiral staircase. It was quite a climb but after a few minutes they arrived in a large square room at the top. The stairs had been lighted but the tower room was not, until Alessa clicked an old-fashioned toggle switch which bathed the room in yellow light from a single high lightbulb.

"Who's going to see?" she said when Will raised his eyebrows at her. "Everyone down there is drunk."

They looked around the tower room. Its walls were whitewashed and flaking away in places. The room was cluttered with more building materials and work had started on the front wall, removing loose paint with a power tool that stood on a workbench. The corners of the large room were buttressed with exposed stone.

"Bingo!" Will said, pointing to a huge bell mounted above on a vast wooden beam. Beneath it was a carved face in the form of a large stone medallion, set in the centre of a side wall. There were two white marble statues on plinths either side of the entrance stairway: one of a wild boar and the other of a hunter with a bow. The boar had a metal arrow stuck in its side, but the iron fletching had at some point corroded and snapped off. Will looked around the room and spied the end of the arrow on the middle sill of the three high front windows. He reached up and brought it down, holding it to the end of the metal shaft.

"What a shame," he said quietly. "It loses the effect. I wonder if they'll put it back on. I hope they don't just throw it away."

He realised that Alessa wasn't paying any attention to him. He put the rusted arrow fletching back on the sill and joined her. She had walked over to the stone face set in the wall and was standing under the huge old bell, staring at the face. It was a large round marble disc depicting an old, bearded man with long ragged hair. His mouth was an oval opening and his eyes were round holes filled with black stone. Somehow the face had a look of anguish.

"Do you recognize it?" Alessa asked, keeping her voice low.

He frowned, trying to remember. "It's the weirdest thing, but it does remind me of something, though I can't think what."

"It's not the original, it's a replica, though I've seen the real thing in Rome. This one isn't full size, though. The real one is taller than me."

"It's slightly scary."

"It's a copy of the *Bocca della Verità*; the Mouth of Truth. I saw the original with my parents when I was about ten. It's just inside a church but you have to queue to get close to it because all the tourists want to see it. The idea is that you stick your hand inside the mouth and if you tell a lie it bites your hand off."

"Charming!" Will said, and then he stared as she put her hand into the mouth and jerked as if it were being bitten off. "Roman Holiday!" he said suddenly. "That old film with Audrey Hepburn and Cary Grant. That's where I remember it!"

She smiled. "You're so cultured, Will! It wasn't Cary Grant, it was Gregory Peck, but you're right about Audrey; no-one could ever forget her.

That's what made *la bocca* famous. If it weren't for that film, no one would know or care, but it's become a sort of icon that you have to visit if you're in Rome for a few days. It's in all the guidebooks. That's why they took me, and being a historian, papà told me the story of it."

She looked wistful, remembering her father. Will noticed and it made him remember the old man too, drinking tea in his sitting room, what seemed like a thousand years ago. There was a pause as they both reflected. Then he gestured at the sculptured face in the wall.

"I wonder what it's doing here."

"We'll never know, I guess. The original one is ancient, a couple of thousand years old I think, but this one was presumably made around five hundred years ago. One of the Medici, perhaps Il Popolano himself, must have decided it would be a good thing to have a copy."

"Remember what Semiramide said in her note in the brooch," Will said, taking back his phone and scrolling back through the photos. He held it so that she could see a picture of the piece of paper where Alessa had written out the translation.

"*Look where your father hunted. Stand under the bell and find the mark of my ring where you feared to lie.*"

He gestured to the mouth.

"That's it. Where you feared to lie. She probably brought her son up here as a little boy and he was scared to put his hand in the mouth in case it got bitten off."

She looked up, suddenly animated.

"And we're standing under the bell, so we've found the right place!"

He reached into the oval mouth and felt around.

"I've still got a hand, and I can't feel anything. You try, you've probably got a smaller hand than me."

Alessa stepped forward and felt around inside the aperture. He turned on his phone light in case there was anything to see.

"I can't feel anything either," she said sorrowfully. "But it's been five hundred years. I suppose it was highly unlikely that we'd find anything after all this time."

Will shone his torch into the nostrils but they were just holes and it wasn't possible to get more than a finger inside. Again he felt around without success. She tried after him, but then gave an exclamation as she kneeled in front of the face.

"What?"

"The mark of the ring," she said.

"Are you sure? It felt smooth to me."

"Not in the nostrils, in the eye, look!"

He looked. The eyes of the face were filled with black stone and coated in dust, but the right eye had a bumpy surface.

"See if there's a brush," she said, gesturing at the stack of building materials. She blew hard at the eye and motes of dust flew off.

He found a clean paintbrush and handed it to her. She used it to remove the dust from the two eye holes, exposing obsidian circles.

"The original *Bocca* has holes for eyes," Alessa said, but on this one the holes are filled in. And there's the mark of the ring." She pointed.

He leaned close and saw what she had seen. On the right eye's black surface was a perfect print of the Medici balls.

"Here is our imprint of the Medici balls," she said. "As if from a ring."

He nodded.

"Good old Pocock. And didn't he say the seal was black?"

"He did. So Semiramide somehow put an imprint of her ring on the stone of the right eye."

He reached into the hole and touched the surface of the eye.

"You know, I don't think this *is* stone," he said. "I think it's sealing wax." He went over to the work bench and found a chisel.

"Well you can't just attack it with that," Alessa said indignantly. "This is an ancient artifact."

"I'll be very gentle," Will lied, and reached into the eye hole with the chisel. He worked for a moment and then brought out the chisel, with a small shaving of black something on the end.

"It's wax, or pitch. Something like that," he said soberly. "Not stone."

They stared at each other.

"So she came up here, or sent a trusted servant," Will said.

"And pushed the note or whatever into the hole."

"And filled up the hole with sealing wax."

"And left the mark of her ring."

"Yes, and then she did the other eye so it wouldn't look unbalanced."

There was a long pause.

"We need to scrape out the seal and see if there's anything behind the bung," Will said. She looked at him in an agony of indecision, then pursed her lips.

"Go on then," she said. "That moronic site manager will probably have the *Bocca* plastered over anyway, so we might as well look before he ruins it."

It was remarkably easy. Will scraped away at the surface and suddenly the wax bung loosened in the hole and he was able to flip it sideways and remove it. He shone his phone light into the hole and his mouth went dry.

"There *is* something, curled up. I need tweezers to get it out."

He went over to the tool bench and searched, followed closely by Alessa. She picked up a pair of narrow-nosed pliers from an open toolbox.

"Let me do it," she said. "I'm a trained art historian whereas you're a clumsy boy who'll probably rip it to shreds."

"But I'm an artist," he said, brandishing the chisel.

She smiled and knelt in front of the stone face. She nudged the curl of paper and it moved. With the greatest of care she gripped it with the pliers, muttering under her breath that she needed silicone-coated tweezers. Then she pulled very carefully and the tube of paper slid out of the stone orbit.

They looked at it. It remained furled into the tight spiral in which it had lain for five hundred years. It was a folded yellow letter, and in the centre could be seen the black lump of a wax seal.

Alessa had brought with her a plastic bag which she had purloined from a shop in Florence. She retrieved it from her gold lamé clutch bag, unfolded it and placed the cylinder of yellowed paper inside.

"We can't open it here," she said. "We need the proper tools and equipment. "If we try to unfurl it, it will break into pieces."

He felt frustrated but knew she was right.

"All right then. Let's take it and get out of here. If we leave it here it could be destroyed with the building works going on, and if we give it to that idiot site manager he'll probably light a cigar with it or something."

"It's stealing," she said.

"It's borrowing," he said. "We're looking after it and finding out its secret. We'll give it back to whoever owns the villa. We just need to find out what it says first."

She nodded.

"I shouldn't accept what you're saying," she said. "I shouldn't, but I'm going to. Let's go. We need to protect it so it doesn't get impacted in any way."

He took the bag so that he could conceal it behind the flap of his unbuttoned jacket if they met anyone. They tidied away the tools and Will put the damaged but intact disc of wax back into the eye hole of the *Bocca della Verità*. They extinguished the light and left the tower room. In a few minutes they regained their car without challenge and drove away from Cafaggiolo, the furled letter held securely in its bag on Will's lap.

It was coming up to midnight when they reached their hotel room, and they were mentally and physically spent. Alessa sat down at the desk and Will handed her the plastic bag with the furled letter inside. She put on her white linen gloves and removed the letter.

"We'll need to rehumidify the paper," she said absently.

"Huh?"

"To stop it cracking when we open it."

"How long will that take?"

"We'll need a few things from a kitchen supplier, and then a day or two for the paper to absorb moisture."

"A *day or two*? I want to open it now!"

She slipped off a glove and tapped the rolled cylinder of paper with her nail.

"Actually it sounds pretty good," she said.

"It does?"

"Yes. It doesn't sound dry and scratchy and echoey, does it? I guess that tower room was a bit damp. It sounds like paper should."

"I'll take your word for it," Will said. "So does that mean we can open it?"

"Let me start very carefully and if it cracks then I'll have to stop immediately. I could do with a lab, right now."

She put the glove back on and then began to unfurl the cylinder, but immediately stopped.

"No, it feels too resistant. I don't want to risk it. It's not ours, after all."

Will wanted to say just open it and we'll read it and if it's a bit damaged it will probably still be legible. But he knew she wouldn't.

"Isn't there any way we can rehumidify it faster than a few days?" he asked desperately.

"We could try a gentle steaming," she said. "Except that we haven't got a kettle. We could buy one tomorrow, though. No kitchen shops open right now."

Will marched over to the little trolley by the bathroom door.

"There's a coffee machine here," he announced, picking it up. "Let's see what we can do with this."

He filled the little machine with a glass of water from the bathroom sink, and switched it on without any coffee or filter inside. Almost immediately it began to heat up, and after a few minutes a thin tendril of steam began to curl from it. Alessa looked at it and grimaced, but she brought the furled letter over and held it in the gentle flow of steam, turning it over and constantly moving it so that it didn't get wet. This carried on for twenty minutes, with Will holding his finger on the switch so that the water kept boiling.

"Let's try that," Alessa said, squeezing the cylinder very slightly to judge its flexibility.

She sat down again at the desk and began to unfurl the letter. This time it worked. After a minute or so of slow-motion unrolling, the letter was flat. It had two horizontal folds and was held together with a black seal, again bearing the mark of the Medici balls from Semiramide's ring. The seal had betrayed its purpose after five hundred years and detached itself from one side of the fold. It no longer sealed the letter.

"Lucky we don't have to rip it open," Will said.

She gave him an old-fashioned look.

"Don't even joke about it."

She turned over the letter and held it for him to see the addressee in a flowing black script.

"Pierfrancesco."

Then she opened the letter slowly and it did not crack on the fold.

"Good paper," she said. "It's not parchment but it's thick and well made. We're very lucky."

She got it flat and held it open.

"*Figlio mio carissimo,*" she began and then translated: "My dearest son."

23

Whoever excommunicates me, excommunicates God.

GIROLAMO SAVONAROLA

7th February, 1497, Florence

It was Shrove Tuesday, the day before the beginning of the Lenten. The usual practice on this last day of *Carnevale* was the consumption of sweetmeats, accompanied by drunken singing of lascivious songs and a few fights. But this was a chastened Florence, commanded now by a pious Dominican friar, Savonarola. The Medici had been deposed and outcast, for it had been a turbulent ten years since Semiramide had kissed Botticelli for one last time in the Palazzo Medici. Apart from a secular painting depicting Calumny of Apelles, Botticelli had attempted to assuage his guilt through religion. Nativities, annunciations and crucifixions dominated his subjects. His brother Giovanni had died four years earlier, and his brother's sons had inherited the house in via Nuova. Botticelli still lived and worked in the house of his nephews. Time and worry had eroded his jovial nature and he had become increasingly mercurial, even though his single night of blasphemous passion with Semiramide on the floor of the Ognissanti convent had never been discovered. The voyeuristic Saltarelli had been stabbed to death by cutpurses before he had exposed Botticelli's secret. Saltarelli's ignominious death was not what the painter would wish on any man, yet it afforded him guilty relief that Semiramide's honour remained unsullied. The problem was that Botticelli himself still remembered that night with perfect clarity, and knew it to be a sin.

The master painter was now fifty-two, his once-golden locks grey and increasingly unkempt, his belly swelling with too much food and wine. His illegitimate son, Pierfrancesco the Younger, would reach his tenth year in less than a month, but Botticelli had not seen him for three years due to the exile of the Medici from Florence. Botticelli recalled seeing the boy only rarely in previous *Carnevale* processions, sitting between Il Popolano and Semiramide in a coach pulled by horses, or playing with his sisters in the gardens of the palace.

Botticelli had kept a low profile. If he had spoken to Lorenzo Il Popolano it was strictly about business. His departure from mythological subjects had lost him much of the humanist Medici patronage, and he had never spoken again with Semiramide. When the Medici had been deposed three years before he had felt a deep despair. They had left the city and now yearned for the fall of the Dominican friar and his pious republic.

Savonarola was increasingly referred to among rich Florentines as the 'mad monk', while his followers the *piagnoni* fanned the flame of this contempt with their increasingly strident demands for 'charitable contributions'. Botticelli's brother Simone, two years his senior, had returned from Naples and moved back into the house on via Nuova. He was an ardent follower of Savonarola, such that Botticelli felt unable to escape the increasingly extreme ideology promulgated by the black-robed friar. Some believed that Botticelli himself was a follower, as he had abandoned all secular forms of art, but this was untrue – Botticelli's moral compass was pointed not to the friar but to God. In his youth Botticelli had been proud and indomitable, but now he felt fearful of everything, and masked it with a grim countenance. He feared Savonarola and his *piagnoni*, but most of all he feared the retribution of *God*. He was filled with a fierce pride about his illegitimate son and yet he could not confess his crime to the Almighty. God, who saw all things, had seen him fornicate upon the floor of His House, so prayer seemed wholly inadequate. The fire and brimstone of Savonarola's sermons only served to make Botticelli more desperate and withdrawn. Without admission of his guilt it was akin to death without a funeral – there was no opportunity to put his mind at rest.

Until today, he thought.

Today would be the culmination of an idea that had come to him two months previously. He had conceived the notion of painting a picture to expose his secret, which he would then *burn*, as a message sent to the heavens. He would put all his skill into the painting and then destroy it. It had been Simone who had put the idea into his head, which was ironic since normally he didn't listen to his brother's thoughts about anything. Two months previously Simone had told him that on Shrove Tuesday, rather than an orgy of consumption before Lent, Savonarola would hold a Bonfire of the Vanities.

Such a bonfire was not a new custom. It had been invented decades before by San Bernardino di Siena, but Savonarola had adopted the practice and made it his own, for it fitted perfectly with his doctrine concerning absolution. The bonfire awaited unlit in the centre of the Piazza della Signoria, guarded by a ring of *piagnoni*, who had for the last several weeks donned their white gowns and gone house to house across the city, demanding 'vanities' such as scarlet cloth, gambling cards, jewellery, scented wigs, books and pagan paintings. They arrived in twos or threes; often aggressive young men who would take by force if nothing were freely offered. Simone had gone with them, and Botticelli had been darkly furious that his hypocritical brother lived in the house supported by him and his art, and yet would cheerfully volunteer his works for burning. On hearing of the proposed bonfire, Botticelli had come up with the perfect answer to the demand for vanities – he would create his painting as a confession, then send it in flames as a 'vanity' to God.

He went into his rear workshop – the one where Saltarelli had spied on him all those years ago – and contemplated the completed painting on its easel.

It was a large tondo, painted on panel in tempera, measuring two and a half braccia in diameter. He had used a spare panel that had gathered dust in his store, the twin of one which he had used a decade before to paint Our Lady with seven angels and a pomegranate. This painting was different, though there were similarities. Our Lady was a good likeness of Semiramide as she now was in her thirties; not one of those long-necked Graces he had put in Primavera, but still beautiful. Beside her on a cloth lay a brooch she had once owned. The Child in her arms had the likeness of his little boy. The Child held a bunch of five keys, and beside him on the coverlet was a pear from which a single bite had been taken, representing the breach of marital faith that Botticelli had caused through his lust. A red carnation lay at the Child's feet to mark Botticelli's love for his son.

The rest of the painting was entirely different. Rather than seven angels there were four, and each was a likeness of his son Pierfrancesco at different ages. He had not seen the child since the age of seven. Botticelli doubted that anyone other than Semiramide herself, and perhaps Il Popolano, would recognise these images, but no matter if they could because the painting was to be destroyed and they would never see it.

Each golden key in the bunch held by the Child had a serpent wound around its shaft, representing the evil that it would unlock. Numbers were shown on the keys in Roman numerals: II, XIIII, XXII, VIIII and I. In the distance behind the four angels was the skyline of Florence, with Ognissanti clearly visible on the river. The sun was behind the church's distinctive tower so that lines of light seemed to radiate from it. The only other character was an old greybeard, who knelt before Our Lady and the Child wearing a red and russet cloak and holding out a letter.

As Botticelli contemplated the finished painting, there was a thunderous knocking on the workshop door. He heard the hymns of the *piagnoni* from the street. He grimaced, but then nodded at the painting and picked it up. The tempera was perfectly dry, but the panel was heavy. In lifting it his arms were almost fully stretched. He carried it out, watched by a solemn Biagio, who had stuck with him through all these years. He put down the panel for a moment and opened the door to the street.

Three white-gowned cocksure youths stood at the door, the leader with his fist raised as if about to hammer on the wood again.

"Give up your vanities and be shriven," the leader yelled so that the whole street might hear, but then quailed before Botticelli's expression. Botticelli was not afraid of these young bullies – he was angry.

"*This* is my contribution," the painter said, lifting the tondo and holding it up before them so that they could see its mastery. "Painted by my own hand and just completed. This is what shall burn."

"We cannot burn a painting of Our Lady," said the leader, shaking his head uncertainly. "It would be sacrilege."

"Do you not understand the symbolism?" Botticelli asked. "See the half-eaten fruit the Child holds? It represents the end of Man's vanity. I have painted it so that it shall represent the end of vanities in the eyes of God. Your friar will understand and approve, even if you do not."

It was an outright lie, but he didn't think the *piagnoni* would understand the true allegory.

"Hand it over then," said the second youth, and the leader glared at him.

"Hand it over to *you?*" Botticelli said with a humourless laugh. "Oh no. I shall bring this to the fire myself, for I have heard tell of vanities mysteriously vanishing on their way to the flames." He waved his arm imperiously, and they stepped back. He snatched up his cloak and swirled it around his shoulders, then placed the large round panel on a handcart that he had ready for the purpose – it was fifteen minutes' walk to the Piazza della Signoria. He padded the panel with a soft cloth behind it, and strapped it in with a cord. It was ridiculous to protect it, he knew, because he was taking it to a bonfire to be burned, but he wanted it perfect until the moment of destruction, so that his message would be clear – here is a perfect painting that the Maestro is sending to God in flames.

He pushed the handcart out into the street, with the painting facing out and upright so that all could see it was a master work. The three white-robed *piagnoni* looked uncertain what to do next. They were used to being in control, but Maestro Botticelli had an undeniable air of command and none of them were brave enough to argue with him.

"You three shall be my escort," Botticelli said to them, giving them a role, and they fell in meekly behind him as he wheeled the handcart along Borgo Ognissanti beside the river, in the direction of the Piazza. Biagio followed the procession to make sure that his master was safe. He wanted to help by pushing the handcart, but he didn't want to reveal his presence so he hung back. A group of urchins and other interested onlookers followed the procession, so that Biagio was soon concealed by the crowd.

Biagio listened to the voices around him, and they were troubled. The locals liked Botticelli, for he was always generous with his purse, but more than that they were tired of this new pious Florence. The spirit had been drained out of the City. Commerce had all but ceased and there was no income to put food in their children's mouths. At first they had flocked to Savonarola's fiery sermons in the cathedral. In a fit of religious fervour they had dared to burn the Medici bank, but that passion was dissipated now. Savonarola had claimed a year gone that Florence would become more glorious, powerful and wealthy than ever before. He had described prophetic visions from the Virgin Mary herself. At first some of his prophesies had seemed to come true, but now the City was on the edge of famine. There had been a poor harvest caused by months of rain, and Florentine mercenaries were engaged in a costly siege of Pisa. Florentines did not feel glorious, powerful or wealthy; they felt close to breaking point. Savonarola told them it was their lack of repentance that was the cause, which did little to quell the growing unrest.

The group around Botticelli and his handcart arrived in the crowded piazza, overlooked by the vast Palazzo della Signoria. In the centre of the piazza a huge octagonal wooden pyramid had been constructed, the height of ten or eleven men from base to top. Seven tiered levels, one for each of the deadly sins, bore the vanities that the *piagnoni* had collected, and the inside of the construction was filled with wood and straw to guarantee a dramatic blaze, as well as small pockets of gunpowder to create impressive sparks. An effigy of Satan topped the pyre. The bonfire was, as intended by Girolamo Savonarola, an awesome spectacle. Whether those in the crowd supported the friar or not, all were keen to see Satan aflame.

Savonarola himself stood on a raised wooden platform beside the pyramid, garbed in the plain black robes of the Dominican order. As usual he was declaiming a puritanical speech to the assembled multitude. He held a burning torch which lit up his olive skin in the dusk, making he himself appear somehow demonic, like the effigy of Satan that topped the bonfire. Biagio stood close to the front and could hear around him both cheers and jeers. The white-clad *piagnoni* were easily visible as they formed a ring around the bonfire to prevent the commoners from snatching valuable objects of vanity from the pyre. They held staves and were ready to use them. The ring parted when Botticelli approached, and his escort continued with him to the foot of the pyramid. Savonarola looked down and immediately recognised the familiar face of the Maestro, and saw the painting that he wheeled on his handcart.

"The Maestro Botticelli brings a painting to the fire, carrying it himself as a humble believer," he shouted, gesturing to the crowd to acknowledge the painter and bowing, his arm outstretched as if to conduct the painter to the pyramid. There was scattered applause and cheers. Like a true politician, the friar had somehow made Botticelli's sacrifice his own.

Botticelli lifted the beautiful painting so that all the crowd could see. He walked forward to the bonfire. He had to clamber up onto the platform and lift the large round panel up after him. He positioned it firmly on the first tier of the bonfire, resting it with the painting upright and facing out. It sat on a sack of rich scarlet cloth. As he climbed down carefully, no longer as spry as once he had been, Savonarola held his torch high and intoned words like a sacrament.

"Thus are the mighty shriven and absolved!"

Biagio could see flecks of spittle flying from the friar's mouth in the torchlight. Savonarola thrust his torch at the base of the bonfire and there was a whoomph as oil-soaked rags caught and burned. A plume of smoke grew, and then the first flames began to flicker out of the pyramid's interior. The crowd grew silent in awe. A wig caught fire and the smell made noses wrinkle. There was a sound of roaring and crackling from within the bonfire, like a dragon being awakened. Small caches of gunpowder went off with minor explosions. An ornate hand mirror shattered in the heat.

Botticelli stood at the bottom of the pyre until the flames reached his painting and the cloth on which it sat began to burn. Then he was thrust back by the *piagnoni* and he turned away, unable in this final moment to see his work consumed by flames. He threaded his way into the crowd, which parted like a sea for him, and was gone from sight. Biagio watched sadly as the flames reached the tondo and began to lick around its perimeter. Savonarola continued to preach hellfire and damnation, but then a bottle flung by someone in the crowd caught him on the side of the head, knocking him to his knees and causing a ripple of laughter.

Attention switched from the fire to the friar. His *piagnoni* flocked around his platform to protect him. There was a particularly loud crack of detonating gunpowder from inside the pyramid. In an explosion of sparks the tondo lifted off the shelf where it rested. Biagio watched it for what seemed a frozen moment as it teetered on the parapet like a coin on its edge, then it dropped and rolled, spinning as it gathered speed. A giant Rus' wool merchant at the edge of the crowd was suddenly confronted by the smouldering panel as it bounced off the edge of the platform and spun through the air towards him. He reflexively caught it, dropping it immediately with a yell of pain as the back of it burned his fingers. He looked up, finding himself with the smouldering tondo at his feet. The crowd roared. Savonarola was climbing unsteadily to his feet. The *piagnoni* stood immobile with staves in their hands like forest brigands, looking at their leader. There was an imperceptible pause. Unwatched, the merchant bent down and snatched up the tondo, using the sleeves of his jerkin to protect his hands. He held up the tondo like a shield. Two *piagnoni* noticed too late and stepped forward but suddenly Biagio was there, shoving one roughly into the other so that they fell in a heap. The cheering crowd parted again like the sea before Moses and then swallowed up the Rus' merchant, who disappeared into the throng.

The merchant was never found and neither did the *piagnoni* find the tondo.

In May of that year, after Savonarola's fanatical zeal led him to defy a direct request from the Pope, he was excommunicated. When in the following year he declined to undergo a trial by fire proposed by a Franciscan preacher, popular opinion turned against him. He was arrested and in May 1498 he was hanged with two of his assistants. The three suspended bodies, still kicking and choking on short ropes, were burned at the very same spot that the bonfire of the vanities had occupied. The ashes of the bodies were piled into carts and carried to the nearby Ponte Vecchio, where they were flung into the Arno to avoid risk either of martyrdom or relics.

24

Awake! for Morning in the Bowl of Night
Has flung the Stone that puts the Stars to Flight:
And Lo! the Hunter of the East has caught
The Sultán's Turret in a Noose of Light.

THE RUBÁIYÁT OF OMAR KHAYYÁM

March, a hotel in Florence

It was well after midnight when Will and Alessa finally managed to open Semiramide's curled-up letter without damaging it. Will yawned and that started them both off. Alessa decided that it would be better to tackle the translation in the morning when she would be fresh. They closed the shutters and clambered into bed. He kissed her but they didn't make love, for sleep overcame them. Will awoke once in the night and padded to the bathroom, then returned to the hollow next to Alessa's warm body. He didn't want to wake her up, so he lay and watched her as she slept. Her breathing was even and her long brown hair was a tumble of curls on the pillow. After a few minutes he joined her in sleep again.

Alessa awoke first in the morning. When Will stirred he found her sitting at the desk in a white towelling robe, one window shutter opened a crack to cast a narrow shaft which caught her in a noose of light. She was scribbling in a notebook, with her laptop at her elbow and Semiramide's letter in its own reverently cleared space. Will leaned down behind her and kissed her neck and said good morning. He massaged her shoulders and the nape of her neck as she worked. She found herself unable to concentrate at the gentle caress of his fingers. Her scalp tingled at his contact. After a while his hands slipped inside the robe and found her nipples, which hardened as his fingers brushed them. Despite her initial determination to carry on with the translation, she gave up, twisting in her seat and lifting her face to be kissed. The academic process paused.

For a while afterwards he lay sated like Mars and she sat thoughtfully Venus-like in bed as she contemplated the quattrocento letter. No satyrs were in evidence, but after a while she slapped him on the bottom and he emitted protesting groans.

"Come *on* Will! You can't just sleep when we've got the most amazing letter in the world to study. Wake up!"

They showered and realised they were hungry. They were afraid a housemaid might come to the room the moment they left, so they put the letter into the room safe. When they went down onto the street they smelled baking, and found *cornetti* and coffee in a café opposite.

Awake and refreshed, they hurried back to the room to find the room had indeed been refreshed. Will went to the safe, having a sudden image of Lucas opening his room safe in Venice and finding the brooch missing. He smiled. Semiramide's letter was secure, and Alessa organised her desk area again, ordering Will to be quiet and leave her in peace. He paced the hotel room, but after five minutes Alessa looked up in exasperation and insisted that he go out for a walk and return in no less than one hour. He did so, prowling the streets of Florence and imagining Sandro Botticelli following those same thoroughfares. He wondered what it must have been like five hundred years previously; no cars, just handcarts and horses, butchers and bakers, musicians and masons and scarlet-cloth makers.

He walked to the Piazza della Signoria and stared at the Palazzo Vecchio – the Old Palace, once known as the Palazzo della Signoria – along with a crowd of other tourists. He found he was standing on a round plaque marking the spot where Girolamo Savonarola, the puritanical Dominican friar, had been burned alive. He looked it up on his phone and found that this had occurred on the 23rd of May 1498. With difficulty he worked his way through the Roman numerals on the plaque to get to that year.

From the Piazza he made his way down to via del Porcellana where it met Borgo Ognissanti. Botticelli's workshop had been along this little street somewhere, when it had still been called via Nuova. He stood at the junction for a while, not far from the Arno, trying to imagine the famous painter within a few yards of him, separated only by time. He found it hard to look at these present-day pockmarked walls and project himself back into that rich history. He felt oddly melancholic, to be right on the spot but unable to step through a gateway into the past. He went down to the Arno and watched its wide brown waters sliding by, turning white as they crossed a weir. A Little Egret was standing at the edge of the weir eating a fish. He recognised the white heron from his childhood in Norfolk. He saw from his phone map that the bridge beyond was the Ponte Amerigo Vespucci, named for an explorer who had given America its name. It was a bright March morning, cool but slowly warming. Will imagined that in Botticelli's day there would have been the stench of fulling mills, but the Florentine air he breathed was fresh and clean.

He returned to the hotel when he judged that a reasonable time had passed. At ten-thirty he let himself into their room and found Alessa slumped back in her chair. She turned to look at him as he came in.

"It's ready," she said, but her voice was thin and stretched, pulling his focus.

"Are you all right?"

"I'm fine. You're just not going to believe the letter, but I've double-checked everything as best I can. Her handwriting is old and shaky and the lettering is different from today, so it's hard and I'm out of practice."

"It's remarkable you can read it at all," he said. "All the s's look like f's and I wouldn't be able to make head or tail of it. To me it's gobbledegook."

She smiled weakly but said nothing, so he held his hand out.

"Let's have a gander then."

She handed him the black and red notebook that she had carried with her everywhere since George had given it to her in Cambridge. Will began to read her translation. After a few sentences he looked up and found her eyes on him. He sat down heavily on the edge of the bed.

3 Marzo 1523
Cafaggiolo

My dearest son,
You were foolish not to listen, but I was wrong to wait so long to speak to you. When I spoke to you in my bed chamber yesterday, you left in such a rage that I could not finish. My maid will hide this letter so it is for your sight only, as I can no longer leave this room. You know I will soon be in God's hands. The physics say I have the crab's spreading claws, which Hippocrates called carcinoma. They pinch me inside and there is naught to be done, so let me be brief.

You accused me of untruths, but what I told you was not a lie.

You are not a Medici.

There. Perhaps the words will burn the page.

In my youth I had an affair of the heart with a man now dead. You were the result of that madness, but the one you call your father never knew you were not of his seed. He and I married for Medici politics and not for love, though passing years and shared joys in time brought affection.

Your true father was Maestro Sandro Botticelli, the painter. Perhaps you will close your eyes to hide these words, and you may hate him, but be not ashamed. His artistic skill was unsurpassed. He was loved by Il Magnifico and the one you knew as your father. He was a great man.

Now to the point, before the crab's claws bite again.

There is a secret of this shameful union which you must destroy before it is discovered. Do you remember the church where you fell and cracked your head? You slept for three days without waking, as God's punishment for my wickedness. Go there alone at night with a coffin pall or some similar large cloth. Bribe the friars to grant privacy if you must ~ they will take coin as charity. Find the painting with an instrument like the one in our library. Remember the letter. Take the note from my maid, on which I wrote five numbers. Press these numbers where you see them on the panel. It will unlatch to expose the secret.

Cover what you find with the pall to conceal it. Carry it from the holy place and burn it.

Forgive me if you can.

Tua madre
~S~

Will put down Alessa's translation of Semiramide's secret letter, and caught Alessa's eye again. She was still staring at him. He blew out his cheeks, then knitted his fingers behind his head and pulled it forward, stretching his neck so that it clicked.

"Well," he said at last. "She was a bit more than his muse."

"Not only that," Alessa said, "but their child Pierfrancesco the Younger wasn't a Medici at all, though of course he lived as one. He's part of the Medici genealogy tree, for Gawd's sake!"

Her voice still sounded reedy. She cleared her throat.

"I'm scared that we've got this," she went on. "I can't think how we'll explain it."

"We'll figure it out," Will said dismissively. "The fact is, we *have* got it, and given what it took to find the letter, it must be genuine. So, if this man was the Younger, who was the Older? I don't remember there being an older one."

"Well, his grandfather was Pierfrancesco, who became known as Il Vecchio. He was the Elder. *His* son was Lorenzo Il Popolano – the Popular – who married Semiramide. They had four or five children I think, and this one was supposedly the heir. That's why he was named Pierfrancesco, after his grandfather, and that's why we now refer to him as the Younger. Otherwise it gets confusing."

"It certainly does," Will agreed fervently. "It would have been good if they'd thought of calling each other something other than Lorenzo or Pierfrancesco."

He shook his head as if to shake something loose from it, chuckling mirthlessly.

"You know, it's only morning but I think I need a drink."

He went to the minibar and found a miniature bottle of wine, flourishing a second one in Alessa's direction.

"Yes please," she nodded.

He opened both bottles and used the provided glasses. They clinked them together.

"This is far more fabulous than we dared think," Will said. "What shall we toast?"

"Botticelli and Semiramide, I think."

They both drank, and Alessa giggled nervously.

"Historians are going to be *so* worked up about this," she said. "It's got everything! Not only was Pierfrancesco the Younger *not* a Medici, but he was Botticelli's child, who has always been assumed to have been a homosexual, because he never married and there are no records of any women."

"So what happened to Pierfrancesco?" Will asked. "Did he go on to greatness?"

"Not really. He carried on the Medici line, or so we thought, for another generation, but he died young, I think. Let me check."

She searched for the Medici family tree and found a good chart.

"Here we are, he married Maria Soderini, but he died in 1525, which is only two years after Semiramide wrote this letter." She tapped the screen. "And here's his son Lorenzino, who was famously unstable. The boy murdered his cousin Alessandro, who was the great grandson of Lorenzo the Magnificent, in the other branch of the family. No-one knows why on earth he did it. I did think briefly of writing my thesis about him, but there isn't much material."

"Perhaps his papa mentioned he wasn't a Medici and he was upset," Will said.

"It actually could be that," Alessa said, her eyes bright. "I finally have an amazing story for my thesis. Lorenzaccio and his murdering ways will now only need to be a brief chapter."

"I thought you said his son's name was Lorenzino?"

"Oh yeah, but he was also known as Lorenzaccio."

He rolled his eyes. "Well of course he was."

"This is one of the greatest discoveries of recent times," Alessa said, her voice becoming more normal with the wine. She didn't seem to be able to stop grinning. She was up now, waving her arms dramatically and pacing around the room.

"It's like...." She cast around for inspiration. "...it's like discovering that Shakespeare had a child with Queen Elizabeth."

He chuckled.

"Young William Tudor. Yes, I do see what you mean."

He ran his hand through his hair. She came over to him and they hugged, holding their wineglasses behind their backs. She pulled back and kissed him on the lips. Her wine had a different taste to his.

"I am *so* excited!" she said. "I feel like I want to sprint down the street and back. I might have to do it." She drained her glass and went back to pacing.

"I wonder what this mysterious secret was," Will said. He went over to the window, opening the shutters so that bright Florentine light spilled into the room.

"We'll never know," Alessa said with a shrug. "Whatever it was, it must surely have been discovered by now."

"You *say* that, but this letter was well hidden and still sealed. It seems like Pierfrancesco the Whatever never read it."

"Which is weird," she said with a frown, "because you'd think he would have gone and looked for it the second he saw the message in the brooch."

"Maybe he never saw that message either," Will said. "Or maybe he was just too furious to listen. I mean, they were practically monarchy, weren't they? It must have been a bit of a downer to be told by his mother that he wasn't a Medici after all. I'm not surprised he was in denial about it."

She turned her mouth down. "Anyway," she said, "the mysterious secret is probably under a multistorey carpark by now."

He didn't say anything but just looked at her, his eyebrows raised, until they both smiled.

"Though it might not be," she admitted at last.

"If it's hidden in a church," Will said, "they tend not to change churches much."

"She's very cryptic though, did you notice? She doesn't want anyone else to find the secret thing. I wonder what on earth it was. It must be quite big if she says to take a coffin pall to wrap it in."

"What exactly is a pall, anyway?" Will asked. "Like a funeral cloth or something?"

"Exactly that, it's a coffin cloth. They used to drape it over the coffin. Today we might use a flag, for example, for a military burial."

"Quite a big secret then. Hopefully not a coffin."

"No, but a pall would be a good big cloth to wrap something in. Maybe a chest of letters or something."

"*Love* letters!" Will said, holding up a finger. "I bet that's it. A box of letters. Everyone always used to write love letters and then get found out and blackmailed."

"They did in Jane Austen's day," Alessa said, somewhat scathingly. "I'm not so sure about Quattrocento Florence."

"I bet they did back then too. If we could find this secret panel, we'd know the truth."

"Yes, but we don't know enough to find it. We don't even know what church she was referring to. She just said the one where he bumped his head."

"Sounds like he really whacked it if he was in a coma for three days. Is there any record of that?"

She shook her head.

"I'd have to research it, but I don't remember any reference. That doesn't mean it didn't happen, but it was five hundred years ago. So much has been lost after all this time, even if it were ever recorded."

"If the secret letters or whatever are still there," Will said slowly, "they could be written by Sandro Botticelli himself, in which case they'd be worth a fortune. Letters from history. He didn't leave any journals or anything. We have to go by what Vasari said about him years later, and he got a few things wrong."

"They would be an extraordinary view into his life, and Semiramide's," she agreed.

"Okay then, let's see what we can work out. The worst that can happen is that the secret *is* under a carpark, and even then we might find it eventually. After all, they found Richard the Third under that carpark in Leicester."

"Yes, and he was killed in a battle in 1485, round about the same time."

"Botticelli would have been putting the finishing touches to Mars and Venus when poor old Richard was turning up his toes."

"All right then," Alessa said, sitting down at the desk. "What do we know?"

They went through Semiramide's letter again and again.

"She doesn't say 'secrets', she says 'secret'," Alessa pointed out. "So perhaps it isn't love letters after all.

"It could still be a box of them. A locked casket, all rusted up."

"I suppose so."

"What about the church? What churches did the Medici frequent in Florence?"

She gave the tiniest of shrugs.

"Well, the cathedral, of course. It could be in the cathedral, but it's massive."

"Yes, but would she talk about the church where he bumped his head if she meant the cathedral? You'd think she'd just say 'the cathedral'. It makes me think it wasn't the cathedral, but another one. Why might he be going to another church?"

"I think they had their own family church, or it could have been one with a private Medici chapel."

"He must have been a boy when he fell down and cracked his head," Will pointed out. "If he was a grown man he wouldn't be likely to fall down and knock himself out, but that's exactly what a boy might do."

"Especially if it were an unfamiliar place and he was exploring."

"Running about when he wasn't supposed to be."

"Yes," she said, and wrinkled her brow thoughtfully.

"Let's get a list of churches and have a look," he said. "But before that, what else do we know?"

They examined the letter yet again.

"We know we start from a painting or a panel in the church," Alessa said. "But then they all have paintings. We also know this painting has got at least five numbers on it."

"And we know it shows some kind of instrument that you might find in a library."

"An *instrument*," Alessa said thoughtfully. "It's an odd word. It makes me think of scientific instruments, but there wasn't much science going on then."

She searched for 'instrument'.

"Oh, we're being stupid! She probably means a musical instrument. A painting containing a musical instrument. What sort of musical instrument might you see in a library?"

"Well, you wouldn't really. If it was in the library it would be decorative, because you want quiet in a library. You'd keep a musical instrument in active use somewhere else entirely, like the music room, or a hall where it's played by your musicians. Not in the library."

"You might have one mounted on the wall, I suppose."

"You might. Or it could be a different kind of instrument, like a globe."

"You'd think she'd say globe if she meant globe."

"Unless she was being cryptic."

They lapsed into gloomy silence for a few moments.

"Maybe a telescope?" she asked hopefully.

"When did globes start being a thing?" Will asked. "I mean, they'd figured out the earth wasn't flat, right?"

Alessa's fingers worked.

"Greek philosophers figured out the earth was round in the fifth century BC," she said. "A Greek called Crates made a terrestrial globe two centuries before Christ, so the library certainly could have had a globe."

He tutted at yet another possibility, shaking his head in frustration.

"So it could be a globe, or it could be a musical instrument. Or a telescope, or anything else we didn't yet think of."

"Semiramide didn't want anyone else to know what she was talking about," Alessa said gloomily.

"So let's go back to churches."

Alessa turned to the computer and searched for Renaissance Florentine churches. A list appeared and she began to count. He watched despondently as she scrolled.

"OK, Wikipedia's got 71 of them, and that probably doesn't include some smaller ones."

"Let's find a list of the most-important ones. The Medici wouldn't have gone to some tiny church."

She searched and a list appeared of top churches to see while visiting Florence:

1. The Duomo
2. Florence Baptistery
3. The Basilica of Santo Spirito
4. The Basilica Santissima Annunziata
5. Santa Croce

6. Santa Maria del Carmine
7. Santa Trinità
8. San Marco
9. San Miniato al Monte – set on a hill overlooking Florence
10. Orsanmichele
11. Santa Maria Novella
12. San Lorenzo – the Medici's parish church
13. Santo Spirito
14. Ognissanti – All Saints' Church
15. Cenacolo di Sant'Apollonia

"Ha, now we're getting somewhere!" Will said, leaning over her shoulder. "Number 12 looks like a good bet. "Oh and Number 14, too, because Botticelli is buried there, so he has a connection. It was his closest church."

"I wonder why on earth he or Semiramide would hide anything in a church in the first place," Alessa said. "It seems such an odd place. It's not in their direct control, and churches are public places so anyone might find it."

"True, although it was behind a secret panel, don't forget. A painting with numbers on it that you have to press."

"It's still rather peculiar. Why would there be a secret compartment in a church?"

"Well, a place to conceal valuables," Will said, waving his arms vaguely. "Hard to know, really. Chalices and candlesticks?"

They were thoughtful for a while.

"This is an *impossible* puzzle," Alessa complained. "I'm all for puzzles, but this was five hundred years ago and Semiramide was deliberately being cryptic so that only her son would get it. We don't stand a chance."

Will picked up the translation and read it for the twentieth time. He frowned.

"I wonder why she says 'remember the letter'. She must be referring to her letter that Pocock found, because she can't mean this one."

"Let's look back at it," Alessa said.

She flipped to the beginning of her notebook and turned a few pages of scribbled notes until she got to the written-out translation of Pocock's letter.

"The main thing she talks about is the brooch," Alessa said. "She tells him about the brooch and that Giuseppe Bronzino, her lawyer, is going to give it to him. I wonder how Isabella d'Este ended up with it instead of her son."

"Remember the letter," Will said again slowly, as if the individual words might suddenly reveal their secret to him. "Maybe the painting we're looking for has got the brooch painted in it, but that is *Mars and Venus* and it's hanging in the London National Gallery. No secret panel there."

"Could anything be concealed in the back of the painting? Those panels are quite thick wood."

He shook his head.

"Absolutely not. I'm lucky enough to have seen the painting off the wall when they were cleaning it, and it's just a panel of poplar wood. No secret compartments, I guarantee. Conservationists have been over every inch of that painting. Anyway, there aren't any numbers in it."

"Any other pictures with the brooch in? If he did one, maybe he did another."

He pursed his lips, but shook his head slowly, absently. Something was on the edge of his memory but he couldn't quite think of it.

"You know what we ought to do," Alessa said. "We could go to the Medici parish church right now and look around. San Lorenzo, in this list."

"Try looking for a painting with numbers on it, you mean?"

"Yes, maybe a fresco, with some kind of musical instrument or globe or something you might find in a library."

"That's a good idea," he said, feeling both impulsive and keen to stretch his legs. "I'm sick of sitting in this room anyway."

"Just before we do," Alessa said, typing furiously on her keyboard, "Let's just see – ah, here we are. San Lorenzo's artworks. So let's try this first one, the Martyrdom of St. Lawrence by Bronzino."

Her tongue emerged as she concentrated and licked her lower lip in a gesture he was coming to recognize –he sometimes did it himself when painting. It made him remember that he had not painted for a long time due to all this chasing around, and he missed it. Then for some reason he remembered the other thing he had not done – he had resolved to take up running to lose his gathering pounds, but had not even bought any running shoes. It occurred to him that it would be good to buy a pair of trainers while he was in Florence. Italians were famous for shoes, although mind you, running shoes probably came from China rather than Italian cordwainers. He remembered running through Richmond Park and that made him think of his distress after breaking up with Lucy. He counted back in his mind. Astonishingly that had been less than a month previously.

"Will!"

He came out of his revery and realized that Alessa had been talking to him.

"Are you all right?" she asked. "You look sad all of a sudden."

He smiled and nodded, putting a hand on her shoulder and feeling her warmth.

"I'm sorry," he said. "I was just thinking about er…buying some running shoes." He patted his stomach.

"Running shoes," she said, tucking in her chin to suggest disbelief. "I'm sure there's a perfectly reasonable explanation. When you have a moment, take a look at this Bronzino."

She tapped the screen and he saw an image of the Martyrdom picture, which seemed to comprise dozens of scantily clad people ranged around Saint Lawrence, who was being roasted over a fire.

"Seems like he was having a bad day," Will said.

"Yes, do you remember the story? Saint Lawrence is the one that was burned alive and told them he was done on that side so they should turn him over. It's been pinched for other stories, though it was probably apocryphal."

"I expect in truth he was screaming his brains out."

"I can't see any numbers though," she went on. "Oh wait, it was painted in 1569 so it wasn't even there in 1523 when Semiramide wrote her letter."

"That's a good point, though," Will said. "We need pictures painted before 1523, but after Pierfrancesco the Whatever was conceived."

"Call him Pierfrancesco the Younger," Alessa said, "or I'm going to have to stab you. But you make a good point. Let me check his birthday."

She typed.

"1487. That's when he was born, so conceived in 1486."

"So it's probably after 1480, unless we're talking about a long trail of love letters."

"1480 to 1523, but probably before 1500 unless her secret was hidden years after it had all happened. That doesn't seem so likely."

"Well, it definitely puts Bronzino's picture out. Shall we look at the rest of them?"

He sighed. "You know, we *could*, or we could go to the church as you suggested and look at real pictures. Besides, I desperately need more coffee."

"All right then," she said, closing the laptop. "I'll bring this with me in case we need to look something up."

She put her laptop into its carry-bag, then they secured Semiramide's letter once more and left the hotel. It was lunchtime and already busy despite being early in the season. They quickly located the Basilica di San Lorenzo on Will's phone and set off, arriving there in twenty minutes after pausing for an espresso.

San Lorenzo was not at all what they had been expecting. To begin with, the unfinished front of the church looked as if the usual ornate marble façade had been ripped off, leaving rough tiers of stone beneath.

They never put the façade on it," Alessa said. "I was reading about it on my phone while we were grabbing a coffee. Michelangelo designed a white marble façade and even made a wooden model of it, but it never got built, so presumably they ran out of money."

It was a different story as soon as they went inside. It had the serene beauty of a cathedral, with an immensely high roof. Tourists stood taking photographs, paused in quiet contemplation or sat in prayer. There was a very slight reverberation which amplified any voice above a whisper, but the overall impression was of an immense, reverent quiet.

They walked down the central aisle and Alessa pointed.

"There's the Bronzino," she said.

"Oh," Will said, looking up at the huge painting. "I was imagining from the picture that it was four feet across, not occupying an entire wall. It just goes to prove it's worth coming in person rather than trying to do everything over the internet."

They began to work methodically around the walls, stopping at each artwork. Some of the pictures were clearly hung paintings and therefore not a feasible cover for a hidden cavity throughout half a millennium. Others were very high up, way beyond the reach of human contact. They quickly found that the church was large and extended into cloisters. There was plenty of art, but nothing which seemed suitable, and nothing bearing numbers or globes or any other kind of instrument. It took them two hours to work around the whole church, by which time they were exhausted by straining their eyes too long looking for suitable paintings. When they had probed into every chapel and corner they met back in the cloisters.

"Well, at least I've seen Donatello's final resting place," Will said, sitting down on the wall and adding gloomily: "No frescoes or paintings with numbers or instruments, though."

"Me neither," Alessa said, sitting down beside him and then looking accusingly at the stone. "Ooh, this is cold! I didn't see Lorenzo the Magnificent's tomb, but he's next door in the New Sacristy. I think he used to be in here but they moved him. Did you know he was only 43 when he died in 1492? They didn't last long without modern medicine. Poor guy had gangrene of the leg, apparently, though it's been hard to establish why. There's been talk of exhumation and a DNA analysis but nothing has ever been done about it."

"They should just let him rest," Will said, looking around the Canons' Cloister with its geometric green hedges and central orange tree. It reminded him of the cloister garden in the Palazzo Ducale in Mantova. "What shall we do now; got any ideas?"

"None at all," Alessa said in frustration. "If only we could find out what she meant! A painting with numbers on it, and an instrument. A church in Florence which may have been this one but we don't know. Something to do with Semiramide's brooch, according to that first letter."

They sat in gloomy silence, thinking. Alessa took out her laptop and connected to the free Wi-Fi, but the connection was running slow.

"We need to go and find somewhere we can connect so I can go on browsing," she said. "Though I have no idea what to look for."

"I don't know about you, but I'm starving," Will said.

"You're always starving," she said, but then she grinned. "All right, I'm hungry too. Those *cornetti* seem an awfully long time ago."

"That's because they were," Will said. "Let's have some food and hope we get inspiration."

They went to Trattoria Zà Zà because Will's phone said it was well recommended, it was only five minutes walk away, and it had Wi-Fi. It was a charming place, full of interesting things, and quite a few tourists were eating or drinking, even though it was only four in the afternoon and not yet time for dinner. They had a glass of Prosecco and then ordered something called

Tagliere della Zia Giuliana – a plate of salami and cheese and delicious things from someone's Aunt Julie – and remembered having a similar platter in Mantova. They were very hungry and the food tasted wonderful. After that, Will had a steak and Alessa had sea bass. When they had finished, the waiter offered them the menu once more for dessert, and Will's moral resolve to eat less went out of the window as he contemplated the list. He had an English menu rather than Alessa's Italian one, so he was able to understand what was on offer despite one or two amusing translations. Alessa ordered Panna Cotta and he ordered strawberries with lemon juice and sugar, just because the lemon juice accompaniment sounded different from the way the English would do it.

When they were finished and drinking coffee, Alessa asked half-heartedly if he thought she should start up the laptop.

"I'd say yes if I could think of a single thing you could look up," Will said. "I reckon we need to have a night off and think about it some more tomorrow, with clear heads."

She put her hand on his.

"This must be costing you a fortune," she said. "I just want to say thank you. I promise I'll pay you back as soon as papà's money comes in."

It was sweet and he kissed her lightly on the lips.

"Until then you'll have to pay me with your body," he said solemnly. "And to think I nearly decided to stay in Cambridge and paint."

The restaurant was filling up with evening diners when they departed, feeling tired and tipsy. They held hands as they walked.

We ought to go back past Botticelli's workshop," Will said. "Unless you're cold?"

"How gallant of you, Will! I'm fine, though I'm quite tired. Is it on the way back to the hotel?"

"Sort of nearly almost," Will said, rocking his head slowly from side to side. "But it's on the Arno, which would be nice to walk by in the evening."

They strolled for about ten minutes arm in arm, and arrived at the junction of via del Porcellana with Borgo Ognissanti.

"I came here this morning while you were translating the letter," he said. "I think his workshop would have been around there somewhere." He pointed to a building."

She stood and looked.

"It doesn't seem possible," she said after a minute, "that all that beauty could come out of this little street. Where's his church? Ognissanti can't be far away."

"It's just up here I think," Will said. "We could go tomorrow. It's probably locked up now."

She started to walk up the street until she came to the church. There was a piazza in front of it.

"There's the Arno," Will said pointing. "On the other side of the square."

The church door was locked as expected, so they walked across the square to join the river again, and stood gazing down at the slowly moving waters, dark but reflecting the city lights of streets and buildings.

"It's beautiful," Alessa said.

They contemplated the river for a while and then she shivered.

"It is cooling down, though. You can tell it's March. It'll be like an oven here in August. Shall we get back?"

They turned around and looked across the piazza at Ognissanti, which had a stained white marble façade, and a brown tower in the background on the right.

Will frowned.

"I've seen that somewhere," he said absently.

"Seen what?"

He pointed.

"That tower. The shape of it with the church."

"In the guidebook? In your Botticelli book?"

He shook his head slowly.

"I don't know, but I expect it'll come to me. Let's get back then. I'm getting cold now. I wonder if that tiny bar in the hotel is open. I could do with a little something to make me sleep."

"You think I'm going to let you sleep?" Alessa asked archly.

He grinned.

When they got back to the hotel the bar was indeed open but they ignored it and sped upstairs, ripped off their clothes and tumbled into bed. After they had made love, Will found the two glasses from the minibar, which had been replaced by the maid, and poured out a Scotch miniature for himself and a Cointreau miniature for Alessa. She sat up in bed, the sheet covering one of her small, pointed breasts but leaving the other exposed. He lay down next to her and stared at the ceiling. Slowly his eyes closed and Alessa sat beside him, sipping the sweet orange liqueur.

Suddenly Will sat bolt upright, almost spilling her drink.

"Steady!" she protested. "What is it?"

"That tower."

"What tower?"

"The brown one. I mean the one on Ognissanti church. With sunbeams coming out of it."

She frowned.

"You're not making sense."

"I mean, I saw a painting of it with sunbeams radiating from it, as if the sun were behind it."

He scrambled off the bed and started to pull on his underwear, then his trousers. He shrugged into his shirt."

"Where are you going, Will?" she said, still confused.

"I'm not," he said absently. "I'm not going anywhere, I just can't think clearly when I'm stark naked."

He slipped into his shoes and then sat down at the desk and opened Alessa's laptop.

He loaded Google Maps and typed 'Ognissanti' into the search window. He zoomed in and then switched to satellite view, seeing the piazza and the terracotta roof of the church, with a white strip of the marble façade.

"Hey, this is neat," he said. "When you move it around it's in 3D. Look, you can see the brown tower."

She climbed out of bed with the sheet wrapped around herself, then found the white towelling robe and put that on. She joined him and leaned down to the screen.

"Campanile," she said. "It's a bell tower, like at Cafaggiolo. There must be 3D for Florence because it's so famous. They don't do that for Islip! If you look at Islip it's just flat houses which tilt a bit."

"Anyway," Will said, concentrating. The image slid across to the piazza before the River Arno, and then he worked out how to tilt it so that they were looking at the front of the church. He shook his head slightly and pursed his lips.

"It looks familiar, and I can see those beams of light coming out of it in my mind's eye. Definitely a painting, not a photograph."

"A *painting*!" Alessa said. "Well that's getting interesting. I wonder if it's one of the ones you saw today."

"Yeah, but it wasn't all white like that."

"You mean the church front?" Alessa said. "Oh well, that's easy. "A lot of those posh marble façades only got put on much later, in the sixteenth or seventeenth century. Remember San Lorenzo, where we went this afternoon? No façade even after all this time. It must have been expensive to do it, with all that marble."

"I suppose so," Will said, remembering the rough stone front of the Medici church. "That feels right, but I can't think where I saw it."

He stood and paced up and down the room, looking up without really seeing as he tried to remember.

"We've been looking at loads of old buildings and loads of paintings today," Alessa pointed out. "And then we saw about a million in Mantova. You may have seen a painting of Ognissanti somewhere. I feel as if my head is stuffed full of paintings."

"It feels like it was ages ago, though," Will said.

"How ages? Like months? Were you with me?"

He looked at her.

"That's it," he said. "We were on the computer, and you were searching for stuff."

"We've been doing that almost every day."

"No, we were on *my* computer," he said. "In my studio back at home."

She thought back.

"In Cambridge," she said. "I told you I had a degree in computer science and you believed me."

Well, I didn't know what a complete liar you were then," he said with a grin. "But yes, and I know what we were looking for."

"The brooch," she said. "And that's when we found the picture of Isabella d'Este."

"Her fingers moved over the keyboard and the familiar picture of Isabella d'Este came up on her screen."

"No campanile," she said.

"I think there was another one," Will said. "Do it again like we did before. We found loads of pictures."

She tried searching for renaissance pearl brooches but quickly remembered that she had done an image search.

"This had better be good," she said. "Because it was quite fiddly to do. Is there some water somewhere? I need to clear my head."

He found a bottle of water in the bottom of the minibar and washed out her glass before refilling it. When he got back she had found the image of the brooch she had previously saved. The search worked and they started to see many of the images they saw before.

He pointed suddenly.

"That one."

She stopped on a round picture of the Virgin and child surrounded by angels and clicked on it. Sure enough, in the background of the image was a brown building with a campanile. The tower had three sets of windows and emanating from the topmost window were lines of light, as if the sun were behind the tower.

"It *does* look like it," she said, squeezing his arm. "You clever boy."

She flipped to the Google Maps image of Chiesa di San Salvatore in Ognissanti.

"Three windows in the tower," he said, pointing.

She flipped back to the image.

"Three windows," she nodded. "Okay, let's see if we can get a better image than this lousy one."

She clicked and paused.

"It's a Russian painting, hanging in The Hermitage in St. Petersburg," she said. "Not Italian at all, which is odd."

She went to The Hermitage website, which came up in Cyrillic script, but there was an English option, which she selected. She entered 'virgin and child' in the search window and got a cameo, then lots of miniature sculptures and a few paintings. She tried specifying the material as 'PAINT' but no results were found, so she cleared that and selected a hundred images per page. She started to scroll down and they both spotted it easily because it was a tondo, about halfway down. Alessa clicked on the picture and started to read out the details.

"It entered the Hermitage from the Mews Museum in St Petersburg. They don't know the artist but they say it's Russian."

"I wonder how they know that if they don't know the artist," said Will.

Alessa shrugged and started to read out the description.

"*This painting by an unknown artist is likely a Russian copy in the style of a number of works which heralded the arrival of a new period of art in Italy, which was to become known as the High Renaissance. The Madonna feeding the Christ child is very finely painted, and grouped around her are four young boys, presumably angels, who are of varying age and height. The Child holds in its hand a bunch of keys, and an old man kneels at the feet of the Child, holding out a parchment as if making an offering. The blue garment worn by the Virgin is of lapis lazuli. Beyond the figures lies a castle or a church with a tower from which emanate beams of light, perhaps representing the star in the sky at the Birth. The painting was acquired from the Mews Museum in St. Petersburg and is also known by the name of the Madonna and Keys, but the original provenance is lost. At some point in its history the painting was damaged by fire, and the rear of the panel support is blackened at the bottom of the painting. Some repairs of lesser quality have been carried out to the original painting surface, perhaps following fire damage, but the original fine brushwork is largely intact.*"

Will pointed at the brooch pinned to the Madonna's blue gown.

"It looks just like Semiramide's brooch, but it's only got seven pearls. That's why we moved on. Can you get it bigger?"

"It depends on the size of the original picture file," Alessa said. "Let me try. This Hermitage site is actually very good, so there's hope."

The image on the Hermitage site had high resolution. She selected its page and then opened the image in a separate tab so she could zoom up on it. The detail remained clear. She slid the image about on the screen until they could see the brooch.

"That's definitely an orange stone," Will said. "You couldn't mistake that for a ruby."

"Those pearls look a bit messy," Alessa said. She tapped the screen. "These four don't look very much like pearls, more like blobs, and they're too big."

Will stared at the brooch, which occupied about a third of the screen.

"The background is a slightly different colour on this side of the brooch. Instead of the pure lapis lazuli it's a bit lighter. Maybe this was a damaged bit and someone painted it back in."

"Maybe they painted in four pearls when they should have painted five," Alessa said suddenly, and he leaned in with a frown.

"That's exactly what they've done," he nodded. "There's space for five pearls of the right size but some idiot has painted in four bigger ones, and made a right mess of it. As you say, they don't look spherical like the other pearls, they look like blobs. They've tried to do a bit of shading but, well…"

He shook his head.

"So this *could* be Semiramide's brooch," Alessa said excitedly. "In which case, maybe Sandro Botticelli himself painted this picture."

Will pulled over another chair and sat down beside her, as close as he could get so that they could both view the screen.

"If that's true and this is an undiscovered Botticelli, it's worth a fortune," he said. "But we need to work it out. It's got the brooch, and it's got Ognissanti. Then we've got this Madonna, but she's not the usual Botticelli face. You wouldn't mistake her for Venus in the Birth, or one of the graces in Primavera. She must be, what, thirty or so, would you say?"

"Yes, but you know, it could be an actual painting of Semiramide when she was a bit older, instead of an idealised one. Let me check when she was born, I can't remember."

She busied herself for a moment.

"Okay, Wikipedia reckons 1464, so she's thirty in 1494. That's interesting. We reckoned she and Botticelli conceived Pierfrancesco in 1486. So Pierfrancesco would be eight years old in 1494."

"Zoom back so we can see the angels behind her," Will said. She did so and he pointed at the oldest boy. "Bring it up on him."

She did so.

"He could be eight or so years old," Will said. "He's not painted effeminately like a typical Botticelli boy angel, though. I wonder who the other boys are. Did he have lots of brothers?"

"No he didn't," Semiramide said, scrolling left so that the other boys' faces crossed the screen.

"They get younger as you move left," Will said. "And you know what else? I think they're the same boy. They've just been painted at different ages. Here he is only four or five, then it could be six, seven and eight. And I'll tell you what, this is *very* well painted."

"So what on earth does all that mean?" Alessa asked. "He paints Semiramide as the Madonna with a child at different ages. Perhaps their *own* child, Pierfrancesco the Younger. He hints that it's her by putting in the same brooch from Mars and Venus. Why on earth would he do that? It's rather giving the game away."

He shook his head. "I have no idea," he admitted. "I'd think this was Semiramide's mysterious evidence that she says must be destroyed, except that it's hanging in St. Petersburg rather than stuck behind a secret panel somewhere. Maybe it was discovered and went to Russia somehow. And it's a bit too mysterious to be damaging evidence. It's an enigma."

She looked at him.

"Perhaps a puzzle is exactly what it is," she said. "Maybe it's a kind of clue to the fact that he had this illegitimate son that he couldn't tell anyone about."

"He was a painter, after all," Will nodded. "So he wouldn't write down a clue, he would paint it."

"I can't see why he would do it at all, though," Alessa said. "He would get found out because people would recognize Semiramide and the boy and maybe they'd put two and two together. It would be a good way to get himself hanged."

"Maybe he just had to get it out there somehow to stop himself going bonkers. Hard to know what was in his mind, five hundred years later."

"It's an awful lot of maybes," Alessa said.

He smiled.

"Maybe it is," he admitted, "but let's look at the rest of it. What about the Christ Child and his bunch of keys? That's pretty weird, go and zoom in on that."

She found the child and they looked at it.

"Hard to tell as this one's only a baby," Will said. "It *could* be the baby that became the boys behind the Madonna, but babies change so much. Have a look at the keys."

Alessa scrolled until the keys filled the screen, and Will stared at the screen.

"Look at this! Each key has a snake twined around the shaft. A serpent means evil, so he means that each key unlocks something evil."

"Like a mysterious secret that Semiramide wants to get rid of..." Alessa said. "...maybe."

She moved the image down so they could see the whole bunch of keys, and then they both spotted the same thing at once.

"Numbers!" Alessa said.

"Roman numerals!" Will said.

Alessa grabbed her notebook and a pen.

"II is two. XIIII is fourteen in old notation. They'd put XIV now. Then we've got XXII, which is twenty-two. Then another weird one, VIIII, which is nine, I guess. And finally an I for one. Five keys, five numbers, and not in ascending order."

They looked at each other.

"Are you thinking what I'm thinking?" Will asked

"It depends. Are you thinking that this is the combination to open the secret panel Semiramide mentions in her letter?"

"That's exactly what I'm thinking."

"Then yes, me too. So Botticelli, if it was indeed he that painted this, paints Semiramide with his child, then paints his boy at different ages, and finally he says that the key to it all is opened by these numbers and it's somewhere in Ognissanti."

"We've solved it," Will said.

"Well not quite. We just need to know what painting it was that Pierfrancesco liked."

"Not really. We just need to see if Botticelli painted anything for that church, and hope it's managed to survive five hundred years."

She went to the search window and typed 'Ognissanti Botticelli'. The screen immediately filled with the same image, of an old, bearded man in red and white. Alessa clicked and found a Wikipedia article.

PAINTING VENUS

Saint Augustine in His Study is a painting of Augustine of Hippo executed in 1480 by the Italian Renaissance master Sandro Botticelli. It is in the church of Ognissanti in Florence.

She realised she had been holding her breath, and exhaled raggedly.

"That must be the one," Will said. "Now that I see it I remember it. It's in Ronald Lightbown's book about Botticelli."

"Wait a minute," she said. She returned to the painting in the Hermitage and once more zoomed. This time she framed the old man whom they had imagined was a disciple. He knelt at the Child's feet, with his face turned sideways. He had a grey beard and moustache and wore a white skull cap. "Here he is," she said simply. "Old St. Augustine himself, holding out a piece of paper to the Christ child."

"Is there anything written on the paper?" Will asked sharply. She fiddled with the controls.

"No, it's blank. At least it is now. It might have had something which has faded."

"What does it say about this saint?" Will asked.

"Hang on, my brain is bursting. Now I need the description of the Augustine painting."

She began to speed read.

"Botticelli was born in a house in the same street as the church...blah blah blah. Probably commissioned by Amerigo Vespucci's father...the order running the church commissioned Ghirlandaio to do a facing Saint Jerome; both saints were shown writing in their studies. That's it! He's writing, look. Listen to this description.

"*It portrays Augustine of Hippo in meditation inside his study. The precise subject is a legend, probably first found in the 13th century, of a vision Augustine had as he began to write a letter to Jerome in his study at Hippo in 420. The time is shown on the clock by his head as the end of the twenty-fourth hour, counting from the previous sunset. This is the hour of Compline, specified in the legend. A light and sweet odour came into his study and a voice told him that 'he might as soon enclose the ocean in a small vessel, as soon clasp the whole earth in his fist, as soon halt the movement of the heavens as describe the beatitude of the saints without having experienced it', as the speaker was now doing. When Augustine asked who he was, he replied he was Jerome. Augustine later heard that Jerome had died in Jerusalem at exactly that hour.*"

Will clapped his hands together. "*Remember the letter!*" he said. "Semiramide wasn't talking about her earlier letter at all, we just ended up there by serendipity. She was talking about Saint Augustine writing his letter!"

They high fived each other and Alessa drained her water.

"And there's our instrument," Will said triumphantly, pointing at the top left corner of the St. Augustine painting. Some kind of planetary model, not a musical instrument. We were almost spot-on with the idea of a globe, though."

"You know what else?" Alessa said. "Two, fourteen, twenty-two, nine and one are all hours on a twenty-four-hour clock." She tapped the top right of the picture. "This blue ring with the red middle is the clock by his head that the description mentions," she said. "We just have to press those numbers on the clockface and the panel unlocks."

"My God! I wonder when the church opens."

"Well, we can't just start *touching* a Botticelli masterpiece," Alessa said. "I think we need to go public on this now. We need to start with the chief priest of Ognissanti. We can't do this ourselves."

They looked at each other soberly. Will wiggled his eyebrows and put on an innocent expression.

"Will!" she said warningly. "That is *not* going to happen. We are not going to sneak in and start pressing bits on a priceless painting in the hope that all this conjecture is real. We need to go to the authorities and tell them the whole story. The best we can hope for is to be present when someone does try opening the panel."

He grinned.

"I knew that really; it was just a little fantasy for a moment. But we've got to convince someone to believe us. That's going to be an interesting challenge."

Alessa was searching again.

"The church opens at nine thirty," she said. "Let's get some sleep now and be there when the door is unlocked."

It was ten past four in the afternoon of the next day and Will and Alessa were in Ognissanti, standing in front of a confessional stall. Above it was the painting of St. Augustine, painted by Sandro Botticelli in 1480. One thing was immediately obvious – no-one could even touch the painting unless they were perched on top of the confessional stall, because it was high up on the wall. They had spoken to a young priest that morning, and he'd suggested they return for the late afternoon opening, when one of the seniors would meet them. They had found the young man again and he had gone hunting for a senior priest. He had already been gone several minutes and they were beginning to despair when a white-haired old man made a slow and shuffling approach, dressed in a brown habit belted with white cord.

"You are a scholar from England?" he asked Alessa in perfect English, raising his eyebrows at her as he approached. "Welcome to our church. My name is Francesco Mandelli."

Alessa said something about his English in fast Italian, and then switched into English for Will's benefit.

"Thank you, I spent two years in Oxford as part of my theological studies," the old man replied warmly, looking pleased. He gestured at the young man beside him. "Gianluca has told me a little of your extraordinary story. Tell me more."

Once more they recounted their tale about the hunt for the letter and finding it, the decoding of the puzzle, and their conclusion that the painting on the wall above their heads was the one Semiramide d'Appiano meant. When Alessa finished unfolding the story, she ended it by lifting her outstretched arm and pointing up at the red and blue clockface on the artwork. But Mandelli was frowning and shaking his head gently, his lips pursed.

Alessa slowly petered out and looked at the old priest expectantly. He shrugged, gesturing with open hands as if in supplication.

"What?" she asked, frowning.

"Step back and look at the bottom of the panel and the top, Signorina Cooper," Mandelli said in a regretful tone. "What do you see?"

Alessa and Will frowned at the panel.

"Iron brackets holding it in place," Mandelli said, answering his own question. "The painting was moved in the early seventeenth century to its present position in the nave, and the panel is attached to the wall with the four iron brackets that you see."

"It was *moved?*" Alessa echoed in dismay.

"Yes. The painting was moved from the original wall separating the choir from the apse, along with its companion." He pointed over his shoulder at Ghirlandaio's St. Jerome on the opposite wall.

"So you see," Mandelli said gently, perceiving their distress, "there is certainly no cavity behind this painting. The panel is mounted against a solid wall."

He looked sorrowfully at them both.

"I am afraid you are chasing the wild geese."

25

Deeply repentant of my sinful ways
And of my trivial, manifold desires,
Of squandering, alas, these few brief days
Of fugitive life in tending love's vain fires

GASPARA STAMPA: opening lines of Rime Varie CCCXI (1554), translated by Lorna de' Lucchi (1921)

15th March 1523

Even the most dispersed families gather for marriages and burials, unless there is discord. Semiramide had died six days previously, which was a long time to be dead but not buried, considering putrefaction and fear of the plague. Yet it wasn't as if it were high summer, when such a delay would have been ill-advised, but an unusually cool March. It had been necessary for family members to travel to the funeral in Cafaggiolo, for Semiramide was to be laid to rest there with her husband. The small family mausoleum was a white-stone edifice at the foot of the villa gardens beyond a fountain. It surprised many that Semiramide was to lie with Il Popolano here, rather than for them both to be interred in the Florentine chapel where other members of the Medici family lay. It had however been a stipulation of Il Popolano's will that he should lie in his favourite hunting lodge, and where he rested, so must his wife.

As they were outside the city and less tightly bound by its rituals, there had not been the usual procession of priests and family members and women wailing in homage, but instead a simple gathering of close family and friends in the extensive gardens and courtyards of Cafaggiolo. In deference to the six-day delay the coffin was closed, so there were to be no last kisses planted on the madonna's cold cheek, nor any chance for her hand to be clasped one final time by a loved one.

Isabella d'Este had been visiting Florence for political reasons, as Cardinal Giulio di Giuliano de Medici looked likely to become the next pope, perhaps even before the year's end. The Marchioness of Mantova had known the family since her childhood. She remembered Semiramide when she had been an elegant young woman and had towered above young Isabella; the epitome of a beautiful princess. She had been kind and wise. Isabella had made the journey out of the city to pay her respects, but also in the shrewd expectation that the cardinal himself might officiate the proceedings. Alas he was absent, though there were Medici aplenty.

She had travelled to the villa in a guarded coach with young Caterina de Medici, a precocious four-year-old who had lost both her parents when she had been but a month outside the womb. Caterina's aunt Clarice had travelled in the coach too, for she was educating the child. Clarice was a stunning thirty-year-old woman, while Isabella was twenty years her senior and unusually plain, but they were both clever and had quickly found a common interest in fashion. Isabella was famous throughout the northern city states for her remarkable sense of high style, and Clarice had expressed surprise that the marchioness had managed to find such a fetching black dress so quickly. From that moment they had got on agreeably, as the carriage bumped its bone-rattling way along the uneven track from Florence and the guards on horseback patrolled outside. The Medici child had slept for much of the way, but had woken towards the end of the journey, eaten some fruit and then been sick. The nurse and fourth member of the coach had dealt with the problem, and otherwise the expedition had been uneventful.

Once they had arrived in Cafaggiolo, they'd had three days to wait until the funeral, and Isabella had become keenly interested in the manufacture of maiolica, thinking she might take the process back to Mantova's artisans. It was a method of tin-glazing earthenware pottery, started at Cafaggiolo by Il Popolano twenty years previously, and was now well-established in one end of the *Manica Lunga* – the long building that in his day had been used for hunting-dog kennels.

Once the funeral was underway, Isabella had surprised herself by getting a lump in her throat. Her eyes had welled with tears when Semiramide had been laid to rest inside the small white building. After the priestly rituals were over, they had all filed out into the villa's gardens in the diluted March sunlight. Now was the moment to build new relationships, and Isabella stood in the gardens surveying the scene.

Servants brought out glasses of hot wine spiced with ginger, cloves, nutmeg and cinnamon – you had to be Medici to have a ready supply of such exotic spices. The wine lifted people's spirits after the melancholy of the burial. Quite a crowd had assembled to pay homage. Semiramide's heir Pierfrancesco was there, whom they called 'the younger' now, and he was accompanied by his wife and his young son. He was a good-looking fellow, slightly effeminate and not in the least like a Medici, so she supposed he had followed his mother's looks. She frowned as she examined him across the perfectly manicured hedges: he didn't appear to be in mourning; he just looked bilious, as if he had swallowed something unpleasant. His wife Maria was a sweet-faced lady in her mid thirties, and Isabella had stood beside her during the burial ceremony and expressed her condolences. They had conversed for a few minutes. Their young boy Lorenzino was speeding around the gardens and ignoring his nurse. He was certainly a handful, Isabella thought privately. She would have reined him in by now, but his father had made no move to do so, and his young nurse appeared unable to impose order.

A lad of about twelve called Alessandro, from Il Magnifico's branch of the family, sat on a bench reading a book. Somehow he had managed to wheedle a glass of mulled wine out of a servant and it sat on the bench next to him, untouched but gently steaming. Isabella also spotted her traveling companion Clarice, who was talking to a couple she didn't know, and Clarice gave her a little wave which Isabella returned. Pierfrancesco's sisters Laudomia and Ginevra were there, and Isabella calculated that they must now be nearly forty. Laudomia was rather fat, while Ginevra was as thin as a beanpole. The other sibling had passed long ago, Isabella recalled: what had he been called…Alfredo, Averado? She sipped the hot wine and felt it warm the pit of her stomach, then munched daintily on a tiny pastry that a servant had proffered her on a silver tray.

It was clear that much of the crowd were Medici family members. Semiramide had been much liked, and many had taken the trouble to make the gruelling trip to Cafaggiolo from the city. Little Caterina weaved in and out of the crowd just as Isabella had once done herself in such company. The little four-year-old was giggling and playing a chasing game with a boy of her own age called Cosimo, and Cosimo's mother was warning him not to be too rough with her. In Isabella's judgement Caterina was holding her own perfectly well, and at one point shoved young Cosimo headfirst into a hedge when none of the adults were watching. Isabella smiled and covered her mouth with her hand to hide her amusement.

Intermingled with the rich and famous were ordinary guests that Isabella mostly didn't know. There were a few painters and sculptors in attendance, for Semiramide and her husband had been great patrons of the arts. There were servants of course, and Isabella's shrewd eye judged that the housekeeper must have hired young girls from the village to assist, for there were too many present to be part of the usual household retinue. Some showed inexperience, and this was understandable. One could not plan in advance for a funeral, but one also could not be seen to have insufficient servants in attendance.

There were some gentlemen clad in legal garb and after a while Isabella noticed that one of their clerks was passing between groups of nobles and whispering discreetly in their ears. Accordingly, various of the party began to peel off from the gathering and make their way up to the villa. Isabella presumed it was time for the will to be read. Clarice had to go with them, and came over to Isabella to ask her if she would keep an eye on Caterina while she attended the reading. She explained ruefully that Caterina's young nurse could be inattentive when young lords turned her head. Isabella smiled and took the little girl by the hand. Little Caterina had been deserted by her young friend Cosimo. Isabella sat down with her on the bench which had recently been vacated by young Alessandro. Presumably he had to attend the reading too. Isabella had not expected to attend and she was not called. It was a pity in one respect, as she would have liked some small memento of Semiramide. She preferred to remember the tall princess in her youth, rather than the old woman she had become. It was sad how the same person inside could transform so much, trading youthful beauty for a worn-out body.

Caterina was cold and wanted to go up to the house, so Isabella took the little girl's hand and they went in. Fires were burning in all the hearths and tapestries hung across the doors. It was noticeably warmer than outside. Some other guests had come in too. The conversation grew louder, as the wine loosened tongues and the conclusion of the funeral brought relief. The door to the library was closed and a guard stood in front of it, so Isabella presumed that was where the reading was in progress. It would be a momentous affair, for the death of any Medici was significant and generally involved the dispersal of a fortune into many different hands. Tonight there would be a banquet in honour of the departed, and tomorrow they would all take to the coaches and make their way back over the muddy tracks to Florence. From there, Isabella would try to meet Cardinal Giulio, or failing that, she would re-join her own retinue and return to Mantova.

She sat in a corner with Caterina and told her a story. Occasionally the serious voice of a lawyer could be heard intoning inside the closed library, but it wasn't possible to make out what he said, and the guard glared at anyone who approached closely. Caterina got bored and wanted to return to the garden despite the cold, though the light was fading. She complained that smoke from the large fire in the hearth was making her eyes smart. This was nonsense, Isabella thought, but she stood up anyway and took the little girl outside. She waited just outside the door, and a thoughtful servant placed a black woollen blanket around her shoulders as she watched the little girl run around the garden happily.

All at once the door behind Isabella crashed open. She started in surprise to see Pierfrancesco himself, Semiramide's son, come outside.

"My lord," she said, but he ignored her completely and stalked past with a look of fury on his face. A moment later one of the young legal clerks followed him out, flourishing a sealed letter in his hand as if intending to pass it to Pierfrancesco, and holding out a small jewellery box in the other.

"I don't want it!" Pierfrancesco was saying angrily. "Take it away!"

"But my lord," the clerk said nervously, "We are required by the will to hand it to you."

Caterina ran up and sped in a circle around Pierfrancesco until Isabella hurriedly grabbed the little girl and drew her back. Pierfrancesco persisted in ignoring them both, and the lawyer continued to offer the small box and the letter to him.

"Take the letter and burn it!" Pierfrancesco said, in a rage for no reason that Isabella could discern. Suddenly the lord snatched the box from the clerk's hand and turned, hurling it into the garden, where it landed somewhere among the hedgerows. Caterina pulled her hand out of Isabella's and sped after the box as a dog might chase a stick. Pierfrancesco snatched the letter from the lawyer and examined it briefly, noting his own name and the unbroken seal. For a moment he looked as if he were going to rip it in half, but then tossed it to the ground. Then he shook his head in exasperation and picked it up, visibly gathering his self control. He returned it to the clerk.

"Burn it, boy," he said curtly, and then turned on his heel and strode back inside. There was a waft of warmth as the tapestry billowed back, bringing a whiff of hearth smoke. The clerk stood beside Isabella looking indecisive.

"He doesn't want it, whatever it is," Isabella said sympathetically.

"It is from the madonna for his eyes only," the clerk said in anguish. "I will have to consult with my master. I cannot burn it, for it is part of the will."

"If I were you I'd file it away somewhere," Isabella counselled. "He might calm down and decide he wants it, then be furious if you have destroyed it."

The young man looked relieved at this suggestion.

"I will," he said, but then looked out into the garden with fresh worry. "I shall never find the box in this dusk."

"He could not reasonably expect that you should," Isabella reasoned. "He hurled it away and it is lost. It's probably just some small trifle anyway."

The young clerk looked slightly less alarmed and bowed briefly to her.

"Thank you my lady," he said. He held up the letter. "I'll put this somewhere safe." He wiped a speck of mud off it and pushed it into the folds of his legal gown, bowed and took his leave.

Isabella rolled her eyes at all the drama. Then she turned and looked down the garden into the gathering dusk. Clarice had been right – Caterina's young nurse had temporarily vanished, abandoning her duties.

"Come along Caterina!" she called. "It's getting dark and you'll catch your death out here. Your Aunt Clarice won't thank me for that."

Caterina came back after a few minutes and looked around.

"Is the big man gone?" she asked shyly.

"Yes my dear, he has gone back inside."

The little girl was holding something behind her back and now she brought it out and handed it to Isabella. It was the mysterious jewellery box.

"You *are* a clever girl!" Isabella said warmly.

The hinge of the box had broken when it had been thrown across the garden, but somehow the little girl had found it and brought it back. Isabella looked in the box and saw a brooch inside, with a beautiful orange stone and eight pearls in a circle.

"You can have it," the little girl said. "You're nice."

Isabella suddenly felt very touched. She had eight children of her own and her maternal instinct was strong in her.

"Well that is very kind of you," she said. "And now we must go in and find Aunt Clarice before we freeze our bones!"

The little girl turned happily and danced back to the door, slipping through the tapestry curtain and leaving Isabella alone for a moment. She stood and looked down at the pretty brooch. She vaguely remembered it, for Semiramide had worn it several times when Isabella had been a little girl. It reminded her of that halcyon past when everything had seemed possible. What a fool Pierfrancesco had been to discard it so ungraciously. She weighed the brooch thoughtfully in her hand for a moment.

Well why not? She thought to herself. *Pierfrancesco threw it away, and I would like a memento of his mother.*

She slipped the brooch back into its broken box and tucked it into a concealed pocket in her gown.

26

Beauty awakens the soul to act.

DANTE ALIGHIERI

March, Ognissanti, Florence

"This is a disaster! Where was the panel moved from?" Alessa asked the priest in dismay.

"As I mentioned," he said patiently, "I believe it was at the entrance to the old choir."

"So...just over there?" Alessa asked, pointing at the open space in front of the altar.

"Oh no, my dear, the original convent was much bigger and everything was moved around in the 1630s when they redesigned it in the baroque style."

"So where would the choir have been then?" Alessa persisted.

"I really couldn't say," Mandelli said, looking uncomfortable at the determined expression on her face. "We do have the original plans in our little library. I suppose we could look."

"That would be perfect," Alessa said, very sweet now that she had her own way.

The original plans were in a locked oak cabinet in a tiny library in the private area of the church. The cabinet was rarely unlocked and it took the old priest a few minutes, breathing heavily, to locate the key. He spent some more minutes frowning and muttering as he slid open drawers, then finally located the ancient plans of Ognissanti. He spread out the yellowed parchments on a desk, then sat down at it with much creaking of limbs. He fussed around until he found a pair of half-moon reading glasses and slipped them on. Alessa wordlessly handed him her pair of white gloves. He looked surprised but put them on. The plans were not at all easy to follow, but Mandelli was very familiar with the modern layout of Ognissanti and after a few minutes he looked up.

"The original choir was here," he said, tapping the paper lightly with his finger.

"And where is that?"

"Next door," he said, indicating with his eyes and a tilt of his head. "What has become the office of the Carabinieri. *Il Comando Provinciale di Firenze*."

"Not good," Alessa said, and Will raised his eyebrows.

"The military police," she explained glumly.

"Don't worry," Mandelli said. "I know the man in charge very well. He will let us in."

"Are you sure?" Alessa said doubtfully. "I didn't think the carabinieri were so accommodating."

Mandelli gave a dismissive gesture.

"Normally this can be the case, I think," he said with a smile, "but the commander is married to my brother's granddaughter. He is family."

Will and Alessa copied the relevant part of the ancient building plans using a photocopier that may itself have been medieval, as it took two minutes to warm up. Mandelli spoke on the telephone to his brother's grandson-in-law. When he came off the phone he waved a hand as if conferring a benediction.

"He is intrigued. He will give us 30 minutes."

They left the church and turned right. Almost immediately Mandelli turned under the Carabinieri archway and entered the precincts of the police station. They were let through a barrier by a man in a black *carabiniere* uniform with red stripes on his trousers. He looked very impressive. He issued them with temporary passes and ushered them into a waiting room. After a few minutes another *carabiniere* came to collect them, and brought them to the office of the *Comandante Reparto*, a handsome man in his early thirties, who stood up and shook their hands. He gave the old priest a hug.

"I am sorry for my English," said the Comandante to Will, after a burst of Italian between him and Alessa and Mandelli. "It is not so well."

"Please excuse me for my lack of Italian," Will said awkwardly, and Alessa translated. More conversation ensued and then the Comandante looked at the photocopied plans of the church. He frowned at them for a while and then his face cleared and he spoke in Italian.

"Alessa translated for Will's benefit, as they all started to get up.

"He thinks it is what is now the refectory," she said. "He will take us there."

They left the office and set off, passing through three sets of double doors, round a corner, down three shallow steps, and into a refectory where several carabinieri sat eating, their caps on the tables beside them.

"*Troppo lontano*," said the Comandante, shaking his head, and added for Will's benefit, "too much long way."

He backtracked to the entrance door and the wide hall which led to the refectory. Will got out the photocopy again and they studied it.

Will then paced along the wall and stopped after a few steps.

"Around about here?" he asked, and they nodded. It was a plain wall but there was a section where it was recessed a few centimetres deep, raised up so that the base was at waist level. "In fact, it could be exactly here," Will said absently. He walked over to the door and went past it to the opposite side.

"Here's another recess," he called. "This one could be where Ghirlandaio's St. Jerome was located, and the first one could be where Botticelli's St. Augustine lived."

He came back and joined them by the first recess.

"Does anyone have a stepladder?"

Alessa translated and the Comandante's assistant went away, returning after a few minutes with a wooden stool with two steps that unfolded. He said something in Italian and everyone except Will laughed.

"This is the best he can find. He says the better ladder is locked away in the janitor's cupboard," Alessa said. She grinned. "The janitor has to watch out for thieves, he says."

Will smiled too and set up the steps, then gestured to Alessa.

"Do you want to have a look?"

She shook her head.

"You're taller than me. You go up and I'll catch you if you fall!"

Several policemen had finished eating and came out of the refectory, pausing and asking what was going on. The Comandante's assistant told them in an undertone and they gathered to watch.

Will positioned the stool, then went up the steps and stood on the seat. He took out his phone and flicked back through the photos until he found the pictures he had taken of the St. Augustine panel. He worked out where the clock face would have been and studied the surface.

"Nothing," he said regretfully, shaking his head. "Nothing at all."

"Are you sure?" Alessa said, feeling weighed down with disappointment.

He studied the surface again assiduously.

"There just isn't any mark. It's smooth yellow stone. We might not have the right place, or it might have been knocked down centuries ago."

"Let's try the other side," Alessa said glumly. "You never know, they might have swapped them round."

Will came down, feeling very dispirited, and picked up the stool. They all trooped over to the opposite wall and Will set up again in front of the recess and went up the steps to the top of the stool.

"I can't see – oh, wait a minute." He craned his neck upward to the righthand corner of the recess.

"You know, there *is* something," he said, and leaned closer to the wall, his voice taking on an edge of excitement. "Looks like little circles."

He studied his phone screen again and then checked their notes about the Madonna and Keys painting they had found in the Hermitage, murmuring to himself all the while.

"II, XIIII, XXII, VIIII and I. I remember now, weird Roman numerals."

"Yes, older variations," Alessa said with exasperation. "Get *on* with it, Will!"

He ignored her and frowned at a photo of the painted clockface he had taken on his phone.

"This is complicated. So that would be bottom right, then top left, then bottom left, top right, and this other one at the bottom, number one." He pressed as he counted, his tongue protruding from his lips.

Nothing happened.

"One of them felt like it shifted slightly," Will said, his throat dry. The crowd didn't understand what he said except for one man who translated. "We need some oil! I can't push hard enough." He fumbled into his pocket and brought out a Euro coin.

"This might do it."

He tried again using the coin to push the buttons.

"Bottom right, top left, bottom left ..."

There was a sudden loud click in the expectant silence, and Will wobbled on the stool. The crowd of policemen began talking among themselves, but the Comandante held up a finger and they quietened.

"Will," Alessa said, her voice suddenly sounding hoarse. "Come down now. I think the wall moved a bit."

"It did," Will agreed. "That's why I nearly fell off the stool."

He came carefully down the steps, folded them under the stool and put it to one side.

Alessa was looking at the base of the recess. "It's unlatched but it's stuck on something," she said. "Or just rusted up. We need something to push in the crack and get it open."

She looked around at the amassing crowd of *carabinieri*.

"*Avete un coltello?*" she asked them, gesturing with her hand. "*Una forchetta?*" A knife or a fork?

Someone hurried into the refectory and came back with both a knife and a fork. She pushed the knife into the crack and edged the stone slab out a little more. It was reluctant to move. Then she stuck the fork into the widened crack and prised it a little further open. The gap was now wide enough to accept fingers and she and Will both put their fingers to the crack and heaved. Reluctantly the ancient stone door squeaked open and revealed a tall cavity behind it. There was an odd musty smell, as air trapped for centuries was at last released. They stood back and there was a collective gasp as everyone saw a wooden chest inside the cavity, bound with tarnished brass and bearing pictures of icons on its vaulted lid.

A red stone glittered in the end that they could easily see.

"That looks like a huge ruby," Alessa said, leaning in. "My God, we've done it Will. We've found the secret letters or whatever. The evidence that Semiramide wanted to get rid of!"

Will stepped forward and was about to lift out the chest but she stopped him with a hand on his arm.

"I'm sorry," she said, "but we have to wait. We need a conservation team on this."

I was afraid you'd say that," Will said, "but can't we at least lift the lid and see what's in it?"

She looked as if she were going to say no but he looked pleadingly at her.

"Go on then," she said, gulping. "Carefully!"

He lifted the lid and they looked inside, while all behind them craned their necks to see.

"A skull," Will said. "A human skull and those look like femurs. A skull and bones. I was hoping for letters from the great man himself."

"It says 'San Giovanni di Meda' on the front of the box," Alessa said, kneeling down and squinting. "I know what this is, it's a funerary urn. This is the reliquary of a saint."

"Well that's very disappointing, "Will said, his heart sinking.

The policemen pressed closer to see and one involuntarily nudged against Will so that his hand holding the lid of the chest moved back and brushed against the back of the cavity.

"Oh, this is *cloth* at the back, not stone," he said in sudden realisation. "It's just filthy."

He closed the lid and brushed the cloth.

A five-hundred-year-old cloth shroud disintegrated and fell in a shower of dried fibres like confetti, making everyone step back.

The dust of centuries cleared, and the crowd looked in awe at the bright colours of the painting which stood upright in the back of the cavity.

"Botticelli," Will said, and there was a murmur from the assembled. Every Florentine knew *that* word.

The painting was as well preserved as the Mars and Venus he knew so well in London's National Gallery. It would later be established that it was exactly the same size. It was indisputably Botticelli's brushwork; a master work of the most exquisite perfection. It depicted an almost-nude woman like Botticelli's Venus, but older and somehow more real. Shadows and highlights on her ribs and muscles seemed to bring her into three-dimensional perspective.

"That must be Semiramide," he said absently. "Same face as in that Madonna and Keys picture. What an erotic painting, though. I'm not surprised she wanted her son to get rid of it. Ha, look at that!"

He pointed at the pearl brooch hanging on a chain between the naked breasts of the woman in the painting. "We've seen *that* before."

"And this might be Botticelli himself," Alessa said, pointing to the darker-skinned man who stood naked behind the woman and clasped her to him. Her eyes were closed and her head tilted back, but he had paused in the act of lovemaking and looked out of the picture at the viewer. His hair was long and curled but greying. He had a noble face with rosebud lips, heavy-lidded eyes and a firm brow. He looked a little arrogant, or perhaps it was calm certainty.

"Just like the Adoration of the Magi, but older," Will said. This is only the second Botticelli self-portrait in existence."

Alessa took Will's hand and they smiled at each other.

"The painter and his muse," she said.

Behind them, someone started to clap, and then the whole stunned crowd began to applaud.

Epilogue

"The Sun Amidst Small Stars" – Titian's nickname, from:
L'amor che move il sole e l'altre stelle.

DANTE ALIGHIERI, Paradiso

1533, Venice

Tiziano Vecellio, known as Titian by the English, was exasperated. He was in his mid forties, already a well-known master of the Venetian art school, and had painted countless portraits, including many of noble birth. It had been his experience that many of his subjects wanted him to improve their visage, and part of his success was that he would comply. He would change a man's chin to make it firmer, or take weight off a woman's face to make her more pleasing, while still retaining the likeness of the individual. The trick was not to change too much; the removal of a wart or other blemish was one thing, but to make the person unrecognisable was a recipe for disaster.

The source of his frustration was the woman before him, whom he knew well to be famous, clever, strong-minded and *always* to get what she wanted. Isabella d'Este was sixty and looked it. To be frank, she was overweight and as plain as a pikestaff. It was true that she wore the most beautiful finery, complete with a marten fur across her shoulder, and she had asked him to paint her portrait, but he had just asked her how she would like it done.

I'd like you to take forty years off," she had replied unblushingly. "I'd like to be twenty again."

"But madam, he had replied in frustration. "If I paint you aged twenty, which I cannot properly do because I did not know you at that young age, no-one will recognise you."

She studied him.

"You are painting this portrait and I am paying you for this service, yes?" she asked.

He grimaced uncomfortably.

"Yes, madam, but—"

"Splendid, and now let me explain. I have no illusions that I am handsome, Maestro Tiziano," she said. "Please don't imagine that. But let me tell you a secret and I forbid you to repeat it. I am fully sixty years of age and that means that soon I will likely be dead. I have had no other portraits I have ever liked, and many of them I have had destroyed. Your portrait of me five years ago was honest and truthful and I despised it from the moment I set eyes on it. That was because it looked like me."

She smiled at him and her smile was infectious. He smiled back uncertainly.

"At the age of sixty I am not seeking honesty. *This* portrait will be a record of how I looked, Maestro Tiziano. I would prefer it to be a pretty face than not. I really don't think that in a hundred years' time anyone will care that it was, ah, adjusted a little. Now time is short, so let us begin. How would you like me to sit?"

He gave up. She would have what she wanted. Isabella always had what she wanted. Perhaps he should lie about his own age, too. He spent some time posing her as he wanted, then readied a crayon to begin sketching. He would imagine her as a young woman.

"One last thing," she said, pointing to the brooch pinned on her Balzo headdress. "This pearl brooch was, ah, given to me by a man I once knew, but I would not wish him to think I still coveted it. Can you change it? A different colour for the stone perhaps, or a different shape?"

"Of course madam, Tiziano Vecellio said, obsequious now to his client. "I shall retain only its essence."

Acknowledgements

Once again with thanks to my wife Viv, who put up with me disappearing for many evenings to write while I was still holding down a day job. Whenever I was stuck for a twist or how to move on, we would discuss it and she would always come up with new ideas and directions. Thanks also to Matthew Shooter, Karl Clinton and others for their careful proof-reading.

The wonderful Uffizi Museum in Florence deserves an honourable mention as the place in which Primavera and the Birth of Venus are displayed today, and the Medici archive at the time of Frederick Pocock's visit would have been there, though my account of that event is fictional.

London's National Gallery is the place to go if you'd like to see the original Venus and Mars painting, though my suggestion that it was one of two panels is again entirely fictional. I also became a reader in the British Library and recommend a visit there, if only to look in awe at the vast towers of books.

In Florence, the Chiesa di San Salvatore in Ognissanti is even more beautiful today than it would have been as a convent in Botticelli's day. You can see Botticelli's panel of Saint Augustine, complete with clockface, though as described in the text it has been moved from its original position, and my account of the original location in the contemporary Carabinieri offices is fictional.

Last but not least, do visit Mantua (*Mantova*) if you get a chance. It is just an hour's easy train journey from Verona, and the Palazzo Ducale is as described in Will and Alessa's visit there, though alas, you will not find a small room containing Isabella d'Este's personal effects and treasures. If you look at the famous painting of Isabella, though – a poster reproduces it – you'll see that she is indeed wearing a brooch that resembles the one so much sought after in this story.

AFTERWORD

I hope you enjoyed this story. It would be a great help to me if you would give it a star rating of your choice and write a brief review of it. A sentence or two would be sufficient to help more readers discover it. Thank you!

You can follow updates, read book samples and see my paintings on the Milky Way Gallery, https://milkywaygallery.com.

Richard Mitchell

ABOUT THE AUTHOR

Richard John Mitchell was born in Sussex quite a few editions ago, and his curiosity for the world led him to pursue a degree in electronic engineering—a skillset that would shape his successful career as a global leader in information technology analysis. Throughout his professional life, Richard authored extensive works and reviewed the writings of analyst experts, while traversing the globe on various ventures. Recently, Richard embarked on a new chapter as he bid farewell to the corporate world and embraced his true passion of writing. Drawing on his affection for storytelling, he chose the realm of fiction to weave captivating narratives that engage readers' imaginations.

Beyond his literary endeavours, Richard finds solace and creativity in the world of art. He has painted pictures for over three decades, primarily working in oils but also dabbling in watercolours and acrylics. Having a profound admiration for the great artists of the past, he has made a detailed study of the Italian Renaissance, with a particular focus on Botticelli. Among his greatest joys in life are his loving family—four children and two stepchildren who have ventured into the world, and an increasing number of grandchildren. Richard lives in North Yorkshire, near the historically rich city of York, with his lovely wife and two dogs.